I0613394

Charles Thorpe

British Marine Conchology

being a descriptive catalogue, arranged according to the Lamarckian system, of the

salt water shells of Great Britain

Charles Thorpe

British Marine Conchology
being a descriptive catalogue, arranged according to the Lamarckian system, of the salt water shells of Great Britain

ISBN/EAN: 9783337387396

Printed in Europe, USA, Canada, Australia, Japan

Cover: Foto ©Andreas Hilbeck / pixelio.de

More available books at **www.hansebooks.com**

BRITISH
MARINE CONCHOLOGY;

BEING

𝔄 𝔇𝔢𝔰𝔠𝔯𝔦𝔭𝔱𝔦𝔳𝔢 ℭ𝔞𝔱𝔞𝔩𝔬𝔤𝔲𝔢,

ARRANGED ACCORDING TO THE LAMARCKIAN SYSTEM,

OF

THE SALT WATER SHELLS

OF

GREAT BRITAIN,

BY

CHARLES THORPE,

ASSISTED BY

SEVERAL DISTINGUISHED CONCHOLOGISTS,

AND

ILLUSTRATED WITH NUMEROUS DELINEATIONS OF THE
RARER AND UNFIGURED SPECIES.

BY

G. B. SOWERBY AND W. WOOD

LONDON:
PUBLISHED BY EDWARD LUMLEY,
56, CHANCERY LANE.

1844

PREFACE.

THE intent of the following pages, is to supply the collector of British Shells, at a moderate cost, and in a portable form, with a complete descriptive catalogue of all the marine species decidedly indigenous to this country.

The author has endeavoured to compile a work which might suffice for the arrangement of any cabinet of British Shells. For the Bivalves, the useful quarto of Turton has been abridged, the abridgement (if it may be so called) consisting merely in a selection and contraction of the synonyms, the whole substance of the descriptions being retained and frequently enlarged. As no work similarly devoted to the elucidation of the Univalves, and based on the more scientific and natural arrangement of the modern systematists, had appeared ; that section has demanded a stricter comparison of specimens, with the drawings and descriptions of the older writers of the Linnœan School. Much care has been bestowed upon a point neglected hitherto by our authors, the comparison of our native species with those described by the older naturalists, and those contained in the Faunæ of Europe and America.

The land and freshwater shells of Great Britain, having been so ably illustrated in the recent edition of Turton's Manual, the author refraining altogether from that branch of his subject, has restricted his attention to the salt-water species alone.

By the scientific Conchologist the convenience of possessing in a small compass, the description of the species which from time to time, discovered since the days of Montagu, have been scattered through the various periodicals of England and Scotland, can not fail to be appreciated. The exquisite figures, for whose fidelity the name of Sowerby is a sufficient guarantee, illustrating those species chiefly which have been either ill delineated or are altogether as yet unfigured, must cause this work, to be indispensable to every naturalist who may study this branch of Nature's handiworks.

As a preliminary for the arrangement of his cabinet, the reader should consult the SYSTEMATIC INDEX, which contains additional matter and emendations, together with a selection of *unpublished species*, from the MSS of some of our most scientific collectors. This portion has been contributed by Sylvanus Hanley, Esq. who has materially assisted the author in the course of his labours.

His gratitude is likewise due to W. Metcalfe, Esq. of Lincoln's Inn, and William Bean, Esq. of Scarborough as well for the use of their extensive collections, as for their willing communication of much valuable information.

LIST OF THE ILLUSTRATIONS.

21. Bulla Cranchii.
22. Mytilus Exustus, young.
23. Lucina Spinifera, adult.
24. Amphidesma Tenue.
25. Conovulus Albus.
26. Cingula Rubra.
27. Scalaria Treveliana.
28. Mactra Elliptica.
29. Chiton Lævis.
30. Pecten Aculeatus.
31. Nucula Nitida.
32. ⎰
⎱ Sphœnia Binghami.
33. ⎰
34. Turritella Elegantissima.
35. Turritella Unica.
36. Trochus Millegranus.
37. Odostomia Interstincta.
38. Rissoa (Cingula) Brugieri.
39. Cingula Pellucida.
40. Pleurotoma Gracilis.
41. Pleurobranchus Plumula.
42. Cingula Labiosa.
43. Rissoa (Cingula) Beanii.
44. Skenea Serpuloides.
45. Cingula Striatula.
46. Cingula Parva, variety Rufilabris.

We recommend those who desire to possess in one work the figures of all the British shells, to procure the new edition of the Index Testaceologicus by Wood and Hanley.

A LIST

OF THE

WORKS CHIEFLY REFERRED TO.

ADAMS or ADAMS MICR.—Adam's Essays on the Microscope.

ANNALS NAT. H.—The Annals of Natural History.

ARG.—Argenville's Lithologie et Conchiliologie. Paris. 1757.

BERW. TR.—Transactions of the Berwickshire Natural Historical Society.

BL. or BLAIN.—Blainville's Manuel de Malacologie.

BORL. CORNWALL—Borlase's Natural History of Cornwall, 1758.

BORN.—Born's Testacea Musei Cæsarei Vindobonensis. Vienna, 1750.

BROD.—Broderip (in Zoological Journal, &c.)

BROWN IL.—Brown's Illustrations of the Conchology of Great Britain.

BRUG.—Brugiere's " Histoire Naturelle des Vers" in the Encyclopedie Methodique.

CH. or CHEM.—Chemnitz's Continuation of Martini's Conchylien Cabinet.

C. I. or CONC. IL.—Conchological Illustrations by SOWERBY JUNIOR. (Cardium and Nucula.)

CONCH. MAG.—See MAL. MAG.

CUV. or CUVIER.—Cuvier's Regne Animale.

DA COS.—Da Costa's British Conchology.

DESH.—Deshaye's edition of Lamarck, and Monograph (MON. DENT.) of Dentalium.

D. or DIL.—Dilwyn's Descriptive Catalogue of Recent Shells, 1817.

DON.—Donovan's Natural History of British Shells, 1799 to 1803.

DOR. CAT.—Catalogue of the Shells, &c. of Dorsetshire, by R. Pultney, 1813.

EDIN. ENC.—Encyclopædia Edinensis.

EDIN. PHIL. J.—Edinburgh Philosophical Journal.

EDIN. J. OF NAT. SC.—Edinburgh Journal of Natnral and Geographical Science.

ELLIS COR.—Ellis's Natural History of Corallines.

ELLIS ZOOP.—Ellis and Solander's Natural History of many Zoophytes.

E. or E. M.—Encyclopedie Methodique (Plates of Shells).

ENC. BRIT. SUP.—Leach's Article CONCHOLOGY in the Supplement to the third edition of the Encyclopædia Brittanica.

F., FL. or FLEM.—Fleming's British Animals.

FAUN. FRANC.—Blainville in the Faune Francaise.

GMEL.—Gmelin's Systema Naturæ, 1788.

GOULD MAS.—Gould's Invertebrata of Massachussets.

GRAY—Gray in the Philosophical Magazine, 1827, and in Griffith's edition of Cuvier.

GRAY TURT.—Gray's edition of Turton's Manual of Land and Fresh-water Shells.

GUAL.—Gualtier's Index Testarum Conchyliorum.

HÆNING. MON. CRAN.—Hæninghaus's Monograph of Crania.

KNORR.—Knorr's Delices des Yeux et de l'Esprit.

LAM.—Lamarck's Animales sans Vertebres, 1818.

LEACH Z. M.—Leach's Zoological Miscellany.

LEACH CIRRHIP.—Leach's Article Cirrhipedes in the Supplement to the Encyclopædia Brittanica.

LIN.—Linnæus's Systema Natura, 12th edition.

LIN. MUS. ULRIC.—Linnæus's Museum L. Ulricæ Reginæ Sueciæ.

LIN. MANT.—Linnœus's Mantissa Altera, 1764.

LIN. T. or LIN. TR.—Transactions of the Linnæan Society of London.

LIST.—Lister's Historia Conchyliorum.

LIST AN. or LIST AN. ANG.—Lister's Historia Animalium Angliæ,

MACG. or MACG. AB.—Macgyllivray on the Molluscous Animals of Aberdeenshire.

Mag. Z. and Bot —Magazine of Zoology and Botany.

Mag. Nat. or Mag. N. H.—Magazine of Natural History, (London and Charlesworth).

Mag. de Zool.—Magasin de Zoologie, (Guerin's)

Mal. Mon.—Forbes' Malacologia Monensis.

Malac. Mag.—Malacological and Conchological Magazine, (edited by Sowerby).

Mart.—Martini's Conchylien Cabinet.

Mich.—Michaud's Supplement to Drapamaud's Histoire Naturelle des Coquilles terrestres et fluviatiles.

Mont.—Montagu's Testacea Brittanica.

Mont Sup.—Supplement to the above.

Mull. Z. D. or Mull. Zool. Dan.—Muller's Zoologia Danica, 1788.

Payr.—Payraudeau's Catalogue des Annelides et des Mollusques de l'Isle de Corse.

Pen.—Pennant's British Zoology, 1777.

Phil. or Phillipi—Philippi's Enumeratio Molluscorum Siciliæ.

Planc. Conch.—Plancus de Conchis Minus Notis.

Poli.—Poli's Testacea utriusque Siciliæ.

Pult. Dor.—See Dor. Cat.

Reeve.—Reeve's Conchologia Systematica.

Say.—Say in the Journal of the Academy of Philadelphia, (vols. 2 and 5,) American Conchology, &c.

Schroet. Ein.—Schroeter's Einlentung in die Conchylien nach Linné.

Seba.—Seba's Descriptio Thesauri rerum Naturalium.

Sil. J.—Silliman's American Journal of Science.

Sow. Brit. Misc.—Sowerby's British Miscellany.

Sow. Conc. Il.—See C. I.

Sow. G.—Sowerby's Genera of Recent and Fossil Shells.

Sow. Sp. Con.—Sowerby's Species Conchyliorum (Pandora).

Sow. Th.—Sowerby's, Junior, Thesaurus Conchyliorum (Lima and Pecten).

Trans. Berwick. N. H. Soc.—See Berw. Tr.

Tr. Wer.—See Wer. Tr.

Turt. B. or Turt. Biv. or T. Biv.—Turton's Bivalves, being the only portion published of his Conchylia Insularum Brittanicarum.

Turt. D., Turt. Dic. or Turt. C. D.—Turton's Conchological Dictionary.

Voy. de Coq.—Voyage de la Coquille, (Mollusques par Lesson).

Walker.—Walker's Testacea Minuta Rariora.

Wern. T. or Wern. Soc. or Wern. Mem.

Wood's G. C.—Wood's General Conchology.

Z. J. or Zool. J.—Zoological Journal.

Z. M.—Zoological Miscellany (Leach's)

Z. P.—-Proceedings of the Zoological Society of London.

SYSTEMATIC INDEX.

The species not printed in italics, are those whose distinctness is doubtful, or which having only been found after death, have probably been cast ashore from wrecks. The numerals refer to the page at which each species is described.

ANNELIDES.

DENTALIUM.

Entalis, 1 (a).

Tarentinum, 2, f. 6. Young

Dentalis, 2, and Semistriatum, 3.

Album, 2.

Octangulatum, 2.

Labiatum, 3.

(a) According to M. Deshayes, this and the succeeding shell form but one species. We shall not be surprised if this opinion prove correct with regard to the common Kentish specimens, (in abundance at Pegwell Bay) which *we* consider to be the Entalis of the majority of British cabinets.

Læve, 3 (*b*). | *Gadus*, 5, *f.* 62.
Imperforatum, 4. | *Trachea*, 5, *f.* 61.
Clausum, 4. | *Subulatum* (*c*), *f.* 60
Glabrum, 4, *f.* 5.

(*b*) The British Dentalia are peculiarly obscure, few cabinets possessing more than one or two of the larger species. I believe the chief difference of the Læve from the Entalis, consists in its being snowy white, highly polished (like enamel), and perfectly free from those extremely minute longitudinal striulæ, which in perfect specimens will be always found, under the lens, in that species. It is also more attenuated and longer, but this latter character is of little avail for comparison, as this genus is rarely found alive and perfect. This species is chiefly found in the north of England, and the Entalis in the south.

(*c*) Subcylindrical, elongated, polished, pale horn coloured, perfectly smooth, moderately arcuated. Larger aperture contracted, perfectly round, smaller extremity with a minute round perforation, no fissure. Length one inch, breadth at the broadest part nearly a line, at the smaller end, one third of a line. This is the Ditrupa Subulata of Berkely in the Zoological Journal, and the Dentalium Subulatum of Deshayes' Monograph. The

PECTINARIA.	*Conchilega,* 7.
Belgica, 5 (*d*).	*Lumbricalis,* 7.
	Cirrhata, 7.
SABELLARIA.	*Arenaria,* 8.
Alveolata, 6 (*e*).	*Subcylindrica,* 8.
	Setiformis, 8.
TEREBELLA.	*Curta,* 8.
Chrysodon, 6.	*Compressa,* 8.

specimen described came from the N. W. coast of Ireland, and was presented by its discoverer to Mr. Hanley, by whom it was transferred to the valuable collection of W. Metcalfe, Esq.

(*d*) I received from Mr. Bean an arcuated and much more tapering and slender varietv, which perfectly agreed with Muller's figure *(Zool. Dan. t.* 26, *f.* 2.*)* of the sheath of his Amphitrite Auricoma.

(*e*) There are two curious varieties (?) of this shell, the first possessing the honeycomb appearance and parallel tubes of the type, but constructed of coarser materials, is usually termed S. CRASSISSIMA. The tubes of the other have no regular arrangement, and their mouths are devoid of the usual patulous rim. It forms large banks at Margate and Ramsgate, and is the S. TUBULARIA of Chenu's Illustrations Conchiliologiques.

Flexilis (f).

SPIRORBIS.

Nautiloides, 9.

Spirillum, 9.

Granulata, 10, *f.* 64.

Heterostropha, 10. *Young*

? Minuta, 11.

Carinata, 10.

Corrugata, 11, *f.* 65.

Lucida, 11, *f.* 63.

Cornea, 12.

Conica, 243.

SERPULA.

Mulleri, 12, *(S. Vermicularis, Montagu and Turton,) (g). Variety Spirorbis Reversa,* 12. *Variety coiled up in substances to which it cannot attach itself, Solitaria,* 265, *f.* 67.

(*f*) Tube free, subcylindrical, flexuous, elastic, scarcely, if at all, tapering, membraneous, without (for the most part) sand, stones, broken shells, or any foreign substances attached; the lines of growth circular, the thickness not exceeding a crowquill. *Scarborough, from* 6 *to* 8 *inches in length.*

(*g*) I may as well mention that the variety B. of Turton's Dictionary, (p. 152,) is but a V. Triquetra, so located as to be unable to spread at the base. I state this from the possession of a specimen authenticated by Turton. The variety Solitaria, were it not always flattened above and considerably smaller, might easily be confused with Tubularia.

Tubularia, 13. (*Ver-*
metus Semisurrectus ?
Phil. t. 9,*f.* 19.*) f.* 68.
Filograna, 13.
*Vermicularis,*13*(h). f.*66

VERMILIA.

Triquetra, 14. *Variety*
Serrulata, 244, *f.* 53.
Variety coiled up in

(*h*) The variety Tubularia of Turton seems so very distinct, that it was only after continual observation that I assented to Mr. Berkely's synonyms in the Magazine of Natural History. The Vermicularis has a thin keel, (often with two additional smaller ones,) aud the mouth seems armed above with an obtuse tooth-like projection, (the shell being cylindrical cannot be confused with V. Triquetra.) It is rarely found solitary, and the larger end scarcely if at all, projects above the surface. In this state it appears to be the Rugosa of the Conchological Dictionary, p. 154, and bears much resemblance to Mulleri, but that species (at least the Vermicularis of Montague, which is declared by Mr. B. to be the same) has a subquadrate look, for the top is somewhat flattened. When aged the carina and tooth totally disappear, the shell rises at a considerable angle from the surface to which the lower portion is attached, the margin of the aperture becomes circular and reflected, and finally the relics of the successively formed mouths produce the effect of one tube growing out of the other.

(*i*) Transverse, inequivalve, inequilateral, open at the anterior end. Hinge with a transverse heart-shaped moveable tooth common to both the valves, and uniting them by a transverse cavity in each; ligament internal.

(*j*) Transversely oval-oblong, inequivalve, slightly gaping at each extremity. Hinge consisting of a more or less prominent horizontal spoon-shaped tooth which receives the ligament. Palleal scar deeply impressed.

(*k*) Transverse, oval, equivalve, a little open at the sides. Hinge with a spoon-shaped tooth and additional denticles, no lateral teeth. Ligament external.

(*l*) Possibly young Astarte's.

PORONIA (*m*).

Rubra (*Kellia R.* 51.)

MONTACUTA.

Substriata, 51.

Bidentata, 52, *f.* 58,

Ferruginea, 52, *f.* 16.

Oblonga, 52.

Glabra, 245.

M.? Purpurea, f. 14 (*n*).

(*m*) A genus established by M. Recluz in the Revue Cuverienne of last year. Although nearly allied to Kellia, it is evidently a natural genus, and is most easily recognised by the broad ligamental plate. The characters are as follows :—" Ovate or roundish, transverse, equivalve inequilateral, closed. Two cardinal teeth in each valve, (but not as in Kellia on the same side of the umbo.) A ligamental pit running alongside of the single lateral tooth. Muscular impressions oval, equal. No palleal sinus.

(*n*) I received from Mr. Bean of Scarborough some shells thus named. They are so minute as almost to baffle microscopic observation. I perceive, however, two approximate cardinal teeth on the same side of the umbo, and a very indistinct anterior lateral one. These characters are those of Kellia proper. The ligament is very indistinct. The shell is elliptical, smooth, glossy, very inquilateral, pale olive with a purplish tinge at the beaks, pellucid,

b

(o) Not impossibly the young Mya Arenaria.
(p) Scarcely differing from HIATELLA.

(*q*) Most rare. Erroneously in text " not rare."

(*r*) This shell is not the M. Modiolus of Linne, which is really that called Tulipa by Lamarck. I state this from an examination of the typical specimens of that great naturalist.

(*s*) M. Nigra (Gray in Supplement to Parry's Voyage) appears to be the Discrepans of Montagu's Supplement, agreeing very well with the figure. The author's reference to the larger Newfoundland specimens must be expunged, for although extremely resembling them, the British shell may be easily distinguished by the proportionate shortness from the beaks to the ventral edge, (which by age also becomes much incurved,) and its decidedly stronger radiating costellæ, *Frith of Forth.*

(t) The O. Hippopus of Lamarck, stated to be common on the French coast, but not mentioned by our own

British writers as found on our shores, appears to be nothing more than that variety of the common oyster, of which the sides are expanded and the inner margin denticulated near the umbo.

(*Pátella Pellucida*, 131).

(*Patella Testudinalis*, 131,)*f.* 103.

(*Patella Virginea*, 131).

(*Young Pulchella*,132).

Fulva (*u*).

PLEURO- BRANCHUS.

Plumula, 132,*f.* 41.

Membranaceus, 133,*f.*76.

EMARGINULA.

Fissura, 133.

Rosea (*Fissura*, *var.* 133) (*v*),*f.* 79.

FISSURELLA.

Reticulata, Donovan, (*Græca*, 134).

Noachina, 134,*f.* 78.

Nubecula, 251.

PILEOPSIS.

Ungaricus, 135.

Antiquus, 135.

Militaris, 135.

CALYPTRÆA.

Chinensis, 136.

BULLÆA.

Aperta, 137.

Punctata, 137.

(*u*) PATELLA FULVA, *Muller Zool. Dan.* 1, *p.* 24, *t.* 24,*f.* 1, 2, 3.—*Gmel.* 3712.—*D.* 1053. Oval-oblong, depressed, uniform orange or tawney yellow, seemingly smooth, but when magnified decussated by minute longitudinal and transverse striæ; apex submarginal. 0·20. *Found in Rosshire by Mr. Jeffreys.*

(*v*) Higher, rounder at the base and the summit more recurved than in Fissura : tinged with rose-colour internally when taken with the animal alive.

(*w*) A. Heteroclita is mentioned in the text. An examination of Mr. Laskey's figure in the Wernerian Transactions has rendered us extremely doubtful as to what genus it should be placed in. We have never seen the shell which was introduced into the catalogue as an Auricula on the authority of Mr. Fleming. The figure somewhat resembles a reversed Achatina Acicula.

(x) This genus has required considerable revision. Mr. Macgillivray's descriptions (his work appeared subsequently to the printing of most of our sheets), and the

Plicata, f. 13. | *Interstincta,* 173, *f.* 37.

Spiralis, 173. | *Insculpta,* 173.

~~~~~~

examination of the specimens from whence Mr. Hanley's descriptions were taken, have thrown considerable light upon the subject. We have thought it better to erase the descriptions at page 172 and give the following derived from the shells themselves, which not having seen, we had contented ourselves with copying from Fleming.

O. UNIDENTATA, *F. p*. 310.—*not Macg. p.* 154.— TURBO U. *Mont. p.* 324.—*Turt. D. p.* 222. Oblong-conical, solid ; whitish, moderately glossy, smooth ; whorls 5 or 6, not much raised ; aperture one third of the entire length, not at all effuse at the base ; outer lip ovate, striated internally with fine raised spiral lines ; the tooth-like plate horizontal, placed a little higher up than the middle of the pillar lip ; apex blunt. Length full one quarter of an inch, breadth rather more than half the length.

O. PLICATA. *Fl. p.* 310. (*not Macg.*)—Turbo P. *Mont.* p. 325 ?—*Turt. Dic. p.* 222. Closely resembling the last, but although much smaller, the whorls are always as numerous, and often more so (7). The shell too is narrower in proportion to its length, and the whorls are flat and polished.

O. EULIMOIDES. *Hanley in Zoological Proceedings*, 1844. Oblong-turrited, pure white, semi-transparent, polished, smooth ; whorls 5, moderately convex, the last-formed equal in length to the spire ; suture distinct ; aperture oblong, the tooth-like plait in the centre of the columellar lip ; outer lip but slightly convex at the edge, rather effuse at the base, perfectly smooth within: Length two lines, breadth not quite half as much. *Herm near Guernsey.*

O. RISSOIDES. *Hanley Z. P.* 1844. Oblong-conical, white, glossy, smooth ; whorls 5, moderately convex, suture distinct, the last whorl equal in length to the rest of the spire ; aperture occupying two fifths of the length of the shell, ovate, the plait lying so far back on the centre of the inner lip as not easily to be distinguished at first ; outer lip smooth within. *Allied to Eulimoides, but the mouth is far smaller ; breadth half the length, which is two lines. Guernsey. Allied to Fragilis of Michaud, but the whorls are fewer and the outer lip quite acute.*

O. TURRITA. *Hanley in Z. P.* 1843. Turrited, pure white, smooth glossy ; whorls 5, moderately convex ; suture oblique, distinct in the last whorls ; aperture one fourth of the entire length, almost uniform from the projection of the tooth-like plait on the upper part of the columella. 1⅓..⅓, lines.. *Guernsey. Allied to Producta of Gould.*

(*y*) Conical, moderately elevated ; whorls few, subinflated ; aperture rounded, imperfect posteriorly ; lip sharp ; umbilicus deep ; operculum multispiral, the nucleus central.

(*z*) Variety ? Patula, *f.* 83. Spire all but flat, umbilicus obsolete, columella groove broad but very shallow ; aperture patulous ; epidermis very distinct.

Fasciata, 256, *f*. 84.	*Variety Quadrifasciata*
Puteolus (*a*).	(*Turbo Q*. 168). *Va-*
** *Spire produced more*	*riety Canalis*, 257.
or less conoid.	*Variety Bifasciata* (*c*).
Vincta (*Turbo V*. 168)	*Variety? Gracilior* (*d*).
(*b*).	*f*. 86.

(*a*) L. PUTEOLUS. *Turton Zool. Jour.* 3, *p*. 191.— Roundish oblong, oblique, purplish with three deeper bands; aperture roundish or oval. *Devonshire. Thicker than Montacuti or Fasciata, and when full grown has the larger volution considerably produced obliquely.*

(*b*) The young are destitute of markings, of a sea green, with an obtuse carina near the base of the body whorl. In this state it agrees well with Montagu's figure of Canalis.

(*c*) With two broad brown and two narrow white bands.

(*d*) L. GRACILIOR. *Metcalfe MSS.* Resembling Canalis of Turton in being of an uniform horn colour, but the shape is more attenuated, the whorls being produced so that instead of the aperture being as long as the spire it only occupies two fifths of the shell. The outer lip too, is acute, (in the adult of Canalis it is thickened,) and the columellar groove very narrow instead of being wider than in the typical variety.

Turbo Costatus of La-
- *'march*) (*e*).
Marginata, 176 (*Rissoa*
Acicula? *Sow. G. R.*
Acuta? Desmoulin.
C.? Dentifera, 177.
Bryerea (*Chesnelii? Mi-*
chaud on Rissoa).

Semicostata, 178.
Striata, 178 (*Rissoa Spi-*
rata? Sow. G.),*f.* 99.
Disjuncta, 179.
Labiosa, 179, *f.* 42.
Rupestris, 184.
Reticulata (*f*).

(*e*) A curious variety (if indeed no more than a variety) of this species has been figured, (f. 4,) from a specimen forwarded by Mr. Bean as Rufilabris? of Leach, which agrees perfectly with specimens collected by Mr. Sylvanus Hanley at Ryde. The shape, as in Parva, is oblong-conical, the 6 or 7 whorls moderately convex, and the lower ones longitudinally obtusely ribbed. Perfect specimens have very fine spiral striæ. But the mouth is peculiar. It possesses an extremely thick white marginal callus on the outer lip, which is edged with rufous. The aperture is violet, a smoky shade of which forms the uniform colour of the shell. The rufous arched line which usually ornaments the exterior portion of the lip in Parva, is absent.

(*f*) C. RETICULATA. *Fl.* 306.—TURBO R. *Mont. t.* 21, *f.* 1, *p.* 322.—*Turt. Dic.* 212.—(*Lin. Trans.* 3, *t.* 13,

Brugieri, f. 38 (*g*). | *Beanii, f.* 43 (*h*).

f. 19, 20.) Conic, pointed, strong, opaque, dirty white or dull brown; whorls 6, much rounded and well defined, strongly striated both longitudinally and transversely. Aperture nearly orbicular, thickened by a rib; inner lip a litttle reflected, with a slight groove behind it. 0·10. *Pembrokeshire, Kent, and Seaford in Ireland.*

(*g*) R. BRUGIERI, *Fayraudeau, t.'*5, *f.* 17, 8, *p.* 113. Oblong-turrited, strong, glassy white; whorls 7, convex, roughened by narrow longitudinal ribs (about 12 on the body), and distinct spiral striæ; body whorl occupying five twelfths of the length; the outer lip not patulous, with a very broad transversely sulcated margin, and a distinct sinus at the base of the aperture, which is oblong; pillar very strong.

A single specimen of this distinct shell is in the collection of W. Bean, Esq., and I believe was found at Scarborough.

(*h*) Ovate-conical, dull white, strong, not umbilicated, apex rather obtuse; whorls five, rather flat, girt with numerous raised concentric sulci, which in the middle whorls and the upper part of the body-whorl are decussated by numerous costellæ, (at least 20 or 30

Scalariformis (*i*), *f.* 89.

** *Outer lip simple,*
acute (*j*).

(*CINGULÆ Proper*).

Ventricosa, 180.

Subumbilicata, 181.

Interrupta, 182.

Rubra, 182, *f.* 26.

Unifasciata, 182 (*Fulva Michaud on Rissoa fide Recluz*).

---

on each whorl); aperture equal to one third the length of the shell; outer lip strong, striated spirally within. *Scarborough.* 0·10..0·25.. *The description of R. Buccinoides of Deshayes, in the expedition to the Morea, seems to apply to a shell allied to this species.*

(*i*) R. Scalariformis, *Metcalfe MSS.* General appearance of R. Cimex, but more elongated, the suture particularly distinct, the whorls rounded, a grooved space destitute of decussation at the base, the belt above which is peculiarly strong; aperture devoid of spiral striæ, but the exterior ridges forming four or five internal grooves. *Herm near Guernsey.*

(*j*) C. ? Globularis, *Metcalfe MSS.*, *f.* 87. Globose, conic, shining, pellucid, horn-coloured, with 4 whorls, the last considerably the largest, marked by slight lines of growth; aperture oval, the inner lip expanded and partly covering a moderately sized umbilicus; suture not deep. *Length and breadth about one twelfth of an inch. Weymouth.*

(*k*) TURBO PUNCTURA, *Mont. t.* 12, *f.* 5.—*Turt. Dic. p.* 211. Oval, thin, white, generally glossy, rather pointed; spires 5, swollen and well defined, with re-gular fine circular and longitudinal ribs so as to re-semble fine lace, and punctured in the interstices; body whorl with about 12 transverse threads, the penult with 6 or 7, and the rest with fewer and less distinctly defined; aperture roundish oval; outer lip thin and plain, pillar lip a little reflected, with a slight longitudinal groove behind it. 0·10..0·20..*West coasts and Ireland. Fleming considers it to be the young of Reticulata. I have not seen it.*

(*l*) C. PELLUCIDA, *Bean MSS.* Turrited-oblong, pellucid white, glossy; whorls five, very smooth and rounded; suture distinct; apex rather obtuse; aper-ture more than one third the length of the shell, outer lip acute and arcuated. *Rare.* 0·25..0·10. *General shape of Montagu's figure of Ventrosa, but his description will not accurately apply.*

(*m*) Hyaline, turbinate, apex mucronated; aperture subovate, acuminated above; lip acute, sinuated.

(*n*) Variety—smaller and more slender, the whorls being deeper in proportion to their breadth, pellucid bluish white. In the cabinet of W. Metcalfe, Esq.

(*o*) PARTHENIA TURRITA, *Metcalfe MSS.* Turrited, subpellucid white; whorls scalariform, about 6, very distinct but not convex, adorned with numerous

Ascaris, f. 20 (*p*).

CERITHIUM.

Coslatuin, 196.

Turbiforme, 193.

Tuberculare, 193, *f.* 8.

Reticulatum, 193.

---

narrow longitudinal ribs, which are about one third of
the breadth of the interstices, and a single raised
spiral rib situated a little below the middle of each
whorl; two additional rather indistinct lower ones on
the body whorl, which occupies one third the length of
the shell. ⅜...*breadth two fifths of length. Guernsey.
This most beautiful species, from the upper portion of
the whorls being flattened, seems in a fine specimen to
have the ribs tuberculated at their summit, or when
rubbed, even to form a spiral band there. The aperture
is small and squarish ; there is no umbilicus but in perfect specimens, a slight umbilical groove and a very indistinct plait on the columella, but not the contracted
mouth of Odostomia.*

(*p*) TURBO ASCARIS, *Turt. Dic.* 217. Extremely
slender, tapering to an exceedingly fine point, milk
white, semitransparent; whorls 7 or 8, rounded and
well defined by a deep impression, each with 4 or 5
regular equidistant and rather deep spiral grooves ;
aperture suborbicular, the inner lip a little reflected.
*Breadth a fourth of the length, which is not the tenth
of an inch. Seafield Ireland. Rare.*

.(*q*) The two first species alone possess the constant emargination which should distinguish this genus. The others have a more or less distinct sinus, and will probably form a subgenus with the first 8 or 9 species of the second division of our Fusi, to which they are so closely allied that it is impossible with justice to separate them. But as these latter cannot come within the definition of Pleurotoma we have provisionally followed Turton in our arrangement.

(*r*) Will probably prove but a variety of F. Turricula, the depth of the sinus evidently varying in individual specimens.

(*s*) P. Metcalfei, *Reeve MSS.* Elongated-subfusiform, white, with a single subcentral rather broad brownish band on the body-whorl, which runs along the base of the others; whorls 5, not raised, but the suture distinct; adorned with 6 broad, strong, and elevated longitudinal ribs, the interstices smooth; spire about equal in length to the body-whorl; aperture very narrow, outer lip thickened, the emargination at the suture. 0·40...0·12. *A few specimens of this rare shell are in the cabinet of W. Metcalfe, Esq. who procured them on an islet near Guernsey. When worn the entire base is of a chesnut colour.*

(*t*) Voluta Hyalina of Montagu is the young of a foreign Columbella.

c

The author, in common with most Conchologists, has felt the want of good figures of the British shells, the majority of the delineations being inadequate for distinguishing the species. He proposes, in the event of there being a sufficient number of subscribers, to publish *the figures of every British marine shell,* engraved by a first rate artist, at the moderate price (to subscribers only) of fifteen shillings a copy. As the production of this desideratum to British conchologists will entirely depend upon there being at least fifty subscribers, the author will feel obliged to those gentlemen who may be willing to become so, if they will at their earliest convenience announce their intention to him, under cover to the publisher.

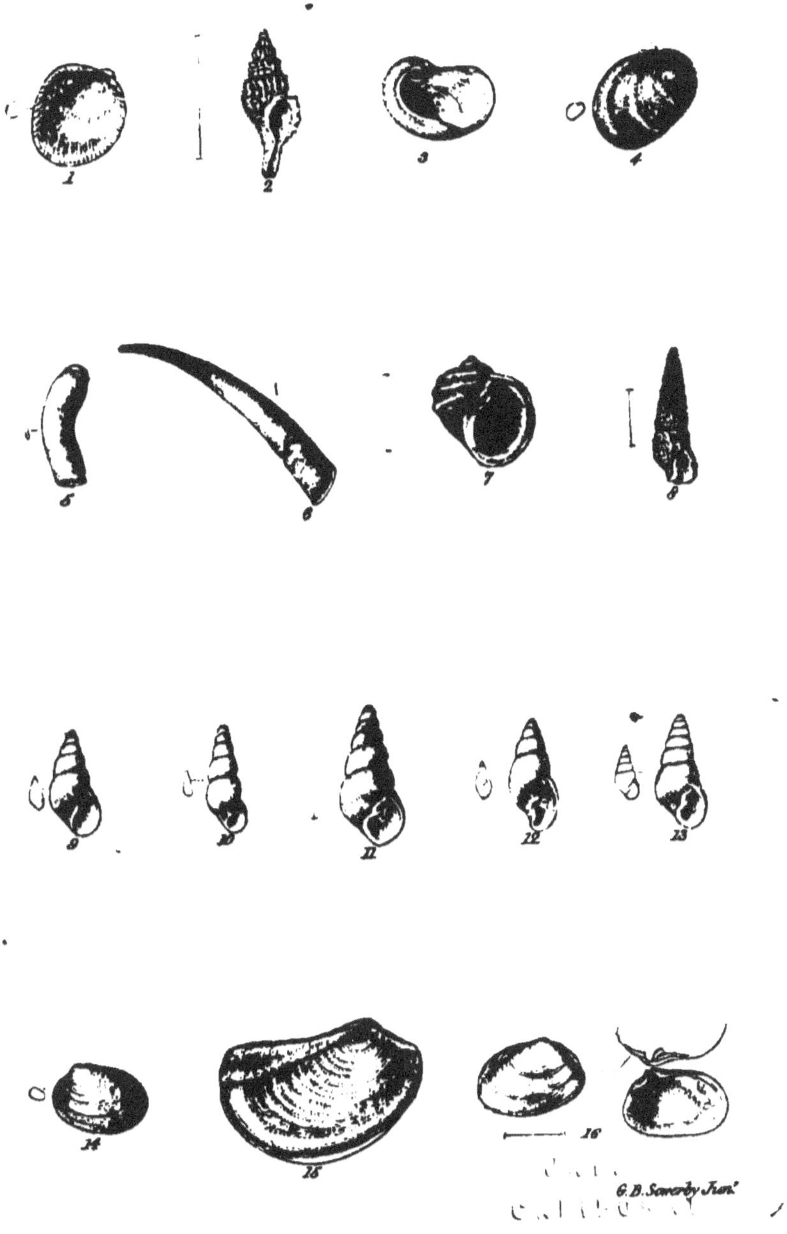

1
2
3
4
5
6
7
8
9
10
11
12
13
14
15
16
G. B. Sowerby Jun.

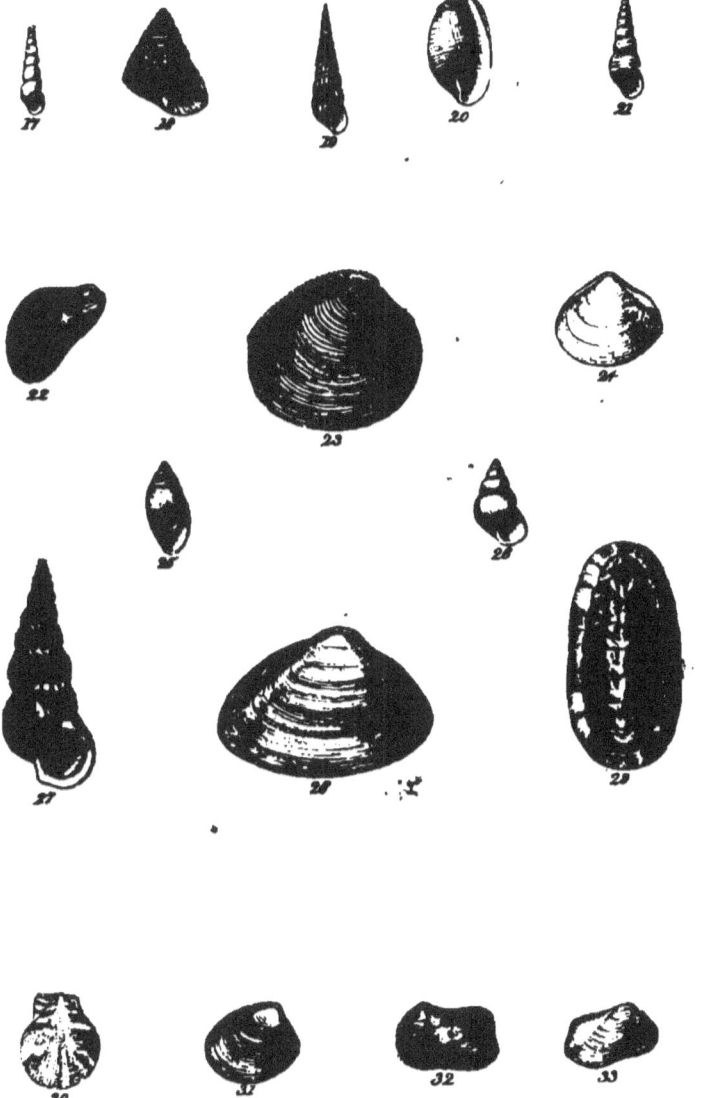

G. B. Sowerby. Jun.ʳ

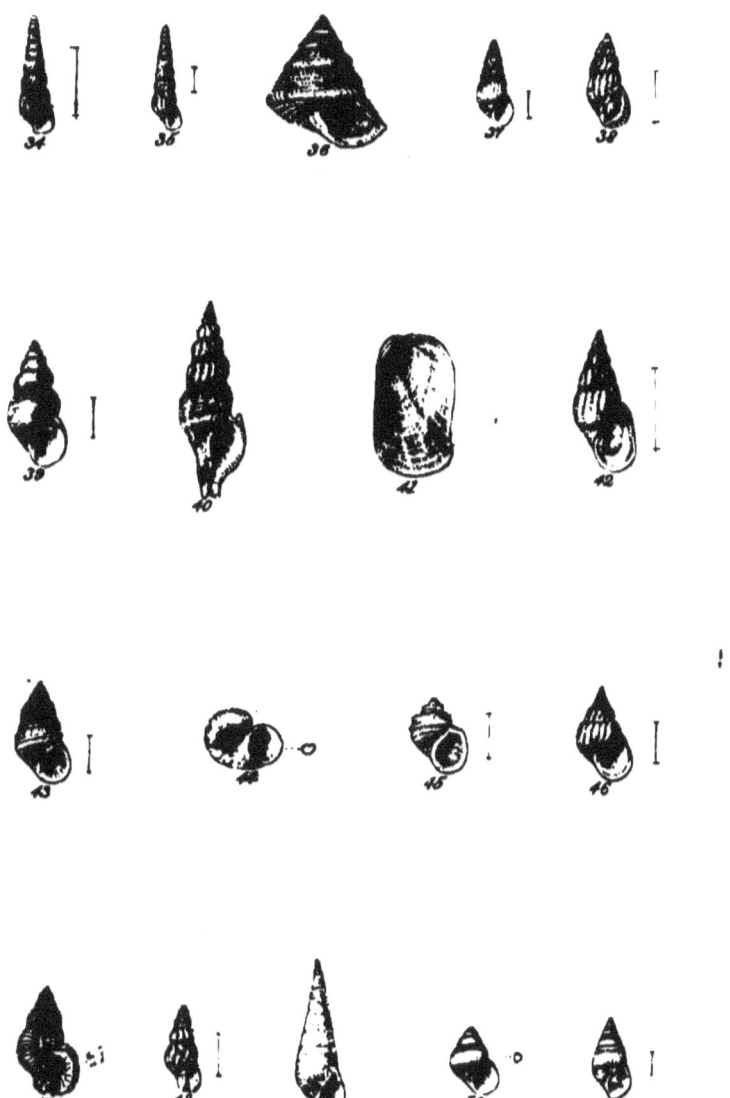

G. B. Sowerby, Jun.

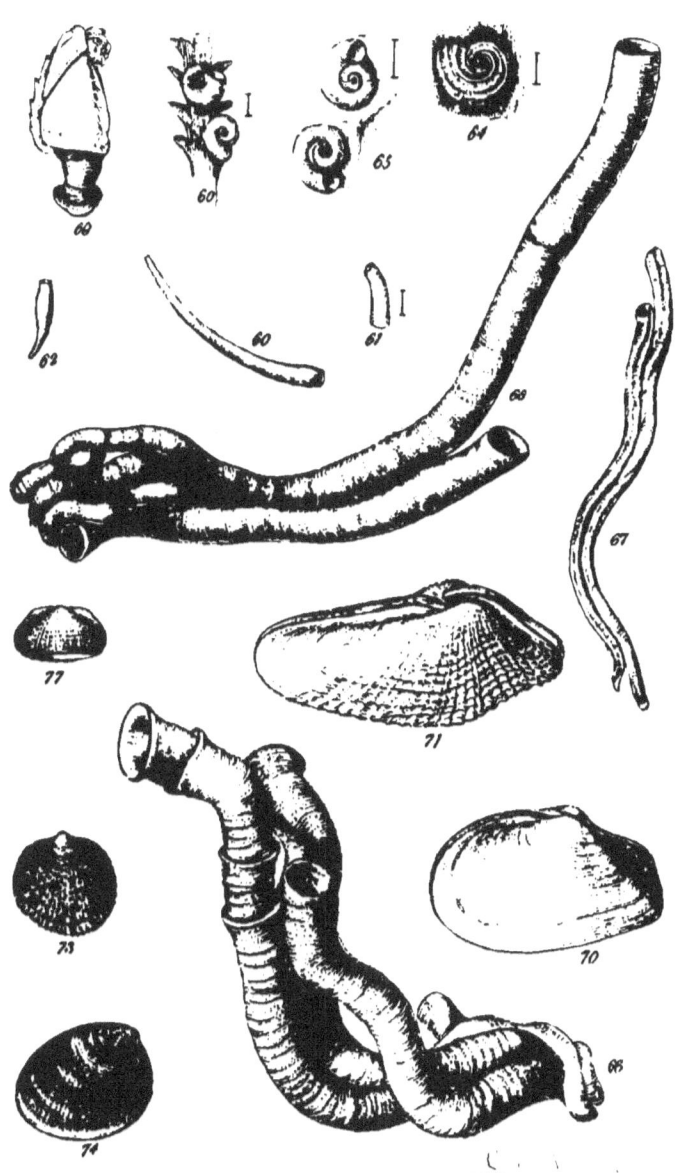

G.B. Sowerby, Jun.r fecit

VII
1 J / 5

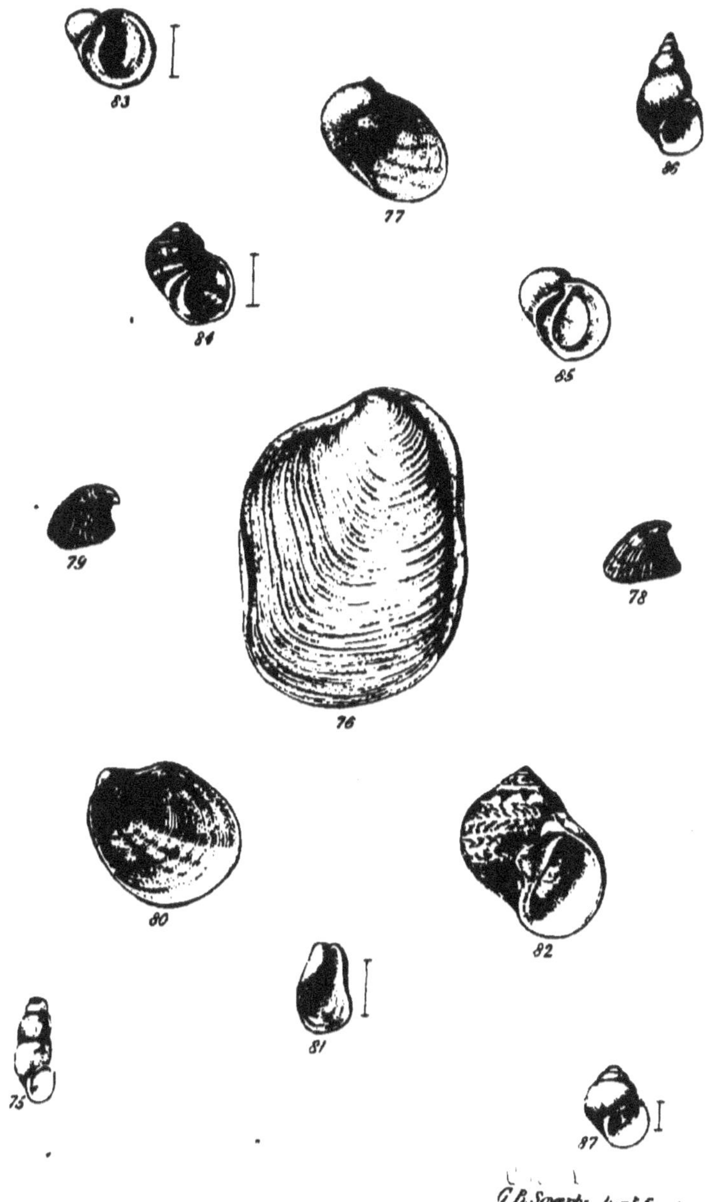

83

77

86

84

85

79

78

76

80

82

75

81

87

G. B. Sowerby Jun.r f.cit.

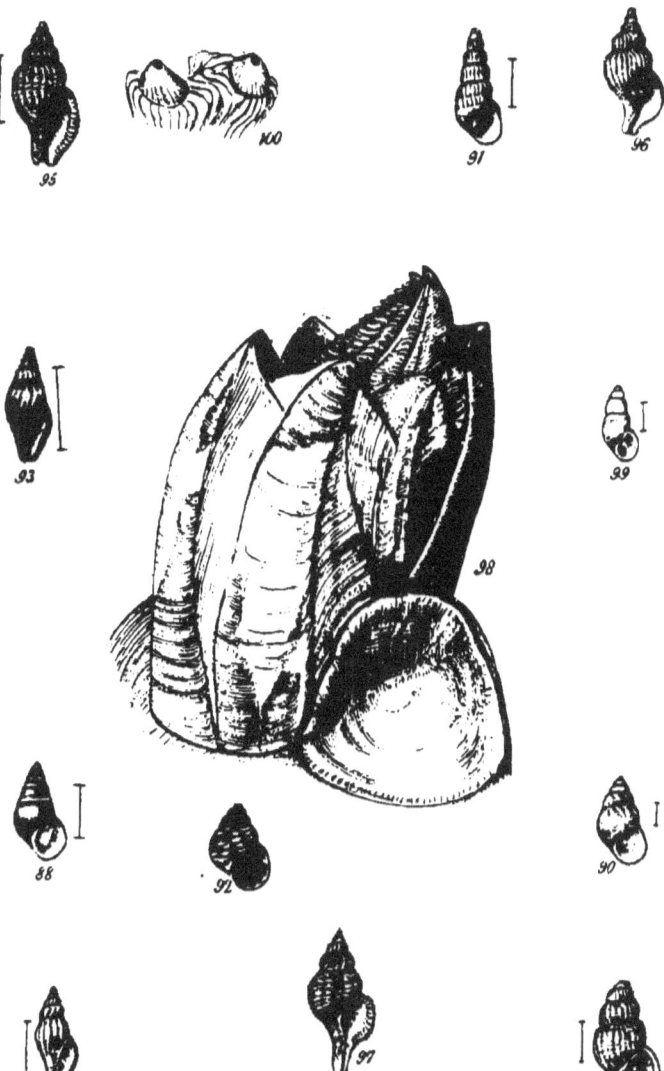

G. B. Sowerby Jun.ᵗ Fecit

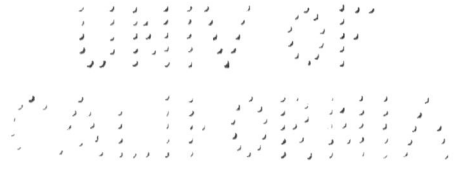

BRITISH MARINE
CONCHOLOGY.

ARTICULATA.

CLASS.—ANNELIDES.

ORDER.—SEDENTARIÆ.

TRIBE.—MALDANIÆ.

GENUS.—DENTALIUM.

Horn shaped, slightly arcuated and almost regular, attenuated insensibly towards the posterior extremity, open at both ends.

D. ENTALIS, *Lin.* 1263.—*D. p.* 1065.—*Arg. t.* 3. *f.* 3.—*Knorr.* 1. *t.* 29. *f.* 1.—*Pen. t.* 4. *p.* 145, *t.* 90. *f.* 154.—*Don. t.* 48.—*Mont. p.* 494.—*Dor Cat. t.* 22. *f.* 10.—*Turt. D. p.* 37.—D. VULGARE, *Da Cos. p.* 24. *t.* 2 *f.* 10.   Slender, tapering, a little curved,

A

opaque, glossy, smooth or marked with a few circular striæ or obscure annulations; white or yellowish white, with mostly a rufous tinge towards the smaller end.

1½. *Common on sandy coasts.*

D. DENTALIS, *Turt.D.p.*37—*An Lin. et auctorum?* Slender, tapering to a fine point, slightly curved, opaque, regularly and closely atriated the whole length, the striæ about 30 or more, with often a few faint annulations at the larger end; white or brownish, mostly rufous at the smaller end. ½ *W. coast, often found in the Gurnard.*

D. ALBUM.—*Turt. D. p.* 256. *and* D. EBURNEUM. *p.* 37.—A little tapering and slightly bent, semitransparent, ivory, white not glossy, often marked with obscure dark purple spots, disposed in longitudinal rows, with about 18 regular fine, raised, longitudinal ribs, and often a smaller intermediate one; lower end not pointed with a roundish oval aperture. ⅛ *W. coast, not rare; differs from the last in having the striæ equally strong throughout and in tapering but slightly.*

D. OCTANGULATUM.—*Don. t.* 162.—*An Lam.* 5. *?* *An Desh. Mon. Dent. in Z. J.* 4. *p.* 181—STRIATULUM. *Turt. D. p.* 37. *(not Gmel)*—D. STRIATUM. *D. p.* 1064. *in part.*—Slender, tapering to a fine point, slightly curved, semi-transparent, with 8 longitudinal angular ribs, between each of which are 3 or 4 very obtuse longitudinal striæ; greyish white, pale rufous or green, with a white tip.—1¾. *Cornwall and Devon, very rare.*

D. Labiatum. *Turt. D. p.* 38.—Nearly cylindrical, very slightly tapering and curved, semi-transparent, ivory white, covered, when fresh, with a black glossy skin, most finely and minutely striated longitudinally; open at the larger extremity, the smaller end truncated, with the flattened surface somewhat undulated in a radiate manner, and finely striated circularly, from the centre of which projects an oval transparent process or lip, terminating in an oval aperture one side of which is cloven half-way down. 1½. *Torbay. Breadth at the open end, one fifth.*

D. Læve. *Turt. D. p.* 256. *and* Politum. *p.* 38. Somewhat cylindrical, slightly tapering and a little curved, semi-transparent, quite smooth and finely polished, white, with generally some irregular grey circular bands which grow darker and more combined together towards the narrower extremity; both ends open, the smaller very obtuse, not truncated, but rounded, with an oval perforation. 1. *Torbay, very rare, not unlike the last. Breadth at smaller end,⅛, at the larger,* 0,20.

D. Semistriatum. *Turt. D. p.* 39. *f.* 68.—Very slender, tapering to a very fine point, glossy, transparent, a little curved, open at both ends, quite smooth on

the upper part, marked below with numerous longitudinal striæ which are very distinct at the point, but grow
fainter towards the middle, and at length totally disappear; clear white with a pale rufous tinge at the
smaller end. 1,1. Breadth at larger end, 0,048. *Dublin
Bay.*

D. IMPERFORATUM. *Walker. f.* 15.—*Mont. p.* 496.
D. p. 1068.—*Adams t.* 14, *f.* 8—*Turt. D. p.* 39.—
Lin. T. 8. *p.* 238—ORTHOCERA. *T. F. p.* 237.—Slender,
slightly curved, whitish, transversely striated, the
larger end a little contracted at the margin, the smaller
end closed and furnished with a small round protuberance. ⅙. *Kent and Cornwall.*

D. CLAUSUM. *Turt. D. p.* 39.—Slender, slightly
tapering, nearly straight, semi-transparent, horn colored
or yellowish white, irregularly striated longitudinally,
open at the larger end, with the opposite end closed and
obtuse. 1. *at larger end* ⅛. *Calves Island, W.
Ireland.*

D. GLABRUM. *Mont. p.* 497.—*Turt. D. p.* 40.—
Lin. T. 8. *p.* 239.—D. MINUTUM. *D. p.* 1068.—*An
Lin* 1264? CÆCUM. *G. Flem, Edin. Ene.* 7. *p.* 67. *t.*
204. *f.* 7.—ORTHOCERA. *G. F. p.* 237.—Cylindric,
arcuated, smooth, glossy, white, perfectly smooth;
aperture orbicular,, the other end closed, rounded, sub-
marginated. 0,0833...0,0167. *Not uncommon at
Biddeford Bay and Barnstaple, Devon.*

D. Gadus. *Mont. p.* 496 *t.* 14. *f.* 7.—*Turt. D. p.* 40.—*Lin. T.* 8. *p.* 238.—*D. p.* 1067.—*An* D. Coarc-tatum. *Desh in Z. I.* 4. *p.* 193.—Subpellucid, sub-arcuated, tapering to a small point, pervious, contracting a little towards the larger end, white, glossy, perfectly smooth. ⅜. 0,0622. *British Channel, not rare.*

D. Trachea. *Mont. p.* 427. *t.* 14, *f.* 10.—*Turt. D. p.* 40.—*Lin. T.* 8. *p.* 239.—*D. p.* 1068.—Ortho-cera. t. *f. p.* 237.—Subcylindric, arcuated, ferrugin-ous brown becoming pale towards the smaller end, which is closed, truncated and furnished with a small round protuberance; marked with regular transverse striæ, or annulations, aperture round, the margin not contracted. ⅛. 0,125 *Milton in Devonshire, rare, in sand.*

Tribe.—AMPHITRITEANÆ.

Genus.—PECTINARIA.

Tube free, solitary, regular, conical, subcylindraceous, open at both extremities, membronaceous or papyra-ceous, covered externally with grains of sand or minute stones.

P. Belgica. *Lam.* I.—Sabella. B. *Gmel* 3749.— S. Granulata ? *Lin.* 1268.—*Mont. p.* 544.— S. Tubiformis. *Pen* 4. *t.* 92. *f.* 163.—*Don. t.* 133. Simple, straight, gradually tapering, the grains of sand so flatter.cd on the surface as to appear one uniform smooth level. *Common on sandy shores, abundant at Shellness, in Kent.* 2¼. ¼.

Genus.—SABELLARIA.

Tubes gregarious, forming one mass, resembling honey-combs on the upper surface, composed of sand, broken shell and small stones; apertures cup-shaped,

S. Alveolata. *Lam.* 1.—Sabella a. *Lin* 1268.—*Mont. p.* 540—*Pen. t.* 92. *f.* 162.—*(Ellis Coral. t.* 36.) *Don. t.* 139.—With numerous tubes placed parallel to each other, contiguous but not interfering, apertures somewhat expanded. *Common, Margate, near Tenby, near Weymouth, &c.*

Genus.—TEREBELLA.

Tube solitary, elongated, cylindraceous, attenuated and pointed at its base, pervious only at the apex, composed of agglutinated sand or shells. ·

T. Chrysodon.—Sabella. C. *Mont p.* 546.—*An Lin.* 1269.—*Mart. f.* 29, 30.—Tube free, cylindrical, about as large as a goose-quill, composed of sand, fragments of shell or small flat pieces of stone cemented on a tubular membrane which is smooth within : mouth furnished with numerous long fibres of the same texture.

projecting in a subfunnel shape but generally somewhat compressed sideways. 4 to 6. *Devonshire, Margate, &c. not uncommon, buried in the sand between high and low water mark.*

T. CONCHILEGA. *An Lam.* 1 ?—SABELLA. *C. Pult. Dor. p.* 54.—*Mont. p.* 347.—S. RUDIS, *Pen.* 4. *t.* 26. *lower fig.*—AMPHITRITE OSTREARIA ? *Cuvier.*— Tube membranceous, sparingly covered with shells, usually in large fragments, attached to old bivalves in flexuous or serpentine manner; mouth not funnel-shaped nor fibrous. 3 or 4. *Common, Margate, &c.*

T. LUMBRICALIS.—SABELLA. L. *Pult. Dorset. p.* 53.—*Mont. p.* 549.—Tube affixed in a serpentine manner upon stones, shells, &c., strong, composed of coarse sand, sometimes mixed with fragments of shells, firmly cemented together in a rough fashion. 2 or 3. $\frac{1}{4}$. *Common, often entwined with Serpula Vermicularis and Vermilia Triquetra.*

T. CIRRHATA. *Gmel.* 3112.—SABELLA. C. *Mont. p.* 550.—Tube free, thick, fragile, tapering a little, composed of sand mixed a little with clay, slightly agglutinated together, soft when moist, crumbly when dry. 6 or 7. $\frac{1}{2}$. *In a muddy bottom, in an inlet running up near Kingsbridge, between high and low water mark.*

T. ARENARIA.—SABELLA. A. *Mont. p.* 532.—Tube extremely fragile, free, cylindrical, not tapering, composed of pure sand, slightly cemented together, without an internal membrane. *Common on the Dorset coast, about the thickness of a Raven's quill.*

T. SUBCYLINDRICA.—SABELLA. S. *Mont. p.* 552.— Tube long, subcylindrical, slender, fragile, not attached, composed of fine sand and minute bits of broken shells, cemented together on a fine membrane, adhering by their flat sides. *Diam.* 0,10. *Salcomb bar.*

T. SETIFORMIS —SABELLA. S. *Mont. p.* 553.— Tube free, long, slender, gradually tapering to half its diameter, composed of very fine fragments of shells and minute flat bits of stone, agglutinated together at their edges, lying on each other subimbricately, and standing oblique towards the larger end. 3 or 4. diam. double that of a hog's bristle. *In sand, Salcomb Bar, Devon.*

T. CURTA.—SABELLA. C. *Mont. p.* 554.—Tube upright, affixed at the base to the shingles, near which it is merely membraneceous and not covered as elsewhere, by sand and minute bits of flat stones or uniform fine sand on a tough membrane; diameter that of a crow quill, slightly tapering. 1. *Closely gregarious in the inlet near Kingsbridge.*

T. COMPRESSA.—SABELLA. C. *Mont. p.* 555.—Tube short, broad, and extremely flat, composed of large fragments of bivalves (chiefly Pectens) which are irregularly disposed, often imbricated, but invariably with the concave side outwards, which leaves a narrow perforation. *Torcross, Devonshire, in deep water.*

TRIBE.—SERPULACEÆ.
Tube solid and calcareous.

GENUS.—SPIRORBIS.

Tube testaceous, twisted into a spiral discoid orb; lower surface flat and affixed.

S. NAUTILOIDES. *Lam.* 1.—SERPULA SPIRORBIS. *Lin.* 1265.—*List. t.* 553. *f.* 5.—*Mart. f.* 21. *A. B. Pen.* 4. *p.* 145. *t.* 21. *f.* 155.—*Da. Cost. t.* 2. *f.* 11.—*Mont. p.* 498. —*D.' p.* 1073.—*Turt. D. p.* 149. *Don. t.* 9.—Opaque, white, with three or four regular lateral whorls, rounded on the upper part and a little wrinkled; umbilicated in the centre; base flat, spreading. *Variety.* With the mouth erect and sometimes a whorl or two turning a little spirally upwards. ⅛. *Excessively common on lobsters, &c.*

S. SPIRILLUM. *Lam.* 2.—SERPULA. S. *Lin.* 1264. *Turt. D. p.* 150.—*Dor. Cat. t.* 19. *f.* 27.—*D. p.* 1072 *Mont. p.* 499.—*Lin. T.* 8. *p.* 240.—*Reversed var.—* SINISTORSA. *Mont. p.* 504.—*Walk. f.* 134.—Glossy white, semi-transparent, orbicular, regular; whorls two or three, slightly wrinkled, and mostly placed laterally, the base not at all spread but quite cylindrical, with a central perforation, which sometimes goes quite through, mouth often turning a little upwards, exactly circular, not thinner than the rest of the shell, but appearing as if regularly cut off, with the whorls rising one upon the other. 1¼. *on Fuci and Sertulariæ, Weymouth, &c.*

S. GRANULATA.—SERPULA. G. *Lin.* 1266.—*D. p.* 1074.—*Mont. p.* 500.—*Don. t.* 100.—*Turt. D. p.* 150.—*Lin. T.* 8. *p.* 241.—SER SULCATA. *Lin. T.* 3. *p.* 254.—Opaque, white, with two volutions, deeply grooved longitudinally or in a spiral direction, and transversely wrinkled, especially in the furrows, aperture round. ⅙. *Milton, &c. tolerably common.*

S. HETEROSTROPHA.—SERPULA. H. *Mont. p.* 502. *Lin. T.* 8. *p.* 242.—*D. p.* 1075.—*Turt. D. p.* 151. —Strong, spiral, dull dirty white, with two or three reversed volutions placed laterally, furnished with longitudinal ridges, one along the back, and another on each side, rough, wrinkled transversely; base flat and somewhat spreading; aperture orbicular and invariably placed opposite the suns apparent motion. 0,076. *Not uncommon, Kingsbridge bay, &c.*

S. CARINATA. SERPULA. C. *Mont. p.* 502.—*Lin. T.* 8. *p.* 242.—*D. p.* 1074.--*Turt. D. p.* 151.—Dull,

opaque, white, spiral, outer whorl rising into a carinated ridge on the top, the middle concave and somewhat
pervious, inner volutions inconspicuous, base a little
spreading; aperture round. 0,0625. *Salcomb Bay, on
shells.*

S. CORRUGATA SERPULA. C. *Mont. p.* 502.—*Lin.
t.* 8. *p.* 242.—*D. p.* 151.—*Turt. D. p.* 151.—Strong,
spiral, white, roughened by transverse wrinkles, a small
portion only of the second volution visible; centre
umbilicated; aperture orbicular. ⅛. *Not rare on
slate rocks at Milton, stronger than Spirillum and
never exposing so much of the interior volution.*

S. MINUTA.—SERPULA. M. *Mont p.* 505.—*Turt.
D. p.* 150.—*Lin. T.* 8. *p.* 241.—*D. p.* 1072.—Very
small, spiral, dirty white, with two or three lateral volutions, wrinkled transversely, sometimes with a slight
longitudinal furrow on each side, forming a ridge or
carina along the back. 0,02. *Heteroclite and not
easily distinguished from Heterostropha except by its
size, rounded base and habits. On Corallina Offici-
nalis.*

S. LUCIDA.—SERPULA. L. *Mont. p.* 507.—*Lin.
T.* 8. *p.* 243.—*D. p.* 1075.—*Turt. Dic.*—SERP.
REFLEXA. *Adams in Lin. Tr.* 5. *p.* 4. *t.* 1. *f.* 31. 2.—
Irregular, heterostrophe, pellucid, glossy, white, always
more or less spiral, sometimes lateral, with two or three

whorls, sometimes the whorls turn upon each other, with the aperture projecting upwards and not unfrequently the spires are unconnected. *On Pertulariæ (especially Abrietina) W. and E. Coast.*

S. CORNEA.—SERPULA C. *Lin. Tr.* 5. *t.* 1. *f.* 33, 4, 5,—Regular, rounded, pellucid, brownish horn colored, with three whorls. *A doubtful species.*

S. REVERSA.—SERPULA R. *Mont. p.* 308.—*Turt. D. p.*—Subcylindrical reversed, rugose, white, much wrinkled transversely, more or less spiral and tapering, sometimes with three or four volutions pretty regularly placed laterally, (sometimes the smaller end is projecting and the larger end coiled, either laterally or upon each other and open in the middle.) Diam. ⅓. *Devonshire, on Pecten Opercularis.*

GENUS SERPULA.

Tube solid, calcareous, irregularly twisted, grouped or solitary, sessile; aperture terminal, rounded, very simple.

S. MULLERI. *Berkely in Mag. Nat.* 7.—S. VERMICULARIS, *Muller, Zool. Dan.* 3. *p.* 9. *t.* 86. *f.* 7. *to* 9. Cylindric, white, gradually tapering, generally terminating in a fine point and wrinkled transversely, attached throughout the whole surface : a double infundibuliform operculum. *Common.*

S. Tubularia. *Mont. (not Turt.)—D. p.* 1083.—
Pen. p. 362.—*D. p.* 1083.—*Johnston Mag. N. H.* 7.
p. 126.—*Flem in Edinb. Enc.* 7. *p.* 67. *t.* 204. *f.* 9.
—S. Arundo. Turt. D. *p.* 155.—Berkely in *Z. I.* 3.
p. 229. tab. sup. 18. f. 2.—*An Mart. f.* 15.?—Round,
tapering, opaque, white, slightly wrinkled transversely ;
the smaller one affixed, subconvoluted irregularly,
sometimes only flexuous, the larger part is detached
frequently for half its length and ascends in a considerable angle from the base, though rarely perpendicular ;
the erect part is nearly straight or slightly flexuous,
but always turning with the sun : aperture orbicular :
no operculum. *4 or 5 diam. at larger end,* 0,20—
Torcross in Devon, Falmouth.

S. Filograna. *Lin.* 1265.—*Lam.* 12. *Planc. Conch.*
App. t. 19. *f. A. B.*—*SEBA.* 3. *p.* 10. *f.* 8. *and* 19. *a.*
S. Complexa, *Turt. D. p.* 153.—With extremely
close-set, confused by intermingled ramose hair-like
tubes ; white, the tube scarcely if at all tapering, rarely
if ever affixed to other substances, almost always forming masses by itself. *Rare, Devon.*

S. Vermicularis. *Lin.*—*Lam. (not var b)*—Tubus
Vermicularis, *Ellis Corallines, t.* 38. *f.* 2.—S. Tu-
bularia. *Turt. f.* 84. *p.* 154.—S. Triquetra.
Mont. p. 50., *not Mont., Sup. p.* 157.—Strong,

14

sesile, opaque, dirty white or tinged with red, irregularly twisted and contorted, sometimes nearly straight or but slightly flexuous, roughened with transverse wrinkles usually more or less carinated and often with a smaller ridge on each side of the dorsal one : operculum corneous and striated. *On old shells, &c. not uncommon.*

VERMILIA.

Testaceous, cylindraceous, laterally affixed, insensibly attenuated towards the posterior end, more or less twisted ; aperture orbicular, usually armed with from one to three teeth.

V. Triquetra, *Lam.* 2.—Serpula. *T. Lin.* 1265. *(not Born)—Mont. Sup. p.* 157.—*Turt. D. p.* 152.— *Sow. G.—D. p.* 1078.—*Sow. Brit. Misc. t.* 31. *(good)* —Flexuous, fixed throughout its entire length, clear white, (rarely pink) the base more or less flattened and spreading, and the dorsal portion with a very distinct sharp simple keel, thus rendered triangular, smooth. 2. 0,167. *Extremely common on Oyster Shells, &c.*

V. Scabra. *Lam.* 7.—Affixed, serpentine, slender, about five minute denticulated dorsal keels. *Cornwall.*

Class CIRRHIPEDA.

Shell either sesible or elevated on a flexible tendinous

pedicle ; valves sometimes moveable and distant, sometimes soldered together, lined internally by the mantle.

ORDER SESSILIA.

Affixed and not pedunculated : aperture superior and anterior.

GENUS CORONULA.

Sessile, suborbicular, seemingly one entire piece, conoid or retuse conical, truncated at the extremities ; substance thick, hollowed interiorly by radiating cells : operculum with four obtuse valves.

C. DIADEMA. *Lam.* 1.—*Bl. t.* 86.*f.* 4·—LEPAS D. *Lin.*—*Ch. f.* 843.—*List. t.* 445. *f.* 288.—*Born. t.* 1. *f.* 5. 6.—*Wood, G. C. t.* 4.—*Da. Cos. t.* 7. *f.* 2.— *Don. t.* 56. *f.* 1. 2.—*Turt. D. p.* 75.—*D. p.* 24.— BALANUS. D. *Mont. p.* 13.—*Brug. p.* 171.—Sub-compressed, hemispheric, dirty white, with twelve compartments, six depressed, flat, and striated transversely, the others, which are alternate, are prominent with four five or six elevated longitudinal ridges and transverse striæ ; at the top is a deep cavity, funnel shaped, hexagonal within, at the bottom of which is the aperture, the ribs are also furnished with divisions or cells in a radiated manner and lined with a coriaceous membrane. *Diam.* 2 *to* 3. *Rare, except in Scotland and its isles.*

Genus BALANUS.

*Conical or elongated-conical, composed of six unequal
pieces or valves, closed at the sides upon a more or
less firm testaceous flat base : shell open at the top,
operculum of four moveable valves.*

B. Communis. *Pultney.—Mont. p.* 6.—*Dor. Cat.
t* 2. *f.* 12.—Lepas Balanus, *Lin.* 1107.—*D. p.* 14.
—*Pen.* 4. *p.* 72. *t.* 37. *f.* 4.—*Don. t.* 30. *f.* 1.—
Turt. D. p. 77.—*Ch. f.* 820.—*Born. t.* 1. *f.* 4.—
B. Sulcatus. *Lam.* 2.—*Brug. p.* 1. 63.—Strong, rugged, cinereous-brown, compartments unequal and
frequently indistinct, composed of irregular and longitudinal striæ or ridges ; conical, detached shells often
perfectly round at the base and sloping upwards;
aperture not large in proportion : operculum of four
valves, transversely striated, with a longitudinal furrow
on the two longest. *Diam. at base,* 1.—¾. *Not
uncommon but local.*

B. Vulgaris. *Da. Cos. p.* 248. *t.* 17. *f.* 7.—
List. t. 444. *f.* 87.—*List. Ang.* 5. *f.* 41.—Lepas
Balanoides. *Lin ?—D. p.* 16.—*Turt. D. p.* 77.—
Wood G. C. p. 44. *t.* 7. *f.* 3.—*Pen.* 4. *t.* 37. *f.* 5.
—*Don. t.* 36. *f.* 2.—*Mont. p.* 7.—*List. t.* 444. *f.* 287.
—*Ch. f.* 826.—B. Balanoides. *Brug. p.* 166.—
An B. Ovularis ? *var. Lam.* 8?—Subconical, some-
times much depressed, valves divided by a deep longi-

tudinal furrow. smooth, white, frequently deeply grooved at the base, posterior compartments the largest; aperture proportionately larger than in the last; operculum of four valves, the two upper slightly striated transversely, the others smooth. *Diam. up to ½. Common every where.* *

B. Rugosus. *Mont. (not Lam. 23.) p.* 8.—*Ch. f.* 824 ?—*Dor. Cat. p.* 25. *t.* 2. *f.* 10.—Lepas R. D. *p.* 17.—*Lin. T.* 8. *p.* 25. *t.* 1. *f.* 5.—*Turt. f. D. p.* 76.—*An* L. Borealis. *Don.* 5. *t.* 160 ? *An* B. Ovularis, *Lam.* 8 ?—Subcylindrical, usually divided into six compartments by furrows which become broad towards the top, where the shell spreads into angulated points and is often as wide as at the base ; valves irregular the post ones broader, sometimes wrinkled or striated

---

* B. Tintinnabulum. *Da Cos. p.* 250.—*Brug. p.* 165.—*Lam.* 3.—*Mont. p.* 10.—Lepas T. *Lin.* 13. —*D p.* 22—*Turt. D. p.* 75.—*&c. &c.*—has no just claim to be considered a native species, being only taken from the bottom of ships arriving from warmer climates.

* Lepas Radiatus. *Turt. D.*—*Wood. G. C. t.* 7. *f.* 7.—cannot be considered either native or naturalized, having only been found on the bottom of a ship.

longitudinally, often smoother; aperture large, inner margin ridged transversely; operculum quadrivalve, not striated, angulated, erect. *Dorset, &c. Diam.* 0,40.

B. SCOTICUS.—LEPAS S. *Wood. G. C. t.* 6. *f.* 3. *p.* 10.—*Turt. D. p.* 76.—Conical, with six valves, dirty white; valves longitudinally ribbed, unequal, striated transversely at the base. ¾.. ½. Scotland on Mytilus modiolus, Lin.—*This brief description is all that is given by Mr. Wood, saving that he farther states that the operculum resembles that of Tintinnabulum, I regard it as of rather doubtful distinctness.*

B. PUNCTATUS. *Dor. Cat. p.* 25. *t.* 1. *f.* 10. *(not Lam: nor Brug.)*—*Mont. p.* 8. *t.* 1. *f.* 5.—LEPAS P: *Wood. G. C. p.* 46.—*D: p.* 15.—*A. Turt. D. p.* 78.— *An* L. CORNUBIENSIS: *Pen.* 4. *p.* 73. *t.* 37. *f.* 6. *?*— *An* B. CRENATUS *? Brug. p.* 168.—Very rugged, brown, valves indistinct, usually punctured, base spreading but little and scarcely broader than high; anterior valve always provided with two connecting shoulders; operculum of four valves, the upper one with a few longitudinal ridges, (the edges of the superior and anterior valves generally closely united at the top, indented or notched, punctated and interlocking. *S. Devon, common on Patella Vulgata.*

B. COSTATUS: *Mont. p.* 11.—LEPAS C. *Don. t.* 30.

f. 2.—Turt. D. p. 78.—*Lin: T.* 8. *p.* 24:—*Wood. G:*
C: p. 46.—*D. p.* 18.—White, somewhat conical, nearly
closed at the top and rather spreading at the base; with
numerous, nearly equidistant, strong, rounded ribs,
radiating from the top to the base. ⅓. *W: Coast of
England, Wales, and Ireland.*

B. CLAVATUS, *Ellis Zoop. p.* 198. *t.* 15. *f.* 7. 8.—
Mont: p. 10.—*Dor: Cat. p.* 25: *t.* 1. *f.* 6.—B. FISTU-
LOSUS. *Brug. p:* 166.—LEPAS. C. *Wood. G. C. p.* 45.
t. 7. *f.* 2.—L. ELONGATUS. *Ch. f.* 838.—*D. p.* 17.
Turt. D. p. 77.—L. BALANOIDES. *var. Pen.* 4. *p.* 73.
t. 37. *f.* 5*A.—Don. t.* 36. *f.* 1.—Elongated-clavate,
broader at the top than at the base; dirty white; valves
three wide and three narrow, wrinkled longitudinally
and faintly striated transversely : operculum quadrivalve, obliquely striated. 2: ⅜. *Sandwich, Weymouth.
Not improbably an elongated variety of* RUGOSUS.

B: CONOIDES. *Mont. p.* 12.—LEPAS C. *Don. t.* 30.
f. 3.—*Lin: T.* 8. *p.* 24.—*Turt. D. p:* 77.—*Wood. G.
C. p.* 42.—*D. p.* 18.—*An* B. LÆVIS. *Brug ?*—Conical, with smooth valves, pointed at the apex : aperture
very small. *Diam.* ⅜. *On Anatifa Lævis.—Donovan's
figure is purplish white, and whether from the style of
engraving or not, appears reticulated by longitudinal
and fine transverse striæ.*

B. ALCYONII.—LEPAS A. *Turt. D. p.* 76.—Somewhat conic, white or brownish white, with six very unequal and irregularly sized valves which terminate in rather acute points; aperture large, oval or roundish, lid of four valves, the two uppermost smooth, pointed, gaping a little at top and protuding in the middle into a kind of keel. *Diameter and height* ⅛. *On Alccyonium and Flustra, Weymouth.*

GENUS ACASTA.

Sessile, oval, subconical, composed of separable pieces, valves six, laterally united, unequal; the basis an orbicular, internally concave, testaceous lamella; operculum quadrivalve.

A. MONTAGUI. *Leach. Cirrhip.*—*Lam.* 1.—BALANUS SPONGEOSUS. *Mont. Sup. p.* 2. *t.* 7. *f.* 4, 5, 6.—*Bl. t.* 85. *f.* 3.—*Dor. Cat. p.* 25.—LEPAS S. *Turt. D. p.* 78.—*D. p.* 27.—*Wood. G. C. p.* 47.—Livid brown with a purple tinge towards the summit; valves six, wrinkled, sharply pointed, the three anterior the broader and shorter; operculum quadrivalve, the two anterior pieces rough with decussated striæ, the two posterior longer and a little hooked forwards. ⅓. *Portland Reach, in sponge, rare.*

GENUS PYRGOMA.

Sessile, univalve, subglobular, ventricose, convex above,

perforated at the apex ; aperture small, elliptical.
Operculum bivalve.

P. ANGLICUM. *Sow. G. f. 7.—Reeve t. 10. f. 7.*
—ADNA A.'*Leach.—An* P. SULCATUM ? *Philippi. p.*
252. t. 12.f. 24. Not uncommon in Devonshire, very
small.

GENUS CREUSIA.

Sessile, fixed, orbicular, convex, conical, quadrivalve ;
valves unequal, united, distinguished by their
sutures : operculum internal, bivalve.

C. VERRUCA. *Lam. 3.—*LEPAS V. *Ch. f. 834·—*
Turt. D. p. 79.—Gmel. 3212.—Wood G. C. p. 57.
*t. 9. f. 5.—*L. STRÖMIA. *Muller, Zool, Dan. 3. t. 94.*
*f. 1.—D. p. 19.—*OCHTHOSIA S. *Philippi. p. 251.—*
*Bl. t. 85. f. 4.—*STRIATA. *Pen. 4. p. 73. t. 37. f. 7.*
BALANUS S. *Da. Cos. p. 250.—Mont. p. 12.—*
L. INTERTEXTA. *Don. t. 36. f. 1.—*CLITEA V. *Sow.*
*G. f. 2.—Reeve. t. 8. f. 2.—*Compressed, white, the
valves strongly ribbed obliquely to each other and finely
striated across the ribs, the margin of the base irregularly serrated : aperture oblique, perfectly closed by
an operculum, and so obscure that it is difficult to find,
except when alive. ¼. *Not uncommon. Kent, Devon,*
Dorset.

ORDER PEDUNCULATA.

Body supported by a tubular coriaceous flexible peduncle

*whose base is affixed to marine substances. Mouth
almost inferior.*

GENUS ANATIFA.

*Compressed at the sides, composed of five valves, which
are contiguous and unequal, the lower lateral ones
being the larger.*

A. LÆVIS. *Lam.* 1.—*Philippi. p.* 252.—*Brug. p.*
62.—LEPAS ANATIFERA. *Lin.* 1109.—*D. p.* 32.—
Ch. f. 852.—*Don. t.* 7.—*Dor. Cat. p.* 26. *t.* 2. *f.* 3.
—*Mont. p.* 15.—*Wood. G. C. t.* 11.—*Knorr.* 2. *t.*
30. *f.* 4. 5.—*Turt. D. p.* 71.—PENTELASMIS A.
Leach.—*Reeve. t.* 12.—P. LÆVIS. *Bl. t.* 84. *f.* 3.—
Compressed, polished, and bluish white ; the two lower
valves large and somewhat triangular, longitudinally
wrinkled and obsoletely striated radiatingly from the
lower anterior angle : the two upper valves angulated
on each side, top rounded, (these likewise are nearly
smooth) ; dorsal valve long, slender, rounded, smooth
down the middle and sulcated on each side ; membrane
and peduncle usually reddish. *Length of shelly part,*
1¼...1. *On ship's timber, common.*

A. STRIATA. *Lam.* 4.—*Philippi. p.* 252.—*Brug.*
p. 64.—LEPAS ANSERIFERA ? *Lin.* 1109.—*D. p.* 31.
—*List. t.* 440. *f.* 283.—*Ch. f.* 856.—*Don. t.* 162.
f. 2.—*Mont. p.* 17.—*Turt. D. p.* 72.—Much resem-

bling the last species but is strongly striated radiatingly,
the lower valve from the lower anterior angle and the
superior one from the upper posterior angle, these are
crost by fine striæ; the angles of the valves are much
more sharp and pointed and particularly the apex; the
dorsal valve is compressed at the sides and brought to
a fine carinated edge; bluish white; membrane and
peduncle orange red. *Drifted wood, Devon, rare,* 1. 1⅜.

A. Sulcata.—Lepas S. *Mont. p.* 17. *t.* 1. *f.* 6.
—*Lin. T.* 8. *p.* 29.—*Dor. Cat. p.* 26.—*Turt. D. p.* 72.
—*Wood. G. C. p.* 68. *t.* 12. *f.* 1.—*D. p.* 31.—Compressed, subtriangular, dirty yellowish white, shorter
than the last; lower valves with fifteen strong ribs
diverging from the lower anterior angle, that which runs
along the front is larger than the rest and forms a margin, the two superior valves form a pointed apex and
narrow downwards to a point; furnished with seven or
eight ribs, with smaller intermediate ones diverging
from the posterior margin; dorsal valve somewhat
compressed, with a smooth subcarinated edge; pedicle
short and dusky. ½. ¼. *Dorset, rare.*

A. Fascicularis.—Lepas F. *Ellis, Zoop, t.* 15. *f.*
6.—*Mont. p.* 557. *and Sup. p.* 5. *and p.* 163.—
Lin. T. 8. *p.* 30.—*Turt. D .p.* 72.—*Wood. G. C. p.*
62. *t.* 10. *f.* 4.—*D. p.* 31.—Lepas Dilatata. *Don.*
t. 104.—A. Vitrea. *Lam.* 5.—Compressed, with five

valves whieh are either smooth or nearly so, very thin and light, horn-colored, the two upper valves ending in a point above the dorsal and somewhat bending back at the apices ; dorsal valve dilated at the base and forming a prominent acute angle, terminating the carinated upper portion : pedicle generally very short. 1. *Rare, Devon, near Milton.*

Genus POLLICIPES.

Shell consisting of five principal elongated trapezi form pieces, surrounded with a number of smaller ones similarly shaped, all sharp pointed at the apex and forming together an irregular laterally compressed cone, supported on a thick scaly coriaceous peduncle.

P. Scalpellum. *Lam.*—Lepas S. *Lin.* 1109.— *Gualt. t.* 106. *f. C. ?*—*Muller. Zool. D.* 3. *t.* 94. *f.* 1, 2.—*E. t.* 166. *f.* 7.—*Dor. Cat. p.* 26. *t.* 2. *f.* 8. —*Don. t.* 166. *f.* 1.—*Turt. D. p.* 74.—*D. p.* 30.— *Mont. p.* 18. *t.* 1. *f.* 3.—*Wood. G. f. p.* 61. *t.* 10. *f.* 3.—Scalpellum Vulgare. *Leach.*—*Reeve. t.* 13.—Much compressed, the sides nearly parallel to each other for about half the length from the base, light brown, dull, rather rough, without any striæ, faintly wrinkled in some parts and covered with short hairs;

valves thirteen, those on the dorsal valve in transverse
rows, the three lower valves on each side to which the
peduncle is fixed, are very small, the two next larger,
the superior one the largest, running a little oblique
to the rest, and is pointed at the top; the dorsal valve
is compressed, the edge rounded at the base, and running into a sharp process about half-way up, from
whence it turns in a diagonal line to cover the edge of
the two superior valves : the upper part truncated obliquely to the front. *Sandwich and Plymouth, rare.*

P. CORNUCOPIA. *Leach.—Lam.* 1.—*Reeve. t.* 14.
f. 1.—PENTALEPAS P. *Bl. t.* 84. *f.* 3.—LEPAS. POL-
LICIPES. *Gmel.* 3213.—*Ch. f.* 851. 2.—*Arg. t.* 26. *f.*
D.—Wood. G. C. p. 60. *t.* 10, *f.* 2.—*Knorr.* 5. *t.*
13. *f.* 7.—*D. p.* 29.—*Mont. Sup. p.* 6. *t.* 28. *f.* 5.—
Turt D. p. 74.—Compressed, erect, solid, eight principal smooth convex white valves, besides numerous
irregular small ones environing the base : four larger
valves obtusely pointed above; membrane dark; pedicle coriaceous, bluish ash-colored and shagreened.
0,80. *without the pedicle. Rather doubtful, very rare.*

GENUS CINERAS.
*Body pedunculate, entirely enveloped in a thick mem-
branaceous integument, with a large anterior opening*

B

at the top for the passage of the cirrhi. To this club-shaped integument are attached five small narrow distant testaceous valves two situated at the sides of the aperture, one dorsal, the rest terminal.
C. VITTATA. *Leach.—Lam.* 1.—*Reeve. t.* 15.— LEPAS V. *Wood. G. C. p.* 69. *t.* 12. *f.* 2. 3.—*D. p.* 33.—LEPAS MEMBRANACEA. *Lin: T.* 11. *t.* 12. *f.* 2. —*Turt. D. p.* 73.—*Wood. G. C. p.* 20.—Somewhat oblong, gradually sloping into the stalk, obliquely truncate at top, fleshy, flattish, with five small white linear testaceous valves, the two upper rather oblique, the two lower with a strong hook-like process in the middle of each projecting inwardly aud curving a little upwards to the point; the back valve gibbous in the middle, extending above to the termination of the upper pair, where they meet and form a projecting angle and reaching below nearly to the commencement of the stalk which is as long as the body ; pale blue with three broad dark blue stripes on each side. 1...½. *Smaller variety.* Uniform dark horn-colored, the stalk not sloping. *Poole and Devon, on planks of wrecked vessels.*

GENUS OTION.

Pedunculated, entirely enveloped in a membranaceous integument, which is ventricose above and surmounted by two horn-like truncated tubes turning

*backwards and open at their extremity. Rather a
large lateral aperture. Several articulated ciliated
cirrhi; testaceous valves very small, five, separate,
two semilunate at the sides of the aperture, one exceedingly minute dorsal and others equally minute
terminal.*

O. Blainvillii. *Leach.—Lam* 2.*—An* O. Cuvieri
Reeve. *t.* 16.*?—*Lepas Cornuta. *Lin. T.* 11. *t.* 12.
f. 1.*—Turt. D. p.* 73.—Stalk longer than the body,
enlarging towards the base; white regularly marked or
clouded with three purplish brown broken longitudinal
lines on each side, which partially extend down the stalk.
Length, 2. *of tubular protuberances,* ⅜. *On wood
from wrecks, Devon, Poole.*

Class CONCHIFERA.
*Shell, with two valves, sometimes but rarely furnished
with differently shaped accessorial ones.*

Order DYMYARIA.
With at least two internal muscular scars.

Family TUBICOLARIA, Lam.
Enclosed in or attached to a shelly tube.

Genus TEREDO, Lin.
*Valves equal, largely open above and below, placed at
the larger extremity of a tube open at both ends.*

B 2.

T. Navalis. *Lin.* 1267.—*Dil. p.* 1089.—*Pen.* 4. *p.* 147.—*Mont.* 527.—*T. Biv.* 14. *t.* 2. *f.* 1, 2, 3.—*F. p.* 454.—*Lam.* 1.—*Sow. G.*—*Reeve. t.* 21.—Tube more or less flexuous and tapering, semi-concamerated near the smaller end; pallets spoon-shaped, convex on the outside and concave within, terminating at one end in a linear elongation which is straight or a little flexuous, and truncate at the other; valves ear-shaped behind, one with a curved denticle on the margin above the teeth. *Diam.* ¾. *In timber.*

T. Bipennata. *Turton, Dic.* 184. *t.* 11. *f.* 38, 39, 40.—*T. Biv.* 15.—*F.* 454. *Gray. Phil. Mag.* 1827.— Tube thicker and stronger, not at all concamerated; pallets very long and slender, somewhat curved and feathered on each side; valves ear-shaped behind, oblong, reflected on the outer margin and detached all round the circumference on the under side, an oblique rib on the margin above the teeth. *Diam.* ¼. *Exmouth.*

T. Malleolus. *Turt. Biv. p.* 255. *t.* 2. *f.* 19.—*F. p.* 454.—Tube consisting of a slight testaceous deposit on the surface of the chamber, the termination of which is slightly concamerated; valves ear-shaped behind, auricles reflected, pallets transverse and mallet-shaped; striæ on the triangular processes remote. *Diam.* ¼. *Torbay.*

T. NANA. *Turt. B. p. 16. t. 2. f. 6, 7.—F. p. 455.*
—Valves rounded and without auricles behind, a strong
conic tooth on the margin above the teeth which points
rather obliquely. *Diam. ¼. Torbay. Not unlike a
young Xylophaga, but destitute of the jointed internal
rib.*

FAMILY.—PHOLADARIA, LAM.
*Without a tubular sheath ; hinge aided by accessary
valves, or very widely gaping posteriorly.*

GENUS.—PHOLAS, LIN.
*Transverse ; hinge margin rolled outwards ; a rib-like
tooth proceeding from the cavity under the beaks.*

* *Valves divided by a longitudinal groove.*

P. CRISPATA. *Lin. IIII.—Mont. p. 23.—T. Biv.p.
6.—Don. 3. t. 62.—Dil. 40.—Lam. 7.—Ch. f. 872,3,
4*—Oblong, rounded and gaping posteriorly ; obliquely
truncated and open anteriorly ; posterior portion roughened by numerous thin waved concentric ridges, with
obsolete radiating furrows ; anterior portion rather
smooth ; hinge margin reflected, smooth ; apophysis
linear. 2...3. *Common.*

P. PAPYRACEA. *Turton, B. 2. t. 1. f. 1. to 4.—F.
456.—Sow. G. f. 3.—Reeve, t. 24. f. 3.*—Oblong ;

posterior side inflated, closed, with oblique concentric wavy subdenticulated ridges dorsally, the ventral area smooth ; anterior side open, truncated, (and continued when perfect in a thin coriaceous expanding cup,) with merely coarse concentric lines of growth ; the back with two small accessorial appendages, with the edges of the valves reflected at the posterior end, so as to form a kind of double obtuse keel, which reaches as far as the longitudinal groove, near the end of which is a kind of raised joint where the accessorial valves are fixed ; apophysis rather short and flat; an erect somewhat triangular and rather concave plate on the hinge margin. ¾. 1½. *Torbay.*

The young (P. LAMELLATA. *Turt B. 5. t.* 1. *f.* 5, 6.) being destitute of the posterior ventral area, gapes, and is rounded and not truncated anteriorly.   It is devoid also of the accessorial valves.

P. TUBERCULATUS. *Turton, B. 5. t.* 1. *f.* 7. 8.— *F.* 547.—Open at the posterior end, which is subroscated ; with a rough tubercle on the margin above the teeth, and a single oval calcareous plate at the hinge extending to the posterior extremity : posterior area with rough ribs which disappear anteriorly. ¾....1½. *Torbay.*

P. STRIATA. *Lin.* 1111. *D. p.* 37.—*Don. t.* 117.—
Mont. 26.—*Turt. B.* 11.—P. CLAVATA. *Lam.* 9.—
P. NANUS. *Pult.* 27.—*Wood, G. C. t.* 16. *f.* 1, 2, 3,
4, 8.—*Ch. f.* 867, 8, 9.—*Reeve. t.* 24. *f.* 2.—*Sow. G.*
f. 2.—Transverse, conoid, posteriorly short, tumid and
rounded, anteriorly produced and subcompressed;
posterior area strongly reticulated by arched striæ,
elsewhere slightly striated except a smooth triangular
space at the posterior ventral margin; one large
rounded accessary plate over the hinge before which is
a lengthened one a third connects the ventral edges;
apophysis long slender and curved. ½...1. *Ship's*
timber.

* * *Valves not divided by a groove.*

P. DACTYLUS. *Lin.* 1110.—*D. p.* 35.—*Lam.* 1.—
Mont. 20.—*Turt. B.* 8.—*Ch. f.* 859.—*Don. t.* 118.
—*Sow. G.*—*Reeve.* 24. *f.* 1.—*F.* 457.—Transversely
elongated, beaked posteriorly and rounded anteriorly;
with concentric waved muricated ridges and indistinct
radiating striæ towards the beaks; hinge margin reflected and supported by numerous small plates so as
to form quadrangular cells; four accessary plates. 4 or
5. *Common.*

P. CANDIDA. *Lin.* 1111.—*Don. t* 132.—*Mont.* 24.
—*Turt. B.* 10.—*D. p.* 36.—*F. p.* 457.—*Lam.* 3.—*Ch.*

861, 2.—Oblong, rounded at both ends, nearly closed posteriorly, covered with raised prickly concentric striæ, which posteriorly form rather distant radiating rows of prickles but not ribs; hinge margin reflected, covered by a single elongated accessorial plate; a tooth like process on the hinge ascending obliquely and anteriorly. 1...2½. *Common.*

P. PARVA. *Mont.* 22. *t.* 1. *f.* 7, 8.—*Turt. B. p.* 9. —*F.* 457.—*D. p.* 38.—P. DACTYLOIDES. *Lam.* 4.— Ovate, posteriorly beaked and rough with reticulated rather prickly striæ; fold above the hinge without cells; a smooth tubercle on the inner margin above the teeth; a single accessorial valve at the hinge. ¾...1¼. *South Coast.*

GENUS.—XYLOPHAGA. TURTON
Globular-oval, equivalve, very open at the anterior side and closed behind, furnished with accessorial valves about the hinge. Hinge without the long curved tooth under the margin, no ligament.
X. DORSALIS, *Turt. B. t.* 2. *f.* 4, 5.—*Sow. G.*— *Reeve. t.* 22.—*F. p.* 455.—Valves rounded, without auricles and closed behind, furnished with a longitudinal jointed rib on the inside and a corresponding external groove; a triangular striated projection in the front of each valve. 0,40. *Torbay.*

Genus.—GASTROCHÆNA. Lam.

Equivalve, somewhat wedge shaped, with a very large, oval, oblique, anterior opening between the valves; the posterior extremity nearly closed; hinge linear, marginal and toothless.

G. Modiolina. *Lam.* 3.—Mya Dubia. *Pen.* 4. *t.* 44. *p.* 82.—*Mont. p.* 28.—G. Pholadia. *Turt. B. t.* 2. *f.* 8, 9. *p.* 18.—G. Hians. *Fl. p.* 458.— Oblong, opaque, dirty white, finely striated concentrically, margin from the beak to the ligament nearly straight, then rounded anteriorly; the oblique posterior truncation extended beyond the middle of the ventral margin; a narrow border in front of the beaks (which are nearly terminal and rather prominent) where the valves are in contact. ⅓...1. *In Limestone, near low water mark.*

Genus.—GALEOMMA. Turton.

Equivalve, equilateral, transverse, with a large open gape at the ventral margin; hinge without teeth; ligament partly internal.

G. Turtoni. *Turton, in Z. J.* 2. *p.* 362. *t.* 13. *f.* 1.—*Desh. in Lam.* 6. *p.* 180.—*Sow. f.* 1, 2, 3.— Tumid in the middle and gradually sloping to the sides which are rounded and closed, dull milky white, the surface covered with short close-set transverse

interrupted opaque lines very irregularly disposed
which gives the margin a serrated appearance; beaks
rather prominent, hinge margin nearly straight, ventral
edge rather rounded; gape extending the whole breadth.
¼...½. *Guernsey, English channel.*

TRIBE.—SOLENIDES.

*Transversely elongated, destitute of accessory pieces
and gaping only at the sides; ligament external.*

GENUS.—SOLEN. LIN.

*Equivalve, transversely elongated. gaping at both ex-
tremities; beaks very small, always short : cardinal
teeth small, varying in number, sometimes none and
rarely a pit between them.*

* *Hinge terminal, shell posteriorly truncated.*

S. Vagina. *Lin.* 1113.—*D. p.* 57—*Lam.* I.—*Don.*
4. *t.* 110.—*Pen.* 4. *p.* 83.—*Mont. p.* 48.—*Turt. B.
p.* 79·—Subcylindrical, more compressed towards the
truncated anterior end; posterior end slightly oblique,
shortest, strictured at the margin; pale yellow longitudinally striated and annulated with brown : a single tooth
in each valve; teeth flattened on the rubbing surface;
the opposite sides strengthened by a rib. 1...5. *Common.*

S. Novacula. *Mont. p.* 47.—*Turt. B. p.* 80.—
F. p. 459.—A single strong, curved, blunt tooth in each
valve; shell destitute of the terminal stricture. ½.
Nearly resembling the following but differing by the
number of its teeth and the absence of the lateral ones.

S. Siliqua. *Lin.* 1113.—*D. p.* 58.—*Lam.* 4.—*Ch.*
29.—*Don. t.* 46.—*Pen.* 4. *p.* 83. *t.* 45. *f.* 20.—
Mont. p. 46.—*Turt. B. p.* 80.—*F.* 459.—Straight,
with an olive brown cuticle which is darkest posteriorly;
a single tooth and a remote lateral lamina in one valve,
in the other, are two besides a lateral inclined tooth
corresponding with the opposite lamina. 1...7.
Common.

S. Ensis. *Lin.* 1114.—*D. p.* 59.—*Lam.* 5.—*Ch. f.*
29, 30.—*Don. t.* 50.—*Pen.* 4. *p.* 83.—*Mont. p.* 48—
Turt. B. p. 82.—*F. p.* 459.—Linear, slightly curved,
the cuticle olive brown, both the ends somewhat
rounded; two teeth in one valve, one in the other, one
of the lateral teeth grooved; hinge not terminal; posteriorly rounded. ¾...6. *Common.*

* * *Hinge not terminal; posteriorly rounded.*

S. Pellucidus. *Pen.* 4. *t.* 46. *f.* 22.—*Mont. p.* 49.
—*Turt. B. p.* 83.—*D. p.*60,—*F. p.*549.—S. Pygmæus.

Lam. 6.—Pellucid, fragile, rounded at both ends, hinge margin nearly straight, the ventral slightly curved : a single tooth in one valve and two in the other, besides contiguous lateral processes. ⅟...1. *Sandy bays.*

S. Legumen. *Lin.* 1114.—*D. p.* 61.—*Lam.* 11.— *Ch. f.* 32, 3, 4 —*Don. t.* 53.—*Pen.* 4. *p.* 84. *t.* 46. *f.* 24.—*Mont. p.* 50.—*F. p,* 459.—Psammobia. L. *Turt. B. p.* 90.—Linear, rounded at both ends, hinge margin nearly straight, ventral edge slightly curved so as to render the posterior end the narrower; smooth, yellowish, thin, pellucid, with fine lines of growth; hinge strengthened by an oblique internal rib, a single tooth in one valve and two in the other, besides lateral teeth which are simple in one valve and winged at the other. ⅟...4. *Ireland and Wales, common.*

S. Coarctatus. *Gmel.* 3227.—*D. p.* 64.—*Lam.* 17.—*Ch. f.* 45.—S. Antiquatus.*Lam.* 15.—*Mont. p.* 52.—Psammobia. A. *Turt. B. p.* 91.—*F.* 460.— S. Cultellus. *Pen.* 4. *t.* 46. *f.* 25.—S. Centralis. *Say. (fide Jay)*.—Oblong, rounded at the extremities, hinge margin slightly convex, ventral rather concave; white, subpellucid, merely striated by the lines of growth, which are more conspicuous at the extremities;

hinge central, with a single tooth in one valve (sometimes a second rudimentary one) and two in the other,
behind which the margin is callous. 1...2. *Rare.*

S. Declivis.—*Turt. Con. Dic. p.* 164. *t.* 22. *f.* 80.
—*F. p.* 460.—*List. t.* 321.—Oblong, rounded at the
extremities, dorsal margin slightly convex, ventral
straight; thin, semi-transparent, with a dark brown
cuticle, irregularly and concentrically striated, beaks
subcentral; sloping gradually to the extremities;
slightly indented before the beaks; teeth strong, two
in each valve, one of them concave and in one valve
one is oblique, behind which the margin is callous.
$\frac{3}{4}$...2. *Scilly Isles.*

S. Fragilis. *Pult. Dor. p.* 28.—*Mont. p.* 51.—
F. p. 460.—Psammobia Tœniata. *Turt. B. p.* 85.—
Oblong, rounded at the extremities, a little contracted
in the middle, dorsal and ventral edges subparallel,
thin, transparent, smooth, with a greenish cuticle, sometimes marked with a longitudinal reddish stripe from the
hinge towards the ventral margin; beaks subcentral;
in one valve two erect teeth, one of which is pointed the
other with one subulate tooth : an internal longitudinal
rib. $\frac{1}{4}$...0,95.

S. Candidus Remeri.—S. Strigilatus. *Turton.*
B. p. 97. *t.* 6. *f.* 13.—*Mart. f.* 43.—*F. p.* 439.—
Elongated oblong, breadth twice and a half the length,
ends rounded, uniform white, marked with coarse ridges
of growth, and anteriorly with curved radiating strigils;
beaks subcentral, anterior slope with divaricating striæ;
ventral edge straightish, subincurved in the middle;
an oblique and erect tooth in each valve (in one valve
the former rudimentary) nymphæ distinct. 0,80...1,6.
Cornwall.

S. Scopula.—Psam. Scopula. *Turt. B. p.* 98. *t.*
6. *f.* 11, 2.—*E. p.* 439.—Kidney-shaped, subequilateral, oblong, glossy white, ventral edge strongly incurved in the middle, striated in two directions anteriorly
(oblique striæ not more than 20.): all the teeth erect.
$\frac{3}{4}$...$\frac{3}{4}$. *Exmouth.*

GENUS.—PANOPEA.

Equivalve,transverse, unequally gaping at the ridges,
a conical cardinal tooth in each valve, and on one
side a short ascending compressed, not exserted
callus. Ligament external, fixed on the callosities.
P. Arctica. *Deshayes.*—Glycimeris. A. *Lam.* 2.
—Pghlycimeris. *Bean in May. N. H.* 8. *f.* 51. *p.*
563.—White under a yellowish wrinkled epidermis,

very thick, oval, inequilateral, gaping at both ends, coarsely wrinkled transversely ; beaks subcentral, from which two longitudinal ridges cross the shell like the letter V.; posteriorly a little rounded, anteriorly obliquely rounded, the edge incurved : a single conic tooth and two muscular impressions in each valve. 2¼... 3,5. *Scarborough, rare. Much shorter in breadth than the Mya Glycimeris of Linneus, having rather the outline of Mya Truncata.*

TRIBE.—MYARIA.

Having a broad spoon-like tooth in each valve or in one only : gaping at one or both extremities.

GENUS.—MYA.

Transverse, gaping at both extremities, with one large dilated projecting and nearly vertical cardinal tooth in the left valve and with a hollow in the opposite valve ; ligament internal, short, thick, and inserted in the hollow of the primary tooth on the one side, and in the pit of the other valve.

---

* The real PANOPEA GLYCIMERIS. (*Mya. G. of Lin.* —*Don. t.* 142.—P. ALDROVANDI, *Lam.* is still too doubtful a native to be at present inserted in our Catalogue.

M. Truncata. *Lin* 1111.—*D. p.* 42.—*Lam.* 1.
—*Ch. f.* 1, 2.—*Don. t.* 92.—*Pen. t.* 41. *f.* 14.—
Mont. p. 32.—*Turt. B. p.* 31.—*F. p.* 463.—Ovate,
ventricose, truncated anteriorly, rounded posteriorly,
ventral edge nearly straight; dull white under a tough
yellowish wrinkled cuticle, marked with coarse striæ of
growth: tooth rounded obtuse entire and projecting
forwards. 2...2,5. *Common in chalk.*

M. Arenaria. *Lin.* 1112.—*D. p.* 42.—*Lam.* 2.—
Ch. f. 3, 4.—*Don. t.* 85.—*Pen. p.* 79. *t.* 42.—*F. p.*
463.—*Mont. p.* 30.—*Turt. B. p.*32.—M. Acuta and
Mercenaria. *Say.*—Ovate, rounded at both extremities but slightly attenuated and produced anteriorly,
convex, thick, dull white under a wrinkled brown epidermis; inside glossy white; hinge composed of a
rounded projecting tooth and a smaller acute one by its
side. 3...5,5. *Common.*

M. Nvregica. *Turt. Lin. t.* 4. *p.* 178.—M. Striata. *Mont. Lin. T.* 11. *p.* 188. *t.* 13. *f.* 1.—Lyonsia
S. *Turt. B. p.* 35. *t.* 3. *f.* 6, 7.—*F. p.* 463.—Oblong,
thin, equivalve, semi-transparent, pearly white under a
brownish epidermis, rounded at one end, waved and
truncated at the other; tooth not fixed. ½...1. *Rare.*

M. Decussata. *Mont. Sup. p.* 20.—*F. p.* 463.—
Ovate, waved at the margin, white with irregular concentric ridges decussated by regular concentric striæ ;
umbo obtuse recurved and not central ; a broad erect
tooth in one valve, in the other a projecting plate with a
small indenture for the reception of the tooth of the
opposite valve. ½. *Rare.*

Genus.—ANATINA.

*Transverse, subequivalve, gaping at both valves or in
one only; no cardinal teeth, one broad primary
tooth in both valves projecting interiorly: a lateral
plate running obliquely under the primary teeth.*

* *Teeth transversely fixed.*

A. Convexa. *Turton. B. p.* 44. *t:* 4. *f.* 1, 2.—
Mya. C. *Wood. G. C. p,* 92. *t.* 18. *f.* I.—*Turt. C.
D. p.* 100.—Amphidesma C. *F. p.* 431.—Mya.
Declivis. *Don. t.* 82.—Oval-oblong, angular and
slightly truncated anteriorly, rounded posteriorly, very
convex, light and brittle, rusty white, with irregular
concentric striæ ; beaks close and and subcentral ; teeth
narrow and very central. 1½....2½. *Paignton.*

A. Pubescens. *Turt. B. p.* 45. *t.* 4. *f.* 3.—Amphidesma. P. *F. p.* 431. --Mya. P. *Mont. p:* 40.—
Turt. C. D. p. 99. *f.* 35.—M. Declivivis. *Lin. T.*

8. *p.* 36.—*Dor. Cat. p.* 27. *t.* 4. *f.* 6.—*Wood. G. C.*
p. 93. *t.* 18. *f.* 3.—A. MYALIS. *Lam.* 9.—THRACIA.
P. *Kiener t.* 2. *f.* 2.—Oblong, depressed, angular and
truncate anteriorly, rough, striated transversely, brownish
white; beaks nearly central, the points crossing each
other at the tips; teeth projecting and running obliquely
to the anterior side with a cavity or notch behind and
small erect denticle inside, with an oblique rib from the
tooth towards the truncated end. *Torbay and Plymouth.* 2½...3¼.

A. TRUNCATA. *Turt. B. p.* 46. *t.* 4. *f.* 6.—AMPHI-
DESMA. T. *F. p.* 431.—Convex, wedge-shaped, posteriorly very short and obliquely subtruncated, anteriorly
attenuated and truncated; rough, striated transversely,
dirty white; teeth projecting a little inwards but running obliquely *(thus distinguished from Distorta,)*
front margin forming nearly a straight line. ½....¾.
In rocks, Torbay.

* * *Teeth projecting horizontally inwards.*

A. DECLIVIS. *Turt. B. p.* 47.—MYA. D. *Mont. t.*
1. *f.* 2.—AMPHIDESMA. D. *F. p.* 432.—Oval-oblong,
slightly compressed, angular truncated and open anteriorly, white, minutely shagreened, posteriorly broad
and rounded. 1....1¼. *Torbay. Distinguished from*

Pubescens by the large oval projecting teeth, which extend forwards and have no lateral attachment.

A. PRÆTENUIS. *Turt. B. p.* 48. *t.* 4. *f.* 4.—MYA. P.*Pen.* 4. *p.* 160. *t.* 50. *f.* 1.—*Mont. p.* 41.—*Lin. t.* 8. *p.* 37.—*Don. t.* 176.—*Wood. G. C. p.* 94. *t.* 24. *f.* 7, 8, 9.—*Dor. C. t.* 4. *f.* 7.—*Turt. C. D. p.* 101.— AMPHIDESMA. P. *F. p.* 432.—Oval, flat, narrower rounded and open anteriorly, posteriorly slightly shorter and rounded, rough, white; teeth oval and projecting. 1...1½. *Torbay. Distinguished from Declvisi by the rounded anterior extremity.*

A. DISTORTA. *Turt. B. p.* 48. *t.* 4. *f.* 5.—MYA. D. *Mont. p.* 42. *t.* 1. *f.* 1.—*Pen.* 4. *p.* 161.—*Lin. T.* 8. *p.*'37.—*Wood. G. C. p.* 98.—*D. p.* 45.—*Turt. C. D. p.* 101.—AMPHIDESMA. D. *F. p.* 432.—Convex, variously shaped, nearly closed, the margin generally indented and the teeth rounded and projecting inwards. 1. *Torbay.*

A. ARCTICA. *Turt. B. p.* 49. *t.* 4. *f.* 7, 8.—MYA. ARCTICA. *Lin.* 1113 ?—Oblong, convex, posteriorly truncated, anteriorly with two transverse ridges, one along the back margin, the other running obliquely to the angle of the front margin; beaks terminal, posterior,

prominent ; teeth rounded and projecting inwards. ½.
.⅞ *Dublin Bay.*

Tribe.—MACTRACEA.

Equivalve, frequently gaping at the lateral extremities,
with the ligament internal or partly external .

Genus.—LUTRARIA.

Inequilateral, transversely oblong, or rounded, gaping
at the extremities; hinge with either a somewhat
complicated tooth, or two, one of which is simple
with an adjoining deltoid hollow which is oblique
and prominent within; no lateral teeth ; ligament
internal, attached in a pit.

L. Oblonga. *Turt. B. p.* 64. *t.* 5. *f.* 6.·—Mya. O.
Gm. 3221·—*Ch. f.* 12.—Mactra Hians.*Don. t.* 140.
—*Mont. p.* 101.—*Pen.* 4. *p.* 196.—*Lin. T.* 8. *p.* 74.
—*Dor. Cat. p.* 33. *t.* 2. *f.* 4.—*D. p.* 146·—*Turt.*
D. p. 85. *f.* 41.—*Da. Cos. t.* 17. *f.* 4.—L. Solen-
oides. *Lam.* 1.—*Bl. t.* 77. *f.* 3.—*Sow. G. f.* 1.—
L. Hians. *F. p.* 464.—Oblong, posteriorly short and
rounded, anteriorly produced and obtuse, margins
subparallel, the dorsal slightly incurved ; yellowish or
reddish white under a thick dusky epidermis, irregularly
wrinkled transversely : hinge with a grooved flattish
tooth locking between two. 2¾...5½. *W. Counties.*

L. ELLIPTICA. *Lam.* 2.—*Turt. B. p.* 65.—MACTRA
LUTRARIA. *Lin.* 1126.—*D.p.* 146.—*Ch. f.* 240,1.—
List. t. 415, *f.* 259.—*Don.* 2. *t.* 58.—*Pen.* 4. *p.* 195.
t. 55. *f.* 3.—*Mon. p.* 100.—*Lin. T.* 6. *t.* 16. *f.* 3, 4.
—*Dor. Cat. p.* 32. *t.* 5. *f.* 11.—*Turt C. D. p.* 84.—
L. VULGARIS. *F. p.* 464.—Oblong, subequivalve,
marked only by the lines of growth and remote obsolete
ridges, longer anteriorly, rounded and slightly gaping
at both ends, yellowish white under a thin close cuticle.
2...3½. *In sand, about low water mark.*

L. COMPRESSA. *Lam.* 4. *and* L. PIPERATA. *Lam.* 5.
—MACTRA. P. *Gmel.* 3261.—LISTERA. C. *Turt. B.*
p. 51. *t.* 5. *f.* 1, 2.—*D. p.* 142.—*Ch. f.* 21.—*E. M.*
t. 257. *f.* 4.—MACT. COMPRESSA. *Mon. p.* 96.—
TELLINA PLANA. *Don. t.* 64. *f.* 1.—*Da. C. p.* 200.
t. 13. *f.* 1.—*Bl. t.* 77. *f.* 2.—Rounded-triangular,
thin, compressed, yellowish white, finely but irregularly
striated transversely, semi-pellucid ; beaks very small
and central ; a distinct lozenge edged with a raised
line ; a single tooth in one valve locking into a bifid in
the other, no lateral teeth. 1¼...1½. *Muddy shores.*

GENUS.—MACTRA.

Transverse, inequilateral, subtrigonal, sides slightly
gaping; beaks prominent ; one primary compressed

*tooth in each valve, and an adjacent heart-shaped
cavity, two lateral compressed teeth situated near
the hinge and inserted; ligament internal and
placed in the pit of the hinge.*

* *Lateral teeth striated.*

M. Solida. *Lin.* 1126.—*D. p.* 140.—*Lam.* 23.—
Pen. 4. *p.* 123. *t:* 55. *f.* 2.—*Ch. f.* 229, 230.—*Don.
t.* 61.—*Mont. p.* 92.—*Lin. T.* 8. *p.* 70.—*Dor. Cat. p.*
32. *t.* 6. *f.* 6.—*Turt. C. D. p.* 81.—*Da. Cos. t.* 14.
f. 6.—Sub-triangular, strong, opaque, sub-equilateral,
slightly depressed from the beaks at both extremities,
nearly smooth, with a few concentric antiquated ridges,
dull dirty white; inside glossy and white. 1½...1¾.
Common.

M: Truncata. *Mont. Sup. p.* 34.—*Turt B. p.* 68.
—*F. p.* 427.—M. Subtruncata. *Don. t.* 126.—
M. Crassatella. *Lam.* 33.—Triangular, equilateral,
solid, depressed from the beaks at both extremities, so
that the sides almost form a rectangle at the prominent
beaks; convex, solid, opaque, dull yellowish white,
sub-angulated anteriorly, irregularly striated by the
lines of growth: umbones large and prominent, slopes
striated. 1½...1½. *Teignmouth and Scotland.*

M. SUBTRUNCATA. *Mont. p* 93. *and Sup. p.* 34. *t.*
27. *f.* 1.—*Lin. t.* 8. *p.* 71. *t.* 1. *f* 11.—*Pen.* 4. *t.* 55.
f. 1.—*Dor. Cat. p.* 38. *t.* 5. *f.* 10.—*D. p.* 141.—
Turt. B. p. 70.—*Turt. C. D. p.* 82.—*F. p.* 427.—
Oval-triangular, inequilateral, convex, not thick, yellowish horn colour, regularly striated transversely, one
side truncated, the other produced in a straight line to
a rather acute point ; beaks not central, tumid and prominent, without curvature. 0,60...0,80 *Common.*

* * *Lateral teeth smooth.*

M. STULTORUM. *Lin.* 1126.—*D. p.* 138.—*Pen.* 4.
p. 193. *t.* 52: *f.* 1.—*Mont. p.* 94.—*Don. t.* 106.—
Turt B. p. 72.—*Dor. Cat. t.* 8: *f.* 3. *p.* 32.—*D. p.*
138.—*Turt. C. D. p.* 81.—*F. p.* 427.—*Da. Cos. p.*
196. *t* 12. *f.* 3.—*E. M. t.* 256. *f.* 3.—Sub-triangular,
transparent, convex equilateral, slightly striated concentrically, drab-colour with narrow pale rays; the
striæ are rough at the anterior angle, from which to the
beak the depression has an obtuse mesial prominence,
the depression at the opposite extremity is less distinct,
and the mesial more prominent and compressed : beaks
and inside purplish. 2...2¼. *Common.*

M. CINEREA. *Mont. Sup. p.* 26.—*Turt. B. p.* 73.
—*F. p.* 428.—Sub-triangular, narrower than the last,
transparent, convex, sub-equilateral, truncated at the

sides, pale brown with a few very obscure white rays; beaks prominent, incurved, from which there is a depression to both extremities : inside pale with a tinge of blush. 1½...2¼. *Weymouth. &c.*

M. GLAUCA. *Gmel.* 3260.—*D. p.* 144.—*F. p.* 428. —*Mont. p.* 571.—*Don.* 4. *t.* 125. *Pen.* 4. *p.* 192.— *Lin. T.* 8. *p.* 68.—*Turt. B. p.* 74.—M. HELVACEA. *Lam.* 5.—*Ch. f.* 232.—M. NEAPOLITANA.*Poli. t.* 18. *f.* 1, 2, 3.—Oval, flattish, inequilateral, faint irregular glaucous rays on a pale ground, finely striated transversely; beaks recurved,with a narrow gape under them. 2½...3½. *Very rare, Cornwall.*

M. FRAGILIS: *Turt. B. p.* 74. *t.* 4. *f.* 10.—*An Ch. f.* 235.—*F. p.* 428.—Oval-oblong, compressed, nearly equilateral and smooth, pale yellowish white, transparent, angulated at the more produced side by a rib which runs obliquely from the hinge to the margin; beaks pointed with a depression under them on the shorter side. 1½....2. *Guernsey, very rare.*

GENUS.—LEPTON. TURTON.
Flat, nearly orbicular, equivalve, inequilateral, a little open at the sides, hinge of one valve with a single tooth and a transverse linear lateral one on each

*side ; of the other valve, with a cavity in the middle
and a transverse deeply cloven lateral tooth on each
side, the segments of which divaricate from the
beak.*

L. Squamosum. *Turt. B. p.* 62. *t.* 6. *f.* 1, 2, 3.—
F. p. 429.—Solen S. *Mont. p.* 565.—*Wood. G. C.
p.* 140.—*D. p.* 70.—*Turt. C. D. p.* 164.—Pellucid,
thin, white, obscurely wrinkled concentrically, punctured in a scalc-like manner; beak small, pointed;
inside glossy, with small longitudinal radiating striæ.
0,40...0,5. *Torbay and Tenby.*

L. Nitidum. *Turt. B. p.* 63.—*F. p.* 49.—Glossy,
slightly striated concentrically, not punctured, horn
coloured. 0,20...¼. *Torbay.*

Genus.—GOODALLIA. Turton.

*Triangular, equivalve, inequilateral, closed : hinge
with two teeth in one valve and a triangular cavity
between them, in the other valve a single tooth :
a lateral simple tooth in each valve on the produced
side.*

G. Triangularis. *Turt. B. p.* 77. *t.* 6. *f.* 14.—
F. p. 429.—Mactra T. *Mont. p.* 99. *t.* 3 *f.* 5.
—*D. p.* 143.—*Turt. D. p.* 82.—Strong, smooth,

opaque, white or brown; beaks very prominent, obtuse; inner margin toothed. 0,17...¼. *Rare.*

G. MINUTISSIMA. *Turt. B. p.* 77. *t.* 6. *f.* 15.—*F. p.* 429.—MACTRA M. *Mont. Sup. p.* 37.—*D. p.* 143. —*Turt. D. p.* 83.—Resembling the last but not quite so angular nor so long in proportion, and the inner margin quite entire. *Devon and Cornwall. Minute.*

GENUS.—ERVILIA. TURTON.

Oval, equivalve, inequilateral, closed; hinge with a single erect tooth closing between two small divergent ones in the opposite valve; lateral teeth none: ligament internal.

E. NITENS. *Turt. B. p.* 56. *t.* 19. *f.* 4—*F. p.* 431. MYA N. *Mont. Sup. p.* 165.—*Wern. T.* 1. *p.* 375. *t.* 8. *f.* 4.—*Wood. G. C. p.* 101.—*D. p.* 47.—*Turt. D. p.* 102—Oval, flattish, pale pink, a little tapering at the longer side and rounded at both, finely and regularly striated transversely; beaks prominent, margin entire. 0,17. ¼. *Scotland and Devon.*

GENUS.—KELLIA. TURTON.

Somewhat globular, equivalve, closed; hinge with two approximate teeth and a remote lateral tooth in one

*valve, and a concave tooth and remote lateral one in
the other : ligament internal.*

K. Suborbicularis. *Turt. B. p.* 57. *t.* 11. *f.* 5, 6.
—*F. p.* 430 —Mya. S. *Mont. p.* 39. *and* 564. *t.* 26.
f. 6.—*Lin. T.* 8. *p.* 41.—*Wood. G. C. p.* 111.—*D. p.*
55.—Sub-orbicular, equilateral, very convex, yellowish white, with slight concentric striæ; ventral
edge nearly straight, ends rounded; cuticle thin, greenish, prismatic. ‡. *Roots of sea-weed.*

K. Rubra. *Turt. B p.* 58. *t.* 11. *f.* 7, 8.—*F. p.*
430.—Cardium R. *Mont, p.* 83. *t.* 27. *f.* 4.—*Wood.
G. C. p.* 213.—*D. p.* 131.—*Walk. t.* 3. *f.* 86.—Oval,
inequilateral, reddish and very finely shagreened (often
paler or covered with a rough green or brown coat;
beaks prominent, subterminal, under which the margin
slopes in an incurved manner towards the smaller end:
inside glossy purple. 0,80...0,10. *Roots of sea-weed.*

Genus.—MONTACUTA. Turton.

*Oval or oblong, equivalve, inequilateral, mostly closed;
hinge with two teeth in each valve and a cavity
between them; lateral teeth none : ligament internal.*

M. Substriata. *Turt. B. p.* 59. *t.* 11. *f.* 9. 10.
—*F. p.* 465.—Ligula S. *Mont. sup. p.* 25.—Mya

c 2.

S. *d. p.* 47.—*Wood. G. C. p.* 102.—*Turt. D. p.*
103.—Oval, convex, slightly contracted in the middle,
white or yellowish white and semi-transparent, with
obscure and rather remote longitudinal raised striæ ;
beaks prominent, not quite central, teeth in one valve
obscure. *Adhering to Echini by slender filaments.*

M. BIDENTATA. *Turt. B. p.* 60.—MYA B. *Mont.*
44. *t.* 26. *f.* 5.—*Lin. Trans.* 8. *p.* 41.—*Wood.*
G. C. p. 99.—*D. p.* 45.—*F. p.* 465.—*Turt. C. D.*
p. 102.—Oval, sm)oth, rather produced at one end,
whitish, but not glossy, and frequently covered with a
rough coat; beaks nearer the broader end ; one of the
teeth oblique and spoon-shaped. ⅜. *in length. In*
old oyster shells.

M. FERRUGINEA. *Turt. B. p.* 60.—MYA F. *Mont.*
p. 22. *t.* 26. *f.* 2.—*Wood. G. C. p.* 100.—*D. p.* 46.
—*Turt. C. D. p.* 102.—*F. p.* 465.—Oblong, slightly
striated transversely, white, often covered or blotched
with an ochraceous coat; beaks placed near one end,
obtuse; one of the teeth in each valve erect, the other
much bent inwards and sloping downwards. ⅜....⅜.
Scotch and Western Coast.

M. OBLONGA. *Turt. B. p.* 61. *t.* 11. *f.* 11. 12.—

F. p. 465.—Oblong, smooth, glossy, all the teeth
erect. ⅛...¼: *Sand in Torbay, closely resembling the
last.*

GENUS.—MESODESMA. DESHAYES.

*Oval, transverse or triangular, and usually shutting
close : hinge with a narrow central spoon-shaped
pit for the ligament, with an oblong and simple
tooth on each side of it.*
M. DEAURATA.—MACTRA D. *Turt. B. p.* 71. *t.*
5. *f.* 8.—*F. p.* 427 —*An* MES. DENTICULATA ? *Gray
in Grif. Cuv.—An* MES. JAURESII ? *Mag. de Zool.*
—Oblong. flattish, inequilateral, rounded at the elongated side and obtusely truncated at the other, opaque,
strong, dull greyish white under a shining bronzed skin
reflecting metallic lustres, coarsely and irregularly
striated transversely, with a few coarser ridges towards
the hinge; beaks rather prominent and pointed, a little
inclined to the longer side. ⅞...1¼. *Exmouth, rare.*

M. DONACILLA. *Desh in Lam.*—AMPHIDESMA. D.
Lam. 2.—DONAX PLEBEIA. *Mont. t.* 5. *f.* 2. *p.* 107.
—*Turt. B. p.* 127.—*Dor. Cat. p.* 38. *t.* 5. *f.* 13.—
Turt. C. D. p. 102.—*F. p.* 434.—*D. p.* 102.--
ERYCINA P. *Sow. G. f.* 3.—*Reeve. t.* 45. *f.* 4—Ovate
triangular, wedge-shaped, posteriorly very short and

obtuse, smooth, variable in color, being sometimes uniform yellow, pale with three or four chesnut or dark
rays and often yellow with a broad central white
ray edged with chesnut ; inside yellowish. ½...¾.
Teignmouth, usually dead specimens.

M. Castanea.—Capsa C. *Turt. B. p.* 128. *t.* 10.
f. 13.—*F. p.* 434.—Donax C. *Mont. p.* 573. *t.* 17.
f. 2.—*Lin. T.* 8. *p.* 77.—*D. p.* 152.—*Turt. C. D. p.*
42.—Oval-oblong, smooth, pale reddish chesnut with a
deeper longitudinal band from the hinge which curves a
little towards the longer side, strong, glossy ; inside
chesnut the margin entire, hinge with two teeth (one
large the other small) in each valve. ¼...½. *Penzance.*

Genus.—AMPHIDESMA.

*Oval, equivalve, mostly closed, hinge with a spoon-
shaped tooth, adjacent denticles and lateral teeth :
ligament external.*

* A. Prismaticum. *Lam.* 10.—*Turt. B. p.* 52. *t.*
5. *f.* 3.—*F. p.* 432.—Ligula P. *Mont. Sup. p.* 23.
t. 26. *f.* 3.—*Pen.* 4. *p.* 169.--Mya P. *Wood. G. C.
p.* 101.—*D. p.* 47 —*Turt. C. D. p.* 103.—Oblong,

* In British Species, the lateral teeth are only in one
valve.

thin, transparent, glossy, brilliant white, reflecting metallic colours, anteriorly tapering to a point, posteriorly
rounded; beaks small, pointing towards the longer side;
inside smooth, glossy, hinge with a plain denticle and
lateral teeth. *W. Coasts, Scotland.* ½...1.

A. TENUE. *Lam.* 8.—*Turt. B. p.* 53·—*F. p.* 433.—
MACTRA T. *Mont. p.* 572. *t* 17. *f.* 7.—*Pen.* 4. *p.* 194.
—*Lin. T.* 8. *p.* 72.—*Dor. Cat. p.* 33.—*D. p.* 142.—
Turt. C. D. p. 84.—Sub-triangular, equilateral, compressed, thin, glossy white, pellucid, ventral edge
rounded; hinge with a cloven and a remote lateral
tooth in one valve, a single plain tooth in the other.
½...0,40 . *S. Coast.*

A. BOYSII. *Lam.* 7.—*Turt. B. p.* 53. *t.* 5. *f.* 4 &5.
—LIGULA B. *Mont. p.* 98. *t.* 3. *f.* 7.—MACTRA B.
Pen. 4. *p.* 195.—*Lin. T.* 8. *p.* 72. *t.* 1. *f.* 12.—*Dor.
Cat. p.* 93. *t.* 12. *f.* 7.—*D. p.* 143.—*Turt. C. D. p.*
84.—M. ALBA. *Wood, Lin. T.* 6. *p.* 174. *t.* 16. *f.* 9.
to 12.—AMP. A. *F. p.* 433.—Ovate, subtriangular,
rounded at both ends, anteriorly shorter, thin, compressed, glossy white, sloping from the beak at both
ends, ventral edge rather suddenly rounded: a single
umbonal denticle in each valve and a large lateral tooth
on each side in one valve. ½—¾. *Common on Sandy
Coasts.*

56

Tribe.—CORBULACEA.

Inequivalve; ligament internal; one of the beaks always projecting beyond the other.

Genus.—CORBULA.

Regular, equivalve, inequilateral; with a conical, bent, ascending, primary tooth in each valve, a small pit at its side; destitute of lateral teeth; ligament external.

C. Nucleus. *Lam.* 6.—*Turt. B. p.* 39. *t.* 3. *f.* 8 *to* 10.—*Sow. G. f.* 1.—*Reeve. t.* 36. *f.* 1.—Mya Inequivalvis. *Mont. p.* 38. *t.* 26. *f.* 7.—*Pen.* 4. *p.* 126. —*Lin. T.* 8. *p.* 10. *t.* 1. *f.* 6.—*Wood. G. C. p.* 113.— *D. p.* 55.—*Turt. C. D. p.* 107·—*E. M. t.* 230. *f.* 4.—Subtriangular, strong, opaque, generally covered with a brown skin under which it is whitish or flesh color, larger valve convex, regularly striated transversely, inclosing the lesser valve over which the beak projects and curves inwards; lesser valve flattish, with a few longitudinal raised striæ : inside smooth, polished round the margin. ¼....½. *Torbay, &c.*

Genus.—SPHÆNIA. Turton.

Transverse, inequivalve, inequilateral, open at the anterior side; hinge of the left valve with an elevated transversely dilated tooth, of the right valve with a

*concave tooth and small denticle behind it ; no late-·
ral teeth : ligament internal.*

S. BINGHAMI. *Turt. B. p.* 36. *t.* 3. *f.* 4, 5. *& t.* 19.
f. 3.—*F. p.* 465.—Wedge-shaped, covered with a brown
wrinkled skin which extends beyond the anterior end,
truncate at the hinge, with the upper margin often a
little contracted about the middle, gradually tapering to
the open anterior extremity; beaks rather prominent,
with the points not quite opposite but diverging from
each other; inside glossy white with a purplish tint, the
margin short and plain, the concave tooth oblique and
inflected. ¼....½. *Torbay, in rocks.*

S. SWAINSONI. *Turt. B. p.* 37. *t.* 3. *f.* 3. *and t.* 19.
f. 2.—*F. p.* 466.—Oval, wedge-shaped, rounded anteriorly; the concave tooth projecting horizontally
inwards. ¼...¼. *Torbay, in rocks.*

GENUS.—PANDORA.

*Regular, inequivalve, inequilateral, and transversely
oblong ; upper valve flattened, under convex; hinge
with two oblong diverging cardinal teeth in the
upper valve ; the other valve with two corresponding grooves : ligament external.*

P. OBTUSA. *Lam.* 2.—*Sow. Sp. Con. f.* 1, 2, 3.
—SOLEN PINNA. *Mont. t.* 15. *f.* 3.—Ovate, posterior side very short, obtuse and obliquely rounded at

the ventral edge, slightly angular at the dorsal, narrower
than the produced and dilated anterior side; anterior
dorsal edge nearly straight and angular at the end; dorsal edge of the flat valve overlapping the concave one.
0,45...0,80. *Rare.*

P. ROSTRATA. *Lam.* 1.—*Sow. G.—Sow. Sp. Con. f.*
7, 8, 9.—*E. M. t.* 250.—TEI LINA INEQUIVALVIS.
Lin. 1118.—*D. p.* 86.—*Don. t.* 41. *f.* 1.—*Ch. f.* 106.
—P. MARGARITACEA. *Turt. B. p.* 41. *t.* 3. *f.* 11. *to*
14.—P. INEQUIVALVIS. *F. p.* 466.—Oblong, anterior side elongated, with two very obtuse keels near the
dorsal edge, somewhat beaked and slightly truncated:
tooth in the flat valve small and blunt: hinge margin
incurved. 0,70...1,40. *Dawlish and Guernsey.*

TRIBE.—LITHOPHAGI:

Borers, without accessory plates and more or less
gaping anteriorly. Ligament external.

GENUS.—HIATELLA.

Transversely oblong, dorsal and ventral edges sub-
parallel; hinge with the teeth obscure or with one
tooth in one valve received into a cavity in the
other.

H. RUGOSA. *Flem. p.* 461.—SAXICAVA. R. and

Pholadis. *Lam.—Turt. B. p.* 20. *t.* 2. *f.* 10.—
Mytilus R.: *Lin.* 1156.—*Pen.* 4. *p.* 110. *t.* 63. *f.* 72.
—*D. p.* 304.—*Mont. p.* 164.—*Dor. Cat. p.* 39. *t.* 13.
f. 5.—*Turt. D. p.* 113.—*Lin. T.* 8. *p.* 270. *t.* 6. *f.* 3,
4.—*List. t.* 426. *f.* 267.—Rounded posteriorly, subtruncated anteriorly, the ventral edge slightly incurved
near the middle, dull white under a greyish wrinkled
cuticle, coarsely wrinkled transversely. ½... 1¼. *Common,
in Rocks.*

H. Arctica. *Lam.—F. p.* 461.—H. Minuta. and
Oblona. *Turt. B. p.* 24. *t.* 2. *f.* 12, 3.—Solen Minutus. *Lin.* 1115.—*Mont. p.* 53. *t.* 1. *f.* 4.—*Ch. f.*
51, 2.—*Wood. G. C. p.* 139. *t.* 34. *f.* 5, 6.—*D. p.*
69.—*Turt. C. D. p.* 161.—With two diverging spinous
ridges on the anterior slope; closely resembling the
former species in age by the gradual disappearance of
the spinous ridges, but distinguished by the greater
incurvation of the ligamental edge. *The Mytilus
Præcisus of Mont. p.* 165. *t.* 4. *f.* 2. *seems but a
variety of this species.*

GENUS.—AGINA. TURTON.
*Transverse, oval, equivalve, inequilateral, open at the
anterior end; hinge with a single erect conic per-*

forating tooth in each valve, lateral teeth none: *ligament external.*

A. PURPUREA. *Turt. B. p.* 54. *t.* 4. *f.* 9.—MYA. P. *Mont. Sup. p.* 21.—SOLEN P. *F. p.* 459.—Oval, obliquely truncated anteriorly, convex, opaque, under a glossy white cuticle, chalky white, with irregular concentric striæ ; inside glossy white, hinge with a single conic tooth in each valve penetrating a corresponding cavity in the opposite. ⅛...¼. *Torbay, in rocks.*

GENUS.—VENERUPIS.

Transverse, inequilateral, posterior side short, the anterior slightly gaping ; hinge with two cardinal teeth in the right valve and three in the left (sometimes three in each); teeth small approximated, parallel and slightly divergent: ligament external.

V. IRUS. *Lam.* 3.—*F. p.* 451-—DONAX I. *Lin.* 1129.—*D. p.* 156.—*Ch. f.* 268,9.—*Pen.* 4. *p.* 100.— *Mont. p.* 108. *and* 573.— *Don.* 1. *t.* 29. *f.* 2.—*Lin. T.* 8. *p.* 77.—*Dor. Cat. p.* 34. *t.* 12. *f.* 6. *(left-hand.)*— *Turt. C. D. p.* 43.—*Da. Cost. p.* 204. *t.* 15. *f.* 6. *(left-hand)*—PETRICOLA I. *Turt. B, p.* 26. *t.* 2. *f.* 14.—Oblong or oval, but variable in modifications being at times truncated and sometimes rounded, dull dirty white, with rather distant, thin, transverse, subreflected lamellæ and regular close radiating striæ in

the interstices; anterior end mostly gaping,rarely somewhat closed; inside white with frequently a chocolate
blotch at one end, margin entire, hinge subterminal.
¼...¾. *Torbay, in Rocks.*

V. PERFORANS. *Lam.* 1.—*Turt. B. p.* 29. *t.* 2. *f.*
15 *to* 18.—*F. p.* 451.—VENUS P. *Mont. p.* 127. *t.* 3.
f. 6.—*Lin. T.* 8. *p.* 89.—*Pen.* 4. *p.* 111.—*D. p.* 206.
—*Turt. C. D. p.* 245.—Variable in shape, more or less
oblong, angularly truncated at one end (sometimes
rounded at both ends or kidney-shaped and indented)
very inequilateral, with transverse striæ which become
lamellar anteriorly,and minute radiating ones; brownish
or yellowish white, with sometimes a few purple
broken rays and linear ziczacs; inside white, glossy,
with mostly a purple blotch at the larger end, margin
entire; hinge with three erect, long, and somewhat recurved teeth in each valve, two of them cloven, the
lower one in the right valve and the upper one in the
left, entire and much the smaller. 1...2½. *In rocks,
common. The young are compressed, white variously
marked with purple blotches anteriorly.*

TRIBE.—NYMPHACEA.
*Never having more than two cardinal teeth in the same
valve, often gaping at the lateral extremities ; ligament external, umbones usually projecting outwards,*

Genus.—PSAMMOBIA.

Transverse, elliptical or oblong-ovate, compressed, slightly gaping at one side; beaks prominent; two cardinal teeth in the left valve and one in the opposite, no lateral teeth.

P. Tellinella. *Lam.* 1.—P. Florida. *Turt. B. p.* 86. *t.* 6. *f.* 9.—*F. p.* 437.—Oblong, nearly smooth, thin, subequilateral, anteriorly obtusely angulated, posteriorly rounded, yellowish, with either red interrupted rays or zones, but always with one small distinct posterior ray, which only proceeds a short distance from the beaks. ⅓...0,83. *W. Coasts of Ireland.*

P. Costulata. *Turt. B. p.*87. *t.* 6. *f.* 8.—*F.p.*437. —P. Discors. *Philippi.p.* 23. *t.* 3. *f.* 8—Oval-oblong, thin, slightly angular anteriorly where there are about twelve fine oblique radiating ribs; color varying from pale yellow to deep purple and marked with crimson blotches or stripes; transversely striated and minutely so longitudinally; beaks nearly central, a little prominent, not inclining to either side : hinge with a single cloven tooth in one valve locking into two in the other, one of which is slightly cleft. ⅓...1. *Dredged in Torbay and the Channel.*

P. Fragilis. *Turt. B. p.* 88. *t.* 7. *f.* 11,2.—*F. p.* 438.—Tellina F. *Lin.* 1117.—*Ch. f.* 84.—*Turt.*

C. D. p. 166. *f.* 18.—T. Jugosa. *Brown in Wer. T.*
2. *p.* 506. *t.* 24. *f.* 2.—Petricoia Ochroleuca.
Lam.—Oboval, tumid, and broader posteriorly, flexuous and produced anteriorly; thin, brittle, white or
brownish with numerous thin raised unequal striæ,
whose interstices are minutely striated longitudinally;
teeth strong, elevated, two in one valve, a cloven tooth
in the other. 1...1¼. *Ireland, rare.*

P. Polygona. *Turt. B. p.* 96.—*F. p.* 438.—
Tellina P. *Mont. Sup. p.* 27. *t.* 28. *f.* 4.—*Turt. C.
D. p.* 180.—Somewhat orbicular, somewhat truncated
and angular at one end, rounded at the other, with fine
transverse striæ and minute longitudinal ones, the margin uneven; beaks not quite central ; in one valve two
large distant teeth, in the other a large cloven triangular
tooth and a small one near it. ½...⅝. *Frith of Forth.*

P. Laskeyi. *Turt. B. p.* 89.—*F. p.* 438.—Tellina S. *Mont. Sup. p.* 28. *t.* 28. *f.* 3.—Oval-oblong,
smooth, glossy, slightly contracted anteriorly, purplish
white under a yellowish olive epidermis, rounded at one
end, obtusely pointed at the other: two approximate
sub-bifid teeth in one valve, a single tooth in the other.
0,40...¾, *Frith of Forth.*

P. Ferroensis. *Lam.* 2.—*Turt. R.p.*94. *t.* 8. *f.* 1. *F. p.* 438.—Tellina F. *Gmel.* 3235.—*Born. t.* 2. *f.* 5.—*List. t.* 394. *f.* 241.—*D. p.* 77.—*Mont. p.* 55.— *Lin. T.* 8. *p.* 49.—*Dor. Cat. p.* 49. *t.* 6. *f.* 1.— *Wood. G. C. p.* 164. *t.* 45. *f.* 1.—*Turt. C. D. p.* 171. —*Da Cost. p.* 209. *t.* 14. *f.* 1.—T. Trifasciata. *Don. t.* 60.—Oblong, compressed, subequilateral, striated, transparent, and decussated on the flattened anterior slope which is subtruncated at its extremity and defined by a slight elevation in both valves; pale red with paler rays: inside white. ¼...2. *Western and other coasts.*

Genus.—SANGUINOLARIA.

Transverse, somewhat oval, slightly gaping at the lateral extremities; upper margin arched and not parallel to the inferior one : hinge with two approximate teeth in each valve.

S. Rugosa. *Lam.* 4.—S. Deflorata. *F. p.* 461.— Psammobia D. *Turt. B. p.* 93.—Venus. D. *Lin.* 1133.—*D. p* 186.—*Ch. f.* 79 to 86.—*E. M. t.* 231. *f.* 3.—*Pen.* 4. *p.* 96. *t.* 57. *f.* 54.—*Mont. p.* 123. *t.* 3. *f.* 4.—O. Versicolor and Purpurea. *Gmel.*— Ovate-oblong, ventricose, with strong longitudinal and fine transverse wrinkles becoming coarser at the anterior end which is generally more or less stained with

purple; white, pale reddish, yellowish or purple, and
frequently rayed with the latter colour: obsoletely
truncated anteriorly. 1½...2. *S. Coast, rare.*

S. VESPERTINA. *F. p.* 461.—SOLEN V. *Gmel.* 3228.
—*Mont. p.* 54 —*Lin. T.* 8. *p.* 47.—*Dor. Cat. p.* 29.
t. 5. *f.* 1.—*Wood. G. C. p.* 135. *t.* 32. *f.* 2, 3.—*Turt.
C. D. p.* 163.—*Ch. f.* 59, 60.—PSAMMOBIA V. *Lam.*
3.—*Turt. B p.* 92. *t.* 6. *f.* 10. *(young)*—TELLINA
DEPRESSA. *Don. t.* 41.—*T.* ALBIDA. *D. p.* 78.—
Oblong, moderately thick, subequilateral, nearly smooth,
anteriorly slightly angulated, opaque, whitish or pale
straw-colour, rayed with reddish purple; one of the
teeth in one valve, thin laminar and oblique. 1¾...2¼.
S. Coasts.

GENUS.—TELLINA

*Transverse or orbicular, both valves generally flattened,
the anterior side angular and inflexed on the margin with a flexuous irregular ridge; with one or
two cardinal teeth in the same valve and sometimes
two lateral teeth, frequently remote.*

* *Oval, with two teeth in one valve.*

T. LINEATA. *Turt. B. p.* 99. *t.* 7. *f.* 1.—*F. p.* 435.

—*An* T. Braziliana. *Lam.?*—Oval, with crowded concentric striæ, anteriorly shorter and attenuated, thin, semitransparent, white. with a pale red longitudinal stripe down the rounded side: beaks straight and pointed : hinge with two cardinal, one cloven, and a lateral laminar tooth on each side in one valve, in the other but a single cloven cardinal tooth. &...&. *Teignmouth.*

T. Punicea. *Gmel.* 3239.—*D. p.* 90.—*Lam.* 21. —*F. p.* 435.—*Pen.* 4. *p.* 179.—*Lin. T.* 8. *p.* 50.— *Dor. Cat. p.* 30. *t.* 7. *f.* 5.—*Wood. G. C. p.* 170. *t.* 39. *f.* 1.—*Turt. C. D. p.* 171.—*Born. t.* 2. *f.* 2.— *E. M. t.* 291. *f.* 2.—*Ch. f.* 1654,5.—T. Læta. *Mont. p.* 57.—T. Inequistriata. *Don.* 4. *p.* 123.—Elongated oval, subinequilateral, slightly angulated and inflected at the shorter anterior end, rather thin, paler or darker crimson, usually with paler unequal bands, deeply striated transversely ; one of the cardinal teeth bifid, the single lateral in each of its valves contiguous broad and oblique. &...1,16.

T. Fabula. *Gmel.* 3239.—*D. p.* 92.—*Lam.* 24.— *Don. t.* 97.—*Mont. p.* 61.—*Pen.* 4. *p.* 179.—*Lin.. T. p.* 52.—*Dor. Cat. p.* 30. *t.* 12. *f.* 3. *and* 3a.— *Wood G. C. p.* 156. *t.* 45. *f.* 4.—*Turt. C. D. p.*

170,—*F. p.* 435.—Ovate, thin, transparent, glossy, white; anteriorly contracted, posteriorly rounded; one of the valves obliquely striated, the other quite smooth; two cardinal and a single lateral tooth in one valve, only single cardinal in the other. ½...¾. *Common on sandy coasts.*

T. Similis. *Sow. Brit. Mis. t.* 75.—*Mont Ap. p.* 167.—*Turt. C. D. p.* 170.—*Turt. B. p.* 102.—*F. p.* 435.—Oval, with both valves obliquely striated; a lateral tooth in each valve. *Paignton sands, very rare.*

T. Donacina, *Lin.* 1118.—*D. p.* 89.—*Lam.* 27.— *Mont. p.* 58. *t.* 27. *f.* 3.—*Poli.* 1. *t.* 15. *f.* 10.—*Pen.* 4. *p.* 178.—*Lin. T.* 8. *p.* 50. *t.* 1. *f.* 7.—*Dor. Cat. p.* 29. *t.* 12. *f.* 3b.—*Wood. G. C. p.* 161. *t.* 45. *f.* 5.— *Turt. D. p.* 170.—*F. p.* 435.—*Turt. B. t.* 8. *f.* 4. *p.* 103.—Oval-oblong, anteriorly very short and obtusely cuneiform, posteriorly rounded; the posterior dorsal edge but little sloping; yellowish with narrow red, often interrupted rays, semi pellucid; hinge in one valve with a cloven cardinal tooth, an additional simple one and lateral teeth on each side in the other. ½...1. *Guernsey, Devon, Dorset, not common.*

T. BIMACULATA. *Lin.* 1120.—*D. p.* 101.—*Lam.*
52.—*Ch. f.* 127. *E. M. t.* 290. *f.* 9.—*Da. Cos. p.*
213.—*Pen.* 4. *p.* 183.—*Mont. p.* 169.—*Lin. T.* 8. *p.*
57.—*Don. t.* 19. *f.* 1.—*Dor. Cat. p.* 31. *t.* 5. *f.* 7.—
Wood. G. C. p. 192. *t.* 45. *f.* 6, 7.—*Turt. C. D. p.*
178.—*F. p.* 435.—*Turt. B. p.* 104.—Rounded-triangular, nearly smooth; obtusely truncated, a little angular and shorter anteriorly; compressed, variable in colouring, being often white with a deep red oblong spot on each side of the hinge, sometimes uniform whitish, cream coloured or violet, at times with linear purple arrow headed radiating markings *(Turt. B. t.* 8. *f.* 5.*)* or with six (T. SEXRADIATA. *Lam.* 53.—*E. M. t.* 290. *f.* 10.—*Ch. f.* 1326.*)* purplish brown rays; hinge with a single cardinal tooth in one valve, two in the other, two lateral in each. ½...⅝. *W. Coasts.*

T. DEPRESSA. *Gmel.* 3238.—*Lam.* 22.—*D. p.* 91.
—*Pen.* 4· *p.* 179.—*Don. t.* 163.—*Lin. T. p.* 51.—
Dor. Cat. p. 30. *t.* 5. *f.* 2.—*Wood. G. C. p.* 171. *t.*
45. *f.* 3.—*Turt. C. D. p.* 171.—*Turt. B. p.* 105. *t.* 8.
f. 6.—T. SQUALIDA. *Mont. p.* 56 —*F. p.* 436.—T.
INCARNATA. *Poli.* 1. *t.* 15. *f.* 1.—Oval-oblong, anteriorly produced, attenuated and pointed, posteriorly rounded, ventral edge little arcuated in the middle; compressed, pinkish flesh colour or orange, with two

oblique paler indistinct anterior twin rays, finelystriated concentrically; a lateral tooth on both sides in one valve, one only in the other.   1⅓...2.   *W. and Irish coasts.*

* * *Oval, two teeth in each valve.*

T. STRIATA. *Mont. p.* 60. *t.* 27. *f.* 2.—*Turt. B. p.* 106.—*F. p.* 437.—*Lin. T.* 8. *p.* 53.—*Turt. C. D. p.* 169.—Oval-triangular, finely and regularly striated transversely and very minutely so longitudinally, rosy white within and without, deeper towards the hinge; each valve with two lateral teeth.   1...¾.   *S. Coasts, rare.*

T. TENUIS. *Pen.* 4. *p.* 180. *t.* 51. *f.* 2.—*Da Cost. p.* 210.—*Lam.* 25.—*Ch. f.* 117.—*Don. t.* 19. *(3 lower figs.)*—*List. t.* 405. *f.* 251.—*Mont. p.* 59.—*Lin. T.* 8. *p.* 52.—*Dor. Cat. p.* 30. *t.* 5. *f.* 3.—*Wood. G. C. p.* 155. *t.* 44. *f.* 3, 4.—*Turt. C. D. p.* 169.—*Turt. B. p.* 107.—*F. p.* 406.—T. INCARNATA. *D. p.* 87.— Oval-triangular, nearly smooth, very compressed, thin and glossy, whitish, reddish or orange, with generally darker bands; anteriorly attenuated; one of the valves with a lateral tooth.   ½...¾.   *Sandy shores, extremely common.*

T. SOLIDULA. *Lam.* 51.—*Mont. p.* 63.—*Pen.* 4. *p,*
184. *t.* 52. *f.* 2. *and* 2A.—*Lin. T.* 8. *p.* 58,—*Dor.*
Cat. p. 31. *t.* 8. *f.* 4.—*Turt. C. D· p.* 177.—*Da Cos.*
t. 12. *f.* 4.—*List. t.* 405. *f.* 251.—PSAMMOBIA S.
Turt. B. t. 8. *f.* 2. *p.* 95.—*F. p.* 438.—T. ZONATA.
Gmel. 3250.—*D. p.* 100.—Rounded-triangular, thick,
ventricose, somewhat angulated and compressed anteriorly, passing from white into yellow or pink, with
darker bands and obsolete ridges of growth ; hinge
nearly central, with two indistinct cardinal teeth in each
valve, no lateral. ¾...⅝. *Excessively common on*
sandy shores.

* * * *Suborbicular with two cardinal teeth in each*
valve.

T. MACULATA. *Turt. C. D. p.* 173. *t.* 13.—*Turt.*
B. p. 108. *t.* 6. *f.* 7.—*F. p.* 436.—Rounded-oval,
equivalve, flat, thin, whitish brown covered with darker
spots irregularly disposed, and marked wtth numerous
raised striæ, crossed in their interstices by minute longitudinal ones ; inside yellowish white, glossy, two strong
remote lateral teeth in each valve. 1...1¼. *Dredged*
in Bantry Bay.

T. CRASSA. *Pen.* 4. *t.* 48. *f.* 28.—*Gmel.* 3238.—

D. p. 96.—*E. M. t.* 291.*f.* 5,—*Lam. p.* 35.—*List.
t.* 299.*f.* 136.—*Turt. B. p.* 109. *t.* 7. *f.* 2.—*F. p.*
436.—T. PROFICUA. and FAUSTA. *Mont. p.* 69. *and*
64.—T. RIGIDA. *Don. t.* 103.—Suborbicular, thick,
heavy, semitransparent, with one valve less convex than
the other, anteriorly shorter ; white or yellowish (with
usually narrow reddish rays) with crowded transverse
furrows which become coarser anteriorly ; beaks often
pink ; inside yellowish ; a simple and bifid cardinal
tooth in each valve, two lateral in one valve only. ½...2.
S. Coasts.

GENUS.—LUCINA.

*Sub-orbicular, inequilateral, beaks small, pointed and
oblique ; hinge variable, sometimes with two divergent teeth, one of which is bifid but changing with
age ; two lateral teeth, the intermediate one obsolete ;
the posterior nearest the primary ones : two distinct
muscular impressions widely separated, the posterior
one prolonged.*

L. LACTEA. *Lam.* 12.—*Turt. B. p.* 112. *t.* 7. *f.* 4,5.
TELLINA L. *Lin.* 1119.—*D. p.* 99.—*Bl. t.* 72.*f.* 1.—
Ch.f. 125.—*Mont. p.* 70. *t.* 2. *f.* 4.—*Lin. T.* 8. *p.* 56.
—*Dor. Cat. p.* 30. *t* 5. *f.* 9.—*Turt. C. D. p.* 176.—
LORIPES L. *F. p.* 430.—Orbicular, equilateral, with
fine irregular concentric striæ, thin, rather compressed,

white or yellowish; beaks pointed, prominent and curved, lunule small and cordiform; inside polished round the area of the margin; in one valve a single plain tooth closing between two plain ones in the other; internal cavity oblique. ¾. *Torbay and British Channel.*

L. LEUCOMA. *Turt. B. p.* 113. *t.* 7. *f.* 8.—LORIPES L. *F. p.* 430.—Orbicular, rather oblique and inequilateral, anteriorly a little produced and angular, and generally a little flexuous under the beaks posteriorly; convex, chalky white, marked with regular crowded transverse raised striæ and deeper wrinkles (sometimes crossed by extremely fine and close set radiating lines); beaks prominent with a curvature under them; inside and hinge as in *Lactea.* ⅝. *Torbay, British Channel and Guernsey.*

L. ALBA. *Turt. B. p.* 114. *t.* 7. *f.* 6,7.—Orbicular, convex, glossy white, with rather remote regular transverse striæ; hinge with two teeth in one valve, one in the other; internal cavity nearly in a straight line. ⅝. *British Channel and Guernsey. More rounded than the last and with no appearance of longitudinal lines.*

L. ROTUNDATA. *Turt- B. p.* 115. *t.* 7. *f.* 3.—TEL-
LINA R. *Mont. p.* 71. *t.* 2. *f.* 3.—*Pen.* 4. *p.* 182.—
Lin. T. 8. *p.* 56.—*Dor. Cat. p.* 30. *t.* 5. *f.* 8.—*Wood.*
G. C. p. 187.—*D. p.* 99.—*Turt. D. p.* 176.—
PSAMMOBIA R. *F. p.* 438.—Orbicular, convex and
nearly smooth, a little undulated in the circumference,
yellowish white or pale horn color and transparent;
beaks not quite central, rather prominent; inside white,
but not glossy, except the area round the margin; hinge
with two teeth in each valve, one cloven, the other diverging, lateral cavity narrow and nearly straight. 1.
W. Coasts and Ireland.

L. UNDATA. *Turt. B. p.* 115.—*Lam.* 13.—VENUS
U. *Pen.* 4. *p.* 209. *t.* 58. *f.* 3.—*Lin. T.* 6. *p.* 169. *t.*
17. *f.* 17,8.—*Mont. p.* 117.—*Don. t.* 121.—*Lin. T.*
8. *p.* 86.—*D. p.* 197.—*Turt. C. D. p.* 241. *f.* 54.—
Orbicular, convex, with slight concentric striæ, very thin
and brittle, dull yellowish white, slightly undulated at
its margin; beaks subcentral, no lunule; inside glossy
yellowish white : hinge with three teeth (one bifid) in
one valve, two in the other. 1. *Common on sandy*
shores.

L. RADULA. *Lam.* 5.—*Turt. B. p.* 116.—*F. p.* 441.
TELLINA R. *Mont. p.* 68. *t.* 2. *f.* 1,2.—*Lin. T.* 8. *p.*

54.—*Pen.* 4. *p.* 181.—*Wood. G. C. p.* 183. *t.* 42. *f.*
4.5.—*Turt. C. D. p.* 175.—Venus Borealis. *Don.*
4. *t.* 130.—V. Spuria. *D. p.* 194.—Lenticular, convex, dirty white, with numerous raised transverse thread-like striæ (which become indistinct in old shells, towards the margin), the interstices broad and shallow; inside dull chalky white; beaks central, pointed, and a little curved; a small lunule; two teeth (one bifid) in each valve. 1½. *W. and Irish Coasts.*

L. Sinuosa. *Lam.* 17.—L. Flexuosa. *F. p.* 442.
—*Gould. p.* 52.—Tellina F. *Mont. p.* 72.—*Lin.
T.* 8. *p.* 56.—*Wood. G. C. p.* 188. *t.* 47. *f.* 7, 8.—
D. p. 99.—*Turt C. D. p.* 177.—-Venus Sinuosa.
Don. t 42. *f.* 2.—Cryptodon F. *Turt. B. p.* 121. *t.*
7. *f.* 9, 10.—Suborbicular, longer than broad, very convex, pure white, thin, pellucid, marked with minute irregular concentric wrinkles, and a longitudinal furrow extending from the apex parallel to the cartilage slope, and forming a deep incurvation in the margin at its termination: hinge with a single obscure penetrating cardinal tooth. ⅞. *S. Coasts.*

L. Spinifera.—Venus S. *Mont. p.* 577. *t.* 17. *f.* 1.
—*Lin. T.* 8. *p.* 78.—*D. p.* 163.—*Turt. C. D. p.* 231.
—Myrtea S. *Turt. B. p.* 133.—*F. p.* 443.—Oval

triangular, yellowish white, with numerous fine laminar
equidistant slightly reflected cencentric ridges, which
anteriorly become confluent in pairs extending beyond
the edges so as to form a fringe of short obtuse spines,
which turn back and form a cavity for the cartilage
beaks small, subcentral, lunule long and narrow : a
single cardinal and two lateral teeth in one valve, two
cardinal in the other, the lateral obscure. ⚲. *W. Coasts,
rare.*

L. CARNARIA. *Lam.—F. p.* 442.—TELLINA C.
Lin. 1119.—*Ch. f.* 126.—*Mont. p.* 73.—*Don. t.* 47.
—*Lin. T.* 8. *p.* 57.—*Dor. Cat. p.* 31. *t.* 5. *f.* 6.—
Wood. G. C. p. 189. *t.* 40. *f.* 4, 5.—*D. p.* 100.—
Turt. C. D. p. 177.—STRIGILLA C. *Turt. B. p.* 118.
t. 7. *f.* 15.—Rounded oval, inequilateral, more or less
tinged with rose-color, rather compressed. marked in
the middle with oblique longitudinal striæ, which, at
at the shorter end, are curved and flexuous, and at the
produced end with straight ones, which meet the oblique ones and form angles ; beaks near one end : hinge
with two cardinal (one bifid) and a lateral tooth in each
valve. ⚲. *W. Coasts.*

L. PISIFORMIS. *Lin.* 1120.—*F. p.* 442.—*Wood.
G. C. p.* 194.—*D. p.* 102.—*Turt. C. D. p.* 178.—

CARDIUM DISCORS. *Mont. p.* 84.—*Wood. G. C. p.* 214.—STRIGILLA P. *Turt. B. p.* 119.—Somewhat globular, subequilateral, glossy white, with numerous striæ, which anteriorly bend in acute angles towards the hinge; beaks small, inclining a little to one side; hinge with a single plain cardinal tooth on one valve, closing between two (one small) in the other, and a remote prominent lateral tooth. ¼. *Falmouth, extremely rare.*

L. DIVARICATA. *Lam.*—TELLINA D. *Lin.* 1120.— *E. M. t.* 285. *f.* 4.—*Ch. f.* 129.—*Wood. G. C. p.* 195. *t.* 46. *f.* 6.—*D. p.* 102.—CARDIUM ARCUATUM. *Mont:* *p.* 85. *t.* 3. *f.* 2.—*Pen.* 4. *p.* 190.—*Lin. T.* 8. *p.* 153. —STRIGILLA D. *Turt. B. p.* 120.—Orbicular, subequilateral, white, thin, rather convex, with a slight posterior flexuosity, with regular rather distant striæ, which form rather oblique curved lines, and turn off at both the sides nearly at right angles; beaks very prominent; hinge with a single cloven tooth in one valve, closing between two plain ones in the other, a small remote lateral tooth in each valve. ¼. *Teignmouth.*

L. TIGERINA. *Sow.*—VENUS T. *Lin.* 1133,4— *D. p.* 191—*Ch. f.* 390,1.—*E. M. t.* 277. *f.* 4.— *Mont. p.* 119. *t.* 4. *f.* 1.—*Lin. T.* 8. *p.* 86. *t.* 2. *f.* 5. —*Dor. Cat. p.* 35. *t.* 1. *f.* 14.—*Turt. C. D. p.* 240.

—Cytherea T. *Lam.* 53.—*Turt. B. p.* 164. *t.* 12. *f.* 12.—*F. p.* 445.—Orbicular, compressed, white, with longitudinal ribs which are rather flat, very close, numerous, and narrow, and are crossed by still closer set concentric wrinkles ; lunule minute, triangular, sunken; ligament buried; inside white, often tinged with rose-color about the hinge and margin ; palleal scar simple, two cardinal teeth in each valve, a lateral in one, its receptacle in the other. 1. *Guernsey.*

Genus.—DONAX.

Transverse, equivalve, inequilateral, anteriorly very short and obtuse; two cardinal teeth in one or both valves, and one or two lateral teeth more or less apart ; ligament external, short.

* *Inner margin crenulated.*

D. Anatinum. *Lam. Bl. t.* 71. *f.* 2—D. Trunculus. D. *p.* 150.—*(not Lin. nor Lam.* 24.*)—List. t.* 376. *f.* 217.—*Da Cos. t.* 14. *f.* 3.—*Pen.* 4. *p.* 93. *t.* 55.—*Mont. p.* 103.—*Turt. B. p.* 123.—*Lin. T.* 8. *p.* 74.—*Dor. Cat. p.* 33. *t.* 6. *f.* 3.—*Don. t.* 29. *f.* 1. —*Turt. C. D. p.* 41.—*F. p.* 433.—Oblong wedge-shaped, the hinge margin nearly straight, glossy, with numerous simple minute radiating striæ, except at the

anterior end, which is shorter, smooth, and very obliquely truncated; yellowish olive, with two or three
pale rays and darker or lighter bands; inside violet, a
single lateral tooth. &...1¼. *Very common.*

D. Denticulata. *Lin.* 1127.—*D. p.* 151.—*Lam.*
50.—*Ch. f.* 256.—*E. M. t.* 262. *f.* 7.—*F. p.* 433.—
Pen, 4. *p.* 199. *t.* 58. *f.* 2.—*Mont. p.* 104.—*Lin. T.*
8. *p.* 76.—*Turt. B. p.* 124.—*Dor. Cat. p.* 34. *t.* 5.
f. 12.—*Turt. C. D. p.* 41. *f.* 19.—D. Crenuiata.
Don.t. 24.—Ovate wedge-shaped, very obtuse anteriorly,
with numerous fine punctured radiating striæ, white
with purple rays; anterior slope wrinkled transversely;
inside purple, margin denticulated. 0,58...¾. *Not
very common.*

* * *Margin plain.*

D. Complanata. *Mont. p.* 106. *t.* 5. *f.* 4.—*Lin. T.*
8. *p.* 75.—*Pen.* 4. *p.* 198.—*Dor. Cat. p.* 34.—*D. p.*
150.—*Turt. C. D. p.* 42.—*Turt. B. p.* 125. *t.* 7. *f.*
13,4.—*F. p.* 435.—Tellina Polita. *Poli.* 2. *t.* 21.
f. 14,5.—Capsa C. *Sow. G. f.* 8.—Oblong, anteriorly
obliquely but obtusely truncated, posteriorly rounded
but attenuated, smooth, whitish, under a greenish epidermis and marked posteriorly with a single broad whitish

or yellowish ray; somewhat violet within, hinge with two teeth in each valve, and a single lateral one. ¼...1¼. *Torbay and Guernsey.*

D. Rubra. *Mont. Sup. p.* 38.—*Turt. C. D. p.* 43. —*Turt. B. p.* 127. *t.* 10. *f.* 14.—*F. p.* 435.—Wedge-shaped, smooth, uniform pale claret color, posterior edge greatly sloping to an attenuated but rounded extremity, glossy, semi-transparent; beaks prominent, posterior; a single approximate lateral tooth in each valve. ⅓. *Tenby.*

Genus.—CRASSINA.

Suborbicular, transverse, equivalve, subinequilateral, close; hinge with two strong diverging cardinal teeth in the right valve, and two unequal ones in the other; ligament external, broader than long.

* *Margin quite entire.*

C. Scotica. *Turt. B. p.* 130. *t.* 11. *f.* 3,4.—Venus S. *Mont. Sup. p.* 44.—*Lin. T.* 8. *p.* 81. *t.* 2. *f.* 3.— *Pen.* 4. *p.* 204.—*D. p.* 267.—*Turt. C. D. p.* 236.— Astarte S. *F. p.* 440.—Rounded-heart-shaped, rather flat, white, under an olive or chesnut cuticle, very

slightly angular and produced anteriorly, with numerous regular equidistant rounded transverse ribs
becoming obsolete near the side, (especially the anterior) the interstices smooth and broader than the ribs
themselve; beaks somewhat triangularly prominent,
acute and slightly curved; lunule deep and cordiform,
lozenge lanceolate: inside glossy white or cream color;
hinge with two strong teeth in each valve. 1...1¼.
W. and Scotch Coasts.

C. COMPRESSA.—VENUS C. *Mont. Sup. p.* 43. *t.*
26. *f.* 1.—*Pen.* 4. *p.* 209.—CYPRINA C. *Turt. B. p.*
137. *t.* 11. *f.* 21. *to* 23.—ASTARTE C. *F. p.* 440.—
V. MONTAGUI. *D. p.* 167.—V. MONTACUTI. *Turt. C.
D. p.* 243.—Roundish triangular, a little compressed,
strong, thick, flattish, marked with rather distant transverse rib-like striæ, white or covered with a yellowish
brown cuticle; beaks prominent, giving that part a
rather triangular outline; lunule elongated, inside
white, with the margin flat, thin, and entire. ½.
Scotland.

** *Margin crenulated.*

C. DANMONIENSIS. *Lam.*—VENUS SULCATA. *Mont.
p.* 131.—*Lin. T.* 8. *p.* 81. *t.* 2. *f.* 2.—*D. p.* 166.—

Turt. C. D. p. 235.—V. DANMONIA. *Mont. sup. p.*
45. *t.* 29.*f.* 4.—*D. p.* 167.—CRAS. SUL. *Turt. B. p.*
131. *t.* 11.*f.* 1, 2.—ARTARTE S. & D. *F. p.* 439.—
Rounded heart-shaped, rather compressed, white under
a dark brown cuticle, with smooth, strong, regular, equidistant, transverse ridges; beaks subcentral, and inclining; lunule subcordiform, lozenge lanceolate.
1...1¼. *Devon and Ireland.*

TRIBE.—CONCHACEA.

With at least three cardinal teeth in one valve, usually
but not always the same in the other.

GENUS.—CYPRINA.

Equivalve, inequilateral, obliquely heart-shaped, beaks
obliquely bent; hinge with three unequal teeth,
approximate at the base and slightly divergent
above; lateral tooth remote (sometimes obsolete);
ligament external and partly sunk between the
beaks.

C. ISLANDICA. *Lam.* 2.—*Turt. B. p.* 135.—*F. p.*
443.—*Bl. t.* 70. *bis.f.* 5.—*Sow. G.—Reeve. t.* 65.—
VENUS T. *Lin* 1131.—*D. p.* 176.—*List. t.* 271. *f.*
108.—*Ch. f.* 341.—*Pen.* 4. *p.* 205. *t.* 56.—*Mont. p.*
114.—*Don. t.* 77.—*Lin. T* 8. *p.* 83.—*Dor. Cat. p.*
35. *t.* 6. *f.* 5.—*Turt. C. D. p.* 238.—*Da Cost. t.* 14.

f. 5.—Obliquely heart-shaped, thick, ponderous, white, under a coarse brown rather glossy cuticle, aud striated irregularly and conceutrically; beaks pointed, no lunule; inside dull white, margin very entire. 4. *Open Coasts.*

* C. TRIANGULARIS. *Turt. B. p.* 136. *t.* 11. *f.* 19, 20.—*F. p.* 444.—VENUS T. *Mont. p.* 577. *t.* 17. *f.* 3. —*Lin. T.* 8. *p* 83.—*Pen.* 4. *p.* 205.—*D. p.* 173.— *Turt. C. D. p.* 238.—Somewhat triangular, being roundish, with a triangular outline towards the beaks which are produced and equally sloping on both sides, smooth, strong; lunule lanceolate; two teeth and a curved lateral in one valve, three and a lateral in the other. ½. *W. Coasts and Dublin Bay.*

C. MINIMA. *Turt. B. p.* 137.—*F. p.* 444.—VENUS M. *Mont. p.* 121. *t.* 3. *f.* 3.—*Lin. T.* 8. *p.* 81.—*Pen* 4. *p.* 203.—*D. p.* 166.—*Turt. C. D. p.* 236.—Rounded heart-shaped, a little compressed, with broad smooth transverse rather obscure ribs, whitish or flesh color, with four red spots, two near the hinge, two at the margin, and generally two white lines connecting the two upper

* This and the succeeding species are but provisionally considered as of this Genus.

with the two lower ones. ¼...⅜. *Devonshire and British Channel.*

C. ORBICULATA. *Turt. B. p.* 138.—VENUS O. *Mont. Sup. p.* 42. *t.* 29. *f.* 7.—*Pen.* 4. *p.* 208.— *Turt. C. C. p.* 241.—CYTHEREA O. *F. p* 446.— Orbicular, compressed, cancellated, white; beaks small, lunule minute and cordiform; margin plain; two approximating teeth, and a transverse and rather remote one where the margin is angular. ⅜. *Dunbar.*

GENUS.—CYTHEREA.

Equivalve, inequilateral, suborbicular, trigonal and transverse; one valve with four primary teeth, of which three are divergent and approximate at their base, and one remote; three primary divergent teeth in the other valve, with a hollow margin parallel.

C. CHIONE. *Lam.* 22.—*Bl. t.* 74. *f.* 5.—*Turt. B. t.* 8.*f.* 11.*p.* 161.—*F. p.* 445.—VENUS C. *Lin.* 1131. —*D. p.* 178.—*Ch. f.* 343.—*Pen.* 4. *p.* 206. *t.* 54.*f.* 2. —*Don. t.* 17.—*Mont. p.* 115.—*Lin. T.* 6. *t.* 17. *f.* 1, 2. *and Vol.* 8. *p.* 84.—*Dor. Cat. p.* 35. *t.* 6. *f.* 7.— *Turt. C. D. p.* 239.—*Da Cost. p.* 184. *t.* 14. *f.* 7.— Oval, heart-shaped, glossy, smooth, fulvous with obsolete rays; lunule oblong, acute and raised in the middle; cartilage cleft broad; epidermis awny chesnut. 3...4. *W. Coasts.*

C. Guineensis. *Lam.—Turt. B. p.* 161.—*F. p.* 445.—Venus G. *Mont. Sup. p.* 48. & 168.—*Pen.* 4. *p.* 207.—*D. p.* 169.—*Dor. Cat. p.* 35.—*Turt. D. p.* 237.—*Ch. f.* 311,2.—Obliquely heart-shaped, with numerous close-set sharp transverse subimbricated la-mellæ, greyish white, with two or three purplish brown longitudinal rays; lunule cordiform; inside white in-clining to purple towards the margin; both the slopes purple. 1¼...1¼. *Scotland and Weymouth.*

C. Exoleta. *Lam.* 48.—*Bl. t.* 74. *f.* 2.—*Turt. B: t.* 8. *f.* 7. *p.* 162.—*F. p.* 445.—Venus E. *Lin.* 1134. —*Ch. f.* 404.—*List. t.* 291. *f.* 127. *and t.* 292. *f.* 128. —*Pen.* 4. *p.* 209. *t.* 57. *f.* 3.—*Don.* 2. *t.* 42. *f.* 1.— *Mont. p.* 116.—*Lin. T.* 6. *t.* 17. *f.* 9, 10. & 8. *p.* 87. *t.* 3. *f.* 1.—*Dor Cat. p.* 35. *t.* 8. *f.* 5.—*D. p.* 195.— *Turt. D. p.*·241—*Da Cost. t.* 12. *f.* 5—*E. t.* 279. *f.* 5. Suborbicular, subequilateral, compressed, whitish or dull reddish with broken red or purple rays, broad stripes or fine lines and roughened by close-set transverse ca-pillary striæ; lunule heart-shaped, sunken and sub-lamellar; inside white. 2. *Sandy bays.*

C. Lincta. *Lam.* 49.—*F. p.* 445.—Venus Sin-uata: *Gmel.* 3285.—*Turt. C: D. p.* 242.—*List.. t.* 289. *f.* 125. & 290. *f.* 126.—*Dor. Cat. p.* 35. *t.* 1.

f. 13.—V. LUPINUS. *Lin. ed.* 10. *p.* 689—V. LACTEA.
Don. 5. *t.* 149.—*Mont. Sup. p.* 46.—*Lin. T.* 8. *p.*
79.—V. EXOLETA. *Pen.* 4. *p.* 209. *t.* 59. *f.* 1.—
V. EXOLETA. VAR. *Lin. T.* 8. *p.* 87. *t.* 3. *f.* 2.--*D.*
p. 196.—C. SINUATA. *Turt. B. t.* 10. *f.* 10, 11. *p.*
163.—Suborbicular, inequilateral, clear white, polished,
the anterior side oblique less rounded and larger than
the posterior, most elegantly and closely striated transversely; beaks prominently curved; lunule broad;
VAR. with broad longitudinal fawn coloured stripes. 1¼.
W. Coasts.

GENUS.—VENUS:

Equivalve, inequilateral, transverse or suborbicular;
hinge with three teeth in both valves, all approximate
the lateral divergent at their summits; ligament
external; a more or less distinct lunule.

* *Inner margin crenulated.*

V. VFRRUCOSA. *Lin.* 1130.—*Lam.* 7.—*Ch. f.* 229,
300.—*D. p.* 163.—*Turt. C. D. p.* 231.—*Turt. B. p.*
141.—*F. p.* 446.—*Da Cos. t.* 12. *f.* 1. *List. t.* 284. *f.*
122—*Don. t.* 44.—*Mont. p.* 112.—*Pen.* 4. *p.* 201: *t.*
57. *f.* 1.—*Lin. T.* 8. *p.* 78.—*Dor. Cat. p.* 34. *t.* 8. *f.*
1.—*Born. t.* 4. *f.* 7.—Rounded-heart-shaped, tumid,

whitish, often tinged with red, thick, not polished, with coarse transverse ribs which become warty at the extremities, crossed by indistinct radiating striæ, which are usually apparent at the umbones; anterior slope more or less spotted on one side ; lunule cordiform and wrinkled; inside white. 1¾. *English and Irish Coasts.*

V. Cassina. *Lin.* 1130.—*D. p.* 165.—*Lam.* 9.— *Ch. f.* 301,2.—*Lin. T.* 8. *p.* 79. *t.* 2.˙ *f.* 1.—*Turt. C. D. p.* 232.—*Da Cos. p.* 193. *t.* 13. *f.* 4. *(left hand) Turt. B. t.* 9. *f.* 1. *p.* 141.—*F. p.* 446.—Orbicular-heart-shaped, whitish or rusty brown,convex, with transverse smooth plates curving towards the hinge,and nearly meeting each other in an imbricated manner, but not reflected at the sides nor tuberculated ; lunule cordiform. 1. *W. and Irish Coasts.*

V. Discina. *Lam.* 6.—*Philippi. p.* 42.—*Bl. t.* 75. *f.* 6.—V. Reflexa. *Mont. Sup. p.* 40. and 168.— *Wern. Soc.* 1. *p.* 384. *t.* 8. *f.* 1.—*D. p.* 168.—*Turt. C. D. p.* 233.—*F. p.* 446.—*Turt. B. p.* 142. *t.* 10. *f.* 1,2.—V. Rusterucci. *Payraydeau. f.* 26, 7, 8.— Suborbicular, thickish, rather compressed, a little truncated anteriorly, where the transverse plates are thin and reflected, brownish white with usually two or three broken reddish rays ; lunule lanceolate and elevated in the middle into a sharp ridge. 2½. *Devon, Scotland, Bantry Bay.*

*V. CANCELLATA. *Turt. B. p.* 144. *t.* 10. *f.* 3.—*F. p.* 447.—Rounded-heart-shaped, anteriorly angular, white with sometimes a rosy tinge, with nine or ten remote transverse plates which are closely cancellated, the interstices with close set radiating riblets ; beaks prominent ; lunule cordiform. ‡. *Guernsey.*

V. SUBCORDATA. *Mont. p.* 121. *t.* 3. *f.* 1.—*Pen.* 4. *p.* 204.—*Lin. T.* 8. *p.* 82.—*D, p.* 166.—*Turt. C. D. p.* 237.—*Turt. B. p.* 145.—*F. p.* 447.—Subcordate, slightly truncated posteriorly, white, strong, ligamental edge sloping rapidly ; with strong radiating riblike striæ, and remote transverse ridges ; beaks much incurved. ¼. *Falmouth.*

* I feel far from certain that this is really distinct from Turton's Dysera, which is assuredly the Cancellata of Lamarc : for the present species, Mr. Turton gives us as synonyms,—CANCELLATA. *Lin.* 1130. —*Ch. f.* 304. *and* 305.

V. Granulata. *Gmel.* 3277.—*D. p.* 171.—*Lam.*
14.—*Ch. f.* 313.—*List. t.* 338. *f.* 175.—*E. M. t.* 272.
f. 3.—*Mont. p.* 122.—*D. t.* 83.—*Lin. T.* 8. *p.* 85.—
Turt. C. D. p. 240.—*Turt. B. p.* 145.—*F. p.* 447.—
Roundish-heart-shaped, with longitudinal grooves, decussated by raised transverse striæ, yellowish, with
purplish brown spotted rays and streaks, and the anterior slope with letter-like markings of the same color;
lunule heart-shaped and usually darker; inside stained,
especially on the anterior side, with purple. ⅞. *Falmouth and N. Britain.*

V. Fasciata. *Don.* 5. *t.* 170.—*Pen.* 4. *p.* 203.—
Desh. in Lam. vol. 7.—*D. p.* 159.—*Lin. T.* 8. *p.* 80.
Dor. Cat. t. 7. *f.* 3.—*Turt. C. D. p.* 234.—*Da. Cos.
t.* 13. *f.* 3.—*Turt. B. p.* 146. *t.* 8. *f.* 9.—*F. p.* 447.
—V. Paphia. *Mont. p.* 110. *(not Lin.)*—Rounded-
heart-shaped, compressed, subequilateral, with broad
flat transverse unequal ribs, whose edges project a little
beyond the anterior edge, forming a double row of
tubercles; whitish or fulvous, with narrow longitudinal
rays or fine lines of red white yellow or purple; lunule
broad aud heart-shaped. ¾. *Not uncommon.*

V. Dysera. *Lin.* 1130.—*Ch. f.* 287,8,9.—*Turt. C.
D. p.* 237.—*Turt. B. p.* 147. *t.* 9. *f.* 4.—*F. p.* 447.

—V. Cingenda. *D. p.* 161.—V. Cancellata. *Lam.*
12.—*Rceve. t.* 68. *f.* 2.—*E. M. t.* 268. *f.* 1.—
Heart-shaped, with rather distant transverse crenulated
membranaceous ridges and raised longitudinal rib-like
striæ in their interstices, whitish, usually tinged with
flesh-color or brown, spotted or indistinctly edged with
dark brown; anterior slope in one of the valves smooth,
brown or striped with brown; lunule heart-shaped and
brown. 1. *Guernsey.*

V. Laminosa. *Laskey in Wern. T.* 1. *p.* 184. *t.* 8.
f. 16.—*Mont. Sup. p.* 38.—*Turt. C. D. p,* 233.—
Turt. B. p. 148. *t.* 10. *f.* 4.—V. Cancellata. *Don.*
t. 115.—V. Rugosa. *F. p.* 448.—*Pen. t.* 56. *f.* 50.—
Triangular, heart-shaped, produced and pointed anteriorly, with crowded transverse membranaceous plates,
closely striated longitudinally in the interstices, uniform
pale brown. 1. *Not very uncommon.—Resembling*
Gallina.

V. Gallina. *Lin.* 1130.—*D. p.* 168.—*Lam.* 24.—
Ch. f. 308.—*List. t.* 282. *f.* 120.—*Pen.* 4. *p.* 205: *t.*
59. *f.* 2.—*Lin. T.* 6. *t.* 17. *f.* 7, 8, & *vol.* 8. *p.* 82.—
Dor. Cat. p. 35. *t.* 8. *f.* 2.—*Turt. C. D. p.* 234.—
Turt. B. p. 149. *t.* 9. *f.* 2.—*Da Cost. t.* 12. *f.* 2.—
F. p. 448.—V. Striatula. *Mont. p.* 113.—*Don.* 2. *t.*

68.—Triangular heart-shaped, with numerous sloping glossy transverse ridges, which seem crenulated from being crossed by crowded fine rufous lines, whitish or pale brown, with more or less distinct darker rays, the beaks much recurved and the slope nearly smooth; lunule sunken, elongated, heart-shaped, and finely striated longitudinally. 1...1¼. *Most sandy coasts.*

V. Pallida. *Turt.B. p.* 150. *t.* 10. *f.* 5.—*F.p.* 448. —Triangular-heart-shaped, produced anteriorly, thin, semitransparent, uniform white or yellowish white, with rather irregular and somewhat indistinct transverse rib-like striæ, crossed by fine longitudinal lines; beaks prominent, pointed, a little curved; slopes quite smooth; margin thin, with the crenulations visible externally. 1...2. *Dawlish.*

V. Ovata. *Pen.* 4. *p.* 206. *t.* 59. *f.* 3.—*Mont. p.* 120. *Lin. T.* 8. *p.* 85. *t.* 2. *f.* 4.—*Lam.* 87.—*Dor. Cat. p.* 35. *t.* 1. *f.* 15.—*D. p.* 171.—*Turt. C. D. p.* 239.— *Turt. B. p.* 150. *t.* 9. *f.* 3.—Cytherea O. *F. p.* 445. —Oval-triangular, subequilateral, moderately convex, brownish white, with longitudinal grooves, rendered scaly by the transverse striæ; beaks acute and rather nearer the subangulated and flattened anterior slope; impressions obsolete. ¼...¾. *W. and Irish Coasts.*

* * *Margin quite entire.*

V. Substriata. *Mont. Sup. p.* 48. *t.* 29. *f.* 6.—
Pen. 4. *p.* 211.—*Turt. C. D. p.* 245.—*Turt. B. p.*
152.—*F. p.* 448.—Oval, thin, semitransparent, white,
with transverse wrinkles and obscure waved longitudinal
striæ; beaks nearer to one end, small, turning a little to
one side ; anterior tooth long and oblique. ⅓...0,60.
Frith of Forth.

V. Ænea. *Turt. C. D. p.* 248. *f.* 20.—*Turt. B. t.*
10. *f.* 7. *p.* 152.—*F. p.* 449.—Oval, tapering and
elongated anteriorly, posteriorly rounded ; white, under
a shining bronzed skin, convex, with regular close-set
transverse striæ and minute longitudinal lines; beaks
much pointed curved and posterior, lunule elongated;
teeth strong, two cloven in one valve, and one in the
other. l...1¼. *Dublin Bay.*

V. Sarniensis. *Turt. B. p.* 153. *t.* 10. *f.* 6.—
V enerupis S. *F. p.* 452,—*List. t.* 385. *f.* 232.—Oval,
anteriorly truncated and tumid, thick, convex, yellowish
white, mostly marked with numerous red or purplish
ziczac lines often disposed in interrupted rays (rarely
uniform chocolate or fawn color); with numerous
rounded transverse striæ not becoming broader anteriorly ; beaks prominent, recurved ; lunule purple and

heart-shaped; inside white, purple or greenish; two of the teeth bifid. 2. *Guernsey*.

V. SINUOSA. *Pen.* 4. *p.* 213. *t.* 58. *f.* 4.—*Mont. p.* 120.—*Lin. T.* 8. *p.* 90.—*Turt. C. D. p.* 248.—*Turt. B. p.* 154. *t.* 10. *f.* 9.—*F. p.* 449.—Roundish oval, subequilateral, with a longitudinal sinuosity from the beaks, whitish, with flat transverse striæ and obscure longitudinal ones; lunule heart-shaped, subcarinate; inside rich glossy yellow; two of the teeth in one valve bifid, one so in the other. ⅜. *Dublin Bay*.

V. AUREA. *Pen.* 4. *p.* 212. *t.* 60. *f.* 1.—*Mont. p.* 129.—*Lin. T.* 8. *p.* 90. *t.* 2. *f.* 9.—*Dor. Cat. p.* 36. *t.* 13. *f.* 3.—*D. p.* 207.—*Lam.* 56.—*List. t.* 404. *f.* 249.—*Turt. C. D. p.* 247.—*Turt. B. p.* 155. *t.* 9. *f.* 7, 8.—*F. p.* 449.—Oval heart-shaped, tumid in the middle and sloping to each side, anteriorly more produced, closely striated transversely, and very obscurely so longitudinally, lighter or darker yellow with blackish brown or bluish ziczac lines or stripes, variously disposed and often confluent; lunule broad; middle tooth cloven. 1...1¼. *Devon and Cornwall*.

V. VIRGINEA. *Lin.* 1136.—*D. p.* 207.—*Lam.* 57. —*Ch. f.* 457.—*Pen.* 4. *p.* 212. *t.* 58. *f.* 5.—*Mont. p.*

128.—*Lin. T.* 8. *p.* 89. *t.* 2. *f.* 8.—*Dor. Cat. t.* 13. *f.* 1.—*Turt. C. D. p.* 536.—*Turt. B. p.* 156. *t.* 8. *f.* 8.—VENERUPIS V. *F. p.* 452.—Rhombic oval, inquilateral, generally obliquely angular on the anterior side, yellowish white or pale reddish brown, usually variegated marked or rayed with rosy or rich purple, with transverse flat striæ which are broader anteriorly; lunule lanceolate; inside white with generally a rosy tinge; two of the teeth cloven. 1½...2. *S. Coasts.*

V. NITENS. *Turt. C. D. p.* 247.—*Turt. B. p.* 157. *t.* 10. *f.* 8.—*E. p.* 449.—Rhombic oval, tumid in the middle, anteriorly angulated, transparent, horny, with some few scattered longitudinal markings, crowded transverse striæ and indistinct longitudinal ones; only the central tooth cloven. ½. *Dublin Bay.*

V. DECUSSATA. *Lin.* 1135.—*D. p.* 205.—*Lam* 46. —*List. t.* 423. *f.* 271.—*Ch. f.* 455,6.—*Pen.* 4. *p.* 210 *t.* 60. *mid. fig.*—*Don. t.* 67.—*Lin. T.* 6. *p.* 168. *t.* 17. *f.* 11,2. *and vol.* 8. *t.* 2. *f.* 6.—*Mont. p.* 124.— *Dor. Cat. p.* 36. *t.* 6. *f.* 4.—*Turt. C. D. p.* 244.—*Da Cos. t.* 14. *f.* 4.—*Turt. B. p.* 158. *t.* 8. *f.* 10.—Ovate, anteriorly subangulated and broader, not polished, whitish grey or pale rust color, with often purplish brown or rufous spots, rays, or ziczacs ; with decussating striæ (becoming tuberculated anteriorly) of which the longitudinal are the more prominent; lunule indistinct; inside glossy white or yellowish, purple about the cartilage; two of the teeth cloven. 2...3. *Common on Sandy Coasts.*

V. PULLASTRA. *Pen.* 4. *p.* 210.—*Lam.* 47.—*Lin. T.* 6. *t.* 17. *f.* 13,4. *and vol.* 8. *p.* 88. *t.* 2. *f.* 7.— *Mont. p.* 125.—*Dor. Cat. p.* 36. *t.* 1. *f.* 8.—*Turt. C. D. p.* 244.—*Turt. B. p.*—VENERUPIS P. *F: p.* 451. —V. SENEGALENSIS. *D. p.* 206.—Oblong, anteriorly subangulated, reticulated by fine striæ, of which the concentric are the more apparent and become sublamellar anteriorly, white, with purple blotches (rarely grey with dark rays) ; lunule rather obscure ; middle tooth cloven. 1¼...1¾. *Common.*

TRIBE.—CARDIACEA.

Having irregular cardinal teeth, both in form and situation : usually with one or two lateral.

GENUS.—CARDIUM.

Equivalve, subcordiform ; beaks prominent ; inner margin of the valves denticulated or plicated ; hinge with four teeth in both valves, two approximated oblique, cardinal teeth mutually inserted and crossing each other and two remote lateral.

* *Ribs spinous or tuberculated.*

C. ACULEATUM. *Lin.* 1122—*D. p.* 115—*Lam.* 14—
E. M. t. 297. *f.* 5—*Ch. f.* 157—*Pen.* 4. *p.* 187. *t.*
53. *f.* 1·—*Don. t.* 6—*Mont. p.* 77—*Lin. T.* 8. *p.* 62—
Wood. G. C. p. 207. *t.* 51. *f.* 1—*Turt. C. D, p.* 28—
Turt. B. p. 181. *t.* 13. *f.* 6, 7—*F. p.* 420—*(Young,*
C. SPINOSUM. *Sow. Brit. Mis. t.* 32)—Very tumid,
comparatively light, oblique, subangulated anteriorly ;
with about twenty-one ribs armed anteriorly with long
sharp spines (lancet-shaped but round in the old shells)
posteriorly with rather flattened obtuse tubercle, transverse striæ only in the interstices of the ribs. 4. *W.*
Coasts.

C. TUBERCULATUM. *Lin.* 1122—*D. p.* 117—*Lam.*
15—*Pen.* 4. *p.* 88—*Don. t.* 107. *f.* 10—*Mont. p.* 568.
—*Lin. T.* 8. *p.* 64—*Wood. G. C. p.* 210. *t.* 50. *f.* 1, 2
—*Dor. Cat. p.* 31. *t.* 2. *f.* 2.—*Turt. D. p.* 28. *f.*
12.—*Turt. B. p.* 183.—*F. p.* 421.—Subglobular,
ponderous, a little truncated anteriorly, with twenty-
one ribs armed anteriorly with tubercles, posteriorly
with scaly plates; pale chesnut usually with darker
zones, the transverse wrinkles crossing the ribs. 4.
W. Coasts.

C. Echinatum. *Lin.* 1122.—*D. p.* 116.—*Lam.* 12. —*Pen.* 4. *p.* 187.—*Da Cos. t.* 14. *f.* 2.—*Don. t.* 107. *f.* 1.—*Mont. p.* 78.—*Lin. T. p.* 63.—*Dor. Cat. p.* 31. *t.* 6. *f.* 2.—*Wood. G. C. t.* 49. *f.* 1,2.—*Turt. C. D. p.* 29.—*Turt. B. p.* 183.—*F. p.* 421.—*(Youny* C. Ciliare. *Lin. &c.)* Suborbicular, convex, thin, slightly oblique, brown or whitish, with eighteen ribs, armed with numerous inflected sharp white spines, curving towards the cartilage side, the posterior ones thicker and more obtuse; the grooves only striated. 2...2. *Common on sandy shores.*

C: Obovale. *Sow. in C. I.*—C. Elongatum. *Mont. p.* 82.—*Lin. T.* 8. *p.* 67.—*Pen.* 4. *p.* 190.— *Wood. G. C. p.* 214.—*D. p.* 131.—*Turt. D. p.* 31.— *Turt. B. p.* 185. *t.* 13. *f.* 9.—*F. p.* 422.—Oval, inequilateral oblique, produced and subangulated anteriorly, pale rufous, with some obscure darker spots anteriorly, tumid in the middle, with twenty-five prickly ribs, the central flattened and separated by a fine line. ⚷. *Torbay.*

C. Nodosum. *Mont. p.* 81.—*Lin. T.* 8. *p.* 68.— *Pen.* 4. *p.* 189.—*Wood. G. C. p.* 212.—*Turt. B. p.* 186. *t.* 13. *f.* 9—Orbicular and rather flat, equilateral, brown or whitish, very slightly angulated anteriorly,

about twenty-six close-set rounded ribs, thickly clothed
with obtuse round tubercles, which anteriorly project
into very short spines ; beaks central, inside white with
generally a chesnut anterior stripe reaching half-way
down the shell; margin strongly serrate. ⚣. *Torbay*.
*The old shells in this and the succeeding species lose
the tubercles and become wrinkled or scaly all over.*

C. EXIGUUM. *Gmel.* 3255.—*Mont. p.* 82.—*Turt.
B. p.* 187.—*Pen.* 4. *p.* 186.—*Lin. T.* 8. *p.* 61.—
Wood. G. C. p. 212.—*Turt. D. p.* 31.—*F. p.* 422.—
Dor. Cat. p. 31. *t.* 2. *f.* 11.—*D. p.* 114.—C. PYG-
MÆUM. *Don. t.* 32. *f.* 3.—Subtriangular, tumid, subtruncated anteriorly, whitish, rarely pink, with from
twenty to twenty-four ribs clothed with rounded obtuse
tubercles especially about the shorter side, the grooves
of which are not always distinct, but towards the hinge
transversely striated ; inside often rosy, one of the teeth
minute. ⚣. *W. Coasts and Ireland.*

* * *Ribs armed with transverse scales.*

C. EDULE. *Lin.* 1124.—*D. p.* 127.—*Lam.* 31.—
Ch. f. 194.—*Pen.* 4. *p.* 189. *t.* 53. *f.* 3.—*Mont. p.*
76.—*Dor. Cat. p.* 32. *t.* 11. *f.* 1.—*Wood. G. C. p.*
226. *t.* 55. *f.* 4.—*Turt. C. D. p.* 30.—*Da Cos. p.* 180.

E

t. 11. *f.* 1.—*Turt. B. p.* 188.—*F. p.* 422.—Rounded-
heart-shaped, becoming obliquely heart-shaped from
the anterior side being produced by age, dirty white,
with about twenty-six ribs which are rough with transverse wrinkled subimbricated striæ ; inside white,
stained anteriorly with brown.   1¼.   *The common
cockle.*

C. Fasciatum. *Mont. Sup. p.* 30. *t.* 27. *f.* 6.—
Pen. 4. *p.* 191.—*Wood. G. C. p.* 215.—*D. p.* 130.—
Turt. C. D. p. 32.—*Turt. B. p.* 189.—*F. p.* 422.—
(the young of C. Rusticum. fide. Sow. in C. 1.—Orbicular flattish, semitransparent, yellowish or pale
rufous, glossy, with a few dark transverse bands often
disposed in spots on the ribs.   *Not uncommon.*

* * * *Ribs unarmed.*

C. Medium. *Lin.* 1122.—*Lam.* 40.—*Ch. f.* 162,
3,4.—*E. t.* 296. *f.* 1.—*Pen.* 4. *p.* 186.—*Don.* 1. *t.*
32. *f,* 1.—*Mont: p.* 83.—*Lin. T.* 8. *p.* 61.—*Wood.
G. C. p.* 211. *t.* 50. *f.* 3.—*D. p.* 113.—*Turt. C. D. p.*
32.—*Turt. B. p.* 190.—*F. p.* 422.—Tumid, suborbicular, rather truncated anteriorly, yellowish white, with
reddish brown blotches, about fifty radiating ribs which
are rather obscure in the middle but stronger at the

sides especially the shorter where they are crossed by
fine striæ which pass over but do not cut the ribs;
one of the cardinal teeth minute or obliterated in each
valve. *Torquay, not rare.*

C. SERRATUM. *Lin.* 1123.—*Lam.* 25.—LŒVIGA-
TUM. *Pen.* 4. *p.* 188. *t.* 54. *f.* 1.—*Da Cos. p.* 178. *t.*
13. *f.* 6.—*Don. t.* 54.—*Mont. p.* 80.—*Lin. T.* 8. *p.*
65.—*Dor. Cat. p.* 31. *t.* 7. *f.* 6.—*Wood. G. C. t.*
54. *f.* 1.—*D. p.* 123.—*Tnrt. D. p.* 31.—*List. t.* 332.
f. 169.—Oboval, with a brownish olive glossy epidermis, often marbled with white and the various hues of
red, with very obscure longitudinal striæ and very remote transverse ones ; flattish and much produced anteriorly where the striæ become obsolete; within, pale
flesh color.   2...1,67.   *Common.*

C. LEVIGATUM. *Lin.* 1123.—*Lam.* 26.—*Ch. f.*
189.—*Knorr.* 2. *t.* 20. *f.* 4 & 5. *t.* 10. *f.* 7.—SERRA-
TUM. *D. p.* 124.—CITRINUM. *Wood. G. C. t.* 54. *f.*
2.—*Turt. B. p.* 192. *t.* 13. *f.* 5.—*E. p.* 423.—Obovate,
longer than broad, rather oblique, convex, glossy, thin,
pale yellow with the anterior slope chesnut, with obsolete minute radiating striæ except at the sides, inside
stained with purplish rose-color near the hinge, the
margin finely serrated.   1½...1½.   *W. Coasts.*

Genus.—ISOCARDIA.

Equivalve, heart-shaped, ventricose ; beaks very distant, divergent and spirally turned to one side ; hinge with two primary flattened teeth situated under the beak, and with an elevated lateral one under the external ligament.

I. Cor. *Lam.* 1.—*Turt. B. p.* 193. *t.* 14.—*F. p.* 419.—Chama C. *Lin.* 1137.—*D. p.* 212.—*Ch.f.* 483. —*E. t.* 232. *f.* 1.—*Blain. t.* 69. *f.* 2.—*Don.* 4. *t.* 134.—*Pen.* 4. *p.* 214.—*Mont. p.* 134. *and Sup. p.* 50—*Lin. T.* 8. *p.* 91.—*Turt. D. p.* 32. *f.* 17.—*Wern. Soc.* 1. *p.* 385. *t.* 48. *f.* 483.—Heart-shaped, globose, fulvous under a reddish epidermis, nearly smooth; the beaks paler, twisted into a single flat volution, both fronting the hinder side. 4...3½. *Dublin Bay.*

Tribe.—ARCACEA.

Teeth small, numerous and disposed in each valve in a line, which is either straight or interrupted; the teeth mutually inserted.

Genus.—ARCA.

Transverse, subequivalve, inequilateral; beaks remote, separated by the area of the ligament ; hinge linear

*straight, without ribs at the extremities ; teeth nu-
merous, serrated, close-set, alternately inserted into
opposite valves ; ligament external.*

* *Crenulated at the margin.*

A. Noæ. *Lin.* 1140.—*D. p.* 226.—*Lam.* 3.—*Ch. f.*
529.—*Mont. p.* 139.—*Pen.* 4. *p.* 215.—*Lin. T.* 8. *p.*
91.—*Don.* 5. *t.* 158. *f.* 1,2.—*Turt. D. p.* 9. *f.* 58.—
Turt. B. p. 166.—*F. p.* 597.—Oblong, decussated in
a punctured manner, pale rufous with darker oblique
bands, rounded posteriorly, anteriorly angular ; beaks
near one end, very remote, incurved, with a broad smooth
space between them ; ventral edge sinuous and gaping
in the middle ; inside whitish or pale chocolate brown,
½...¾. *Guernsey and W. Coasts.*

A. Fusca. *Don.* 5. *t.* 158. *f.* 34.—*Mont. Sup. p.*
51. *t.* 4. *f.* 3.—*Pen.* 4. *p.* 215.—*Turt. D. p.* 10.—
Turt. B. p. 167.—*F. p.* 397.—Imbricata. *D. p.*
226.—*Ch. f.* 532.—*List. t.* 367. *f.* 207.—Oblong,
uniform brownish white, decussated, angular anteriorly,
the ventral edge shorter, straight and nearly closed.
*W. Coasts.—Resembling the last, but is proportionably
narrower, more convex, with finer decussations, the
margin nearly straight and the beaks very remote.
Rare.*

A. TETRAGONA. *Lam.—Turt. B. p.* 167. *t.* 13. *f.* 1.
—F. p. 398.—Obliquely quadrangular, whitish brown, with granular decussations, tumid at the beaks from which proceed a nearly central rib to the angular point of the opposite margin; hinge not quite straight in consequence of the marginal slope, ventral edge gaping; inside white with a purplish blotch at one end. ⅛...1. *W. Ireland.*

A. BARBATA. *Brown in Wern. Soc.* 2. *p.* 512. *t.* 24. *f.* 3.—*F. p.* 398.—RETICULATA. *Turt. B. p.* 168.— Oblong, rather compressed, rounded at one end and slightly angular at the other, white under an olive brown skin, with numerous nearly equidistant flat radiating ridges, covered with a fine brown downy pile and decussated by minute striæ; ventral edge straight and nearly closed; beaks nearer one end and rather approximated; inside glossy with pale rays. ¼...1,014. *Lough Strangford.*

** *Margin entire.*

A. LACTEA. *Lin.* 1141.—*D. p.* 236.—*Lam.* 17.—*List. t.* 235. *f.* 69.—*Pen.* 4. *p.* 216. *t.* 61. *f.* 2.—*Da Cost. p.* 171. *t.* 11. *f.* 5.—*Mont. p.* 138.—*Don.* 4. *t.* 135. —*Lin. T.* 8. *p.* 92.—*Dor. Cat. p.* 36. *t.* 11. *f.* 5.—

F. p. 398.—A. Perforans. *Turt. D. p.* 9.—*Turt. B. p.* 169. *t.* 13. *f.* 2,3.—Oblong, subequilateral, rounded posteriorly and angular anteriorly, white with a brown velvety epidermis, and crowded longitudinal riblets which are merely crossed by the striæ of growth; beaks distant, the ligamental area black oblong and sunken; inside white, ventral edge but slightly open. ½...¼. *W. Coasts, in rocks.*

Genus.—PECTUNCULUS.

Suborbicular, double convex, equivalve, subequilateral and closed; hinge arcuated, teeth numerous, oblique, serrated; ligament external.

P. Glycimeris. *Deshayes.*—P. Glycimeris, Undatus & Pilosus. *Turt. B. p.* 171. *t.* 12. *f.* 1, 2, 3, 4. —P. P. & P. Marmoratus. *Lam.*—P. Pilosus. *Phillippi.*—*F. p.* 400.—Arca. G. *Lin. Mus. Ulric.*— A. Pilosus. *D. p.* 242.—A. Marmorata. *Gmel.* 3314.—*Ch. f.* 560. & 563.—*List. t.* 247. *f.* 82.— *Knorr.* 6. *t.* 14. *f.* 4.—*Gual. t.* 72. *f.* 6.—*E. t.* 310. *f.* 3.—A. Glycimeris. *Pen.* 4. *p.* 216.—*Lin. T.* 8. *p.* 93. *t.* 3. *f.* 3.—*Turt. D. p.* 7.—Orbicular-ovate, becoming inequilateral by age, white with angular red streaks arranged either longitudinally or transversely (sometimes flesh-coloured with white spots and angular red ones), minutely decussated, the apices obliquely incurved and approximate; inside white or whitish; epidermis velvety. 1¼. *W. Coasts.*

P. Decussatus. *Turt. B. p.* 173. *t.* 12. *f. 5.—F. p.* 400.—Orbicular, depressed, with numerous fine raised decussated lines which are clothed with a short silky brown pile, yellowish white with purple and crimson clouded patches, which are often disposed in ziczac angles; inside glossy white, the disc often stained with dark red, margin very strongly serrated. 1. *British Channel.*

P. Nummarius. *Turt. B. p.* 174. *t.* 12. *f. 6.—F. p.* 400.—Arca N. *Lin.* 1143 ?—*List. t.* 239. *f.* 81.—Lenticular, very finely decussated, yellowish white or cream-color, with numerous round red dots (which very rarely become confluent about the margin and form short lines); beaks tumid and prominent, causing the margin on each side of them to appear a little projecting or as it were slightly eared like a Pecten. ½. *Guernsey and Torbay.*

Genus.—NUCULA.⁓

Oval-triangular or oblong, equivalve, inequilateral, closed; the beaks approximated : hinge with an oblique projecting spoon-shaped tooth in each valve,

and numerous sharp pointed lateral comb-like teeth ;
ligament internal.　,,

* *Margin crenulated.*

N. Nucleus. *Turt. B. p.* 176. *t.* 13. *f.* 4.—*F. p.*
401.—Arca. N. *Lin.* 1143.—*Pen.* 4. *p.* 217.—*Don.*
2. *t.* 63.—*Mont. p.* 141.—*Lin. T.* 8. *p.* 95.— *Dor.*
Cat. p. 37. *t.* 12. *f* 6.—*D. p.* 244.—*Turt. D. p.* 8.—
Da Cos. t. 65. *f.* 62. *(rt. hand.) Ch. f.,*574.—N. Margaritacea. *Lam.* 6.—Obliquely subcordiform, subtriangular, anteriorly produced, cuticle blackish or dark
olive green, (at times with yellowish rays and very
minute striæ) glossy; lunule oval; inside silvery, teeth
about twenty anteriorly, about ten posteriorly ; margin
crenated.　0,40...½.　*Common.*

N. Tenuis. *Turt. B. p.* 177.—*F. p.* 402.—Arca.
T. *Mont. Sup. p.* 56. *t.* 29. *f.* 1.—*Pen.* 4. *p.* 218.—
D. p. 246.—*Turt. D. p.* 11.　Obliquely-heart-shaped,
roundish and nearly smooth, produced and rounded
anteriorly, white or covered with a thin olive skin ;
inside white, a little pearly, margin entire.　¼...⅜.
Scotland.

N. Rostrata. *Turt. B. p.* 178.—*F. p.* 402.—

ARCA R. *Mont. p. 55. t. 27. f. 7.—Pen. 4. p. 217.—
D. p. 245.*—Oval, anteriorly produced, curved and rounded, glossy, pale horn color, with fine regular and reflected concentric striæ, which however become irregular in crossing the very slight longitudinal anterior ribs; central tooth obsolete, margin entire.   ¼...½ *Frith of Forth.*

N. MINUTA. *Turt. B. p. 178.—F. p. 402.*—ARCA. M. *Pen. ¼. p. 216.—Mont. p. 140.—Lin. T. 8. p. 92. —Dor. Cat. t. 1. f. 16.—D. p. 245.—Turt. D. p. 11. f. 98.*—A. CAUDATA. *Don. 3. t. 78.*—Oval, anteriorly produced, curved and truncated, white or yellowish with a few ridges crossing the transverse striæ, margin entire. ¾...½. *Tenby, Sandwich, Scotland.*

ORDER.—MONOMYARIA.
With one siphonal scar.

TRIBE.—MYTILACEA.

Hinge with the ligament marginal, partly inclined, linear, extending along a great part of the anterior border. Rarely foliated and adherent.

GENUS.—MODIOLA.
Subtransverse, equivalve, regular, posteriorly very

short ; beaks almost lateral, inclining to the shorter side ; hinge toothless, lateral, linear ; cartilage sub-internal, situated in a marginal groove ; scar single, sublateral, elongated and hatchet-shaped.

M. RHOMBEA. *Berkely in Z. J.* 3. *p.* 229. *t.* 18. *f.* 1.—Thin, rhombic, gibbous, with transverse subcrenu-lated folds which are posteriorly obscure, and longitu-dinal ribs ; umbones incurved, slightly prominent. Length 0,17. *Weymouth, rare.*

M. MODIOLUS. *Turt. B. p.* 199. *t.* 15. *f.* 3.—ARCA M. *Lin.* 1158.—*Pen.* 4. *p.* 238. *t.* 69.—*Da Cos. p.* 219. *t.* 15. *f.* 5.—*Don.* 1. *t.* 23.—*Lin. T.* 8. *p.* 107. —*Dor. Cat. p.* 40. *t.* 12. *f.* 5.—*D. p.* 314.—*Turt. D. p.* 111.—*E. t.* 219. *f.* 1.—M. VULGARIS, *F. p.* 412. —Oblong, smooth, long, thick, coarse, covered with a blackish skin, anteriorly obliquely dilated, the beaks tumid and obtusely angular ; when half grown thinner, of a horn color and usually clothed more or less with long leaf-like filaments which are entire on both their edges. (M. BARBATUS. *Lin.* 1156.—*Ch. f.* 749.—*Pen.* 4. *p.* 238. *t.* 67. *f.* 2.—*Don.* 2. *t.* 70.) 4 or 5. Common.

M. GIBBSII. *Turt. B. p.* 200.—*F. p.* 413.—*Leach,*

Z. M. t. 72. *f.* 2.—Somewhat triangular, very flat and angular anteriorly, regularly striated transversely, clothed with foliations which are serrated on one side, white and opaque under the cuticle. 2...1¼. *W. Coasts.*

M. Discors. *Turt.B.p.*201. *t*: 15. *f.* 4,5.—F.*p.*413. —Mytilus D. *Lin.* 1159.—*Mont. p.* 167.—M, Discrepans. *Lam.* 15.—*Da. Cost. t.* 17. *f.* 1.—*Pen.* 4. *p.* 167.—*Lin. T.* 8. *p.* 111. *t.* 3. *f.* 8.—*Dor. Cat. p.* 40. *t.* 2. *f.* 1.—*D. p.* 319.—*Turl. D. p.* 112.—Oval, very tumid anteriorly rather pointed and somewhat contracted at the ventral margin; divided into compartments, the central being nearly smooth, the extremes with longitudinal ribs; cuticle green or brownish horn-color; beaks quite terminal, very obtuse and twisted into a single flat volution. 0,44. *W. Coasts and Ireland.*

M. Discrepans. *Turt. B. p.* 202.—*F. p.* 413.— Mytilus D. *Mont. p.* 119. *and Sup. p.* 65. *t.* 26. *f.* 4.—*Lin. T.* 8. *p.* 111. *t.* 3. *f.* 9.—*Pen.* 4. *p.* 241.— *D. p.* 319.—*Turt. D. p.* 112.—Oval, flattish, rounded anteriorly, slightly ribbed longitudinally at both ends; beaks not quite terminal. ¼. *W. Coast and Ireland. Like the last but flatter broader and rounder at the end opposite the hinge, where the ribs are only eight in number, the color too is blacker.*

Gfnus.—MYTILUS.

Longitudinal, equivalve, acute at the base, usually affixed by a byssus ; beaks acute, somewhat straight and terminal ; hinge lateral and usually toothless, ligament marginal and subinternal; scar elongated, clavate, sublateral.

M. Edulis. *Lin.* 1157.—*Ch. f.* 750.—*Pcn.* 4. *p.* 236. *t.* 66. *f.* 2.—*Don.* 4. *t.* 128.—*Mont. p.* 159.— *Lin. T.* 6. *t.* 18. *f.* 13,4.—*Dor. Cat. t.* 12. *f.* 5. *l. hand.* —*D. p.* 309.—*Turt. D. p.* 109.—*Da. Cost. t.* 15. *f.* 5. *l. hand.—-E. t.* 218. *f.* 2.—*Knorr.* 4. *t.* 15. *f* 1.— *F. p.* 411.—Oval-oblong, smooth, posteriorly tumid towards the beaks, curved and somewhat carinate ante-riorly, rich blue under the epidermis; beaks blunt; hinge with four or five teeth. 2. *Common Muscle.*

* *An var.* M. Subsaxatilis. *Williams in Mag. Nat.* 7. *p.* 354,—*An.* M. Galloprovincialis*? Lam.* —Strong, solid, the hinge line longer and very straight, thus forming a more or less distant angle with the ven-tral edge. *I believe it to be a distinct species.*

---

* When beween rocks the posterior edge becomes concave.

* M. Pellucidus. *Pen.* 4. *p.* 237. *t.* 66. *f.* 3.—*Mont. p.* 160.—*Don.* 3. *t.* 81.—*Lin. T. p.* 167.—*D. p.* 310. —*Turt. D. p.* 110.—*Ch. f.* 751.—*Var* Edulis. *F. p.* 411.—Oval, transparent, usually yellowish with dark blue rays, broader than the last, anteriorly straight; only two or three tubercular teeth under the hinge. 2. *Common.*

† My. Striatulus. *Lin. Mant. p.* 548.—*Schræt. Ein. t.* 9. *f.* 16.—*Gmel.* 3358.—*Turt. in Mag. N. H.* 7.—Semitransparent, dark horn-colored, with a few paler zones, marked with numerous slight longitudinal ribs decussated by transverse depressed lines giving them a granulated appearance; front margin a little incurved, hinge margin angular. *Scarborough.*

---

* The Crenatus and Ungulatus are occasionly found on our coast but are not native species.

† Contrary to my usual habit, I have copied the synomyms without verifying them, since I am unable to procure the described shell. In almost every other case reliance may be placed on the foreign synonyms, as much labor has been expended in the comparison of figures.

GENUS.—LITHODOMUS. CUVIER.

Subcylindrical, rounded at both ends; beaks nearly terminal; no teeth; ligamental line nearly straight.

L. LITHOPHAGUS. *Lin.* 1156.—*Lin. T.* 8. *p.* 270. *t.* 6. *f.* 1. *to* 5.—Cuticle green, finely striated by the layers of growth; inside glossy, irridescent. 0,40...1. *Limestone, very rare.*

GENUS.—PINNA.

Longitudinal, equivalve, cunieform, acute at the beaks, gaping at the opposite extremity; beaks straight; hinge lateral and toothless; ligament marginal, linear, very long, almost internal.

P. INGENS. *Pen.* 4. *p.* 115.—*Mont. p.* 180.—*Lam.* 13.—*Mont. p.* 180.—*F. p.* 406.—P. LÆVIS. *t.* 152. —P. INGENS. & FRAGILIS. *Turt. B. p.* 222. *t.* 22. *f.* 1.—Oval-triangular, semitransparent, horn coloured, with concentric arched striæ, a few longitudinal obsolete ridges towards the back; ligamental edge straight, compressed anteriorly, from whence it runs almost directly for two-thirds and then slopes suddenly to the beaks. 6...12. *S. Coasts, deep water.*

P. FRAGILIS. *Pen.* 4. *p.* 114. *t.* 69. *f.* 80.—*F. p.* 406.—P. MURICATA. *Don. t.* 10.—PECTINATA. *Mont. p.* 178.—*Turt. B. p.* 223. *t.* 19. *f.* 1.—Triangular, pellucid, corneous, about eighteen radiating ribs running the entire length of the shell; ventral edge rounded. 2½...6. *S. Coasts.* *Towards the middle posteriorly, the scaly striæ run obliquely to the margin.*

* P. PAPYRACEA. *Turt. B. p.* 224. *t.* 20. *f.* 3.—*F. p.* 407.—Oval triangular, thin, brittle, with nine distant unarmed ribs nearly covering the entire surface; ventral edge slightly rounded; contracted rapidly towards the apex; the open end even. 2¼...4¼. *Devon.*

TRIBE.—MALLEACEA. LAM.

Subinequivalve, foliaceous, ligament marginal; sublinear either entirely simple or interrupted by crenulations or a row of teeth.

GENUS.—CRENATULA.

Subequivalve, flattened, foliaceous, somewhat irregular, no particular aperture for the byssus; hinge lateral, linear, marginal, crenulated; crenations arranged in a straight line, callous, somewhat excavated, receiving the ligament.

C. TRAVISII. *Turton in Mag. N. H.* 7. *p.* 349. *f.*

---

* Muricata, fide Turton, is probably not native.

47.—Rhombic, longer than broad, rounded below, transparent, whitish with pale violet longitudinal interrupted
striæ, very thin and brittle, obliquely truncate at the
top, with a few pale violet spots below; front margin
incurved. ½...1. *Scarborough. Probably the young
of the W. Indian species, which, when mature, is internally of a jet black.*

Genus.—AVICULA.

*Inequivalve, fragile, with the dorsal edge straight and
transverse, the extremities produced, the anterior
one caudiform; left valve emarginate, with a sinus
or notch through which the beard passes; hinge
linear with one tooth in each valve under the beaks;
ligament linear and marginal placed in a long
narrow groove.*

A. Hirundo. *Turt. B. p.* 220. *t.* 16. *f.* 3,4.—*F.
p.* 405.—Mytilus. H. *Lin.* 1159.—*D. p.* 320.—
Turt. D. p. 108 *f.* 7.—*An. Ch. f.* 724,5.?—*An* A.
Tarentina. ? *Lam.*—Rather oblique, smooth or furnished with a few scales about the margin, dull greenish
grey or brown with pale rays; tail rather elongated;
wing large and deep. *Dublin Bay, Torbay and W.
Coasts, rare, up to* 2.

Tribe.—PECTINIDES.

Ligament internal or semi-internal, shell for the most

part regular and not foliaceous in texture.

Genus.—LIMA.

*Longitudinal, subequivalve, auriculated, slightly gap-
ing on one side ; beaks divaricated ; hinge toothless,
the cardinal pit partly external and receiving the
ligament.*

L. Bullata. *Turt. B. t.* 17. *f.* 4,5.—Pecten
Fragilis. *Mont, Sup. p.* 62.—*Pen.* 4. *p.* 223.—
Ostrea F. *Turt. D. p.* 131.—Lima F. *F. p.* 388—
Very convex and much curved outwards on one side with
numerous raised longitudinal striæ, which are a little
undulated, with three or four lesser ones between each of
them ; cardinal margin and auricles oblique. ⅓...1.
Devonshire and Bray in Ireland, rare.

L. Subauriculata. *Turt. B. p.* 218.—*F. p.* 389.
—Pecten S. *Mont. Sup. p,* 63. *t.* 29. *f.* 2.—Ostrea.
S. *Turt. D. p.* 131.—Flattish and subequilateral, a
little unequal at one of the sides (but not so much as in
the last) with longitudinal straight striæ without lesser
intermediate ones ; auricles nearly rectilinear. ¼...¼.
*W. Coasts.   More elongated than the last, the striæ
more remote and nearly straight.*

Genus.—PECTEN.

Free, regular, inequivalve, auriculated, dorsal line

transverse and straight; the beaks contiguous;
hinge toothless, the cardinal cavity entirely internal,
triangular, and receiving the ligament.

* *Ears equal or nearly so.*

P. Maximus. *Pen.* 4. *p.* 219. *t* 62.—*Lam.* 1.—
F. p. 383.—*Turt. B. p.* 207.—*Ch. f.* 585.—*Mont. p.*
143.—Ostrea M. *Lin.* 1144.—*List. t.* 163. *f.* 1.—
Knorr. 2. *t.* 14. *f.* 1.—*E. t.* 285. *f.* 1.—*Don.* 2. *t.*
49.—*Lin. T.* 8. *p.* 96.—*Dor. Cat. p.* 37. *t.* 9. *f.* 3.—
D. p. 247.—*Turt. D. p.* 128.—P. Vulgaris. *Da.*
Cos. t. 9. *f.* 3.—Suborbicular, inequivalve, one valve
being convex white and tinged with yellow towards the
beaks, the other flattish concave towards the beaks and
usually brownish red, or white variegated with pink or
brown; about fourteen radiating rounded ribs. 4 or 5.
The common scallop.

P. Opercularis. *Pen.* 4. *p.* 221. *t.* 63. *f,* 2.—
Mont. p. 145.—*Lam.* 34,—*F. p.* 383.—*Turt. B. p.*
209.—*E. t.* 112. *f.* 2.—Ostrea O. *Lin.* 1146.—*Dor.*
Cat. p. 38. *t.* 9. *f.* 1,2,4,5.—*D. p.* 266.—*Turt. D. p.*
129.—(P. Pictus. *Da. Cost. t.* 9. *f.* 1,2,4,5.)—*List.*
t. 190. *f.* 27.—*Knorr.* 2. *t.* 2. *f.* 2,3.—Suborbicular,
the upper valve the more convex, with from eighteen to

twenty radiating rather convex ribs, which are somewhat roughened by obsolete longitudinal and minute
transverse striæ, and are narrower than their interstices ; the color extremely variable, being yellow,
white, pink, &c., but the lower valve always white.—
*Variety.*P. Lineatvs. *Lam.* 35.—*Da. Cost. t.* 10. *f.*
8.—*Mont. p.* 47.—*Pen.* 4. *p.* 222.—Ostrea L. *Lin.*
T. 8. *p.* 99.—*Dor. Cat. p.* 38.—*D. p.* 266.—The
rays marked each with a longitudinal red line. 2.
Very common.

P. Subrufus. *Turt. B. p.* 210. *t.* 17. *f.* 1.—
Ostrea S. *Don.* 1. *t.* 12:—Equivalve, suborbicular,
equilateral and smooth, uniform rufous brown the
twenty radiating ribs rounded and smooth. *Torbay.*
A few transverse scaly marks towards the margin.

P. Sinuosus. *Pen.* 4. *p.* 222. *t.* 64. *f.* 2.—*F. p:*
384.—*Lam.* 49.—*Turt. B. p.* 210. *t.* 9. *f.* 5.—
Ostrea S. *Gmel.* 3319,—*Lin. T.* 8. *p.* 99.—*Dor.*
Cat. p. 38. *t.* 10. *f.* 3,6.—*D. p.* 262.—*Turt. D. p.*
130.—P. Distortus. *Da Cos. p.* 148. *t.* 10. *f.* 3,6.—
Mont. p. 148.—P. Pusio. *Don.* 1. *t.* 34.—*Sow. G.*—
List. t. 172. *f.* 9.—*Reeve. t.* 114. *f.* 6.—Suborbicular or longitudinally oval, inequivalve, variously distorted, white, pink or brownish, irregularly marbled or

marked with chocolate brown, about forty fine prickly radiating riblets. 1. *S. & W. Coasts, in crevices of rocks.*

P. Glaber. *Pen,* 4. *p.* 223.—*Mont. p.* 150. *and Sup. p.* 59. *t.* 28. *f.* 6.—*F. p.* 384.—*Turt. B. p.* 211. —Ostrea G. *Turt. D. p.* 132.—Equivalve, yellow mottled with rufous brown, with very minute transverse striæ and from seven to ten obscure rounded rays, and numerous grooves in the inside. ⚭. *Scotland, near Dunbar.*

P. Tumidus. *Turt. B. p.* 212. *t.* 17. *f.* 3.—*F. p.* 384.—Ostrea. T. Equivalve, inequilateral, suborbicular, glossy white, transparent and without striæ ribs or sculpture of any kind; one of the sides produced; ears nearly equal. ⚭. *Torbay.*

* * *Ears unequal.*

P. Lævis. *Pen.* 4. *p.* 223.—*Mont. p.* 150. *and Sup. p.* 161. *t.* 4. *f.* 4.—*Turt, B. p.* 213.—*F. p.* 385. —Ostrea L. *D. p.* 131.—O. Similis. *Laskey. Wer. Soc.* 1. *t.* 8. *f.* 8.—Equivalve, equilateral, orbicular, thin, smooth, except a few transverse wrinkles, yellowish white, often marbled with brown, semitransparent; one ear large the other small. ⚭. *Anglesea & W. Coasts.*

P. Obsoletus. *Pen.* 4. *p.* 222. *t.* 64. *f.* 3.—*Don.*
t. 1. *f.* 2.—*Mont. p.* 149. & *Sup. p.* 57.—*Turt.* *B. p.*
213. *t.* 9. *f.* 6.—*F. p.* 385.—Ostrea O. *Lin. T.* 8. *p.*
100.—*D. p.* 263.—*Turt. D. p.* 133.—Ost. Lævis.
Lin. T. 8. *p.* 100. *t.* 3. *f.* 5.—Equivalve, roundish-
oval or oblong, purple reddish or yellowish (rarely
clear white) often variously marbled or spotted; the
surface generally marked with raised ribs towards the
broader end, more or less in number, which are
sometimes defined by a deep transverse line separating
them from the plain part, but always marked with
fine and almost invisible longitudinal irregular and
somewhat undulate striæ over the whole surface. *Torbay
and English Channel.*

P. Varius. *Pen.* 4. *p.* 221 *t.* 64. *f.* 1.—*Mont. p.*
146.—*Lam.* 47.—*F. p.* 384.—Ostrea V. *Lin.* 1146.
--*Don.* 1. *t.* 1. *f.* 1.—*Lin. T.*8. *p.*97.—*Dor.Cat.p.* 38.
t. 10. *f.* 1,2,4,5,8,9.—*D. p.* 260.—*Turt. D. p.* 130.
—*Da Cost. t.* 10. *f.* 1,2,4,5,7,9 —*Ch. f.* 633,4.—
List. t. 180, 181, *and t.* 189. *f.* 23.—Rounded-oblong,
extremely variable in coloring, but not unfrequently
brownish red, with about thirty-two rounded prominent
radiating ribs, armed when perfect, with erect vaulted
scales, the interstices very deep and not striated; ears
very unequal. 1¼. long. *Extremely Common.*

P. Pusio. *Lam.* 55.—*F. p.* 385.—*Turt. p.* 215. *t.* 17. *f.* 2.—Ostrea P. *Lin.* 1146.?—*D. p.* 261.—*Ch. f.* 635,6.—*Knorr.* 4. *t.* 12. *f.* 2.—Oblong-oval, equivalve, with about forty rounded and nearly smooth striæ, which are usually alternately larger and smaller, and very slightly muricated about the margin; variable in coloring, often brownish white with chocolate ziczac bands, or saffron or crimson, the under valve generally pure white. ⅛...⅜. *Torbay, in rocks.*

P. Islandicus. *Turt. B. p.* 216.—*F. p.* 385.— *List. t.* 1057. *f.* 4.—Ribs numerous, rough, unequal, from seventy to one hundred, grouped in pairs or otherwise, reddish, the furrows reticulated. 3...3¼. *W. Scotland, rare.*

Tribe.—OSTRACEA.

Ligament internal or semi-internal; shell irregular and of a foliated texture.

Genus.—OSTREA.

Fixed, inequivalve, irregular, with the beaks more or less separated from each other and becoming unequal by age; hinge toothless, with a cavity which is partly external and in the lower valve becomes elongated; ligament internal

O. Edulis. *Lin.* 1148.—*Pen.* 4. *p.* 225. *t.* 65. *f.* 2.
—*Mont. p.* 151.—*Dor. Cat. p.* 38. *t.* 11. *f.* 6.—*D.*
p. 280.—*Turt. D. p.* 133.—*Lam.* 1.—*List. t.* 193. *f.*
30.—*Ch. f.* 682.—*Da Cost. t.* 2. *f.* 6:—*Blain. t.* 60.
f. 1.—*E. t.* 184. *f.* 7,8.—*F. p.* 392.—Rounded-oval,
rather attenuated towards the beaks, dirty white, rough,
with concentric waved scaly foliations; upper valve less
and flattened ; inner margin very entire. *The common
Oyster.*

O. Parasitica. *Turt. B. p.* 205. *t.* 17. *f.* 6,7.—*F*
p. 392.—*Turt. D. p.* 134. *f.* 8.— Rounded or oblong,
nearly smooth, the upper valve convex, greenish, often
with radiating bands of brown. 1¼. *Attached to
marine substances.—Probably a variety of Edulis and
deriving both form and color from the Pectens, &c. it
may have attached itself to.*

Genus.—ANOMIA.
*Inequivalve, irregular ; with the under valve perfora-
ted near the beak and fixed by an operculum or
tendon ; hinge withont teeth ; ligament internal,
placed transversely under the beak.*
A. Electrica. *Lin.* 1151.—*Turt. D. p.* 1. *f.* 67.—
Turt. B. p. 227. *t.* 17. *f.* 8,9.—*F. p.* 394.—Somewhat orbicular, with the surface a litle undulated, bright,

transparent amber or yellow inside and out, not rough
plaited nor scaly, beaks pointed, not quite terminal;
the lower valve flat, scale-like, and with a large interrupted perforation. 1¼. *W. Ireland.*

A. Ephippium. *Lin.* 1150.—*Pen.* 4. *p.* 232. *t.* 65.
up. fig.—*Don.* 1. *t.* 26.—*Mont. p.* 155.—*F. p.* 395.
—*Don.* 1. *t.* 26.—*Mont. p.* 155.—*Lin. T.* 8. *p.* 102.
—*Dor. Cat. p.* 38. *t.* 11. *f.* 3.—*D. p.* 286.—*Turt.*
D. p. 2.—*Lam.* 1.—*List.* 204 *f.* 38.—*Turt. B. p.*
227. *t.* 18. *f.* 1. *to* 3.—Orbicular-oval, rather rough,
irregularly wrinkled and plaited, when full grown scaly,
dirty white; beaks terminal; inside rich pearlaceous,
white but often stained with greenish or dirty brown;
operculum oval, large, thick, rough. 3. *Common on*
rocky shores.—Probably most of the remaining Anomiæ
are nothing more than varieties, (excepting Aculeata)
as this genus accommodates its shape, sculpture and
coloring to the substance to which it may attach itself.

A. Cepa. *Lin.* 1151.—*D. p.* 287.—*Turt. B. p.* 228.
t. 18.*f.*4.*(young)*—*Ch. f.* 694,5.—*F. p.* 395.—Oblong,
inclining to oval, rather flat, with a rough but not an
undulating surface; under valve not scaly, thin; beaks
terminal; inside more or less rosy, not pearly. 1¼...2.
Guernsey, Torbay, &c.

F

A. Squamula. *Lin.* 1151.?—*Mont. p.* 156 & 561. —*Dor. Cat. t.* 13. *f.*4.—*Turt.D. p.* 3.—*F. p.* 395.— *Turt. B. p.* 229. *t.* 18. *f.* 5,6,7.—Somewhat orbicular, smooth, transparent, flat or a little tumid about the beaks, thin, brittle; operculum tendinous, seldom hard at the base, with a testaceous termination. ⚭. *Common on old shells.*

A. Undulata. *Gmel.* 3346.—*Mont. p.* 157. *t.* 4. *f.* 6.—*Pen.* 4: *p.* 233.—*Dor. Cat. p.* 39. *t.* 11. *f.* 4. —*D. p.* 289.—*Turt. D. p.* 4.—*F. p.* 395.—*Turt. B. t.* 10. *f.* 8,9,10.—Ostrea Striata. *Mont. p.* 153. *and Supp.* 580.—*Don. t.* 45.—Rounded or oblong, very variable in figure, sometimes very convex and opaque, often thin, transparent and flat; upper valve furnished with numerous radiating striæ which cause the margin to be crenated; inside rich green with an irredescent blue border; perforation large, on one side of it a triangular striated cavity; the plug terminating in a thin oval layer, strongly striated transversely and crossed by fine longitudinal lines. 1. *On old shells and crevices of rocks.*

A. Punctata. *Turt. B. p.* 232. *t.* 18. *f.* 11.—*F. p.* 395.—Orbicular, thin, transparent, purplish white, a little truncated at the base; upper valve convex and covered with numerous raised pustular dots, the under valve flat and marked with concave dots; beaks terminal. 1. *Teignmouth, &c. on Crabs, &c.*

A. CYLINDRICA. *Turt. D. p.* 6.—*Turt. B. p.* 232. —*F. p.* 396.—A. CYMBIFORMIS. *Lin. T.* 8: *p.* 104 *t.* 3. *f.* 6.—*Mont Sup.p.*64.—*An. A.* PYRIFORMIS. *Lam.?* —Oval, somewhat cylindrically convex and transversely rugged, but often smooth, brownish, narrower towards the beak which curves over the under valve and ends in an obtuse point. ⅓...⅓. *On Fuci and Sertulariæ.*

A. STRIOLATA. *Turt. B. p.* 233.—*F. p.* 396.— Oval, somewhat cylindrically convex and striated longitudinally, with the beak curved backwards. *Roots of Fuci.*

A. ACULEATA. *Gmel.* 3346.—*Ch. f.* 702.—*Mont. p.* 157. *t.* 4. *f.* 5.—*Pen.* 4. *p.* 233.—*D. p.* 288.— *Turt. D. p.* 4.—*F. p.* 396.—*Turt. B. p.* 233·—Flat, rounded or oblong, sometimes truncated at the top, brown or whitish, armed with numerous radiating prickly striæ on the upper valve. 0,40. *Dover, &c*

A. FORNICATA. *Lam.* 6.—*Turt. B. p.* 234. *t.* 18. *f.* 1, 2, 3.—*F. p.* 396.—Orbicular or inclining to

F 2

oblong, irregularly sinuous at the margin on the sides, with numerous extremely fine radiating striæ only visible towards the margin, the dorsal portion being sculptured by numerous regular transverse ones; hinge pointed, terminal; outside silvery, under the hinge a large hollow vaulted chamber which is much curved on one side and scaly on the outside; perforation round and nearly closed   1½.   *Torbay.*

A. TUBULARIS. *Turt. B. p.* 234.—*F. p.* 396.— Orbicular, whitish, with the beaks terminal; perforation entire all round and produced into a raised cylindrical tube.   ¼.   *Attached to Fuci.*

A. CORONATA. *Bean in Mag. N. H.* 8. *p.* 564. *f.* 52.—Oval, glossy, pale amber, the upper valve concave, smooth, with rather an undulating surface; beaks pointed, not terminal, above which are three or four rows of spines the outer extending beyond the shell giving it a coronated appearance; under valve convex, with an irregular surface and a few indistinct traces of longitudinal striæ.   ½...¼.   *Scarborough.*

TRIBE.—RUDISTÆ.

Ligament, if any, undiscovered, or represented by a tendinous cord which attaches the shell.

Genus.—DISCINA.

Inequivalve, rounded ovate, slightly depressed; valves of equal size and each marked with a central or-bicular disc which in the upper valve is undivided and submammillary in the centre, in the other valve is extremely white and divided by a transverse fissure.

D. Ostreoides. *Lam.—F. p.* 376.—Orbicula Norvegica. *(not Lam.) Sow. Lin. T.* 13. *p.* 468. *t.* 26. *f.* 2.—*Sow, G. f.* 3,4,5.—*Reeve. t.* 126. *f.* 3,4,5. —Upper valve brown with fine longitudinal ribs crossed by concentric wrinkles; margin more or less waved; inside under the apex with two irregular callous ridges; under valve white, concentrically wrinkled, a disc round the fissure to which the peduncle adheres.. 0,40...½. *A Very doubtfnl native species; on ballast.*

Genus.—CRANIA.

Inequivalve, suborbicular; lower valve almost flat, pierced internally with three unequal oblique per-forations; upper valve very convex, strengthened internally with two prominent callosities.

C. Rostrata. *Hæning. Mon. Cran. p.* 3. *f.* 3.— *Desh. in Lam.* 7. *p.* 302.—C. Personata. *Sow. Lin. T.* 13. *t.* 26. *f.* 3.—*Sow. G. f.* I,2.—*Reeve. t.* 128. *f.* 2.—Patella Distorta. *Mont. Lin. T.* 11. *t.* 13.

f. 5.--Ch. f. 687.—Criopus Anomalus. F. *p.* 377.
—Suborbicular, posteriorly retuse; posterior scars
rounded, anterior uniting into one; beak acute; disc
sinuated; margin anteriorly irregular and thickened.
♃. *Zetland, on submarine stones.*

Tribe.—BRACHIOPODA.
*Shell bivalve, affixed to marine substances by contact
or a tendinous cord.*

Genus.—-TEREBRATULA.
*Oval, inequivalve, fixed by a tendinous pedicle; the
upper valve with the beak produced and perforated
or emarginate; under valve with two elongated
. projections issuing from the internal disc, which are
. sometimes variously branched; hinge with two teeth;
ligament internal.*
T. Cranium. *Mont. in Lin. T.* 11. *p.* 188. *t.* 13.
f. 2.—*F. p.* 368.—*Turt. B. p.* 236.—Anomia C.
Turt. D. p. 5.—T. Vitrea. *Flem. in Edinb. Ency.*
7. *p.* 96. *t.* 206. *f.* 2.—Oval, ventricose, semitransparent, thin, brittle, finely shagreened and slightly
wrinkled concentrically, under a dull white skin milk
white, ventral edge slightly truncated; the internal projecting processes of the under valve with a lateral
ramification issuing from the base on one side. ♃.
Zetland, rare.

T. Psittacea. *Lam.* 12.—*Turt. B. p.* 236.—*F. p.*
368.—Anomia P. *Gmel.* 3248.—*Ch. f.* 713.—*D. p.*
296.—*Turt. D. p.* 5. *f.* 42,3,4.—Oval convex, blackish
horn-color, inflected and smooth at the sides, longitudinally striated on the disc ; beak of the upper valve elongated, curved and pointed. 1. *Teignmouth, excessively
rare.*

T. Aurita. *Flem. Phil. Zool.* 2. *p.* 498. *t.* 4. *f.* 5.—
F. p. 369.—T. Costata. *Lowe. Zool. J.* 2. *p.* 105. *t.*
5. *f.* 8,9.—*Desh. in Lam.* 7. *p.* 351.—Regularly ribbed,
the eight ribs on the disc the most distinct and rounded,
obsoletely wrinkled concentrically, the lateral ribs
indistinct; the larger valve broadest in the middle,
semicircular at the margin and narrowed at the apex ;
small valve suborbicular; the hinge margin subtruncated or rather obtusely angular and having the sides
depressed ; inner surface punctated. 0,20....0,30.
W. Scotland.

CLASS.—MOLLUSCA.
ORDER.—GASTEROPODA.
TRIBE.—PHYLLIDIANÆ.
GENUS.—CHITON.

*Shell consisting of eight imbricated testaceous plates,
connected by a more or less coriaceous margin.*

C. FASCICULARIS. *Lin.* 1105.—*Lam.* 5.—*Mont. t.*
27. f. 5.—Dor. Cat. t. 1. f. 1.—*Wood. G. C. t. 2. f.*
6.—Turt. D. p. 34.—*Lam.* 5.—Oblong, apparently
smooth, but when examined with a glass rough like
shagreen, except on the elevated dorsal ridge; margin
surrounded with eighteen tufts of whitish hairs, one at
the junction of each valve and two in front ; dark brown *
or cinereous.   0,80...0,40.   *Common, Margate, Sandwich, Devonshire.*

C. MARGINATUS. *Pen.* 4. *p.* 71. *t.* 36. *f.* 2.—*D. p.*
11.—*Mont. p.* 1.—*F. p.* 289.—*Wood. G. C. t.* 3. *f.* 4.
—*Sow. Conch. Ill. f.* 106. *to* 112.—C. CINEREUS. *Z.*
J. 2. *p.* 99.—*Wood. G. C. t.* 3. *f.* 5.—Oval, carinated,
elevated, anteriorly widened, minutely granulated, granules not united into a determinate figure; margin
also minutely granulated ; color various. *Extremely*
common under stones between low and high water mark.
Average size, ⅝.

C CINEREUS. *Lin.* 1106.?—*Mout. p.* 3.—*F. p.*
289.—*Sow. Conch: Ill. f.* 94. *to* 98.—*Black variety,*
C. ASELLUS, *Lowe. Zool. J.* 2. *t.* 5. *f.* 3,4.—Depressed,
subcarinated, minutely granulated ; granulations on the
central areas arranged in lines ; margin minutely
grained ; color various.   *On stones, &c. low water*
mark, not uncommon. ½.

C. ALBUS. *Lin.* 1107.?—*Mont. p.* 4.—*Sow. Conch.*
Ill. f. 99. 99*a.*, 100.—*Brown variety,* ASSELLOIDES.
Lowe. Zool. J. 2. *t.* 5. *f.* 5.—Oval, depressed, subcarinated, lightly and minutely granulated; margin scaly.
Rare, Oban, &c.—*Differs from Marginatus in the*
large size and regular arrangement of the granules or
rather scales of the marginal integument.

C. LÆVIS. *Mont: p.* 2.—*Lowe. Z. J.* 2. *t.* 5. *f.* 1.
p. 97.—*F. p.* 290.—*Sou. Con: Ill. f.* 101, 101*a.*, 102.
—C. MARGINATUS. *Lin. T.* 8. *t.* 1. *f.* 2.—Apparently
smooth but finely granulated, narrow, carinated ; margin broad, velvety to the eye but really finely reticulated.
$\frac{1}{2}$. *Scotland, rare.*

C. RUBER. *Lin.* 1106.?—*F. p.* 289.—*Sow. Conch.*
Ill. f. 103,4.—*Lowe. Zool. J.* 2. *t.* 5. *f.* 2.—Smooth,
usually mottled red, shining; valves beaked; margin
minutely granular. ⅓. *Dorset, Scotland, but very*
rare, common in Orkney and Zetland.

C. LÆVIGATUS. *Fleming, Edin. Ency.* 7. *p.* 103.—
F. d. 290.—C. LATUS. *Lowe. Zool. J. p.* 103. *t.* 5. *f.*
6,7.—*Sow. Conch. Ill. f.* 113, 113*a.*—Broad, smooth,
subcarinated, the margin smooth ; color white and red,.

variegated.   0,80.   *Scotland, not common, Zetland, plentiful.*

GENUS.—PATELLA.

Univalve. not spiral, shield-shaped or retuse-conic, imperforate, devoid of a marginal fissure, cavity simple ; apex recurved anteriorly.

P. VULGATA. *Lin.* 1258.—*Lam.* 28.—*Mont. p.* 475.—*D. p.* 1032.—*Dor. Cat. p.* 58. *t.* 23. *f.* 1,2.— *List. Ang. p.* 195.—*List. t.* 535. *f.* 14.—*Knorr.* 6. *t.* 27. *f.* 8.—*Bl. t.* 48. *f.* 1.—Extremely variable in form being more or less depressed or conic, scutelliform, the apex subcentral and obtuse, various shades of yellowish sea-green, rough with crowded elevated striæ and about fourteen but slightly raised subangulated riblets frequently marked by a difference of color and scarcely, if at all projecting at the margin ; inside sometimes appearing radiated.   2¼.   *Common Limpet.*

P. PECTINATA. *Lin.* 1259.—*Born. t.* 18. *f.* 7.— *Lam.* 40.—*Bl. t.* 49. *f.* 5.—P. INTORTA. *Don. t.* 146. —*Pen.* 4. *p.* 143. *t.* 90. *f.* 148.—*Mont. Sup. p.* 154. —*F. p.* 286.—*D. p.* 1037.—Oval, somewhat transparent, yellowish brown, with crowded radiating riblets armed with black imbricated scales ; apex much inclined, prominent nearly marginal.   ¾.   *Anglesea, Devon, Frith of Forth, rare.*

P. Pellucida. *Lin.* 1260.—*D. p.* 1042-—*Lam.* 42.
—*List. t.* 543. *f.* 27.—*Pen.* 4. *p.* 143.—*Born. t.* 18:
f. 9.—*Ch. f.* 1620.—*F. p.* 287.—Elliptic, smooth,
polished, pellucid, olive, with interrupted sky-blue
radiating lines; apex near the margin, often obsolete;
margin entire. *Var.* (P. Lævis. *F. p.* 287.—*D. p.*
1043.—*Pen.* 4. *p.* 144. *t.* 90. *f.* 151.—*List. t.* 542.
f. 26.—P. Cœrulera. *Mont. Sup. p.* 152.) coarser,
thicker, ochraceous with azure lines .0,80. *The variety
is found on the roots, the type, on the leaves of Fuci ;
common.*

P. Virginea. *Muller. Z. Dan. t.* 12. *f.* 2,3.—*D. p.*
1052.—*F. p.* 287.—*Desh. in Lam.* 7. *p.* 544.—*Gmel.*
3711.—P. Parva. *Mont. p.* 480.—Oval, obtusely
conical, small, pink, with numerous reddish radiating
lines, smooth, more or less pellucid (becoming by age
opaque and of an uniform colour); apex obtuse, not
central; margin entire. 0,40...0,30. *On stones near
low water mark, not uncommon.*

P. Testudinalis. *Muller and Desh. in Lam.—*
P. Clypeus. *Brown. Ill.—*P. Clealandi. *Sow. Lin.*
T. 13. *p.* 621.—*F. p.* 287.—Oval, white with red
brown or purple spots, faintly striated longitudinally
and still more faintly transversely; summit obtuse,

lateral, tinged with light purple ; margin entire ; inside white with a dark brown muscular impression. ¾, *Bangor, rare, Isle of Man.*

P. PULCHELLA. *Forbes in Mag: Nat. H. 7. p.* 591, *f.* 61.—Ovate, smooth, subpellucid, bluish white with ten or twelve moinliform red rays (becoming by age reddish white and opaque) ; apex acute, submarginal. 0,16...0,20. *Isle of Man.*

P. ANCYLOIDES. *Forbes, Annals Nat. Hist. 5. p.* 108. *t.* 2. *f.* 16.—*An.* P. GUSSONI. *Phillippi. t.* 7. *f.* 7.? —Extremely thin, pellucid, rounded, gibbous, white, seeming reticulated when under a lens ; vertex inclining to the margin ; inside bluish white. 0,16, *Arran. Wonderfully like a marine Ancylus.*

TRIBE.—SEMIPHILLIDIANA.
GENUS.—PLEUROBRANCHUS.
Dorsal and internal, thin, flat and obliquely oval.
P. PLUMULA. *E. p.* 291.—BULLA. P. *Mont. p.* 214. *vig.* 2. *f.* 5. *(animal) and t.* 15. *f.* 9.—*D. p.* 478. —*Lin. T.* 8. *p.* 123.—Ovate-oblong, depressed, pellucid, thin, glossy yellowish white tinged with brown at one end, the other minutely convoluted on the back or upper part (the convolution making but one turn) strongly wrinkled concentrically, and marked with two

or three ray-like indentations running from the margin towards the apex; the pillar lip slightly turned inwards. ⅓...⅓. *Devonshire, &c. not common.*

P, MEMBRANACEA. *F. p.* 291.—LAMELLARIA M. *Mont. in Lin. T.* 11. *p.* 184. *t* 12. (*f.* 3. *animal*) *f.* 4. —Ovate, excessively thin, flat, with a minute lateral whorl, silvery tinged with pink. 2. *English Coast, rare.*

TRIBE.—CALYPTRACIANÆ.
Shell always external.

GENUS.—EMARGINULA.
Conical, shield-shaped, the vertex inclined to one side ; internal cavity simple ; posterior margin cleft or emarginated.
E. FISSURA. *Lam.* 1.—*F. p.* 364.—PATELLA F. *Lin.* 1261.—*D. p.* 1054.—*Pen.* 4. *p.* 144. *t.* 90. *f.* 151.—*List. t.* 543. *f.* 28.—*Don. t.* 3. *f.* 2.—*Mont. p.* 490.—*Dor. Cat. p.* 59. *t.* 23. *f.* 4.—Conical, white or yellowish with close set prominent radiating ribs, can‧cellated in the interstices by transverse striæ, pellucid, apex reflected ; margin crenated ; slit narrow and long. *variety* (ROSEA. *Bell in Zool. J.* 1. *t.* 4 *f.* 1.) apex higher and more recurved ; inside rose-colored. ⅓...⅗. *E. Coasts.*

GENUS.—FISSURELLA.

Shield-shaped or depressed conical; concave within; the vertex with an oblong or ovate perforation, destitute of a spire.

F. GRÆCA. *(of British authors not Lamarc)—F.p.* 364.—PATELLA G. *Pen.* 4. *p.* 144. *t.* 89. *f.* 153.— *D. p.* 1056.—P. RETICULATA. *Don. t.* 21. *f.* 3.— Elliptic, white, greenish, brownish or white with green rays, with strong narrow unequal radiating ribs, decussated by raised concentric coarse wrinkles; perforation simple, more or less oblong, apex truncated; inside white or rayed with brown; the margin waved and crenulated; *young* (F. APERTURA. *F. p.* 364.— PATELLA A. *Mont. p.* 491. *t.* 13. *f.* 10.) with a reflected subspiral apex. 0,43....1. *Common on the Kentish Coast.*

F. NOACHINA. *Sow. Conch. Il. f.* 15.—*Desh. in Lam. t.* 7. *p.* 604.—PATELLA N. *Ch. f.* 1927,8.—*D. p.* 1055.—P. FISSURELLA. *Mull. Z. Dan. t.* 24. *f.* 4, 5.6.—CEMORIA. FLEMINGII. *Leach. Brit. Shells, t.* 10. *f.* 4,5.—PUNCTURELLA. *Lowe. Z. J.* 3. *p.* 78.— Patelliform, conical, whitish, with strong longitudinal ribs; the vertex intorted, a canal becoming broader as it descends runs from the apex and terminates in a perforation; perforation oblique, produced within as a short vaulted canal, ½. *Argyleshire. very rare.*

Genus.—PILEOPSIS.

Obliquely conical, anteriorly recurved, the apex nearly spiral; aperture of a roundish oval; anterior margin the shorter, acute and subsinuated; the posterior larger and rounded; an elongated, arcuated, transverse muscular scar under the posterior margin.

P. Ungarica. *Lam.* 1.—Patella U. *Lin.* 1259. —*D. p.* 1034.—*Pen.* 4. *p.* 143. *t.* 90. *f.* 147.—*Don. t.* 21. *f.* 1.—*Mont. p.* 486.—*Knorr.* 6. *t.* 16. *f.* 3.— *Mart. f.* 107.—Capulus U. *Sow. G, f.* 1.—*F. p.* 363. —White or pink under the brown epidermis which has a pilose margin, rough with raised coarse radiating striæ; the apex spiral and acuminated; inside white or pink. ⅓. *Not common, on rocks and shells in rather deep water.*

P. Antiquata.—Patella A. *Lin.* 1259.—*Dor. Cat. p.* 51.—*Mont. p.* 485.—*List. t.* 544. *f.* 31.— *Mart. f.* 111,2.—Capulus A. *F. p.* 364.—P. Mitrula. *Lam.* 2.—Patella M. *D. p.* 1035.—White, thick, opaque, the layers of growth forming rough concentric sublamellar ridges; inside white; apex obtuse. 1⅓. *Rare.*

P. Militaris.—Patella M. *Dor. Cat. p.* 51.—

D. p. 1035.—*Don. t.* 171.—*Mont.* 488. *t.* 13. *f.* 11.
—*An List. t.* 544. *f.* 32.?—CAPULUS M. *F. p.* 364.
—Subpellucid, subconic, white, finely striated both
ways so as to give the shell a somewhat cancellated
appearance ; vertex much reflected, recurved and
tnrned to one side, descending almost to the edge of the
shell; aperture round and even ; inside glossy white;
epidermis brown and pilose. ⅟. *Rare, Weymouth.*

GENUS.—CALYPTREA.

*Conoid, the summit vertical, imperforated and pointed;
internal cavity with a spiral septum or a convolute
chamber.*

C. CHINENSIS. F. p. 362.—PATELLA C. *Lin.* 1257.
—*Mont. p.* 489. *t.* 13. *f.* 4.—*D. p.* 1017.—*Mart. f.*
121,2.—*List. t.* 549. *f.* 39.—P. ALBIDA. *Don. t.* 129.
—C. LÆVIGATA. *Lam.* 2.—Very thin, subpellucid,
subconic, pale brown or whitish, much compressed and
rounded at the margin ; vertex central, terminating in
a very small subspiral volution ; slightly wrinkled concentrically and rough with short concave scales partially
or entirely ; inside glossy, white, furnished with a subspiral columella extending from near the margin to the
end and forming the external subvolution, which is

* *The* CREPIDULA *of Turton in Zool. J. is not native, being taken from the bottom of an American vessel.*

broad, flat, thin, and stands obliquely to the side of the shell. ♀. *Cornwall.*

Genus.—BULLÆA.

Extremely thin, somewhat involute on one side, and destitute of a columella or spire ; aperture large and expanded.

B. Aperta. *Lam.*—Bulla A. *Lin.* 1183.—*Sow. G. f.* 1.—*D. p.* 477.—*Ch. f.* 1354,5.—*Don. t.* 220.— *Mont. p.* 208. *vig.* 2. *f.* 1.3.—*Da. Cos. t:* 2. *f.* 3.— Suborbicular, thin, glossy, pellucid, brittle, white, slightly wrinkled, no external convolution or umbilicus ; inner lip very small, slightly involuted, visible to the end ; aperture occupying nearly the whole of the shell. 0,70. *Devonshire, Kent, &c., common.*

B. Punctata. *Clark. Z. J.* 3. *p.* 339.—Bulla P. *Adams. Lin. T.* 2. *t* 1. *f.* 6, 8.—*F. p.* 294.—Ovate-oblong, extremely thin, white, pellucid, glossy, marked with transverse dotted lines ; inner margin arcuated ; apex obtuse with a very shallow umbilicus. 0,10. *Exmouth and Torquay in pools at the lowest spring tide, very rare.*

B. Pruinosa. *Clark. in Z. J.* 3. *p.* 339.—Sub-globose, subopaque, dead frosted white, delicately reticulated, appearing as if covered with fine gauze, circumference of the upper part somewhat constricted (as if a thread had been tightly tied round it) ; columellar margin arcuated, a little reflected and in the middle of it a flexure or notch; apex rather rounded and slightly umbilicated. 0,30...0,20. *Budleigh, Salterton, Devon.*

B. CATENATA. *Forbes.*—BULLA C. *Mont. p.* 215. *t.* 7. *f.* 7.—*D. p.* 478.—PUNCTATA. *variety, F. p.* 294.—Pellucid, white, glossy, closely and finely striated transversely all over, the striæ when magnified seem interwoven or formed into links like a chain; apex obtuse with a visible involution ; aperture extremely large, occupying nearly the entire length of the shell; *var.* Frosted, less diaphanous, with a more transparent zone taking in eight or ten of the catenæ which are more strongly defined; subumbilicated. 0,10. *Devon, rare.*

BULLA.

Ovate-globose, involute, devoid of columella or projecting spire ; aperture the entire length of the shell, outer lip with an acute edge.

B. LIGNARIA. *Lin.* 1184.—*Lam.* 1.—*D. p.* 480.— *Bl. t.* 45. *f.* 8.—*List. t.* 714. *f.* 71.—*Knorr.* 6. *t.* 37-*f.* 4.—*Mont. t.* 194,5.—*Pen.* 4. *p:* 116.—*Mont.*

p. 205.—*F. p.* 292.—Oval-oblong, thin, brittle, sub-pellucid, yellowish brown with numerous transverse striæ of a lighter color giving the shell the appearance of veined wood, apex depressed into a subumbilicus ; aperture large extending the whole length of the shell, contracted above; inside glossy white, columella visible to the end. 2. *Cornwall and Devon.*

B. Akera. *Gmel.* 3434.—*Mont p.* 219.—*F. p.* 292.—*(Ch. f.* 1358.)—*D. p.* 482.—*Dor. Cat. p.* 43. *t.* 22. *f.* 12.—B. Resiliens. *Don.* 3. *t.* 79.—B. Fra-gilis. *Lam.* 10.—*Bl. t.* 45. *f.* 7.—Oval, extremely thin, pellucid, horn-colored, elastic, somewhat wrinkled longitudinally ; apex obtuse, convoluted, canaliculated, the volution even with the body ; aperture large at the base, much contracted above, the outer lip extremely thin and not adhering to the body whorl ; pillar lip a little thickened and white, columella visible to the end. ¾...,040. *Southampton, Poole, Guernsey, rare but local.*

B. Hydatis. *Don. t.* 88.—*F. p.* 292.—B. Am-pulla. *Pen.* 4. *p.* 116.—Subglobular, translucent, with a brownish epidermis; minutely striated spirally; apex concave but not exhibiting volutions; aperture interrupted by the rounded body whorl, widened below;

pillar lip rounded, but the pillar not visible to the end.
Rare.

B. CRANCHII. *F. p.* 292.—Subcylindrical, translucent, horn-colored, the strong spiral striæ in bands,
slightly waved by indistinct lines of growth; aperture
narrow, rendering the continuation of the pillar less invisible; the latter is straight, a little reflected, forming
a pillar cavity and is slightly waved where it joins the
outer scarcely projecting lip; apex concave, without
visible whorls. 0,60...0,40. *Plymouth Sound.*

B. STRIATA. *Brug. Lam.* 3.—*List. t.* 714. *f.* 72.—
B. AMYGDALUS. *D. p.* 480.—B. AMPULLA. *Mont.. p.*
206. *t.* 7. *f.* 1.—*Mart. f.* 202,4.—*F.p.*293.—Oblong-
oval, smooth, glossy, opaque whitish mottled and veined
with light chesnut; no external volution but in its place
an umbilicus; on the lower end of the pillar lip the
shell is thickened and of an opaque white, but this does
not extend up the shell; columella not visible to the
end. ⅜. *Falmouth, in sand, rare.*

B. ZONATA. *Turton in Mag. Nat. H.* 7. *p.* 352.—
Oval, solid, opaque, with regular, rather broad alternate
zones of white and fulvous or pale rufous brown, and
transverse lines of very minute raised dots; apex

umbilicated and as well as the pillar pure white. ⅓...
0,20. *Near Land's End, Cornwall. The shape not
unlike Lignaria but is conical-oval and the volutions
more loosely connected.*

B. HYALINA. *Turton in Mag. Nat. H.* 7.—Oval,
transparent, smooth, crystalline, the aperture dilated at
the base, pillar slightly umbilicated; crown flattened,
channelled, umbonate. *Newcastle, not uncommon,
Land's End.—Not unlike Umbilicata but is shorter,
more oval, and the aperture more dilated.*

B. UMBILICATA. *Mont. p.* 203. *t.* 7. *f.* 2.—*Turt.
D. p.* 22.—*F. p.* 293.—*Lin. T.* 8. *p.* 129.—*D. p.*
497.—Oblong-oval, smooth, white; apex rounded and
umbilicated ; aperture extremely narrow, extending the
whole length of the shell and dilating a little at the
base. ⅓...0,062. *In sand, Falmouth.*

B. TRUNCATA. *Adams in Lin. T.* 5. *t.* 1. *f.* 1,2—
Mont. p. 223. *t.* 7. *f.* 5.—*F. p.* 293.—B. RETUSA.
Lin. T. 8. *p.* 128.—*D. p.* 497.—Subcylindric,
opaque, white, the upper part longitudinally striated,
the lower plain; apex truncated and largely umbilicated showing the involutions ; aperture linear, dilated
slightly at the base and contracted most in the middle.
⅓. *Devon and Cornwall.*

B. Obtusa. *Mont. p.* 223. *t.* 7. *f.* 3.—*F. p.* 293.
—*(Walk.t.* 3. *f.* 62.*)*—*Lin. T.* 8. *p.* 128.—*Dor.*[*Cat.*
p. 44. *t.* 18. *f.* 14.—*D. p.* 497.—*(Adams. t.* 14. *f.*
28.*)*—Moderately strong, subcylindrical, opaque, white,
longitudinally wrinkled; apex convoluted, obtuse, whorls
four or five, very little produced; aperture nearly the
length of the shell, narrow and rather more compressed
in the middle, dilated at the base; iuner lip thickened,
smooth, white. 0,20...0.10. *Kent and Devon.*

B. Cylindracea. *Pen.* 4. *p.* 117. *t.* 59. *f.* 85.—
Don. t. 120.—*Mont. p.* 21. *t.* 7. *f.* 2.—*List. t.* 714.
f. 70.—*F. p.* 293.—*D. p.* 496—*Dor. Cat. p.* 43. *t.*
18 *f.* 22.—Cylindrical, narrow, involuted, white, semi-
transparent: smooth, umbilicated at the apex, aperture
narrow, linear, slightly dilated at the base; outer lip
straight; pillar lip with an indistint fold. ½...0,20.
S. Coasts.

B. Alba. *Turton Z. J.* 2. *p.* 364. *t.* 13. *f.* 6.—*F.*
p. 294.—Ovate-oblong, slightly striated longitudinally,
white, unspotted, the vertex umbilicated, three transverse
punctured striæ at each extremity. ½- *British Channel.*

Tribe.—LAPLYSIANÆ.

Genus.—LAPLYSIA.

* *Shield dorsal, subcartilaginous, semicircular, ad-*
hering by one side and covering the branchial
cavity.

A. Depilans. *Lin.* 1082.—*Pen.* 4. *p.* 42. *t.* 21. *f.*
21.—A. Hybrida. *Sow. Brit. Misc. t.* 53.—*F. p.*
290.—Animal purplish with black spots; shell amber
brown. *On sea-weeds a little beyond low water mark.*

A. Punctata. *Cuv. Moll. t.* 1.*f.* 3, 5.—*Flem. Ed.*
Enc. 14. *p.* 623.—*F. p·* 291.—Animal brown with
white spots. *Bay of Kirkwall, Scotland.*

A. Viridis. *Mont. Lin. T.* 7. *t.* 7.*f.* 1.—*E. p.* 291.
—Animal green; no shell. *Devon.*

Tribe.—COLIMACEA.

Spiral, but without any exterior projections except the
striæ of growth ; outer lip frequently reflected ; no
real operculum.

~~~~~~

* It is scarcely if at all possible to distinguish Aplysiæ
by the shells.

Genus.—AURICULA.

* *Suboval or oval oblong ; aperture longitudinal, quite entire at the base and contracted above or its margins disunited ; pillar with one or more plaits; outer lip either reflected outwards or simple and sharp edged.*

A. Personata. *Desh. in Lam.* 8. *p.* 332.—Carychium P. *Mich. p.* 73. *t.* 15. *f.* 42,3.—Voluta Denticulata. *Mont. p.* 234. *t.* 20. *f.* 5.—Acteon D. *F. p.* 337.—Conovulus D. *Gray. Turt. p.* 225. *f* 144.—Aur. Myosotis. *Lin. T.* 16. *p.* 368.—Voluta Ringens & Reflexa. *Turt. D.*—Turbo Bidentatus. *Walker. f.* 50,53.—Oblong, brittle, smooth, brown or purplish (sometimes nearly hyaline) ; spiro conical, varying in length ; mouth oblong, rather thickened ; peristome slightly reflected ; pillar three or five plaited ; outer lip more or less denticulated. ½. *Clefts of rocks near high water mark.*

A. Bidentata. *Ferussac.—Lin. T.* 16. *f.* 368.— Voluta B. *Mont. Sup. p.* 100. *t.* 30. *f.* 2.—*D. p.* 507.

---

* Voluta Triplicata of Donovan (*t.* 138;—*Mont. Sup. p.* 99.—Acteon T. *F. p.* 337.*)* is not a native species.

CONOVULUS B. *Gray. Turt. p.* 227. *f.* 145.—ACTEON B. *F. p.* 337.—*Variety* A. EROSA. *Lin. T.* 16. *p.* 368. Ovate, ventricose, smooth, shining white; spire short; suture indistinct; mouth oblong, throat smooth, peristome simple, reflected in front and slightly thickened; two of the plaits on the pillar larger than the rest. ½. *Devon, under stones left by the tide.*

A.ALBA. *Gray. An. Ph.* 16. *p.* 370.—*Forbes. Mal. Mon. p.* 12.—VOLUTA A. *Mont. p.* 245.—*Turt. D. p.* 250.—*D. p.* 508.—CONOVULUS A. *Gray. Turt. p.* 227.—VOLVARIA A. *F. p.* 333.—Fusiform, pointed, thin, white, pellucid, slightly striated transversely; whorls six; mouth slender, oblong; pillar two-plaited. 0,10. *The sea coast near the mouth of rivers under stones left by the tide.*

A. FUSIFORMIS.—ACTEON. F. *F. p.* 337.—VOLUTA F. *Turt. D. p.* 251.—Glossy white, transparent, quite smooth, swollen in the middle and tapering to both ends; whorls four, very flat, and only defined by a fine lucid circular line; body whorl very large, occupying more than three fourths of the shell, base rounded and a little reflected; aperture oblong-oval reaching to the top of the primary volution; outer lip very thin and plain; pillar lip smooth, not spreading

G

or reflected, without teeth or folds but furnished with a small oblique gibbosity in the middle. 0,30...0,15. *Exmouth.*

A. Heteroclita.—Voluta H. *Laskey. Wern. Mem.* 1. *p.* 398. *t.* 8. *f.* 1,2.—Acteon H. *F. p.* 337. —Glossy, white, veined like ivory in a longitudinal direction, with eight or nine reversed whorls which taper slightly to an obtuse point, the body whorl occupying two thirds of the length; aperture narrow not quite half the length of the shell; pillar with one plait. ¼...0,085. *Dunbar.*

GENUS.—TRUNCATELLA. Lowe.

Turrited, the adult cylindrical decollated or obtusely truncated; whorls well defined, either smooth or with longitudinal ribs; aperture oval and short; the peritreme contiguous; lip simple, no epidermis. T. Montagui. *Lowe. in Z. J.* 5. *p.* 303.—Turbo Truncata. *Mont. p.* 300. *t.* 10. *f.* 7.—*Turt. D. no.* 65.—Turritella T. *F. p.* 303.—Cylindrical, smooth, glossy, pellucid, thin, horn-colored, with four spires; the apex abrupt as if broken; whorls much raised, the suture deep; aperture suborbicular, slightly mar- ginated, reflecting a little on the pillar lip—variety (rare) longitudinally striated or marked with cre- nulæ in the sutures. 0,20...0,07.—*Young,* Turbo

SUBTRUNCATA. *Mont. p.* 300. *t.* 10. *f.* 1.—*Turt.*
D. no. 64.—TURRITELLA S. *F. p.* 303.—Pellucid
yellowish white, with six or seven rounded smooth
whorls separated by a deep depressed line, gradually
tapering to an obtuse point; aperture suborbicular,
inclining to oval,—variety, faintly striated longitudinally, somewhat glossy. 0,20...0,05. *Southampton
and Salcomb in drift sand.*

TRIBE.—NERITACEA.

*Fluviatile or marine, semiglobular or depressed oval,
destitute of a columella; aperture semicircular with
an oblique straight pillar-lip.*

GENUS.—NATICA.

*Subglobular, operculated, umbilicated; aperture en-
tire, semicircular; inner lip oblique, toothless,
callous; the callosity modifying the umbilicus and
sometimes covering it; outer lip sharp, always
smooth within.*

N. MONILIFERA. *Lam.* 16.—N. GLAUCINA. *F. p.*
319—*Pen.* 4. *p.* 344.*t.* 90.*f.* 1.—NERITA G.*Mont.p.*
469.—*List. An. Ang. t.* 3.*f.* 10.—*List. t.* 568. *f.* 19.
—*Da Cos. p.* 83. *t.* 5. *f.* 7.—*D. (in part) p.* 978.—
Strong, smooth, glossy, livid or purplish flesh color,
ferruginous or chesnut about the acute apex, paler when

G 2

young and with bands of spots and streaks; whorls six,
the body whorl very large and ventricose, the others
small in proportion ; rounded, produced and somewhat
lateral; aperture suboval, sublunate; outer lip rather
thin and even ; pillar lip rather thick and reflected,
forming a large and deep umbilicus; operculum horny.
1. *Common on sandy shores.*

N. Rufa. *F. p.* 319.—Nerita R. *Mont. Sup.* 150.
t. 30. *f.* 3.—Smooth, purplish, with a white band
round the top of the volutions and two others on the
body whorl ; pillar lip forming a large projection over
the cavity behind and producing an indentation on each
side of it. ♀. *England and Scotland, rare.—Second
whorl proportionably larger than in the preceding.*

N. Nitida. *F. p.* 319.—Nerita N. *Don. t.* 144.
—Mont. Sup. p. 149.—N. Mammilla. Var. *C. D. p.*
985.—Glossy, white, the spire short; whorls five,
nearly flat, the suture nearly obliterated; umbilicus
half closed. ♀. *Diffused but rare.*

N. Alderi. *Forbes in Malac. Monens. p.* 31. *t.* 2.
f. 6,7.—*An* N. Valenciennesi ? *Payr. t.* 5. *f.* 23,4.
—Spire produced, of five whorls, divided by a shallow
suture, body whorl largest and rounded, the upper ones

nearly flat, smooth purplish brown, with two bands of plain yellow which are bordered by two narrow bands of white spotted with brown, lower part of the body whorl white, a dark brown band bounds and enters the umbilicus which is neither grooved nor striated ; pillar lip brown and white, slightly reflected on the umbilicus. Young, with the spire less produced. 0.60. *Dover, Isle of Man, &c.*

N. GLABRISSIMA. *Forbes.*—NERITA G. *Brown. Wern. Mem.* 2. *p.* 532. *t.* 24. *f.* 12.—N. SULCATA. *Turt. D. p.* 124. *t.* 56,7.—NATICA S. *F. p.* 320.— Globular, semitransparent, bluish white ; whorls four, with remote oblique longitudinal striæ, swollen, well defined ; pillar lip flat, projecting a little in the middle over the cavity behind, which is long and deep. ⅛. *Dublin Bay.*

N. HELICOIDES. *Johnston in Trans. Berwick. N. H. Soc.* 1835.—Ovate-conical, smooth, white, immaculate, covered with a yellowish epidermis; whorls five, rounded, separated by a channelled suture, the spire produced and rather obtuse ; aperture pure white with a small fissure on the pillar. 0,60...0,40. *Berwick Bay.*

N. Tuberosissima. *F.p.* 320.—Nerita T. *Mont.*
Sup. p. 150. *t.* 29. *f.* 5.—Pellucid, white, whorls four,
marked with four spiral broken tubercular ridges, the
upper volutions small; umbilicus large. ⅛. *Dunbar,*
very rare.

N. Intricata. *F. p.* 319.—Nerita I. *Don. t.*
167.—N. Canrena. *Mont. Sup. p.* 148.—N. Canrena. var. M. *D. p.* 978.—Smooth, livid, with bands
of sagittate ferruginous lines; umbilicus large and furnished with two spiral ridges and two grooves. ½.
Weymouth, rare.

N. Pallidula. *F. p.* 320*—Nerita P. *Don. t.*
16. *f.* 1.—*Mont. p.* 468.—*D. p.* 986.—*Da Cos. t.* 4.
f. 4.—Turbo Pallidus. *Turt. D. p.* 192.—Lacuna
P. *Turt. in Z. J.* 3. *p.* 190.—Smooth, thin, subpellucid, brownish yellow, depressed, but three whorls,
the last extremely large, pillar lip white with a very
wide groove leading to the deep umbilicus; outer lip
very effuse. ½...⅜. *On sea-weeds at low water mark,*
common.

N. Lacuna. *F. p.* 320.—Helix L. *Mont. p.* 428.
t. 13. *f.* 6.—*D. p.* 917.—*Lin. T.* 8. *p.* 201.—Turbo
L. *Turt. D. p,* 193. *t.* 25. *f.* 87, 89.—Lacuna Montacuti. *Turt. in Z. J.* 3. *p.* 191.—Thin, pellucid,

subglobose, light horn color, with four tumid smooth
whorls, the body one large, the two uppermost very
small and somewhat lateral ; aperture large suboval,
outer lip extremely thin membranaceous; pillar lip
thick, white, grooved with a long canal terminating in a
small but deep umbilicus. ‡. *Devon, &c.*

GENUS.—IANTHINA.

Ventricose, conoid, thin, transparent ; aperture trian-
gular: columella straight, produced beyond the base
of the outer lip, which has a sinus in the middle of
it ; no operculum.

I. COMMUNIS. *Lam.* 1.—*F. p.* 326.—I. FRAGILIS.
of most writers.—*Bl.t.*37.*f.* 1a. *(good).*—I. BICOLOR.
Menke. p. 140.—*Philippi. p.* 164.—HELIX IAN-
THINA. *Lin.* 1246.—*Knorr.* 2. *t.* 30. *f.* 2,3.—*List. t.*
572. *f.* 24.—*Turt. D. p.* 58.—*D. p.* 938.—Depressed,
conoid, obtuse, nearly smooth, a few indistinct spiral
striæ on the base, the whorls flattish, violet beneath,
pale lilac above, body whorl obtusely carinated; whorls
four, pillar rectangular to the outer lip; aperture
broader than long, columella straight and short. *Diam.*
up to 1. *but rarely so large, not common but sometimes*
found in Cornwall and Ireland.

I. EXIGUA. *Lam.* 2.—*Sow. G. f.* 2,3—*Lesson. voy.*

de Coq.—Mag. N. H. 7. *p.* 352.*—D'orb. Mol. Cub.
—D'orb. Mol. Amer.—Bl. t.* 37. *bis. f.* 1.—Oval, a
little swollen and slightly carinated in the middle,
violet, marked with very oblique elegant longitudinal
striæ which turn at the subcarinate part in an obtusely
angular direction; spire produced and pointed. 0,40...
0,30. *Land's End, Cornwall, very rare.—More conical than Fragilis, the whorls rounded and more distinctly defined, the mouth not so proportionately
spread, by which it appears somewhat spindle shaped.*

I. Pallida. *Thompson's Annals of Nat. Hist.* 5. *p.*
96.*t.*2.*f.*2.—*An.* I. Nitens. *Phil.t.*9.*f.* 16?—Ovate,
obtuse, pale, all the whorls strongly rounded, the suture
deep; aperture large, longer than broad, semiovate,
columella curved, outer lip rounded and acutely edged.
¾. *Clare.*

Genus.—SCISSURELLA. D'orbigny.
*Shell with a depressed spire, the outer lip notched with
a deep slit following the growth of the volutions,
obliterated to within a short distance of the margin
and forming a sort of keel upon the back of the shell.*
S. Crispata. *Fleming. p.* 366.—White; whorls
three, increasing rather rapidly from the slightly elevated apex and sloping with a gentle convexity from the

suture to the keel, marked with numerous fine decussated arched longitudinal ribs which are coarser above than below; under side with a central cavity from which the whorl extends a little convex to the keel; aperture suborbicular, outer lip thin, the inner reflected. *In shell sand at Noss Zetland, after a storm.*

GENUS.—VELUTINA.
Aperture circumscribed, no pillar, body-lip oblique.

V. LÆVIGATA. *F. p.* 326.—HELIX L. *Lin.* 1250. —*Don.* 3. *t.* 105.—*Walk. f.* 17.—*Pen.* 4. *t.* 86. *f.* 139.—*Mont. p.* 382. *and Sup. p.* 140.—*Lin. T. p.* 222.—*Dor. Cat. p.* 56. *t.* 18. *f.* 9.—*D. p.* 971.— Thin, fragile, imperforate, subpellucid, flesh-colored, with eight volutions, the body whorl extremely large, the others very small very little produced and lateral; apex compressed; transversely wrinkled and slightly striated longitudinally or spirally, covered when fresh with a rough brown epidermis which generally rises into regular equidistant membranaceous spiral ridges; aperture suborbicular, dilated, margin thin. 0,60. *Shellness and Devon.*

V. OTIS. *F. p.* 326.—HELIX OTIS. *Turt. D. p.* 70. —(*Walk. t.* 1. *f.* 17)--Semitransparent, glossy, whorls three, smooth, longitudinally oblong ; aperture oblong, body lip a little thickened and flattish. 0,08. *Inter· stices of rocks covered at high water, Devonshire.*

Trire.—MACROSTOMÆ.

Auriform, with the aperture very wide and the margins disunited ; without an operculum or columella:

Genus.—SIGARETUS.

Subauriform, suborbicular ; inner lip short and spirally intorted ; aperture entire, dilated, rounded oblong, not nacreous ; margins disunited.

S. Perspicua.—Helix P. *Lin. not Gmel.*— S. Haliotoideus. *F. p.* 360.—Bulla H. *Mont. p.* 211. *t.* 7. *f.* 6. *(Animal—vignette.* 2. *f.* 6.*)—Lin.T.*8. *p.* 123.—*Dor. Cat. p.* 43. *t.* 22. *f.* 5.*—Helix H. *var.? D. p.* 973.—S. Convexus. *Blainv. t.* 42. *f.* 2.—Suboval, ear-shaped, extremely thin, white, pellucid, glossy, smooth but not quite destitute of wrinkles; aperture oval, not quite extending to the apex which is small, obtuse, and laterally convoluted, scarcely making two volutions; the body of the shell very small and only turning a little inwards spirally ; inner lip visible to the end. ¾...½: *Devon, rare.*

S. Tentaculatus. *F. p.* 360.—Lamellaria. T

Mont. in Lin. T. 11. *p.* 186. *t.* 12. *f.* 5,6.—More depressed and opaque than the preceding. *Devon.*

Genus.—HALIOTIS.

Ear-shaped, usually depressed; spire very short, sometimes depressed and sublateral; aperture extremely dilated, ovate-oblong and, when perfect, entire; disc, with perforations disposed in a line running parallel to the left margin.

H. Tuberculata. *Lin.* 1256.—*List. t.* 611. *f.* 2. —*Knorr.* 1. *t.* 17. *f.* 1.—*Mart. f.* 148,9.—*D. p.* 1009. —*Pen.* 4. *p.* 141. *t.* 88. *f.* 144.—*Don. t.* 5.—*Mont. p.* 473.—*Dor. Cat. p.* 57. *t.* 22. *f.* 1,2.—*Da Cos. t.* 2. *f.* 1,2.—Ovate-oblong, depressed convex, spirally striated, with irregular longitudinal more or less distinct rather distant folds; brownish outside, often variegated with green, beautifully irridescent within; apex with a single spiral turn, slightly produced, umbilical cavity very small; inner lip inflected. 3. *Guernsey.*

Tribe.—PLICACEA.

Shell with plaits on the pillar, and the aperture narrow.

Genus.—TORNATELLA.

Convolute, oval-cylindrical (usually striated transversly

*and destitute of an epidermis) ; aperture oblong
and entire, the outer lip sharp-edged ; one or more
plaits on the pillar.*

T. FASCIATA. *Brug.—Lam.* 3.—VOLUTA TORNA-
TILIS. *Lin.* 1187.—*D. p.* 503—*Mont.p.*231.—*List.t.*
835.*f.* 58.—*Mart. f.* 442,3.—*Pen.* 4. *t.* 71. *f.* 86.—
—T. TORNATILIS. *F. p.* 336.—Ovate-conical, with
fine spiral striæ, pinkish flesh-colored with two white
bands; spire exserted and acute; columella with a
single fold; outer lip thin, slightly rounded. 0,80.
Sandy Bays.

TRIBE.—SCALARIANÆ.

*Shell devoid of plaits on the columella; the margins
of the aperture united in a circular form.*

GENUS.—SCALARIA.

*Subturrited, with longitudinal elevated, subacute in-
terrupted ribs; aperture rounded ; the margins
united, marginated and reflected.*

S. COMMUNIS. *Lam.* 5.—S. CLATHRUS. *F. p.* 311.
—TURBO C. *Lin.* 1237.—*Pen.* 4. *p.* 129. *t.* 82. *f.*
3D.—*Borl. Cornwall. t.* 28. *f.* 9.—*List. t.* 588. *f.*
51.—*D. p.* 854.—*Knorr.* 1. *t.* 11. *f.* 5.—*Mart. f.*
1434.—T. CLATHRATULUS. *Don. t.* 28. *upper figures.*

—Turrited, imperforated, whorls ten, smooth, crossed
by about ten distinct contiguous somewhat oblique and
rather strong ribs; whorls rounded and deeply divided
by the separating line; colour white or whitish with chocolate amorphous marking which however frequently
are arranged as interrupted bands on the ribs.   1½.
*Kentish Coast, &c.—The operculum is black, coria-
ceous and spirally striated.*

S. CLATHRATULUS. *F. p.* 311.—TURBO C. *Walker.
t.* 2. *f.* 45.—*Lin. T.* 8. *p.* 171. *t.* 5. *f.* I.—*Mont. p.*
297. *and Sup. p.* 124.—*D. p.* 854.—Imperforate,
turreted, narrow, snowy white, thin, transparent, eight
obtuse whorls adorned by about fifteen crowded lamellar
contiguous ribs, the intermediate spaces smooth ½....
0,20.   *Rare*

S. TURTONI. *F. p.* 311.—TURBO T. *Turt. D. p.*
208. *f.* 97.—T. CLATHRATUS. *Don. t.* 28. *lowest fig.*
—Strong, pale brown with two or three dark spiral
bands; whorls about twelve, rounded, pointed, crossed
by about as many ribs, which are but little raised
rounded and bent at the suture; interstices spirally
striated ; lips white, pillar lip a little reflected. 2¼...¾.
England and Ireland.

GENUS.—CYCLOSTREMA. FLEMING.

Spire short ; transverse ridges on the body whorl, disjoined from the pillar by a crenulated groove.

C. ZETLANDICA. *F. p.* 312.—*Mont. Lin. T* 11. *p.* 194. *t.* 13. *f.* 3.—Conical, white, apex obtuse, whorls five, tumid, ribbed spirally and longitudinally, with angular tubercles at the point of decussation, the spiral ridges most prominent at the base where the longitudinal ones disappear; aperture nearly orbicular and marginated. 0,18. *Zetland.*

GENUS.—SKENEA. FLEMING.

Spire depressed and destitute of spinous processes ; suture deep.

S. DEPRESSA. *F. p.* 313.—SERPULA CORNEA. *Adams. Lin. T.* 5. *t.* 1. *f.* 33.—HELIX D. *Mont. p.* 439. *t.* 13. *f.* 5.—Brown, whorls three or four, rounded, wrinkled across, with a deep groove for the separating line; above, the whorls are nearly on a level, their central edge bending suddenly at the suture and forming a deep groove ; beneath, with a large central cavity exposing the volutions; aperture circular, detached from the body whorl, sometimes slightly reflected. 0,08. *At the roots of Fuci, not uncommon.*

S. SERPULOIDES, *F. p.* 313.—HELIX S. *Mont.*

Sup. p. 147. *t.* 21. *f.* 3.—*(young.—Walk.t.*1. *f.* 23.*)*
—White, smooth, glossy, subopaque ; whorls three,
round, nearly on a level above ; beneath with a central
cavity, round which there are traces under a high mag-
nifying power of diverging lines of growth ; aperture
circular, with the margin a little reflected. 0,10. *Not
uncommon from deep water.*

S. Divisa. *F. p.* 315.—Turbo D. *Adams. Lin. T.*
3. *p.* 254—White, glossy, subpellucid ; whorls three or
four, rounded, nearly on a level above, the lower half of
each whorl spirally striated ; beneath, with a large central patulous cavity exposing the whorls ; aperture circular and usually detached from the body-whorl. 0,08.
Common in deep water.

Tribe.—TURBINACEA.

*Turrited or conical; with the aperture oblong or
rounded, not expanding, and the margins disunited.*

Genus.—TROCHUS.

*Conical, the spire elevated, sometimes shortened; the
periphery angulated or subangulated often thin and
acute ; aperture transversely depressed, the margins
disunited above ; columella arcuated, more or less
projecting at the base ; operculated.*

* Umbilicated.

T. Magus. *Lin.* 1228.—*D. p.* 774.—*Lam.* 21.—
List. t. 641. *f.* 32.—*Knorr.* 6. *t.* 27. *f.* 4.—*Mart. f.*
1656.—*Pen.* 4. *p.* 127. *t.* 80. *f.* 107.—*Don. t.* 8. *f.* 1.
---*Mont. p.* 283 —*Lin. T.* 8. *p.* 151.—*Dor. Cat. p.*
48. *t.* 16. *f.* 1.—*F. p.* 321.—T. Tuberculatus. *Da*
Cos. p. 44. *t.* 3. *f.* 1.—Depressed-conical, thickish,
with indistinct spiral striæ, whitish with confluent purplish red radiating streaks; body whorl somewhat
flattened and subtuberculated above, a raised spiral
striæ near the base of each of the six whorls; base
slightly convex, umbilicus large and deep. Breadth, 1.
Common.

T. Umbilicatus. *Pen.* 4. *p.* 126.—*Mont. p.* 286.
—*Ch. f.* 1685.—*Da. Cost. t.* 3. *f.* 4.—*Dor. Cat. t.*
16. *f.* 7,8.—T. Cinerarius. *Don.* 3. *t.* 74., *three*
middle figures.—T. Obliquatus. *D. p.* 779.—Strong,
depressed, rounded at the top, the apex depressed and
not pointed; volutions five and nearly even, suture
fine; white or greenish with longitudinal purplish
waved or ziczac lines and obsolete spiral striæ; aperture compressed, angulated umbilicus large and perforated to the apex. ⅜...¾. *On Fuci, near low water*
mark ; very flat when young.

T. CINERARIUS. *Lin.* 1229.—*List. t.* 641. *f.* 31.—
Ch. f. 1686.—*Don. t.* 74., *upper and lower figures.*—
Pen. 4. *p.* 127.—*D. p.* 779.—*Mont. p.* 284.—*F. p.*
322.—*Lam.* 65.—T. LINEATUS. *Da Cost. p.* 43. *t.* 3.
f. 6.—*Dor. Cat. p.* 43. *t.* 16. *f.* 11,2.—Conical,
spirally striated, cinereous with fine approximate undulated brown longitudinally oblique lines; whorls little ·
elevated, the suture slender; apex rather pointed;
mouth angulated; umbilicus small but deep. ⅜...⅜.
Common on Fuci at low water mark.

T. TUMIDUS. *Mont. p.* 280. *t.* 10. *f.* 4.—*Lin. T.* 8.
p. 153.—*Dor. Cat. t.* 16. *f.* 9,10.—*F. p.* 322.—
T. PETHOLATUS. *D. p.* 776.—Strong, subconical,
tumid, with five projecting but not rounded volutions,
ashy grey, yellowish (or rarely dark purplish brown)
always more or less streaked with fine obscure undulated
longitudinal lines, and striated closely delicately and
spirally ; apex small but not taper ; suture deep ; body
whorl angulated at its lower edge, the base slightly
rounded, the umbilicus small and distinct. ¼. *Devon
and Dorset.*

T. PERFORATUS. *Smith in Wern. Tr.* 8. *p.* 99. *t.*
1. *f.* 3,4.—Subconic, strong, greenish ash with fine
obliquely longitudinal reddish brown lines under a thick

shagreen like brownish drab epidermis, spirally striated; whorls five, slightly rounded, apex obtuse, base subcarinated and a little rounded beneath; aperture subquadrangular, pearly within; umbilicus small but long. ⅝—¾. *Kyles of Bute.*

* * *Imperforated.*

T. CRASSUS. *Mont. p.* 281.—*Lin. T.* 8. *p.* 154.— *Dor. Cat. p.* 48. *t.* 17. *f.* 3. *& 7.—D. p.* 796.—TURBO LINEATUS. *Da Cos. p.* 100. *t.* 6. *f.* 7.—*Don. t.* 71.— *F. p.* 323.—TR. PUNCTULATA. *Blaim. Faun. Franc. t.* 11. *f.* 2.—Strong, thick, subconic, whorls five, rounded, the suture small and depressed, apex moderately pointed but generally worn ; cinereous or light brown covered with fine close set purplish brown ziczac lines or vice versa; base convex; aperture rounded, pillar lip white, and concave in the middle, in front of which is a blunt tooth ; outer lip acute, edged internally with purplish black ; umbilicus indistinct, if any. 0,80. *On rocks about mid-tide, not uncommon.*

T. GRANULATUS. *Born. t.* 12. *f.* 9,10.—*Blain. Fauna. Franc. t.* 10. *f.* 5.—*Lam.* 53.—T. PAPILIOSUS. *Da Cos. p.* 38. *t.* 3. *f.* 5,6.—*Don.* 4. *t.* 127.— *Dor. Cat. p.* 48. *t.* 16. *f.* 5,6.—*F. p.* 323.—*D. p.* 800.

T. TENUIS, *Mont. p.* 275. *t.* 10. *f.* 3.—Conic-orbicu-
lar, thin, very oblique, eight scarcely convex whorls
adorned with crowded elevated transverse granular striæ,
pale usually ornamented with reddish chesnut spots;
base large in proportion, convex, its spiral granular
striæ usually with distinct chesnut dots, imperforate or
all but so, aperture large, angular, the nacre brilliant.
1¼. *S, Coasts.*

T. ZIZIPHINUS. *Lin.* 1231.—*D. p.* 799.—*Gualt.*
t. 61. *f. C.—Mart. f.* 1594.—*List. t.* 616. *f.* 1.—
Knorr. 3. *t.* 14. *f.* 2.—*Pen.* 4. *p.* 126. *t.* 80. *f.* 103.
—*Da Cos. p.* 37. *t.* 3. *f.* 3,4.—*Don. t.* 52.—*Mont. p.*
274.—*Dor. Cat. p.* 48. *t.* 16. *f.* 3,4.—*F. p.* 323.—
Lam. 46. *and* T. CONULOIDES.? *Lam.* 47.—Conic,
the apex acute, whorls seven or eight, flattened, separated by a smooth circular ridge, obsoletely striated
spirally (often with three spiral smaller raised ridges)
livid or reddish with broad wavy longitudinal darker
streaks; the ridges often articulated; aperture somewhat compressed, angulated, inside pearly; base
flattish with circular spotless ridges, imperforated.
1...⅞. *Common.*

T. EXIGUUS. *Mont. p.* 277.—T. EXASPERATUS.
Pen. 4. *p.* 126.—*F. p.* 323.—T. CONULUS. *Da Cos.*

*t. 2. f. 4.—Don. t. 8. f. 2.—*T. Minutus. *D. p.* 797.
—An. Mart. 1529.?—T. Erythroleucus. *Lam.* 69.
— Conic, strong, with six volutions wrought with four
or five small spiral crenated ridges, and defined by a
broad and more elevated ridge finely cut diagonally
with striæ so as to resemble a twisted cord, the interstices finely striated in the same direction; cinereous
brown or purplish, the larger ridge usually red (sometimes spotted with white) the pointed apex rich crimson,
base imperforate; aperture angulated, white, not pearly.
⅜...¼. *Sussex and Dorset.*

T. Striatus. *Lin.* 1230.—*D. p.* 797.—*Mont. p.*
278.—*F. p.* 323.—T. Conicus. *Don. t.* 155. *f.* 1.—
T. Erytroleucus. *Turt. D. p.* 191.—*Dor. Cat. p.*
48. *t.* 18. *f.* 2.—Conical, the apex acute ; whorls six
or seven, flat, scarcely defined, wrought with eight or
nine fine spiral ridges intersected by very fine longitudinal striæ, cinereous with interrupted longitudinal
dark purplish brown lines (sometimes dull crimson or
purplish with darker lines); aperture angulated, pearly;
base flat, with fine circular ridges, imperforated. ⅜...¼.
Not common, in Cornwall and Devon.

T. Martini. *Smith, Wern. Tr. t.* 1. *f.* 26. *p.* 99.
—Conical, citron or flesh-colored streaked with nearly

equidistant reddish brown irregularly shaped spots; whorls flat, with five or six minute tuberculated spiral ridges, the lower one the strongest; apex acute, suture distinct, base imperforate flat, subconcave, with numerous concentric tuberculate ridges; aperture nacreous, compressed. 0,80. *Isles of Man, Dublin, &c.*

Genus.—TURBO.

Conoid or subturrited, the periphery never compressed; aperture entire, rounded, not modified by the penult whorl, the margin disunited above; pillar arcuated flattened and not truncated at the base, an operculum.

T. Littoreus. *Lin.* 1232.—*List. t.* 585. *f.* 43.— *Lam.* 24.—*D. p.* 817.—*Born. t.* 12. *f.* 13,4.—*Mart. f.* 1852.—*List. An. p.* 162.—*Mont. p.* 301.—*F. p.* 298.—Ovate, imperforated, thick, transversely striated, variable in colouring, often yellowish grey often with narrow bands whorls five, the separating line shallow, the whorls, except the [last little convex; outer lip joining the body at an acute angle; columella white, throat chocolate brown. Variety—scarlet. 0,80. *Common Periwinkle.*

T. Petræus. *F. p.* 298.—*D. p.* 820.—Helix P. *Mont. p.* 403.—Strong conical, opaque, purplish brown,

nearly smooth, whorls five, the body occupying nearly
two-thirds of the shell, apex acute; aperture lunated,
outer lip considerably projecting, piilar lip smooth flat,
somewhat spreading and as well as the corneous operculum and the interior dark purple. ⅓...⅓. *S. Devon,
variety.*—Blotched or irregularly streaked with white
or rufous on the upper part of the body whorl.

T. RUDIS. *Mont. p.* 304.—*Don. t.* 33.*f.* 3.—*Lam.*
29.—*F. p.* 298.—*D. p.* 818.—*Lin. T.* 8. *p.* 159. *t.* 4.
f. 12,3.—*Dor. Cat. t.* 18. *f.* 6.—Ovate, thick, strong,
with five ventricose whorls well defined by the suture;
yellowish grey or brown, usually striated transversely;
spire rather prominent and pointed; aperture suborbicular, inner lip thick, a little reflected. *The very
young, deep brown and more slender.* ⅓. Common.

T. TENEBROSUS. *Mont. p.* 303.—*Turt. D. p.* 197.
—*F. p.* 298.—*D. p.* 817.—*Dor. Cat. p.* 49. *t.* 18. *f.*
15.—Strong, short, conic, nearly as broad as long,
dark chocolate with five ventricose spires, the body
whorl occupying about half the length of the shell,
apex obtusely pointed; aperture suborbicular; outer
lip thin, dark purplish brown within. ⅓. *Kent, Dover,
not uncommon.*

* T. FABALIS. *Turton. Z. J.* 2. *p.* 366. *t.* 12. *f.* 10.
—*F. p.* 298.—Subglobular, very obtuse, smooth, with
three hardly produced volutions, chesnut with obscure
pale bands (often covered with a grey coat which conceals the markings and color); bands about twelve,
apparently interrupted so as to give the surface a
chequered appearance; pillar and throat chesnut.
0,09. *Scarborough.*

T. CASTANEA. *Gmel.—D. p.* 836.—T. HIPPO-
CASTANUM. *Lam.*—T. MAMIMILLATUS. *Don. t.* 174.
—*F. p.* 299.—*Lin. T.* 8. *p.* 166.—*Mont. Sup.p.* 126.
—Whorls five, slightly rounded, pale chesnut, spirally
striated with raised dots, a few ridges of larger ones
giving the shell an angulated appearance; length and
breadth subequal; aperture rounded. 0,80. *Scilly
Isles.—A doubtful native.*

T. CRASSIOR. *Mont.p.* 309. *and Sup. p.* 127. *t.* 20.
f. I.—*D. d.* 820.—*Lin. T.* 8. *p.* 159.—*Walk. t.* 2. *f.*
34.—*F. p.* 299.—T. PALLIDUS. *Don. t.* 178. *f.* 4.—
LACUNA C. *Turt. Z. J.* 3. *p.* 192:—Conoid, thick,

---

* In all probability the fry of the preceding or of
some other species of this genus.

opaque, under a pale brown much wrinkled epidermis polished opaque milk white; whorls tumid and deeply divided, the last subcarinated at the base; the outer lip joining the body nearly at right angles ½...½. *Kent.*

T. Quadrifasciatus. *Mont. p.* 328. *t.* 20. *f.* 7.— *F. p.* 299.—*Lin. T.* 8. *p.* 167.—*D. p.* 845.—Lacuna Q. *Turt. in Z. J.* 3. *p.* 191.—Conical, spirally striated, glossy, yellowish horn-colored, with four ochraceous bands (sometimes faint and nearly obliterated) the body-whorl slightly carinated at the base ; spire somewhat produced ; pillar flattened, with a small groove ending in an umbilicus ; operculum membranceous, smooth, yellowish. 0,30. *On sea weeds, a little beyond low water mark, common.*

T. Vinctus. *Mont. p.* 307. *t.* 20. *f.* 3.—*Lin. T.* 8. *p.* 167.—*D. p.* 844.—Lacuna V. *Turt. in Z. J.* 3. *p.* 192.—Oblong-conical, smooth, with six rounded whorls and the summit rather obtuse, subpellucid, rufous horn-color with four purplish or chesnut brown bands (which rarely unite into two larger ones) ; aperture suborbicular, the outer lip very thin, the inner thick, furnished with a narrow channel (which however is more dilated than in the last) terminating in a small umbilicus; body whorl not carinated. ⅛. *Devon, on Algæ.*

T Armatus. *D. p.* 829. *(young.)*—T. Calcar. *Mont. Sup. p.* 137. *t.* 29. *f.* 3.—*Ch. f.* 1786,7.— Delphinula C. *F. p.* 312.—Whorls four, the upper ones depressed and forming a flat summit; pale pink, round, with large smooth lanceolate spines, radiating in straight lines from the body ˉand part of the second whorls, about thirteen in number; base convex, with a central cavity; · aperture orbicular. ⅓. *Iona.— Possibly a young Rugosus.*

T. Decussatus. *Mont. p.* 322. *t.* 12. *f.* 4.—*F. p.* 299.—*An* T. Pellucidus. *Lin. T.* 3. *p.* 66. *t.* 13. *f.* 33,4.?—T. Arenaria. *D. p.* 839.—Subpellucid, somewhat glossy, white, the apex not very pointed; whorls five, rounded, well defined, strongly striated longitudinally and decussated by extremely fine striæ; aperture suboval, contracted above, outer lip thin, inner lip not spreading. ⅛...0,012.· *Salcomb Bay, rare.*

T. Margarita. *Lowe. in Z. J.* 2. *p.* 107. *t.* 5. *f.* 10,11.—*F. p.* 299.—Helix M. *Mont. Sup. p.* 143. —*Wern. Mem.* 1, *p.* 408. *t.* 8. *f.* 5.—Margarita

H.

Vulgaris. *Leach. fide. Sow. in Malac. Mag.*—Whorls four, rapidly increasing, the body whorl very large, smooth, glossy, greenish, sometimes with one rufous spiral band (when bleached brownish white); pillar cavity wide; rounded, the spire short and blunt; aperture suborbicular, nacreous, outer lip thin and prominent retrally, where it joins the body nearly at right angles, pillar lip reflected; operculum finely striated spirally. ⅛...⅜. *On fuci, not very uncommon.*

T. Carneus. *Lowe. in Z. J. 2. p. 107. t. 5. f. 12,3.*—Margarita C. *Sow. in Malac. Mag. p. 25.* —*Sow. Conch. Il. f. 9.*—Subconical, the spire short, apex elevated and acute; whorls four, girt with regular elevated rather distant striæ; aperture large, suborbicular, anteriorly subangulated; umbilicus large and deep, *Scotland (Oban.)*

T. Subcarinatus.—Helix S. *Mont. p. 438. t. 7. f. 9.*—Cingula S. *F. p. 305.*—Trochus Rugosus. *Brown. in Wern. Mem. 2. p. 520. t. 24. f. 5.*—Subpellucid, white, finely striated longitudinally, whorls three, the last large, the others small but little produced and placed somewhat laterally; body whorl with two spiral ridges at the base and another near the suture; umbilicus wide and deep, aperture oval, outer lip

projecting considerably, inner reflected and spreading
into a sharp angle elevated on the body whorl. *Base*
0,010. *Devon.*

T. Nivosus. *Mont. p.* 326.—*F. p.* 300.—*Lin. T.*
8. *p.* 163.—*D. p.* 889.—Smooth, glossy, white, rather
slender and tapering to an obtuse point; whorls five or
six, much rounded and deeply divided by the suture;
aperture suboval; inner lip and columella quite smooth
and even ; imperforated. 0,077....0,025. *S. Devon,*
very rare.

T. Neritoides. *Ch.f.*1684.—*An* T. Neritoides.
Lam. 27.?—T. Retusus. *Lam.* 28.—*Blain. Faun.*
Franc. t. 12. *f.* 6.—Nerita Littoralis. *Lin.* 1253.
—*List. t.* 607. *f.* 39, 40, 41, 42, 44.—*Lis. An. Ang.*
t. 3. *f.* 11, 12, 13.—*Knorr.* 6. *t.* 23. *f.* 8.—*Pen.* 4. *p.*
141. *t.* 87. *f.* 143.—*D. p.* 989.—*F. p.* 318.—*Da.*
Cos. t. 3. *f.* 13 *to* 16.—*Don. t.* 20. *f.* 2.—*Lin. T.* 8.
t. 5. *f.* 15.—*Dor. Cat. p.* 57. *t:* 16. *f.* 15 *to* 16. *and*
t. 20. *f.* 2,3.—*Mont. p.* 467.—Semiorbicular, thick,
strong, smooth, plain light or orange yellow red or
brown, sometimes prettily mottled or chequered brown,
or yellow and white and rarely banded ; whorls four or
five, the body whorl very large, the rest small and
lateral (sometimes quite flat, sometimes rather produced)

H 2.

the suture indistinct; aperture suborbicular, sublunated, sometimes inclining to oval, margin thickened within, edge acute, pillar lip somewhat spreading, flattish. *Common.*

GENUS.—ODOSTOMIA. FLEMING.

Conical, aperture ovate, peristome incomplete above, and furnished with a tooth on the pillar.

O. UNIDENTATA. *F. p.* 310.—TURBO U. *Mont. p.* 324. *t.* 21. *f.* 2.—VOLUTA U. *Lin. T.* 8. *p.* 131.— *D. p.* 508.—Conic, strong, smooth, glossy, subpellucid, white, the apex rather obtuse; whorls five or six, not much raised; aperture suboval, outer lip plain; pillar with one tooth near the middle. 0,20....0,09. *Not common, Margate, Salcomb Bay.*

O. PLICATA. *F. p.* 310.—TURBO P. *Mont. p.* 325. —VOLUTA P. *Lin. T.* 8. *p.* 131.—*D. p.* 509.—Strong, conic, smooth, glossy, subpellucid, white, usually tinged with purple or pink at the tip, with rather an obtuse apex; whorls five or six, not much raised; aperture suboval; outer lip plain; pillar with one tooth near the middle. 0,20...0,083. *Devon, rare.—General appearance of Cing. Ullvæ.*

O. SPIRALIS. *F. p.* 310.—TURBO S. *Mont. p.* 322.

t. 12. *f.* 9. *(Walk. t.* 2. *f.* 46.*)*—Voluta S. *Lin. T.*
8. *p.* 130.—*D. p.* 508.—Pellucid, conic, glossy, white ;
whorls four or five, nearly flat, the body marked with
spiral ridges half way from the base, the rest finely
ribbed longitudinally ; suture with a very fine spiral
ridge, apex rather obtuse ; aperture suborbicular, pillar
lip turning inwards and forming an apparent small
denticle or plait which runs spirally some way up the
columella. 0,08...0,040. *Salcomb Bay, Devon.*

O. Interstincta. *F. p.* 310.—Turbo I. *Adams.*
in Lin. T. 3. *p.* 66. *t.* 13. *f.* 23,4.—*Mont.* 324. *t.* 12.
f. 10.—Voluta I. *Lin. T.* 8. *p.* 131.—*D. p.* 509.—
Glossy, white, tapering, with five rather flat, but finely
ribbed volutions, the suture fine, the apex obtuse ; aperture suboval ; pillar lip a little reflected, with a single
small tooth. 0,08...0,022. *Very rare, Devon.*

O. Insculpta. *F. p.* 310.—Turbo I. *Mont. Sup.*
p. 129.—Voluta I. *D. p.* 509.—Subpellucid, white,
tapering, the apex obtusely pointed ; whorls six,
rounded and regularly striated spirally ; aperture subovate ; pillar lip a little reflected, with a small cavity
behind. ⅛. *Devon, rare.*

O. Sandvicensis. *F. p.* 310.—" The three spired

elegantly reticulated Turbo with a one toothed oval aperture." *From Sandwich, rare.—Walk.* 15, *t.* 2. *f.* 55.

Genus.—CINGULA.

Aperture with the peristome complete, being united above.

* *Outer lip thickened by a rib.*

C. Cimex. *F. p.* 305.—Turbo C. *Lin.* 1233.— *Mont. p.* 315.—*Lin. T.* 8. *p.* 161.—*Dor. Cat. p.* 49. *t.* 14. *f.* 69.—*Don. t.* 2. *f.* 1.—T. Cancellatus. *Da. Cost. p.* 104. *t.* 8, *f.* 6,9.—With four strong, conic, cancellated, white, well defined volutions, the decussating striæ so coarse as to cause the interstices to appear deeply punctured ; apex rather obtuse ; aperture suboval, margin thick, outer lip crenated internally. ⅛...0,55. *Kent, not uncommon, Devon and Cornwall, rare.*

C. Calathisca. *F p.* 305.—Turbo C. *Mont. Sup. p.* 132. *t.* 30. *f.* 5.—*D. p.* 821.—Brown, conical ; whorls six, with numerous longitudinal and spiral ribs, the pits formed by whose intersection are more numerous than in the preceding species, forming eight rows on the body whorl and four in the next, outer lip denticulated within. ⅛. *Rare, W. Scotland & England.*

C. STRIATULA. *F. p.* 305,—TURBO S. *Mont. p.*
306. *t.* 10. *f.* 5.—*D. p.* 857,—*An. Lin.* 1238.?—*Lin.*
T. 8. *p.* 172.—*Dor. Cat. p.* 50. *t.* 14. *f.* 10.—*T.*
CARINATUS. *Da. Cost. p.* 50. *t.* 14. *f.* 10.—Whorls
four or five, flat above, white (semipellucid when recent)
rather strong, base wrought with fine spiral striæ, which
towards the upper part rise into three distant elevated
membranaceous ridges, the furrows deep and rounded at
the bottom; strongly striated longitudinally from top to
base (chiefly conspicuous in the interstices); apex not
very pointed; aperture suborbicular, angulated above,
marginated. 0,20...0,17. *Kent, Cornwall, not common.*

C. COSTATA. *F. p.* 305.—TURBO C. *Adams in Lin.*
T. 3. *p.* 65. *t.* 13. *f.* 13,4.—*Mont. p.* 311. *t,* 10. *f.* 6.
—*D. p.* 860.—*Lin. T.* 8. *p.* 174.—*Walk. f.* 47.—*T.*
CRASSUS. *Adams Micr. t.* 14. *f.* 20.—Strong, subpellucid, glossy, white, with four or five much raised and
well defined volutions, furnished with strong ribs
which terminate on the body whorl in a strong spiral
rib, and finely striated transversely (the striæ most conspicuous in the interstices); apex rather obtuse; aperture suborbicular, lip a little expanded, a groove behind
it extending behind the pillar to the aperture. 0,20...
0,05. *Devon, Dorset, Pembrokeshire, (in drift sand)
not uncommon, in Scotland rare.*

C. PARVA. *F. p.* 306.—*Da Cos. p.* 104,—TURBO
P. *Mont. p.* 310.—*D. p.* 857.—*(Walk. t.* 2. *f.* 43.)
Lin. T. 8. *p.* 171.—*Dor. Cat. p.* 50. *t.* 19. *f.* 4.—
T. LACTEUS. *Don. t.* 90.—T. ÆREUS. *Lin. T.* 3. *p.*
66. *t.* 13. *f.* 29 *and* 30.—Strong, conical, coarsely
ribbed longitudinally, variable in coloring, being glossy
white, dark chesnut or pale rufous (sometimes variegated, or dark with the ribs white); ribs strong and distant, from nine to eleven on the body whorl; aperture
suborbicular, outer lip strengthened by a rib. ⅜. *Common in drift sand, Kent, Devon, &c. &c.*

C. MARGINATA. *F. p.* 306.—TURBO M. *Mont.*
Sup. p. 128.—*Wern. Mem.* 1. *p.* 406. *t.* 8. *f.* 13.—
T. ARCUATUS. *D. p.* 859.—Subcylindrical, white,
·stroug, finely striated spirally; the whorls six, with
about as many longitudinal ribs which become obsolete
at the suture; aperture patulous. ⅜., *breadth* ¼. *less.*
Guernsey and Dunbar, rare.

C. CONIFERA. *F. p.* 306.—TURBO C. *Mont. p.*
314. *t.* 15. *f.* 2.—*D. p.* 859.—*Lin. T.* 8. *p.* 173.—
Dor. Cat. p. 50. *t.* 19. *f.* 6.—Strong, taper, white,
the apex rather obtuse; whorls six, each with about
twelve longitudinal undulated ribs, interrupted only by
a fine suture, the interstices at the top of the whorls

formed iuto small cavities (giving the shell a denticulated appearance) the ribs crost by most minute spiral
striæ; aperture oval oblique, strongly marginated,
pillar lip not reflected. ½...0,08. *Weymouth, rare.*

C. DENTICULATA. *F. p.* 306.—TURBO D. *Mont.
p.* 315.—*D. p.* 859.—*Lin. T.* 8. *p.* 173.—Conic,
subpellucid, white, the apex obtuse; whorls six. each
with nine or ten coarse ribs projecting at the top of each
spire and forming indentations as in the last; aperture
suborbicular, outer lip thickened by a rib, pillar lip
smooth and indented, with one or two small tubercles
at the base adjoining the ribs. 0,22...0,11. *Weymouth.*
—*The ribs are not undulated as in the preceding, but
run obliquely to the left.*

C. SEMICOSTATA. *F. p.* 307.—TURBO S. *Mont. p.*
326. *and Sup. p.* 129. *t.* 21. *f.* 5.—*D. p.* 837.—
Lin. T. 8. *p.* 162.—T. ELEGANS. *Lin. T.* 3. *p.* 66. *t.*
13. *f.* 31,2.— Short, conic, white, obtusely pointed;
whorls four or five, rounded and well defined; wrought
with faint ribs and fine obsolete transverse striæ on the
body whorl, the ribs not extending to the lower part
where the striæ are most conspicuous; aperture suborbicular, pillar lip slightly reflected.   0,04...0,08. *I*a
sand, Devon.

H 3.

C. BRYEREA. *F, p.* 307.—TURBO B. *Mont. p.* 313. *t.* 15. *f.* 8.—*D. p.* 858.—*Lin. T.* 8. *p.* 172.—*Dor. Cat. p.* 50, *t.* 19, *f.* 7.—Strong, conic, glossy, white; whorls seven, well defined, somewhat rounded, smooth, but longitudinally ribbed; ribs seventeen or eighteen, all but contiguous; aperture oval; outer lip strong, pillar lip replicate, smooth.—Variety, with stronger and fewer ribs (not above twelve.) 0,22. *Weymouth.*

C. STRIATA. *F. p.* 307.—TURBO S. *Adams. Lin. T.* 3. *p.* 66 *t.* 13. *f.* 25,6.—*Mont. p.* 312.—*Lin. T.* 8. *p.* 173.—*D. p.* 859—*(Walk. t.* 2. *f.* 49.)—Strong, Subpellucid, glossy, white; whorls four or five, well defined, much raised, furnished with strong longitudinal ribs and spiral striæ which are chiefly conspicuous in the interstices, apex rather obtuse; aperture suborbicular, lip a little expanded, bordered by a strong sulcated rim, a ridge rises at the upper angle of the aperture, and runs transversely backward, then turns downward and joins the margin of the lip behind, this ridge is bordered above by a fine depressed line where the longitudinal ribs terminate. ⅛...0,04. *Not rare, Dorset, &c., &c.*

C. DISJUNCTA. *F. p.* 307.—TURBO D. *Mont. Sup. p.* 128.—*Wern Mem.* 1. *p.* 405. *t.* 8. *f.* 3.—*Turt.*

D, p. 219.—Rather slender, pointed, white, quite smooth; whorls six, much swollen, divided by a very broad and deep band, which is flat at the bottom or concave in a slight degree and not angular as in most other shells, giving the whorls the appearance of being disunited ; aperture suborbicular, pillar lip reflected with a perforation behind it. 0,20...0,07. *Scotland, rare.*

** *Outer lip not thickened by a rib.*

C. Labiosa. *F. p.* 307.—Turbo L. *Mont. p.* 400. *t.* 13. *f.* 7.—*Lin. T.* 8. *p.* 164.—*Dor. Cat. p.* 149. *t.* 18. *f.* 16.—*D. p.* 840.—T. Membranaceus. *Adams. in Lin. T.* 5. *p.* 2. *t.* 1. *f.* 14,5.—*Turt. D. p.* 203.— Somewhat conic, tapering to rather a fine point, pale horn-colored, sometimes with oblique obscure brown lines, semitransparent, usually purple at the tip; whorls six or seven, slightly rounded, well defined. with from fifteen to eighteen longitudinal more or less distinct and rounded ribs on the two last but one volutions, and on the upper part of the body whorl, smooth elsewhere; mouth glossy, oval, dilated, equal to half the length of the shell, rounded below; lip expanded, thin, a little reflected; pillar lip spread ; columella within undulated and forming a slight eleva- tion. ⅓...0,08. *Common.*

C. VENTRICOSA. *F. p.* 307.—TURBO VENTROSA. *Mont. p.* 317. *t.* 12. *f.* 13.—*D. p.* 840.—*Lin. T.* 8. *p.* 164.—*Dor. Cat. p.* 49. *t.* 18. *f.* 12*a.*—T. EBUR-NEUS. *Adams. t.* 14. *f.* 15.—*Walk. f.* 36.—Smooth, glossy, thin, with six much rounded whorls, light pellucid horn-colored (appearing black when the animal is present); apex moderately pointed; aperture suborbicular, closed by a thin wrinkled corneous operculum, margin almost entire the whole way round. $\frac{1}{8}$...0,04. *Kent, &c.*

C. AURICULARIS. *F. p.* 307.—TURBO A: *Mont. p.* 308.—*D. p.* 844.—*Lin. T.* 8. *p.* 166.—Conic, smooth, subpellucid, light horn-colored; whorls five, much rounded and deeply divided by the suture; apex moderately pointed and usually darker; aperture suboval or ear-shaped; outer lip thin; inner much reflected, forming an angle about the middle behind which is a narrow umbilicus. $\frac{3}{8}$...0,217. *Southampton.*

C. ULVÆ. *F. p.* 308.—TURBO U. *Pen. p.* 132. *t.* 86. *f.* 120.—*Mont. p.* 318.—*Da Cos. p.* 105.—*D. p.* 840.—*Lin. T.* 8. *p.* 104.—*Dor. Cat. p.* 49. *t.* 18. *f.* 12.—Opaque, dark or rufous brown, the apex moderately pointed; whorls five to seven, nearly flat, the suture small; aperture suboval, inner lip reflected on the pillar, forming a slight depression but not an umbilicus; operculum corneous, rayed with arched striæ from the inner margin. *Up to ⅝...⅞. On Ulvæ and mud, about highwater mark, common but local, rare on open coasts.*

C. SUBUMBILICATA. *F. p.* 308.—TURBO S. *Mont. p.* 316.—*D. p.* 841.—*Lin. T.* 8. *p.* 165.—*Dor. Cat. p.* 50. *t.* 18. *f.* 12*b.*—Smooth, rather glossy, conical, the apex rather obtuse ; whorls four or five, very tumid, the body whorl occupying above half of the shell ; aperture oval, outer lip even, inner a little reflected, forming a subumbilicus. ⅛...0,06. *Weymouth.—Differs from Ventrosus in the aperture not being contracted above and in the greater proportional width of the base, from Ulvæ, in the whorls being more tumid and in its umbilicus.*

C. INTERRUPTA. *F. p.* 308.—TURBO T. *Adams. in Lin. T.* 3. *t.* 1. *f.* 16,7.—*Mont. p.* 329.—*Lin. T.* 8. *p.* 166.—*D. p.* 841.—*An. Don. t.* 178. *f.* 2.?— Conic, pellucid, glossy, white with interrupted longitudinal ochraceous streaks, chiefly on the two basal whorls and frequently forming two rows of oblong spots on the body ; whorls five, not much rounded, the apex moderately pointed ; aperture suborbicular, outer lip not very thin, inner reflexed. ⅛...0,04. *Devon and Cornwall, common at Margate in drift sand.*

C. Rubra. *F, p.* 308.—Turbo R. *Adams. Lin. T.*
3. *p.* 66. *t.* 13. *f.* 21.—*Mont. p.* 320.—*D. p.* 838.—
Lin. T. 8. *p.* 162.—Pellucid, smooth, glossy, reddish
brown (also very rarely white); suture fine, apex
pointed; whorls five, rounded; aperture suborbicular,
a little reflected on the pillar. ⅓. *or more, breadth
scarcely one-third its length.—Cornwall, &c.*

C. Vitrea. *F. p.* 308.—Turbo V. *Mont. p.* 321.
t. 12. *f.* 3.—*D. p.* 838.—Helix V. *Lin. T.* 8. *p.* 213
—Thin, pellucid, white, smooth, slender, subcylindrical; whorls four, the suture deep, apex rather obtuse;
aperture suboval, contracted above, outer lip thin, inner
slightly thickened. ⅓..0,043. *Whitsand Bay, Cornwall.*

C. Unifasciata. *F. p.* 309.—Tubbo U. *Mont. p.*
327. *t.* 20. *f.* 6 —*D. p.* 839.—*Lin. T.* 8. *p.* 163.—
Smooth, conic, white, with one (or rarely two) purplish brown bands on the body whorl; whorls five,
very little raised and divided only by a small line;
outer lip thin and somewhat expanded, the inner
spreading on the columella; imperforate. ⅓...0,05.
*Southampton and Devon, rare.—If there be two bands
they occupy no larger space than the single would.*

C. Cingilla. *F. p.* 309.—Turbo C. *Mont. p.* 328.

t. 12. *f.* 7.—*D. p.* 841.—*Lin. T.* 8. *p.* 165.—T. TIT-
TATUS. *Don. t.* 178. *f.* 1.—T. GRAPHICUS. *Turt. D.
p.* 200. *f.* 34.—*Brown, Wern. Mem.* 2. *p.* 521. *t.* 24.
f. 6.—Conic, subpellucid, obscurely striated, except at
the base where the striæ are strong; whorls six, horn-
colored with chesnut brown bands (usually three on the
body and two on the other whorls); apex uniform brown
and moderately pointed; aperture suboval, contracted
above; outer lip thin and not expanded, inner slightly
thickened; imperforate. ⅜ .,0,04. *Plymouth and
Salcomb.*

C. ALBA. *F. p.* 309.—TURBO A. *Adams. Lin.* 3. *p.*
66. *t.* 13. *f.* 17,8.—Whorls six, not much rounded,
smooth, glossy, subpellucid, pale brown or with brown
spiral bands; about sixteen longitudinal rounded and
slightly waved ribs on the body whorl; aperture suborbicular; pillar lip a little reflected, outer lip thin.
0,10. *Common on Roots of Fuci.*

C. SEMISTRIATA. *F. p.* 309.—TURBO S. *Mont.
Sup. p.* 136.—*D. p.* 842.—Conical, the apex obtuse,
white; whorls five or six, rounded, well defined, smooth
in the middle, striated spirally above and below, the striæ
extending to the body whorl as far as the junction of
the lip; aperture subovate, angulated above. ¼...0,20.
Southern coast of Devon,

C. DISPAR. *F. p.* 309.—TURBO D. *Mont. Lin. T.*
11. *p.* 195. *t.* 13. *f.* 4 —Grey, striated spirally,
wrinkled obliquely; whorls four, the body one large
and subcarinated at the base, the rest small, and usually
worn; aperture suborbicular, dark purple with a single
white band near the lower extremity. ¼...0,20. *Poole.*

C. RUPESTRIS.—RISSOA R. *Forbes. in Annals. Nat.
His.* 5. *t.* 2. *f.* 13.—Translucent, white with seven flat
whorls which are almost smooth; round the summit of
each runs a spiral striæ which gives a marginated
appearance to the suture; body whorl slightly carinated
and spirally striated below the carination, a few obsolete
striæ sometimes appear above; mouth pear-shaped, not
margined; pillar lip broad and slightly replicated.
0,20. *Isle of Man.*

C. HARVEYI.—RISSOA. H. *Thompson. Annal. Nat.
His.* 5. *p.* 97. *t.* 2. *f.* 11.—Oblong, obtuse, white,
whorls angulated above, concave in the middle, longitudinally ribbed; ribs twenty-four on each whorl, angulated both above and below; the body whorl girt below
with three transverse elevated belts, apex obtuse, whorls
four or five; aperture scarely angulated above, lip
simple. 0,17. *Clare, Ireland.—Allied to Excavata
of Philippi.*

C. TRISTRIATA.—RISSOA T. *Thompson. Annals. Nat. His. 5. t. 2. f.* 10.-- Conic, volutions five and a half, rounded, smooth, with spiral rows of tawny spots; body whorl very large; aperture roundish oval; no umbilicus; three striæ wind round the summit of each whorl. ½. *Youghal, Ireland.*

C. BALLIÆ.—RISSOA B. *Thompson Annals. Nat. His. 5. t. 2. f.* 9.—Elongated, white, apex obtuse, five slightly rounded whorls, deeply marked longitudinally with somewhat distant striæ; aperture ovate, margin of the mouth thin, base of the body whorl spirally striated. ½. *Youghal, Ireland.—Not unlike Odos. Spiralis.*

C. PALLIDA.—TURBO P. *Mont. t.* 21. *f.* 4. *p.* 325. —PHASIANELLA P. *F. p.* 302.—Smooth, white, rather slender in shape, with six or seven whorls tapering to a moderately fine apex; whorls not much raised but separated by a well defined suture; aperture suborbicular, outer lip arcuated, a faint duplicature on the pillar lip forming a small umbilicus. ½...0,04. *Rare, Salcomb Bay, in sand.*

GENUS.—PHASIANELLA

Oval or conical, solid, aperture entire, oval, longer than broad, the margins disunited above, the right lip

*sharp and not reflected. columella smooth, attenu-
ated at the base.*

* *Acalcareous or horny operculum.*

P. PULLUS.—TURBO P. *Lin.* 1232.—*Lam. p.* 31.
—*D. p.* 822.—*Born. t.* 12.*f.* 17,18.—*Don. t.* 2. *f.* 2.
to 6.—*Mont. p.* 319.—*Dor. Cat. p.* 49. *t.* 14. *f.* 1.
to 3.—TURBO PICTUS. *Da Cost. t.* 8. *f.* 1. *to* 3.—
CINGULA P. *F. p.* 308.—Ovate, smooth, glossy, with
four or five rounded volutions, the body whorl forming nearly half the shell, the apex rather obtuse;
coloring extremely variable, always more or less,
streaked, spotted or lineated and generally pink or
purple, with dark undulated lines or spotted with white
(sometimes purplish brown with white spots); aperture
suborbicular or large; operculum strong and calcareous.
⅜. *Common on S. Coast.*

P. STYLIFERA. *Turt. Z. J.* 2. *p:* 367. *t.* 13. *f.* 11.
—VELUTINA S. *F. p.* 326.—Oval, yellowish horn-
color, becoming rufous on the pillar side, transparent,
quite smooth; volutions five, the two lower very tumid,
the three upper abruptly minute; aperture suborbicular,

---

* Except in Stylifera, which is only placed in this
Genus pro tempore.

the margin disunited at the top and very thin ; no operculum. 0,08. *Torbay, on spines of Echinus Esculentus.*

GENUS.—EULIMA. Risso.

*Elongated, subulate, smooth, polished, often inflected
or distorted and often presenting flattened con-
tinuous varices, the base always devoid of cleft or
umbilicus; aperture oval-oblong, rounded below,
terminating above in an acute angle ; pillar simple,
narrow, short and arcuated, right lip slightly thickened, simple and obtuse.*

E. Polita. *Deshayes in Lam.* 8. *p.* 453.—Turbo
P. *Lin.* 1241.—*D. p.* 881.—Helix P. *Mont. p.* 398.
—*Dor. Cat. p.* 51. *t.* 19. *f.* 15.—T. Levis. *Pen.* 4.
p. 130. *t.* 79. *upper fig.*—T. Albus, *Don. t.* 177.—
E. Anglica. *Sow. Conc. Il. f.* 5.—Phasianella P.
F. p. 301.—Elongated, turrited, solid, ivory white,
perfectly smooth, extremely glossy ; whorls narrow,
flattened, contiguous, apex very pointed ; aperture very
small, ovate, acuminated above. ¼,...0,20. *Cornwall,
Devon and Dorset, rare.*

E. Decussata.—Helix D. *Mont. p* 399.—Phasi-
anell. D. *F. p.* 302.—Slender, white with eight for
nine whorls which are very slightly raised and strongly
and regularly striated longitudinally, decussated by very

minute striæ, suture fine, apex acute, aperture narrow, suboval, contracted at both ends; outer lip somewhat expanded and a little thickened at the back, inner lip very slightly reflected. 0,30....0,10. *Weymouth, very rare.*

E. Subulata. *Desh. in Lam. p.* 455.—Turbo S. *Don. t.* 172.—*D. p.* 881.—Helix S. *Mont. Sup. p.* 142.—*Dor. Cat. p.* 55. *t.* 19. *f.* 14.—E. Lineata. *Sow. Conc. Ill. f.* 13.—Phasianella S. *F. p.* 301. --Subulate, very narrow, smooth, polished white with two narrow spiral yellowish brown bands at the base of each whorl; suture indistinct, whorls nearly flat; aperture lengthened, rounded below, contracted above, outer lip nearly straight. 0,60. *England and Scotland, rare.*

Genus.—TURRITELLA.

Turrited, not pearly; aperture rounded, entire, margins disunited above, the outer lip with a sinus; operculum horny.

T. Terebra, *F. p.* 302. *(not Lam. 1.)*—Turbo T. *Lin.* 1239. *in part.*—*Pen.* 4. *p.* 130. *t.* 81. *f.* 13.— *Mont. p.* 293.—*List. t.* 591. *f.* 57.—*An. Martini. f.* 1425.?—*D. p.* 871.—*Don. t.* 22. *f.* 2.—*Dor. Cat. p.* 51. *t.* 15. *f.* 5, 6,—*(Da Cos. t.* 7. *f.* 5,6.)—*List. An. Ang. t.* 3. *f.* 8.—About sixteen scarcely convex whorls, terminating in a fine point and girt with numerous raised spiral striæ, of which three are usually more prominent, reddish or purplish brown (often light and variegated with darker shades); aperture orbicular (subquadrangular in the young), outer lip round and thin, pillar lip nearly straight. 1⅛. *breadth at base* ⅝. *Devonshire.*

* T. BICINGULATA. *Lam—*T. EXOLETA. *Fl.—List. t.* 592. *f.* 60.—TURBO CINCTUS. *Don. t.* 22.—*Da Cos. t.* 7.*f.* 8.—*Mont. p.* 295.— Turreted, very finely striated transversely, marbled with brown white and rufous, whorls convex, with two broad prominent rounded transverse belts. 2. *Lincolnshire and Lancashire, (fide Da Costa.) a doubtful species.*

T. ELEGANTISSIMA. *F.p.*303.—TURBO E. *Mont. p.* 298. *t.* 10.*f.* 2.—*D.p.*856.—*Lin. T.*8.*p.*209—*(Walk. f.* 39.*)*—TURBO ACUTUS. *Don. t.* 179. *f.* 1.—Glossy, semipellucid, white, with from nine to fifteen flat spires well defined by the separating line and terminating in

* T Duplicata. *(F. p.* 308.—*Lam.* 1.—Turbo. D of Linnean writers) rests on too doubtful authority as a native species, to be inserted in our catalogue.

a fine point ; with regular equidistant, slightly oblique longitudinal furrows which are moderately deep but not not so broad as the corresponding ridges ; aperture suborbicular, a little angulated both above and below, the inner lip somewhat reflected. ¼...0,06. *Kent, Cornwall, Devon, &c.*

T. UNICA. *F. p.* 303.—TURBO U. *Mont. p.* 299. *t.* 12. *f.* 2 —*D. p.* 860.—*(Walk. f.* 40.)—*Lin. T.* 8. *p.* 174.—*T.* ALBIDUS. *Adams. t.* 14. *f.* 17.—Glossy, pellucid, white, with nine whorls which terminating in a fine point are rounded, separated by a deep suture and wrought with fine longitudinal somewhat undulated ridges or striæ, whose interstices are extremely delicately and transversely striated ; aperture suborbicular inclining to oval. 0,20. *Sandwich.*

T. SIMILLIMA. *F. p.* 303.—TURBO S. *Mont. Sup. p.* 136.—*D. p.* 856.—*Wern. Mem.* 1. *p.* 406. *t.* 8. *f.* 15.—White, slender, with eight slightly elevated whorls adorned with fourteen distant ridges parallel with the axis of the shell and narrower than the interstices ; aperture subovate. ⅜. *Jura.*

T. NITIDISSIMA. *F. p.* 304.—TURBO N. *Mont p.* 299. *t.* 12. *f.* 1.—With nine extremely slender smooth pellucid white spires, terminating in a fine point; whorls greatly raised and much rounded, suture deep; aperture suborbicular, inner lip a little reflected. ⅛. *Falmouth, in sand, very rare.*

T. INDISTINCTA. *F. p.* 304.—TURBO I. *Mont. Sup. p.* 129.—*D. p.* 860.—Glossy brown, with darker spiral bands, the suture deep; whorls eight, flattened, with numerous waved longitudinal ridges which are wanting on the lower part of the body whorl, where the spiral striæ are most conspicuous, these last occupy only the interstices and those but faintly. 0,20...0,09. *Sandwich and Loch Broom, Scotland; rare.*

T. CARILATULA. *F. p.* 304.—*(Walk. t.* 11. *f.* 44.) —T. SUBARCUATUS. *Lin. T.* 3. *p.* 66. *t.* 13. *f.* 27,8. Whorls seven to ten, bent towards the apex, with numerous longitudinal ribs; aperture contracted and marginated. *England.—An obscure species.*

T. FULVOCINCTA. *Thompson Annals Nat. His.* 5. *p.* 98.—With about eleven whorls, transversely ribbed, spirally striated, whitish with a single fulvous band winding round the volutions. *Nearly* 0,33. *Near Dublin.*

ZOOPHAGA.

*Shell spiral and enveloping ; aperture either canalicu-
lated or notched.*

TRIBE.--CANALIFERA.

*With a longer or shorter canal at the base of the
aperture; the outer lip not changing its form by
age.*

GENUS.—CERITHIUM.

*Turreted ; the aperture oblong, oblique, terminated at
. its base by a short canal which is either truncated
or recurved, never notched; a groove at the upper
part of the right lip; a small horny, orbicular
operculum.*

C. COSTATUM. *F. p.* 357.—STROMBIFORMIS C.
Da Cos. p. 118. *t.* 8. *f.* 14.—STROMBUS C. *Don. t.*
94.—*Mont. p.* 255.—*Lin. T.* 8. *p.* 142.—*Dor. Cat. p.*
46. *t.* 14. *f.* 14.—*D. p.* 678.—Turreted, dark brown,
with ten or eleven whorls furnished with numerous fine
close-set longitudinal ribs and an elevated spiral - line
turning round the bottom of each volution and becoming
double at the base of the shell; aperture suborbicular,
outer lip a little expanded, inner lip smooth, with a
short canal. ⅝. *Devon, Cornwall, rare.*

C. Turbiforme. *F. p.* 357.—Strombus T. *Mont.*
Sup. p. 110. *t.* 30. *f.* 7.—S. Costatus. *var. D. p.*
679.—Brown, whorls seven, well defined by the suture,
destitute of a thread-like spiral line at the base of each,
longitudinal ribs about eighteen, base smooth ; aperture
suborbicular, outer lip thickened at the margin and a
little spreading. ⅟₄...0,08. *Iona, rare.*

C. Tuberculare.—Murex T. *Mont. p.* 270
and Sup. p. 116.—*Lin. T.* 8. *p.* 150.—*D. p.* 758.—
Terebra T. *E. p* 346.—Whorls nine or ten, slender,
taper, tuberculated, chesnut brown, separated by a slight
depression, the apex pointed; aperture small, oval,
ending in a canal somewhat enclosed by the columella
turning inward. ⅟₄. *Drifted sand, Devon and Sandwich, rare.*

C. Reticulatum.—Murex R. *Mont. p.* 272.—
D. p. 758.—*Lin. T.* 8. *p.* 150.—*Dor. Cat. t.* 14. *f.*
13.—Strombiformis R. *Da Cos. p.* 117. *t.* 8. *f.* 13.
—Terebra R. *E. p.* 346.—Pale rufous brown, strong,
slender and tapering to a very fine point ; whorls eleven
or twelve, reticulated by four spiral ridges and somewhat oblique longitudinal striæ ; suture small and not
deep ; aperture oval, angulated above, contracted below
into a slight canal ; outer lip thin, base not reticulated.
⅜...⅛. *Common in Cornwall.*

I

C. Subulatum.—Murex S. *Mont. Sup. p.* 115.
t. 30. *f.* 6.—*D. p.* 759.—Terebra S. *F. p.* 347.—
Whorls fifteen, slender, little raised, defined by a purplish brown spiral line, with two spiral rows of beads
divided by a depressed line, and longitudinally striated;
base smooth, dark brown; aperture small. *Sound of*
Mull, near Scalasdale, Scotland.

C. Adversum.—Murex Adversus. *Mont. p.* 271.
D. p. 758.—*Lin. T.*8.*p.*151.—Turbo Reticulatus.
Don. t. 159.—Turbo Perversus. *Walk. t.* 11. *f.* 48.
Terebra P. *F. p.* 347.—Turbo Punctatus. *Adams.*
t. 14. *f.* 121.—Turreted, opaque, light brown; whorls
ten or eleven, depressed, reversed, tuberculated, tapering
to a fine point; three spiral rows of tubercles on each,
the middle one the smaller; aperture oval, ending in a

---

* To this Genus belongs the Turbo Tubercularis.
Pennant. 4. *p.* 129. *t.* 82. *f.* 111., which is the Murex
Fustatus of Montague and the Cerithium Granulatum
of Lamarc. I have not added it to my catalogue since
it is an African shell and rests on very doubtful authority,
as a native species. *Lister. t.* 122. *f.* 18. is a good
representation of it; Maton's M. Fuscatus. is also
foreign, and is known as Melania Matoni, Gray.

straight canal; base with two or three smooth spiral
ridges. ⅜...0,011. *Sheerness and Devon.*

GENUS.—PLEUROTOMA.

*Turreted or Fusiform; terminating below in a more or
less elongated and straight canal; outer lip with a
transverse fissure or notch near the suture.*

P. GRACILIS. *F. p.* 354.—MUREX G. *Mont. p.*
267. *and Sup. p.* 586. *t.* 15. *f.* 5.—*D. p.* 742.—*Lin.*
T. 8. *p.* 143.—*Dor. Cat. p.* 46. *t.* 14. *f.* 18.—M.
EMARGINATUS. *Don. t.* 169. *f.* 2.—Slender. tapering
to a fine point, yellowish with lighter and brown bands;
whorls little rounded, with eleven or twelve very convex,
obtuse longitudinal ribs interrupted at the suture by a
depressed spirally striated space, the spiral striæ at the
base strong and rather distant; aperture oval, canal moderately long, rather open. ⅜...¼. *Deep water, not
uncommon.*

P. SINUOSA. *F. p.* 354.—MUREX S. *Mont. p.* 264.
t. 9. *f.* 8.—*Lin. T.* 8. *p.* 145.—*D. p.* 745.—Strong,
thick, white; whorls six, tapering to a fine point, little
convex, with seven longitudinal, strong, much elevated
and arched ribs which do not extend to the fine suture,
finely and regularly striated transversely, the striæ most
conspicuous in the interstices; aperture narrow and

oblong-oval, canal short and not much contracted, at the upper angle is a deep sinus; outer lip slightly thickened by a rib. ¾...¼. *Weymouth, rare.*

P. SEPTANGULARIS. *Turton.*—MUREX S. *Mont. p.* 268. *t.* 268. *t.* 9. *f.* 5.—*Don. t.* 179. *f.* 4.—*D.p.*244. —FUSUS S. *F. p.* 350.—Tnrreted, subfusiform, strong, somewhat glossy, light purplish brown; whorls seven or eight, smooth, with seven almost uninterrupted obtuse longitudinal ridges, the interstices little concave and broad; aperture oblong oval, ending in a short canal, outer lip sharp at the edge, thickened at the back, contracted and a little indented above. ⅝...¼. *Devon and Cornwall, rare.*

P. BOOTHII.—FUSUS B. *Smith. in Tr. Wern.* 8. *t.* 1. *f.* 1.—Subfusiform, strong, deep chocolate brown; apex acute, whorls eight, rounded, closely spirally and strongly striated with numerous slightly oblique longitudinal ribs which do not cross the broad and concave suture; aperture oblong-ovate, smooth, white and furnished with two longitudinal purple belts, pillar lip with a brownish purple spot above; outer lip thick, flattened on the edge, a slightly rounded sinus above, canal short and wide. 0,69...¼. *Rothesay Bay.*

P. LINEARIS. *Turton.*—MUREX L. *Mont. p.* 261. *t.*
t. 9. *f.* 4.—*Lin. T.* 8. *p.* 148.—*D. p.* 745.—FUSUS L.
F. p. 350.—M. ELEGANS. *Don. t.* 179. *f.* 3.—Subfusiform, turreted ; whorls seven or eight, rounded, light
brown, with nine or ten ribs crossed by elevated striæ or
ridges, the summits of which are purplish brown and
form fine spiral thread-like lines (the ridges are rarely
uniform brown) up to the acute and dark (usually purple) apex; aperture oval, terminating in a straight
canal, outer lip thickened at the back by a rib, inner
margin crenated. ⅜...⅜. *Devon and Cornwall.*

P. CHORDULA. *Turton.*—MUREX C. *Turt. D. p.*
350.—FUSUS C. *F. p.* 350.—Conic, brown, a little
tapering to a rather obtuse point; whorls five; rounded,
the body occupying more than half the length ; spirally
striated and adorned with fifteen wire-like contiguous
ribs which bend in the middle towards the outer lip ;
aperture narrow oval, ending in a short canal; outer
lip thickened externally by a rib. 0,17...0,06. *Drifted
sand, Dublin Bay.*

P. TREVELLIANUM. *Turton. in Mag. Nat. Hist.*
7. *p.* 350.—*Macg. Aberd. p.* 172.—Oval, fusiform,
yellowish white, with six or seven volutions which are
very closely striated and flattened at their tops ; mouth

ovate-oblong, lip thin, canal rather short. *Scarborough.*
*—Extremely like Fusus Turricula but is more inflated,
the striæ twice as many, and has a distinct notch at
the upper angle of the outer lip.*

P. SMITHII. *Forbes in Annals Nat. Hist. 5. p.* 107.
t. 2. f. 14.—Fusiform, turreted, when magnified seems
most delicately striated, yellowish white with numerous
spiral bands of yellowish brown; whorls eight, slightly
rounded, slightly angulated above, with twelve strong
longitudinal ribs, sutures deep ; aperture oblong lanceolate, much shorter than the spire, lip thickened by a
rib, canal short and slightly inclined. 0,40. *Arran.*

P. COARCTATA. *Forbes Annals Nat. His. 5. t. 2.
f.* 15. *p.* 107.—Dusky white, with obscure rufous spiral
bands, narrow fusiform, strong, spirally striated ; whorls
seven, slightly rounded, with seven strong longitudinal
ribs ; aperture narrow lanceolate, beak moderate. 0,40.
*Arran.—Narrower than the last, and the mouth and
beak longer and much more attenuated.*

P. DECUSSATA. *Macgyl. Aber. p.* 172.—Elongated, fusiform, rather thick, yellowish white, with the
spire tapering to a fine point ; suture distinct ; whorls
rounded, with longitudinal ribs narrower than their

interstices, and numerous spiral thin laminæ traversing the interstices and decussating the ribs on which they form small oblong tubercles; mouth ovate oblong, the canal very oblique and elongated. ⅓. *Aberdeen.*

P. RETICULATA. *Brown. Illus. t.* 38. *f.* 43,4.— *Macgyl. Aber. p.* 173.—Oblong-fusiform, thin, dull white, with the spire tapering to a rather obtuse point, and somewhat convex in outline, with numerous longitudinal narrow ribs dividing on the body (whose breadth is rather less than the length of the spire) into several raised lines, and all reticulated with transverse raised lines; whorls slightly subangulated above, the space between the angle and the distinct suture convex and sloping; mouth oblong, narrow, deeply sinuated at the suture, lip thin, canal very short. 0,17...0,50. *Aberdeen, &c.*

GENUS.—FUSUS.

Fusiform or subfusiform, canaliculated at the base, ventricose below or in the middle, without varices ; spire elevated and elongated ; outer lip not notched; pillar smooth ; operculum horny.

* *Whorls destitute of longitudinal ribs.*

F. Antiquus. *Lam.* 11.—*F. p.* 348.—*Mac. Ab. p.*
168.—Murex A. *Lin.* 1222.—*D. p.* 724.—*Mart. f.*
1292. *and* 1294.—*List. t.* 913. *f.* 4.—*List. An. Ang.*
t. 3. *f.* 1.—*Don. t.* 31.—*(Da Cos. t.* 6. *f.* 4.)—*Dor.*
Cat. t. 17. *f.* 4.—M. Despecius. *Pen.* 4. *p.* 124. *t.*
78.—*Mont. p.* 256.—Ovate-fusiform, ventricose, whitish (reddish when young) faintly striated transversely ;
whorls very convex, seven or eight, apex pointed ;
aperture suboval, patulous; outer lip plain, tail short ;
inside yellowish. 5. *Common.*

T. Corneus. *F: p.* 348.—*Mac. Ab. p.* 169.—
Murex C. *Lin.* 1224.—*List. t.* 913. *f.* 5.—*List. An.*
t. 3. *f.* 4.—*Pen.* 4. *p.* 124. *t.* 76. *f.* 99.—*D. p.* 733.
—*Don. t.* 38.—*Mont. p.* 258.—*Dor. Cat. p.* 47. *t.* 17.
f. 5 —*(Da Cos. t.* 6. *f.* 5.)—F. Islandicus. *Lam.* 15.
—Fusiform-turreted, strong, white, transversely striated ;
whorls rounded, eight, the suture deep ; aperture oblong
oval ; epidermis brownish. 2. *N. Coast, Dorset.*

F. Carinatus. *Lam.* 13.—Murex C. *Pen.* 4. *p.*
77. *f.* 96.—*Don. t.* 19.—*Turt. D. f.* 95. *p.* 88.—F.
Despectus. *F. p.* 348.—Strong, oval, dull yellowish
white ; whorls seven, the first very inflected and covering
more than half the shell, faintly striated transversely,
the upper part of each somewhat sloping to the next,

thus distinctly defining the whorls; the four first volutions with two distinct elevated ridges winding round
the middle which gradually disappear in the smaller
ones; aperture wide oval, ending in a slightly reflected
open canal; inside pale yellowish white, outer lip very
thin, inner lip spread. 3...1½. *Dublin Bay, rare.*

F. RETROVERSUS. *Fleming in Wern. Mem. 4. p.*
498. t. 15 f. 2.—F. p. 349.—Whorls five, sinistral,
transparent, rounded, increasing rapidly (giving the
shell a bellied appearance) smooth and glossy; aperture
oblong, outer lip joining the body whorl at an acute
angle ; pillar straight, slightly scooped out at the apex
for the canal, which is shallow regular and short; lines
of growth scarcely perceptible. 0,08. *Zetland.*

* *Whorls with longitudinal ribs.*

F. TURRICOLA. *F. p.* 349.—MUREX T. *Mont. p.*
262. *t.* 9. *f.* 1.—*D. p.* 744.—*Lin. T.* 8. *p.* 144.—*Dor.*
Cat. p: 47. *t.* 14. *f.* 15.—PLEUR T. *Blainv. Faun.*
Franc.—Macg. p. 171.—M. ANGULATUS. *Don. t.*
156.—Turreted, white and somewhat glossy, the apex
acute ; whorls seven, tapering, rather depressed, and flat
at the top, ribbed longitudinally, striated transversely,

suture strong; aperture narrow-oblong, ending in a broad canal. ¼...¼, *Kent.*

F. BUCHANENSIS. *Macg. Aberd. p.* 170.—Fusiform, rather thick, dull grey, the spire tapering to a small nipple-shaped point; whorls six, moderately convex, with prominent obtuse strong ribs (the last with twelve, the two first glossy pale brown and devoid of them) separated by wider concavities and nodulose by the decussations of strong spiral dusky raised lines; suture distinct; mouth narrow-oblong, nearly half the length of the shell; canal narrow moderate and straight, lip thickened by a rib and crenated. ¼...0,08. *Aberdeen,* *Allied to P. Smithii. and F. Linearis.*

F. PROXIMUS. *F. p.* 349.—MRUEX P. *Mont Sup.* 118. *t.* 30. *f.* 8.—*D. p.* 744.—White, with longitudinal ribs, the whorls six, slightly compressed, flattened near the deeply dividing suture, destitute of spiral striæ; aperture ovate-oblong, ending in a short canal, which spreads somewhat at the termination; outer lip remarkably broad and reflected. 0,80. *Dunbar.*

F. COSTATUS. *F. p.* 349.—MUREX C. *Pen.* 4. *p.* 125.—*Don. t.* 91.—*Mont. p.* 265.—*D. p.* 743.— *Lin. T.* 8. *p.* 144.—*Dor. Cat. p.* 46. *t.* 14. *f.* 4.—

BUCCINUM C. *Da Cos. p.* 128. *t.* 8. *f.* 4.—Subfusi-form-turreted, variable in color, being chocolate or partly mixed with white, yellowish white with fine spiral brown streaks or pale dead uniform white; whorls six, tapering, with nine elevated longitudinal ribs, otherwise smooth, often glossy; aperture narrow, canal scarcely contracted and nearly straight; outer lip usually thickened with an external rib, its edge acute; inner lip but slightly replicated. 0,30...⅓. *S. Wales, Devon, Cornwall.*

F. ATTENUATUS. *F. p.* 350.—MUREX A. *Mont. p.* 266. *t.* 9. *f.* 6.—*Lin. T.* 8. *p.* 143.—*D. p.* 742.— Most slenderly fusiform, uniform yellowish white, the suture very fine; whorls scarcely raised, eight, tapering to a fine point, destitute of striæ, with nine equidistant strong longitudinal ribs which are arched or undulated as they rise in the middle of each volution; aperture narrow, contracting a little at the canal, which is moderately long and nearly straight; outer lip thickened at the back by a rib; inner lip plain. ⅓...0,014. *Devonshire, very rare.*

F. NEBULA. *F. p.* 350.—MUREX N. *Mont. p.* 267. *t.* 15. *f.* 6.—*Lin. T.* 8. *p.* 143.—*Dor. Cat. p.* 46. *t.* 14. *f.* 16.—*D. p.* 743.—PLEUROTOMA N. *Blainv.*

Faun. Franc.—Turreted, subfusiform, variable in colour, yellowish white, purplish brown or rufous, rarely blush colour with the decussated striæ white, suture very fine, apex acute; whorls eight, scarcely elevated between the longitudinal ribs, slightly but elegantly reticulated; aperture narrow, oblong-oval, ending in a canal turning a little on one side; outer lip sharp, the inner replicate smooth and glossy. ½...0,20. *Devon, not common.*

F. Rufus. *F. p.* 350.—Murex R. *Mont. p.* 263. —*Lin. T.* 8. *p.* 145.—*D. p.* 744.—Slenderly fusiform, pale rufous brown or chesnut; whorls six, tapering, adorned with fifteen or sixteen small longitudinal ribs, striated spirally; aperture narrow-oblong, ending in a short canal; outer lip smooth, rarely thickened by a rib, pillar lip smooth. 0,30...½. *Margate, Sandwich, Devon, Dorset, Wales.*

F. Minimus. *F. p.* 350.—Buccinum M. *Mont. p.* 247. *t.* 8. *f.* 2.—*Lin. T.* 8. *p,* 139.—*D. p.* 639.— B. Brunneum. *Don. t.* 179, *f,* 2.—Turreted, subfusi-form, strong, varying from light to dark chesnut brown, whorls five, with ten much elevated longitudinal ribs decussated by transverse striæ: aperture oval, outer lip twisted internally; canal short and straight. 0,20...0,10 *Devon, rare.*

F. Accinctus. *F. p.* 350.—Murex A. *Mont. Sup. p:* 114.—*Laskey Wern. Mem.* 1. *p.* 402. *t.* 8. *f.* 14. —Yellowish white with an obsolete brown band (consisting of four colored lines) on the middle of the body whorl continuing to the apex; whorls seven, finely striated spirally, adorned with longitudinal ribs which are highest and bent in the middle; aperture oblong, canal short. $\frac{1}{3}$...0,08. *Frith of Forth, rare.*

F. Gyrinus. *F. p.* 351.—Murex G. *Mont. Sup. p.* 170.—*Laskey Wern. Mem. p.* 401. *t.* 8. *f.* 10.— Brown, strong, short, conic, and tumid; whorls four, with numerous spiral rows of brown tubercles (eight on the body whorl three on the succeeding.) $\frac{1}{4}$....$\frac{1}{8}$. *Frith of Forth.*

F. Purpureus. *F, p:* 351.—Murex P. *Mont. p.* 260. *t.* 9. *f.* 3.—*Lin. T.* 8. *p.* 148.—*D. p.* 745.— Fusiform, dark purple with sometimes a few spots or blotches of white; whorls nine or ten, rounded and tapering to an extremely fine point, furnished with nineteen or twenty slightly oblique ribs decussated by numerous sharp elevated ridges which render the shell extremely rough and almost cancellated; aperture narrow, oval, terminating in a straight canal; outer lip thin, margin white and crenated by the striæ;

pillar obliquely striated and somewhat tuberculated.
½...¼. *Devon, rare.*

F. MURICATUS. *F. p.* 351.—MUREX M. *Mont.*
p. 262. *t.* 9. *f.* 2.—*Lin. T.* 8. *p.* 149.—*D. p.* 746.—
Fusiform, strong, white or flesh-colored under a red
epidermis, the smooth apex acute; whorls seven, tapering,
ventricose, seemingly tuberculated from the numerous
longitudinal ribs being decussated by the strong elevated spiral striæ; aperture oval, terminating in a long
slender canal which together rather exceed the length
of the shell, outer lip sharp and dentated at the edge,
the margin crenulated within. ½...¼. *Salcomb Bay,
Dorset, rare.*

F. BARVICENSIS. *F. p.* 351.—*Johnston in Edinb.
Phil. J.* 13. *p.* 221.—Ventricose, white ; whorls six,
armed with longitudinal furbelowed ribs (thirteen on
the body whorl) which are continued obliquely across
a flattened space at the suture in elevated striæ, and terminate on the rather long beak, which is slightly
ascending and smooth at the extremities; aperture
round inclining to oval, with the lips smooth. ½...¼.
Berwick.

F. BAMFIUS. *F. p.* 351.—MUREX B. *Don. t.* 169.

f. 1.—*Mont. Sup. p.* 117.—*Lin. T.* 8. *p.* 149.—*D. p.* 742.—PLEUROTOMA B. *Macg. Aber. p.* 171.— Whorls six, rounded, white or rufous, with numerous longitudinal plaits which in young shells are raised and sharp especially at the suture, sometimes with indistinct spiral ridges; aperture rounded, the inner lip concave, the outer rounded, base attenuated, canal produced and bent slightly to the left. ¾...⅜. *Sandy Bays.*

F. FENESTRATUS. *Turton. Mag. Nat. His.* 7.— Oblong-fusiform, ivory white, with numerous longitudinal ribs which are reticulated by transverse striæ; volutions eight, swollen; the tail produced, a little turned to the left; mouth white, smooth; the tip papillary. 1¼...⅜. *Cork.—In shape resembling Corneus, but the whorls are much more rounded and deeply divided, the tail not so elongated, the reticulations rather coarse and slightly granular.*

F. NORWEGICUS. *Turton Mag. N.H.* 7.—STROMBUS N. *Ch. f.* 1497,8.—*Gmel.* 3520.—*D. p.* 675.—Quite smooth, ivory white; volutions six, rather flat, the lower one ventricose; aperture twice as long as the rest of the shell and pure white; outer lip much dilated and smooth on the inner margin, the edge sharp and slightly reflected; pillar smooth. 5...2. *Scarborough.*

F. Turtoni. *Bean. Mag. N. H.* 1. *p.* 493. *f.* 61.—
Fusiform, white under a brown epidermis, covered with
slightly elevated spiral lines which are broader than the
intervening spaces and crossed by numerous lines of
growth; whorls nine, a little elevated in the middle, from
which they gradually slope to the separating line; aperture pale violet, ovate, nearly equal in length to the
spire; canal wide and short; outer lip a little dilated
and very thick; inner lip smooth, glossy and much
spread on the pillar. 4½...2. *Scarborough.*

Genus.—PYRULA.

*Subpyriform, canaliculated at the base, ventricose
above, no varices; spire short, sometimes almost
retuse; pillar smooth; outer lip not notched.*

P. Carica. *Lam.* 2.—*F. p.* 347.—Murex C. *Gmel.*
3545.—*D. p.* 722. —*Mart. f.* 744. *&* 756,7.—*Knorr.*
1. *t.* 30. *f.* 1. *&* 6. *t.* 27. *f.* 1.—*Turt. D. p.* 86. *f.* 26.
—Pyramidal, thick, dull reddish grey with a few chocolate brown longitudinal markings near the inner lip,
irregularly striated and somewhat scaly lengthways;
about the canal are a few transverse striæ, on which
there is a broad raised rather oblique rounded protuberance; whorls six, hardly raised, armed above with a
row of pointed protuberances which on the body whorl
become large, triangular and concave, upper whorls

finely striated spirally ; mouth equal to four-fifth's of
the shell, triangular, inside polished white, lip broad
and thin, 6...4. *N. Ireland, most rare.*

GENUS.—TRICHOTROPIS. SOWERBY.

*Ovate-fusiform, with the apex pointed ; the aperture
ovate, with a short oblique narrow canal, the outer
lip thin and denticulated, the inner reflexed but
leaving exposed a rather large umbilical groove.*

T. UMBILICATUS. *Macgy. Aberd. p.* 330.—FUSUS
U. *Brown in Wern. Mem.* 8. *p.* 98. *t.* 1. *f.* 2.—TR.
ACUMINATUS. *Malac. Mag.—Annals Nat, H.* 8.—
Ovate-turreted, white or reddish white, with fine deeply
impressed oblique striæ ; whorls convex, seven, obliquely flattened above, longitudinally marked with fine
but deep striæ and spirally with compressed rounded
strong ribs, six or seven on the very large and ventricose
body whorl, between each pair of which is a smaller
and three small ones near the distinct suture ; spire
slender; aperture ovate, broader behind, canal very
small and oblique, inner lip reflexed but not concealing
the umbilicus from which a groove extends nearly to
the canal. 0,58...¼. *Aberdeen, &c.*

GENUS.—MUREX.
Oval or oblong, canaliculated at the base; with external

*rough, spinous, or tuberculated varices ; aperture
rounded or oval ; varices at least three, the lower
uniting obliquely with the upper in longitudinal
series ; a horny operculum.*

M. ERINACEUS. *Lin.* 1216.—*D. p.* 690.—*Lam.* 48.
—*Macgy. Aber. p.* 168.—*Knorr.* 4. *t.* 23. *f.* 3.—
Born. t. 11. *f.* 3,4.—*Pen.* 4. *p.* 123. *t.* 76. *f.* 95.—
Don. t. 35.—*Mont. p.* 259.—*Dor. Cat. t.* 14. *f.* 7.—
(Da Cos. t. 8. *f.* 7.)—TRITON E. *F. p.* 356.—Oval-
oblong, rough, strong, angulated, dirty white or brownish,
with seven or eight produced and contabulated whorls,
the apex pointed ; whorls with six or seven rugged prominent varices, crossed by transverse elevated striæ, the
whole shell (when not worn) imbricated by small
arched scales ; aperture oval, canal tubular, outer lip
thickened by a rib, inner edge dentated.   1¾...0,80.
Common.

TRIBE.—ALATA.

*With a longer or shorter canal at the base of the aper-
ture ; outer lip changing its form by age and sinuated below.*

GENUS.—ROSTELLARIA.

*Fusiform or subturreted, terminating below in a beaked
canal ; outer lip dentated or entire, more or less*

*dilated and winged by age and having a sinus con-
tiguous to the canal.*

R. Pes. Pelecani. *Lam.* 5.—*F. p.* 359.—*Macgy.
Aber. p.* 173.—Strombus P. *Lin.* 1207.—*D. p.* 656.
—*Mart. f.* 848,9,0—*List. t.* 865. *f.* 20—*Knorr.* 3—.
t. 7. *f.* 4.—*Pen.* 4. *p.* 122. *t.* 75. *f.* 94.—*Don. t.* 4.
Mont. p. 253.—*Dor. Cat. p.* 46. *t.* 15. *f.* 7.—Aporr-
hais Quadriferus. *Da. Cost. p.* 136. *t.* 7. *f.* 7.—
Turreted, reddish grey, with ten ribbed or rather tuberculated whorls, on the body whorl are two rows of
smaller tubercles beneath the larger ones; outer lip
much expanded, digitations three, acute, divaricate;
basal canal oblique and subfoliated. 1...0,33. *Devon,
Dorset, Scotland.*

Tribe.—PURPURIFERA.

*Base of the aperture with either a short posteriorly
ascending canal, or an oblique semi-canaliculated
notch, directed backwards.*

Genus.—CASSIS.

*Inflated; aperture longitudinal, narrow, terminated
at the base by a short canal, abruptly reflected
backwards; pillar with transverse plaits or wrinkles,
outer lip often dentated.*

C. Bilineata. *Flem. p.* 339.—Buccinum B.

212

Mont. p. 244.—B. DECUSSATUM. *Pen.* 4. *t.* 79. *lower figs.*—B. PORCATUM. *Pult. Dor. p.* 41.—*List. t.* 998. *f.* 63.—Glossy brown with spiral bands of brown spots; whorls five or six, the upper part set round with two series of tubercles; outer lip slightly toothed, pillar lip rugged and granular. 1 to 2. *Weymouth, Dunbar, Plymouth Sound, rare.—I have copied this description from Fleming as I have never met with an authenticated specimen in a British cabinet ; he further adds " in the specimen sent me, the whorls have numerous fine waved spiral striæ." It is certainly a young shell and not improbably the adult is the common W. Indian Testiculus.*

GENUS.--PURPURA.

Ovate, either smooth, tuberculated or angular ; aperture dilated, terminating below in an oblique, sub-canaliculated emargination ; columella flattened, terminating acutely below.

P. LAPILLUS. *Lam.* 30.—*F. p.* 341.—*Macg. Aber. p.* 166.—BUCCINUM L. 1202.—*D. p.* 613.—*Mart. f.* 1111,2,3,4. *and* 1128,9.—*List. t.* 965. *f.* 18,9.— *Knorr.* 6. *t.* 29. *f.* 4.—*Pen.* 4. *p.* 118. *t.* 72. *f.* 89.— *Don. t.* 11.—*Mont. p.* 239.—*Dor. Cat. p.* 44. *t.* 15. *f.* 1,2,3,4,9,12.—*Da Cos. t.* 7. *f.* 1,2,3,4,9,12.—Ovate acute, whitish often banded with brown or yellow, thick, often nearly smooth, often with strong spiral striæ and longitudinal fine elevated membranaceous ones; apex small and pointed; aperture oval, outer lip thick, toothed (but not always) internally. 2 ..1. *Extremely common and excessively variable.*

Genus.—DOLIUM.

Thin, ventricose, inflated, usually subglobose, rarely oblong, with transverse belts ; the outer lip dentated or crenulated its entire length ; aperture longitudinal, emarginated at the base.

D. Perdix. *Lam. 7.—F. p.* 342.—Buccinum P. *Lin.* 1197.—*D. p.* 583.—*Mart. f.* 1078.—*List. t.* 984. *f.* 71.—*Knorr.* 3. *t.* 8. *f.* 1.—*Mont. p.* 244. *t.* 8. *f.* 5. —*Dor. Cat. p.* 44. *t.* 15. *f.* 14.—*Pult. Dor. p.* 41.— Suboval, with five or six volutions, the body whorl very large and tumid, the others small in proportion, marked with flat transverse ridges which are broader than the interstices, yellowish brown, marbled and spotted with white ; aperture large and oval, the outer lip thin and plain, inner lip a little umbilicated. 1., *but the foreign specimens infinitely larger. Weymouth.*

Genus.—BUCCINUM.

Oval, or oval conical ; aperture longitudinal, base notched, no canal ; pillar not flattened, turgid above.

B. Undatum. *Lin.* 1204. *—D. p.* 633. *--Lam.* 1.—
Macgy. Aber. p. 162.—*Mart. f.* 1206,7,8,9,0.—*List.*
t. 962. *f.* 14,15.—*Knorr.* 4. *t.* 19. *f.* 1.—*List. An.*
Ang. t. 3. *f.* 2,3.—*Pen.* 4. *p.* 121. *f.* 90.—*Mont. p.*
237.—*Don. t.* 104.—*Dor: Cat. p.* 45. *t.* 17. *f.* 6.—
(Da Cos. t. 6. *f.* 6.)—*F. p.* 342.—*Variety,* B. Striatum. *Pen. t.* 74. *f.* 91.—*Reversed variety, Born. t.* 9.
f. 14,15.—*Ch. f.* 892,3.—*Variety, with an elevated*
circular rib at the top of each whorl.—B. Carinatum.
Turt. D. p. 13. *t.* 26. *f.* 94.—*F. p.* 343.—Ovate-
conic, ventricose, with seven or eight rounded whorls,
whitish, tinged more or less with red yellow or brown,
(when young somewhat variegated) transversely grooved
and striated, undulately ribbed obliquely coarsely and
longitudinally, and decussated by very fine longitudinal
striæ; aperture white or yellow, smooth within. 3¼.
Common Whelk.

B. Donovani. *Gray in Beechey Zoology.*—B. Gla-
ciale. *Don. t.* 154. *(not Lin. nor Lam.) Mont. Sup.*
p. 109.—*Lin. T.* 8. *p.* 136.—*F. p.* 343.—Whorls nine,
tapering, obsoletely striated spirally, finely striated longitudinally, white with a reddish tinge, the upper whorls
with longitudinal waved furrows, the body whorl with a
spiral ridge. 2...0,84. *Zetland and Orkney, very*
rare.

B. Humphreysianum.*Bennet in Z. J.* l. *p.*898. *t.*
23.—*An List. t.* 963.*f.* 17.—B. Anglicanum. *F. p.*
343.—Ovate-conical, thin, horn-colored, with eight
convex whorls, closely and finely striated transversely;
striæ slightly waved and crossed by very minute longitudinal lines, dirty flesh-colored (the body whorl frequently
adorned with three double bands of brown irregularly
spotted with white); pillar smooth and white; aperture
horn-colored, the lip white, slightly thickened and reflected at the margin; canal very short with a slight
tinge of violet behind it. 2...1. *Cork, rare.*

B. Ovum. *Turton in Z. J.* 2. *t.* 13.*f.* 9.—*F. p.* 343.
—Oval, inflated, thin, ivory white, smooth; whorls six,
and tumid, the spire very short in proportion; outer lip
thin and short. 1¾...1. *Plymouth, very rare.*

B. Acuminatum. *Brod. in Z. J.* 5. *p.* 44. *t.* 3.*f.*
1,2.—Conical, subulate, tapering gradually from the
angle of the body whorl to the acuminated apex, white
or brownish white; whorls ten, tinged with elevated
striæ, which together with those which are intermediate
and less elevated have a granular appearance; epidermis
brown; mouth milk white with the edge of the tip a
little reflected and the pillar strongly marked with one
plait in the advanced stage of growth; basal furrow
deep, canal large. 4,70....2. *Torquay.*

B. Fusiforme. *Brod. Z.J.5. t.3. f.3. p.*45—Ovate-oblong, fusiform, white ; whorls seven, ventricose, with numerous longitudinal subgranulose ribs, crossed by frequent transverse striæ. The ribs cease upon the lower part of the body whorl, leaving the base simply striated transversely; pillar smooth. 1½...⅝. *Cork, rare.*

B. Lineatum. *Da Cos. p.* 130. *t.* 8. *f.* 5.—*Don. t.* 15.—*Mont. p.* 245.—*Lin. T.* 8. *p.* 136.—*Dor. Cat. p.* 45. *t.* 15. *f.* 5.—*D. p.* 626.—*Mart. f.* 1186. *to* 9. —*F. p.* 344.—B. Pediculare. *Lam.* 49.—Minute, strong, conic, smooth, with five or six volutions, regularly banded with alternate lines of dark chocolate brown and white (sometimes white with the dark lines irregular in their distance) ; apex sharp and pointed; aperture oval, outer lip a little spreading, smooth within. ¼...⅜. *Dorset, Devon, rare.*

B. Pictum. *F. p.* 344.—Purpra P. *Turt. in. Z. J.* 2. *p.* 365. *t.* 13. *f.* 8.—Oblong conical, glossy, whitish with ochraceous blotches usually disposed in a reticulated manner; whorls eight, decussated ; aperture not quite half the length of the shell, outer lip smooth. 0,40...0,17. *British Channel.*

B. Hepaticum. *Pult. Dor. p.* 41.—*Mont. t.* 243.

t. 8. *f.* I.—*Dor. Cat. p.* 44. *t.* 15. *f.* 13.—*Lin. T.* 8. *p.* 135.—*D. p.* 605.—Oblong-conical, strong, brownish or olive brown, with seven or eight rather tumid, strongly divided whorls, somewhat glossy, with numerous longitudinal ribs which near the suture, are so divided by a spiral line or depression as to form small knobs; a few spiral striæ at the base, apex sharp; outer lip thick, denticulated or striated internally, inner lip with a pad above. 1...⅞. *Rare, Purbeck and Weymouth.*

B. RETICULATUM. *Lin.* 1204.—*D. p.* 637.—*Lam.* 14.—*List. t.* 966. *f.* 21.—*Mart. f.* 1162,3.—*Born. t.* 9. *f.* 16.—*Pen.* 4. *p.* 122. *t.* 72. *f.* 92.—*Don. t.* 76. —*Mont. p.* 240.—*Dor. Cat. p.* 45. *t.* 15. *f.* 10.—*D. p.* 637.—NASSA R. *F p.* 340.—Oblong-conical, variable in coloring, more or less tinged with ashy brown; whorls seven or eight, tapering to a point, wrinkled with transverse elevated striæ and obtuse broad longitudinal ribs; aperture suboval; outer lip not margined, denticulated within; inner lip replicated, glossy white, sometimes faintly crenated.—Variety, lip not denticulated. *Up to* 1¼...¾. *usually* 1...½., *very common.*

B. MACULA. *Mont. p.* 241. *t.* 8. *f.* 4.—*Lin. T.* 8. *p.* 138. *t.* 4. *f.* 4.—*Dor. Cat. p.* 45 .*t.* 15. *f.* 8.—*D. p.* 638.—B. MINUTUM. *Pen.* 4. *p.* 122. *t.* 79.—

K.

B. COCCINELLA. *Lam.* 45.—NASSA INCRASSATA. *F. p.* 340.—*Macg. Ab. p.* 165.—*Variety with a varix,* TRITONIA VARICOSA. *Turt. in Z. J.* 2 *t.* 8. *f.* 4.— Oblong-conical, whorls six or seven, apex pointed; with longitudinal ribs and transverse striæ, variable in colouring, being mottled rufous, brown and white, pale lilac, uniform rufous; aperture suborbicular; outer lip gibbous on the back, denticulated within; inner lip replicated and finely denticulated; base of the canal with a constant small brown spot. ½...¼. *Common, not unlike the preceding species.*

B. AMBIGUUM. *Pult. Dor. p.* 42.—*Mont. p.* 242. *t.* 9. *f.* 7.—*Lin. T.* 8. *p.* 138. *t.* 4. *f.* 5.—*Blain. Faun. Franc. p.* 178.—*Dor. Cat. p.* 45. *t.* 18. *f.* 19. —*D. p.* 638.—NASSA A. *F. p.* 340.—Subconic, short, thick, strong, white; whorls six, finely striated and armed with distant longitudinal ribs which swell into knobs at the sutures; aperture suborbicular, outer lip thickened by the rib and slightly denticulated, inner lip replicated, with generally two faint distant folds 0,58. ...¾. *Weymouth, Portland, Poole, rare.*

B. CINCTUM. *Mont. p.* 246. *t.* 15. *f.* 1.—*Lin. T.* 8. *p.* 139.—*D. p.* 639.—*Dor. Cat. p.* 45. *t.* 14. *f.* 17. —Nassa C. *F. p.* 340. Oblong-conical, subfusiform white with rufous spiral lines in the middle of each whorl; whorls six or seven, nearly even, strongly striated transversely at the base, finely and closely ribbed longitudinally and obsoletely striated in the interstices spirally; apex sharp; aperture narrow and oval; outer lip thickened with a broad external rib and denticulated within, at its base near the end is a small rufous spot and another at the upper angle of the aperture, from these two obsolete broken lines gird the base of the shell. ‡ *Weymouth, very rare.*

B. TUBERCULATUM. *Turt. D. p.* 16.—NASSA T. *F. p.* 341.—Taper, white, but not glossy; whorls six, rounded and well defined, sculptured by numerous strong longitudinal ribs which are crossed by transverse lines, thus seeming tuberculated; aperture oval, the outer lip thin and toothed within; the inner lip strongly marked with oblique striæ and ending in a short, reflected, rather cloven canal. 0,60...0,16. *In sand, Exmouth.*

TRIBE.—COLUMELLARIA.

No canal at the base of the aperture, but a subdorsal

* Whether to consider the Voluta Hyalina of Montague as a Mitra or as a Buccinum I know not, having

*notch which is more or less distinct ; pillar furnished
with plaits.*

Genus.—MARGINELLA.

*Oval-oblong, smooth ; the spire short ; the outer lip
margined externally with a varix ; base of the aperture slightly emarginated : pillar with nearly equal
plaits.*

M. Donovani. *Payraudeau.*—Voluta Lævis. *Don.
t.* 165.—*D. p.* 527.—*Lin. T.* 8. *p.* 133.—Erato L.
Reeve. t. 285. *f.* 3.—Cypræa Voluta. *Mont. p.* 203.

---

never met with the shell in any cabinet. It is most
assuredly not a Cancellaria, which Mr. Fleming
(from whose labors I have freely drawn) has considered it
I transcribe the description from the Testacca Brittanica,
V. Hyalina. *Mont. Sup. p.* 101. *t.* 29. *f.* 5.—
Pellucid, white, smooth, tapering to an obtuse point,
with six flat volutions scarcely defined by the separating
line ; body whorl more than half the length of the shell ;
the aperture contracted, the base truncated and canaliculated ; outer lip smooth ; columella plicated with seven
or eight fine thread-like striæ that originate from behind
the pillar lip, length one quarter of an inch, breadth
more than one third its length. *Dunbar.*

t. 6. f. 7.—M. Voluta. *F. p.* 335.—Conoid, convo-- lute, whitish, polished, strong, smooth ; extreme volu- tions two, very small; aperture linear, both lips denticulated, the inner very faintly, outer lip much thickened and very white; columella subplicated. ⅛. *Devon.*

M. Catenata.—Voluta C. *Mont. p.* 236. *t.* 6. *f.* 2. *and Sup. p.* 104.—*F. p.* 332.—*Lin. T.* 8. *p.* 132. —*D. p.* 527.—Oblong-oval, strong, subpellucid, po- lished, white with four bands of articulated opaque white oblong and small rufous spots or streaks; upper volution scarcely defined, the apex indented and invo- luted: aperture the whole length of the shell, linear; outer lip thin but not marginated and obsoletely denti- culated; pillar with strong and two faint folds. ⅛...⅜. *Cornwall and Guernsey:*

Genus.—VOLVARIA.

Cylindraceous, convolute, the spire scarcely prominent ; aperture narrow, as long as the shell ; one or more plaits on the lower part of the pillar.

V. Pallida. *F. p.* 333.—Voluta P. *Lin.* 1189.— *D. p.* 527.—*List. t.* 714. *f.* 70. *left hand fig.*—*Mont. p.* 232.—Bulla Cylindracea. *Da Cos. t.* 2. *f.* 7.— B. Pallida. *Don. t.* 66.—Smooth, glossy, white, cylindric; upper volutions extremely small and scarcely defined by the suture, the apex obtuse; aperture narrow, nearly extending the entire length of the shell and spreading a little at the base; outer lip thin; pillar with four strong folds. ½...¼. *Tenby, very rare.*

Tribe.—INVOLUTA.

Shell destitute of a canal, but having the base of the aperture effuse or notched and its whorls so compressed and convolute that the last almost or entirely conceals the rest.

Genus.—OVULA.

Turgid, attenuated at each extremity, subacuminated; margins convolute; aperture longitudinal, narrow, effuse at the extremities; pillar lip toothless.

O. Patula. *Sow. in Z. J,* 4. *p.* 161.—Bulla P. *Pen.* 4. *p.* 117. *t.* 70. *f.* 85a.—*Don. t.* 143.—*Mont. p.* 207.—*Lin. T.* 8. *p.* 121.—*Dor. Cat. p.* 43. *t.* 12. *f.* 8.—*D. p.* 475.—Volva P. *F. p.* 331.—Oblong, smooth, white, pellucid, the upper end extending beyond the body, the base more extended; aperture large, terminating in a short canal at each end, most contracted at the top; columella twisted, forming a subumbilicus; outer lip plain and very acute. ¼...1. *Weymouth.*

GENUS.—CYPRÆA.

Ovate or ovate-oblong, convex, the margins involute ;
aperture longitudinal, narrow, toothed on each side,
effuse at the extremities; spire all but concealed.

C. EUROPEA. *Mont. p.* 200. *and Sup.* 88.—*Macgy.*
Aber. p. 175.—*List. An. Ang. p.* 168. *t.* 3. *f.* 17.—
List. t. 706. *f.* 57.—*D. p.* 467.—*F. p.* 330.—C.
PEDICULUS. VAR. EUROPEAN. *Lin.* 1180.—*Don. t.* 43.
—*Pen.* 4. *p.* 115. *t.* 70.*f.*82.—*Da. Cos. p.* 32. *t.*2. *f.*
6.—C. COCCINELLA. *Lam.* 66.—*Blain. Faun. Franc.*
t. 9a. f. 1.—Oval, glossy, with transverse elevated striæ
and usually intermediate smaller ones, or bifurcated,
livid flesh-coloured often with three dark spots on the
tumid back which is always devoid of a longitudinal
sulcus; outer lip and under part white.—Young, C
BULLATA. *Mont. p.* 202. *t.* 6. *f.* 1.—Pellucid, the
striæ indistinct, outer lip not thickened, the apex
slightly produced and formed into two or three convo-
lutions. *Common, Kent, &c.*

ORDER.—CEPHALOPODA.

SECTION.—POLYTHALAMIA,
Chambered Shells.

GENUS.—ORTHOCERA.
Straight or but slightly arcuated, subconical, striated

externally by numerous longitudinal ribs, chambers formed by transverse septa perforated by a tube which is either central or marginal.

O. LEGUMEN. *Lam.* 6.—*F. p.* 237.—NAUTILUS L. *Lin.* 1164.—*D. p.* 350.—*Gualt. t.* 19. *f. P.—Turt. D. p.* 121.—*(Walk. t.* 3. *f.* 74. *N)—Mont. Sup. p.* 82. *t.* 19. *f.* 6.—*Lin. T.* 8. *p.* 118.—White, smooth, glossy, transparent, somewhat flattened, a little concave on one side, without marginal ridge on either side, a little curved, slightly tapering or nearly of equal diameter at both ends, the extremes a little rounded and contracted ; joints eight or nine, divided by oblique lines, the anterior or larger end oblique and margined, with an obtuse syphon which rises above the margin and a considerable aperture near the concave side.—*Variety,* N. RECTUS. *Mont. p.* 197. *t.* 19. *f.* 4,7.—*Turt.D. p.* 121.—*Walk. f.* 74.—Straight and subcylindrical.—*Variety,* N. SUBARCUATUS. *Mont. p.* 198. *t.* 6. *f.* 5.—*Turt. D. p.* 122.—The three anterior chambers more globose than the rest. 0,12 *Margate, &c., in fine sand.*

O. COSTATA. *F. p.* 236.—NAUTILUS C. *Mont. p.* 199. *t.* 14. *f.* 5.—*D. p.* 348.—*Turt. D. p.* 122— *Lin. T.* 8. *p.* 120.—Straight, subcylindrical, with from five to twelve raised articulations which are adorned with from four to seven longitudinal ribs; aperture extended in a conic central syphon. ⅓. *Sandwich, allied to Nautilus Raphanus of Linnæus.*

O. Jugosa. *F. p.* 236.—Nautilus J. *Mont. p.* 198. *t.* 14. *f.* 4.—*Turt. D. p.* 123 —*Lin T.* 8. *p.* 119. —*An.* N. Obliquus. *Lin.?*—Opaque, brown, tapering, subcylindrical, very slightly curved, with nine somewhat globular joints marked with many longitudinal ribs; terminal joint of the smaller end produced and longer than those which are near it; aperture produced to a conic syphon. 0,16. *Kent, &c. in fine sand.*

O. Bicarinata. *F. p.* 237.—Nautilus B. *Mont. Sup. p.* 86.—*Turt: D. p.*123.—*D. p.*349.—Somewhat cylindrical, curved, tapering a little to a rounded point; joints eleven, rather globular with two slight longitudinal ribs, one along the arc, the other on the opposite side; the larger end terminating in a produced syphon. ⅜. *In fine sand.*

O. Linearis. *F. p.* 237.—Nautilus L. *Mont. Sup. p.* 87. *t.* 30. *f.* 9.—*Turt. D. p.* 123.—*D. p.* 351.— Dentalina L. *Macg. p.* 40.— Glossy white, transparent, smooth, a little flattened, linear, quite straight, of nearly equal size throughout or slightly tapering,

K 3.

furnished with faint and rather oblique ribs at the narrower end only, which disappear about half way up and are not quite regular in their size ; the smooth or upper termination produced obliquely into a syphon, the upper end rounded. 0,28. *In fine sand, near Dunbar.**

NODOSARIA.

Elongated, straight or slightly arcuated, subconical, rendered nodulous by the inflation of the chambers ; nodules quite smooth (i. e. not longitudinally ribbed) chambers numerous, rather tumid, divided by transverse septæ which are perforated either in the centre or near the margin.

N. Spinulosa,—Nautilus S. *Mont. Sup. p.* 86. *t.* 19. *f.* 5.—*Turt. D. p.* 123.—*D. p.* 349.—Orthocera S. *F. p.* 236.—Pale chesnut, with three very globular joints covered with spines which all incline to the posterior end ; upper bulb a little elongated to form

---

Closely allied to this species, if indeed distinct is the Dentalina Davidsoni. *Macg. Aberdı p.* 321.— Subarcuated, considerably tapering, somewhat compressed, marked in its whole length with transverse crenulated furrows and convex frosted ridges; of twelve somewhat oblique cells, the last much larger ; aperture small and circular ; colour hyaline. 0,16. *Aberdeen.*

syphon.—*Variety*, slightly curved and tapering with eight not so much inflated; joints, and covered with tubercles rather than spines. ⅜. *In fine sand.*

N. Radicula. *Lam.* 1.—Nautilus R. *Lin.* 1164. —*D. p.* 348.—*Mont. p.* 197. *t.* 6. *f.* 4. *& t.* 14. *f.* 6.—*Turt. D. p.*122—*Lin. T.* 8. *p.* 119—Orthocera R. *F. p.* 236.—Straight, opaque brown, the joints transverse, smooth, usually eight or nine often less, subglobose; variable in respect to the terminal joint, in some the aperture is extended to a conic point, in others it is only a small round opening on the extreme articulation which is globose; the smaller end in some is rounded, in others conic and pointed. ⅓ *Sandwich.*

Genus —SPIRULA.

Cylindrical, thin, semitransparent multilocular, partially twisted in a discoid spiral form, the whorls disunited, the last produced in a straight line; chambers transverse, equally distant, concave above, with a lateral interrupted syphon; aperture orbicular.

S. Peronii. *Lam* 1.—.S. Australis. *F. p.* 227.— *Bl. t.* 6. *f.* 1.—*E. t.* 465. *f.* 5.—Nautilus Spirula. *Lin.* 1163.—*Mart. f.* 184,5.—*D. p.* 345.—*List. t.* 550. *f.* 2.—*Gualt. t.* 9. *f. E.*—*Knorr.* 1. *t.* 2. *f.* 6.

—*Turt. D. p.* 117.—With five smooth whorls, partitions slightly depressed externally, clear white, pearly within. Diameter of the coil, ¼. *Aberdeen, Kerry, Belfast, Clare*

Genus.—SPIROLINA.

Multilocular ; the last whorl or two spiral and discoid; volutions contiguous, the last one terminating in a straight line : septa straight, perforated by a tube.

S. Subarcuatula *F. p.* 277.—Nautilus *S. Mont. Sup. p.* 80. *t.* 19. *f.* 1.—*Walk. f.* 73.—*Turt. D. p.* 121.—White, glossy, semi-transparent, with 12 joints the first four or five nearly straight and separated by oblique raised and more opaque lines ; the rest curling spirally inwards and divided by radiating lines ; the back margin furnished with a raised edge and slightly indented by the division of the joints, the front margin obtusely rounded ; aperture oblique with a small syphon at the upper point. ⅜ *In fine sand.*

S. Semilitua. *F. p.* 227.—Nautilus. *S. Lin.* 1163.—*Mont. p.* 196.—*D. p.* 346.—*Turt. D. p.* 121. —*Lin. T.* 8. *p.* 118.—*Mart. f.* 186. Opaque brown, elongated, subarcuated, chambers diminishing in size to the mouth, which is contracted, outer margin rounded, the partitions of the chambers raised on all sides ; syphon produced nearly in a line with the back. *Rare, Sandwich and Sheppy.*

S. CARINATULA. *F. p.* 277.—NAUTILUS. *C. Walk. f.* 72.—*Adams. t.* 14. *f.* 37.—*Mont. p.* 195.—*Turt. D. p.* 120. Whitish, transparent like glass, oblong, arched at the back, scarcely, if at all raised into a keel like ridge ; joints seven, regularly decreasing, the terminal one globular ; aperture linear, oval, minute. *In fine sand, Sandwich, rare.*

GENUS.—VERMICULUM. MONT.
MILLIOLA. LAM.

Transverse, ovate-globose, or elongated, multilocular ; chambers transverse, encircling the axis of each other ; aperture very small, situated at the base of the last whorl, either orbicular or oblong.

V. INTORTUM. *Mon. p.* 520.—*F. p.* 233.—*Wern. Mem.* 4. *t.* 15. *f.* 3.—*Mac. Ab. p.* 37.—MILIOLA PLANULATA. *var. B. Lam?*—SERPULA SEMINULUM. *Lin.* 1264.— *D. p.* 1070.—*Dor. Cat. t.* 19. *f.* 31.—S. OVALIS. *Lin. T.* 5. *t.* 1. *f.* 28, 29, 30.— Suboval, compressed, opaque, glossy white; compartments three or four, the interior ones varying in shape

and size, some being proportionably longer than others
(the larger and more orbicularly shaped variety has
sometimes five, one of which is extremely small' and
linear) these subvolutions defined by a depression and
wrinkled transversely ; aperture compressed, semilunar.
0,10. *Common on all sandy shores.*

V. Subrotundum. *Mont. p.* 522. *t.* 14.*f.* 9.—
Flem. Wern. Mem. 4. *p.* 565. *t.* 15. *f.* 4.—*F. p.* 233
—*Macg. Ab. p.* 36.—Serpula. *S.Turt. D. p.* 155.
Suborbicular, subcompressed, smooth, glossy, opaque
white, composed of three compartments, the middle one
elevated above the rest on the upper side, not visible
beneath : aperture small, angulated : margin in live
shells yellow. 0,4. *Not so common as the last.*

V. Bicorne.*Mont. p.* 519.—*F. p.* 234.—Serpula
B.Walk. t. 1. *f.* 2.—*Turt D. p.* 156.—*Adams. t.*14.
f. 2.—Chambers three, the middle one small, raised or
depressed, the last suboval, compressed, striated longitudinally on the longer side from the aperture : the other
side smooth : contracted towards the mouth which is
very small and orbicular. *Sandwich and Reculver.*
0,08.

V. Oblongum. *Mont. p.* 522.—*Flem. Wern. Mem.*

4. *p. 565. t.* 15. *f* 5.—*F. p.* 234.—*Macg. Ab. p.* 37.
—SERPULA O. *Walk. t.* 1. *f.* 4.—*Turt. D. p.* 155.—
Oblong, oval, opaque, glossy white, somewhat compressed ; on one side a single longitudinal suture which
seems to divide the shell into two parts; on the other
side the middle compartment is surrounded by a faint
depression, that separates it from the exterior one, and
is more elevated ; aperture a little produced, oval, the
margin yellow.   0,04...*In sand from Sulcomb Bay,
Devon, rare.*

V. DISCIFORME. *Macg. Aberd. p.* 319. Orbicular, very thin, of four arcuated flattened turns, which
are opaque, greyish or reddish white, moderately glossy,
faintly rugose, striated longitudinally the outer margined
with a bluish white keel ; on one side all the four turns
apparent, on the other, three ; aperture large, direct,
oblong or even linear ; margin parallel, rim thickish
and generally reddish brown, a medial erect tooth extending to more than half the height of the mouth.
0,08...*Aberdeen.   Differs from Intortum in its orbi-
cularity, its lesser thickness, its thinner keel and
much narrower mouth.*

V. PLANATUM. *Macg. Aberd. p.* 319.—Roundish ,
very thin, of three arcuated, much compressed, yellowish

white, rather glossy, opaque, faintly and longitudinally rugose whorls, outer margins thin but no carinate ; all the turns apparent on both sides, the last very large ; mouth large, obovate-oblong, with a slightly thickened and somewhat spreading margin and a medial erect tooth extending to two thirds its height and enlarged and emarginated at the end.   0,08. *Aberdeen.*

SPIROLOCULINA.—MACGILLIVRAY.

Suborbicular, depressed, with the cells curved and opposed to each other in a single plane, and completely exposed or not embracing each other ; the aperture roundish at one end of the last turn.

S. CONCENTRICA. *Macg. Aberd. p.* 36.—MILIOLA. C. *Brown Ill. t.* 1. *f.* 22.   Elliptic-orbicular, concave on both sides, very thin, of about five opposite arcuated cells distinctly separated by a groove ; outer cells externally flattened or slightly convex ; white generally with two brown or blackish streaks on each turn; aperture nearly square with an erect tooth-like process and thick brown margin.   0,04.   *Aberdeen.*

ARETHUSA. MONTFORT.

Cells arranged obliquely and alternately along an axis. with the mouths of all the chambers having an aspect towards the same pole; forming a subturriculated shell.

A. LACTEA. *F. p.* 234.—VERMICULUM. L. *Mont. p.* 522.—*Macg. Ab. p.* 37.—*Flem. Wern. Mem.* 4. *p.* 566. *t.* 15. *f.* 6.—SERPULA. L. *Walk: t.* 1. *f.* 5.— *Turt. D. p.* 156.—*Adams. t.* 14. *f.* 4.—Delicately transparent, with the inner walls of the chambers appearing as white veins; chambers ovate, six or seven, well defined on one side, obscure on the other, contracted towards the mouth. 0,05. *Sandwich, Zetland, Perth, Dunbar.*

GENUS.—LAGENULA. FLEMING.
Shell with a globular body, having a produced neck or tube.

L. SRIATA. *F. p.* 254.—VERMICULUM S. *Mont.*3.*p.* 523.—SERPULA LAGENA *Walk. t.* 1. *f.* 6.—*Turt. D. p.* 157.—*Adams. t.* 14. *f.* 5.—Pellucid, with opaque fine longitudinal striæ, rounded retrally, the mouth slender and produced, with a small round aperture. 0,04. *Not uncommon.*

L. PERLUCIDA. *F. p.* 235.—VERMICULUM P. *Mont. p.* 525. *t.* 14. *f.* 3.—SERPULA P. *Turt. D. p.*

157. *t*. 23.—Bottle shaped, smooth, white, transparent, glossy, with six equidistant longitudinal ribs and a small knob at the base ; neck very long, subcylindrical ; aperture extremely small. 0,09. *Seasalter.*

L. Squamosa. *F. p.* 235.—Vermiculum S. *Mont. p.* 526. *t.* 14. *f*- 4.—Serpula. S. *Turt. D. p.* 158.— Minute, subglobose, marked with undulated striæ like the scales of a fish ; aperture a little produced. *Seasalter.*

L. Globosa. *F. p.* 235.—Serpula. G. *Turt. D. p.* 157 —*Walk f.* 6.—Vermiculum G. *Mont. p.* 523.... Glossy white, transparent, somewhat oval, with a long slender neck and marked with opaque longitudinal lines ; aperture small, orbicular. 0,04. *In fine sand, rare, Sandwich.*

L. Lævis. *F. p.* 235.—*Macg. Ab. p.* 38.—Serpula L. *Turt. D. p.* 157.—*Walk. f.* 9.—Vermiculum L· *Mont. p.* 524. Bluish white, very transparent like glass, with a long cylindrical neck ; more ●blong than the last and the aperture elongated. 0,04. *In fine sand.*

L. Marginata. *F. p.* 235.—*Walk. t.* 1. *f.* 7.—

VERMICULUM M. *Mont. p.* 524.—Nearly ovate, compressed, marginated, white, transparent, glossy, mouth but little produced. *Rare, Reculver, Kent.*

L. RETICULATA. *Macg. Ab. p.* 38.—Ovate-globose considerably compressed, highly glossed, smooth, pellucid, with numerous opaque white internal reticulated markings, bounding irregular areolar spaces; internal cavity simple, the cells being only parietal; aperture terminal, rather large, oval. 0,04...0,03. *Aberdeen.*

L. URNA. *F. p.* 235.—VERMICULUM. U. *Mont. p,* 525. *t.* 14. *f.* 1.—SERPULA U. *Turt. D. p.* 158.— Glossy white, semitransparent, smooth, somewhat globular but sloping rather suddenly like an urn into a short conic neck with a slender appendage or knob at the base. 0,04. *In fine sand, Sheppy Island.*

GENUL.—LOBATULA. FLEMING.
The upper disc occupied by the last formed whorl, the portions of which radiate from the centre to the margin ; the whorls on the lower disc exposed.

L. VULGARIS. *F. p.* 232.—NAUTILUS FARCTUS. *Fichtel. t.* 9. *f. g. h. i.*—SERPULA L. *Mont. p.* 515 & *Sup. p.* 160.—NAUTILUS L *D. p.* 344.—*Adams*

f. 36.—*Walk. f.* 71.—*Turt. D. p.* 120.—Discorbis.
L. *Macg. Ab. p.* 34.—D. Vesicularis. *Blain t.* 5.
f. 3. Compressed, white or yellowish, with a frosted
appearance when much magnified, roundish or inclining
to oblong, convex above and flat beneath ; on the first
volution are six or seven lobed joints separated by faint
crescent shaped lines ; aperture extremely small. *Minute, attached to zoophytes.*

L. Concamerata. *F. p.* 233,—Serpula C. *Mont.
Sup. p.* 160. Nautilus. Dissimilis, *Turt. D. p.* 120
Suborbicular, compressed, flat beneath, slightly convex
above, subpellucid, white, with three irregular volutions,
the external having about nine glossy and tumid cells
of unequal size but usually alternating large and small.
Diam. 0,04....*Devon. Differs from the last by possessing infinitely more minute and numerous cells and
in being devoid externally of that frosted appearance
exhibited by it under the microscope.*

L. Pulchella.—Discorbis P. *Macg. Aberd. p.*
319. Orbicular, depressed, hyaline white, spiral, of
numerous rather small, somewhat oblique regular cells
in three and a half turns ; lower surface rather convex,
even, glossy ; the margin thin but rounded and very
slightly lobate ; the upper surface convex, but with a

central depression in the middle of which is a roundish knob ; the turns distinctly visible on the lower disc, although neither they nor the cells are separated by sulci ; on the upper surface which is occupied, excepting the central part, by the last turn, the cells are a little convex with slight separating depressions. 0,04. *Aberdeen.*

GENUS.—TEXTULARIA. MACGILLIVRAY.

Subpyramidal, compressed, with the summit pointed, the base rounded, having on each side an angular or sinuous grove extending from the summit to the base, and composed of two series of alternating cellules ; the aperture semi-lunar on the inner side of each cellule.

T. OBLONGA. *Macg. Aber. p.* 38. Oblong lanceolate, somewhat compressed, of two alternate vertical series of horizontal, rather convex, depressed, glossy, somewhat tuberculated olivaceous cells. 0,04...0,02. *Aberdeen.*

T. OBTUSA *Macg. Aber. p.* 321. Rather broadly oblong, reddish white, subtruncated at the base, rounded at the apex, much compressed, sloping to the margins which are thin and subcarinated,; of about sixteen alternating cellules, disposed in two series, and horizontal,

unless at the commencement or apex, where they are
vertical or radiating ; their surface convex, strongly gro-
nulated and glistening. *Aberdeen* 0,04....004.

GENUS.—ROTALIA.

*Orbicular, spiral, convex or conoid above, flattened, ra-
diated, and tuberculated beneath, multilocular ;
aperture marginal, triangular.*

R. BECCARIA. *F. p*, 232.—*Macg. Aber. p.* 35.—
NAUTILUS B. *Mont. p.* 186. *t.* 18. *f.* 4.—*Turt.
D. p.* 119.—*Dor. Cat. t.* 19. *f.* 28.—*Walk. f.* 63.—
D. p. 342.—Transparent, white or covered with a brown
skin, convex on one side and flat on the other ; spires
four or five, twisted, with ten joints in the first which
are deeply grooved ; aperture oboval *Reversed var.*
(NAUT. PERVERSUS. *Walk. f.* 64.—*Mont. p.* 187. *t.*
18. *f.* 6.) *Minute. Weymouth, Margate, &c. in
sand.*

R. INFLATA. *F. p.* 232.—NAUTILUS 1. *Mont. Sup
p.* 81. *t.* 18. *f.* 3.—*Turt, D. p.* 120. Brown, opaque,
with three volutions; in the first are three joints which
are exceedingly tumid and rounded, and so deeply divided as to appear like lobes; the aperture somewhat
globular. *Minute. In fine sand.*

Genus—POLYSTOMELLA.

*Sides equal, the last whorl embracing and concealing
the previously formed one.*

P. Crispa Lam.—*Macg. Aber. p.* 33—Nautilus
C. *Lin* 1162.—*D. p.* 341.—*Gualt. t.* 19. *f. A. D.—
Walk. f.* 65.—*Adams. t.* 14. *f.* 30.—*Mont. p.* 187.
& *Sup. t.* 18. *f.* 5.—*F. p.* 228—*Turt. D. p.* 119.—
With. lateral spires, about twenty flexuous crenated joints
in the exterior whorl, marked with elevated striæ   outer
edge carinated; interior   volutions   hidden ; aperture
clasping the body, semicordate, furnished with a small
perforation or syphon. *Kent, Dorset Devon, &c. Not
uncommon, minute.*

P. Rotata.—Nautilus R. *Maton in Lin. T.* 8. *p.*
114.—*Turt. D. p.* 118.—*D. p.* 340.—An Nautilus
C. *Lin* 1162. ?—*Mart. f.* 180—*Mont. p.* 189. *t.* 15.
f. 4. & *Sup. p.* 76.—*F. p.* 228.—Smooth. spiral, with
six joints on the body whorl, marked by as many flexuous elevated striæ radiating from the centre but not
extending quite to the margin ; back strongly carinated,
both sides equally convex, smooth and rather more
elevated in the centre; inner volutions lost after
entering the aperture, which is semicordate, clasping the

body equally on both sides and furnished with a small perforation. *Sandwich, &c. minute.*

P. LŒVIGTULA.—NAUTILUS L. *Mont. p.* 188. & *Sup. p.* 175. *t.* 18. *f.* 7, 8.—*Turt. D. p.* 118.—*D. p.* 341.—*F. p.* 228,—*Lin. T.* 8. *p.* 115. *(Walk. t.* 3. *f.* 67.—*Adams. t.* 14. *f.* 32.*)*—Glossy, smooth, the partitions marked by subelevated flexuous rays, exteriorly subcarinated, sides convex ; mouth triangular with a rim which does not clasp the body whorl ; aperture near the discal edge : chambers about ten. *England and Scotland. minute.*

D. DEPRESSULA.—*Macg. Aberd. p.* 318.—NAUTILUS D. *Mont. p.* 190. & *Sup. p.* 78. *t.* 18. *f.* 9.— *Lin. T.* 8. *p.* 115.—*Turt. D. p.* 118.—*Walk. t.* 3. *f.* 68.—*Adams. t.* 14. *f.* 63.—*D. p.* 341.—*F. p.* 228. Depressed, exteriorly rounded, the chambers and partitions nearly even, about nine, the latter slightly curved and ending at the centre in a pellucid spot. *England and Scotland. minute.*

P. UMBILICATULA. *Macg. Aberd. p.* 317.—NAUTILUS. U. *Mont. p.* 191. & *Sup. p.* 78. *t.* 18. *f.* 1.— *Turt. D. p.* 119.—*Walk. t.* 3. *f.* 69.—*F. p,* 229.—*D. p.* 343.—*Lin. t.* 8. *p.* 115.—Depressed, exteriorly

rounded, partitions sunken, flexuous, with a subtuber-
cular pellucid elevation in the centre. *Minute. Diffused
but not common.*

P. CRASSULA.—NAUTILUS. C. *Mont. Sup. p.* 79. *t.*
18. *f. 2.—Walk. t. 4. f.* 70.—*F. p.* 229.—*Turt. D.
p.* 119.—*D. p.* 343.—*Lin. T.* 8. *p.* 117.—Depressed,
umbilicated, opaque brown, with numerous close-set
joints, shewing part of the interior volution. with numerous close-set elevated joints ; sides similar ; mouth
a little oblique, scarcely clasping the body and furnished
with a syphon. *English, very rare:*

P. GUILIELMINÆ. *Macg. Aberd. p.* 315. Orbicular, disciform, greyish white, considerably compressed,
the sides equally convex, bevelled to a thin subcarinate
margin ; the cells of the last whorl about fifteen, elevated,
narrow, convex, with the concave interstices transversely
sulcated ; the centres elevated ; the end moderately
raised, semilunar, convex, with its sides embracing the
previous turn. 0,02. *Aberdeen.*

P. CRENULATA. *Macg. Aberd. p.* 316. Roundish,
discoid, pale bluish grey, the sides somewhat convex,
the margin rounded, the centres slightly depressed ; the
rays formed by the cells about twenty, curved, convex,

K

and regularly crenato-sulcate, as are their interstices, being marked with concentric grooves and ridges : end of the last cell semilunar, narrow, convex. 0,02. *Aberdeen.*

P. Nautilina. *Macg. Aberd. p.* 317. Nautiliform, with the cells somewhat convex, the margin rounded, the cells of the last whorl about ten or twelve, little convex, narrow smooth glossy but granulated towards the umbilicus which is small, the interstices depressed, curved and somewhat striated : end of the last cell large, cordate, nearly flat, with two series of pores. 0,02. *Not rare at Aberdeen.*

Genus.—NUMMULINA.

Discoid, suborbicular, depressed, with a multilocular spire, with complex walls, and arranged in the same plane ; the two surfaces convex, the margin plain.

N. Marginata. *Macg. Aberd. p.* 34.—Renoidea M. *Brown. Ill. Con. t.* 1. *f.* 25.—Suborbicular, depressed. glossy, convex on one side, conico-convex on the other ; yellowish white, with a very thin broad margin separated by a circular groove from the body of the shell ; the internal spiral tube with few volutions 0,02. *Aberdeen. Some individuals are perfectly orbicular, others less so, some with a slight angle.*

ADDENDA

AND

EMENDATIONS.

The British Dentalium Dentalis is not that described by Linnæus but is the Tarentinum of Lamarck. This conclusion is made from a comparison of Turton's specimen with the Mediterranean species.

SPIRORBIS. CONICA.—HETORODISCA. C. *Flem. Edin. Enc. t.* 205. *f.* 3.—*Fl. Ed. Phil. j. vol.* 12. *p.* 247.—Sinistral, strong, hyaline, triangular.

When young the upper part of the whorl has a distinct groove with a low acute ridge on each side and a very small central cavity. In this state the whorls are two in number, the outer one lateral with a spreading base. The third whorl in its growth not only embraces

the others but ascends and forms the outline of the shell
into a truncated cone, with the mouth at the top sublateral. The groove and central cavity are in this state
less distinct, the latter generally obliterated. *Rare.*
In deep water.

VERMILIA SERRULATA. *Elem. in Edin. Phil. J.*
vol. 12.—SERPULA. S. *Fl. in Ed. Ency.* 7. *p.* 67. *t.*
204. *f.* 8. Translucent, triangular, with a serrated
dorsal ridge; lid single, concave. with a smooth
margin.

BALANUS CRANCHII. *Leach. Enc, Brit Sup.*
Depressed, conical, very spreading at the base; valves
darker or paler purple, crowded with coarse raised
radiating striæ; aperture very small in proportion;
walls at the base, cellular. *Diam.* I. *Rare. Tenby.*

MACTRA ELLIPTICA. *Brown. Ill.—Forbes Mal.*
Mon. p. 48.—*Macg. Aber. p.* 289. Subelliptical.
very thin, yellowish white, smoothish, somewhat glossy,
with faint and very delicate concentric striæ, rather conspicuous lines of growth and slight indications of
radiating'striulæ ; umbones prominent, pointed, recurved
and nearly central : posterior slope convex, the anterior
less so and forming an obtuse angle with the arched

and ventral margin. 0,58...1. *Scotland. Isle of Man, &c. More delicate and more elongated than the young of M. Solida.*

ERVILIA. PELLUCIDA. *Macg. Aber. p.* 341.—
TELLINA. P. *Brown. Ill. Conc. t.* 16. *f.* 22. Ovate-
elliptical, compressed, very inequilateral, rounded at
both ends, semitransparent, glossy, white, concentrically
sulcated, dorsal line concave ; hinge with two slender
divaricate teeth separated by a triangular space. 0,04.
...0,06. *Aberdeen.*

MONTACUTA. GLABRA. *Macg. Ab. p.* 303.—
TELLIMYA. G. *Brown Ill. Con. t.* 14. *f.* 19. Ovate-
oblong, subelliptical, very thin, subpellucid, very
inequilateral, nearly equally rounded at both ends,
convex, white or tinged with brown, nearly smooth,
slightly punctulate towards the margin; inside glossy,
slightly granulated, somewhat irridescent ; in the right
valve an oblique deflexed, adherent concave tooth, and
a white sinus with a conical tooth, the margins channelled for a short space ; in the left valve a sinus with a
concave tooth, the margins plain. 0,25.—0,416.
Aberdeen.

SPHŒNIA COSTULATA. *Macg. Aberd. p.* 301.

Ovate-elliptical, equally rounded at both ends, posteriorly much shorter, umbones small and slightly prominent; convex very thin, semitransparent, glossy hyaline white, concentrically striolate, about 15 radiating little elevated ribs; tooth in the form of an elongated thin lamella of small extent. 0,0834...0,08 *Aberdeen. Only a single valve as yet found.*

TELLINA. PROXIMA. *Smith in Wern. Mem.* 8. *p.* 105. *t.* 1. *f.* 21.—*Macg. Ab. p.* 340. Subovate, compressed, thin, dull brown, with irregular concentric striæ, the umbones very small and nearer the anterior end; hind slope little convex, posterior end rounded, dorsal slope rapidly declining and nearly straight, anterior end subangulated. ¾...1. *Aberdeen, very rare*

CRASSINA ELLIPTICA. *Brown Ill. Conch. t.* 18. *f.* 3.—ASTARTE C. *Macg. Ab- p.* 259.—(*C. Ovata. Brown in Edinb. J. of Nat. Sc.* 1 *t.* 12. *f.* 8. & *C. Depressa of Ill. Conc. t.* 18. *f.* 2. *fide Macgillivray.*) —C. SEMISULCATA *of Jeffreys M. S.* Ovate-elliptical compressed, posteriorly much shorter; dorsal line nearly straight, elongated, with a linear-lanceolate impression; posterior slope concave, the lunule narrow-lanceolate; valves not thick, about twenty two broad scarcely elevated concentric ribs which become obsolete at the sides and are, as well as the interstices, concentrically striated ; cuticle light yellowish-brown : margin entire. 1...1½. *Scotland. I believe this shell is the C. Garensis of some writers. The C. Multicostata of Macgillivray is our Compressa.*

C. SULCATA. *Macg. Aberd.* 229. (*not his synonyms*) Rounded-triangular, subangulated anteriorly, convex ; posteriorly longer ; umbones pointed and contiguous ; dorsal slope convex. the impression lanceolate ; posterior slope somewhat concave, lunule ovate-lanceolate ; valves very thick, with twenty five or more concentric ridges *of the same breadth as the interstices,* which as well as they, are concentrically striated ; cuticle olive brown, margin crenated. 0,8...1. *Aberdeen. Very like Danmoniensis, but in that shell the ridges are much narrower than the furrows.*

C. (*Astarte*) COMPRESSA. *Macgill p.* 261. (*not Turt.*) Ovate-triangular, compressed, posteriorly shorter, umbones pointed ; dorsal slope straight for half its length, then convex with a linear oblong impression ; posterior slope nearly straight to the end of the oblong impression ; valves moderately thick with irregular flattened concentric ridges and shallow sulci obliterated toward the margins ; muscular impressions very large, margin entire; cuticle yellowish brown. 1¼... 1⅘. *Scotland. According to Mr. Macgillivray this is the true Venus Compressa of Montagu and the Astarte C. of Fleming*:

NUCULA NITIDA *Sowerby Conch. Illus. Nucula f.* 20. Ovate-subtriangular, smooth, shining white with an olive colored cuticle ; anterior slope somewhat rounded, posterior nearly straight with a central elevation 0,05....0,4. *Common. North of England.*

MODIOLA FABA. *Gray*—MYTILUS F. *Chemnitz. f.* 761.—CRENELLA DECUSSATA *Macgil. Ab. p.* 229.— MODIOLA GLANDULA. *Totten in Sil. J.* 26. *p.* 367. *f.* 3. *?—Gould Mas. p.* 131. *f.* 87.*?* Suborbicular, transverse, more extended anteriorly, convex, rather thin, pellucid, nacreous, radiatingly striated and marked with concentric striolæ as well as somewhat regularly spaced lines or ridges of growth, producing a decussated appearance ; umbones prominent, a little curved to one side at the point, contiguous and central ; hinge thin, with a sinus and thick angular fold in each valve under the umbo ; margin crenulated. *Scotland and England, rare.*

M. RADIATA *of Brown*, Is closely allied to M. Modiolus, but is smaller, more delicate, covered with a yellow
epidermis under which the white shell is, more especially
at the anterior end, rayed with more or less crooked,
crimson red wavy markings. 1. *Tenby*.

M. NIGRA. Oblong, very short, rounded and narrow
posteriorly, rather dilated anteriorly, margin nowhere
angulated, ventral edge rather incurved ; cuticle yellowish black, sides radiated with raised striæ which
appear granular from the very fine concentric decussations, central area smooth; ligament scarcely visible
externally. *A single small specimen not one inch broad
was found at Scarborough by W. Bean, Esq. Foreign
Shells, (Newfoundland) are triple this size.*

LIMA APERTA *Sow. Th. t.* 22. *f.* 26, 7, 8, 9,—
OSTREA HIANS *Gmel.*—L. TENERA *Turt. in Z.
J.* 5.—PECTEN FRAGILIS *Mont. Sup. p.* 62.—Thin,
subcompressed, obliquely oval-elongated, smooth at the
sides, minutely striated in the middle, very slightly gaping posteriorly, widely so anteriorly; anterior gape
margined by a strong internal rib ; anterior auricles
acute ; hinge area small. *Rare.*

PECTEN ACULEATUS *Jeffreys in Conch. Mag.*—

Sow. Th. Pecten. f. 47.—P. Vitræus. var *Chemnitz.*
f. 637. *b.* Equivalve, suboval, thin, with radiating
striæ armed with elevated minutely prickly dots; ears
unequal, the anterior small; the posterior large and in
one valve strongly emarginated; pale yellow clouded
with red. 0,8...0,9. *Oban.*

P.Nivkps *Macgillivray in Edin. Phil. J.—Sow. Th.*
Monog. Pect. f. 223, 4.—Oval white, rather thin, the
left valve very slightly the larger; ears unequal, the
posterior rather large; ribs fourty, smooth, quadrate
armed with distant erect acute spines; interstices flat.
1¼...1,7. *Bears a strong resemblance to Varius.*
Scotland.

P. Isabella *Macgil. Aber. p.* 225. Rounded-
ovate, subequivalve, little convex, with twenty four
slender compressed rounded ribs having very numerous
elevated thin edged lamellæ rising towards the margin
into triangular compressed pointed spines, the grooves
with transverse scalar lamellæ not extending over the
ridges; ears very unequal, with radiating sulci transverse lamellæ and spines: margin of the upper valve
under the auricular sinus with four free curved conical
spinelets, of which a series is continued to the smooth
and glossy umbo; white, lower valve tinged with pink.
Aberdeen. 0,23....0,27.

CHITON CRINITUS *Penn.—Sowerby Conc. Ill. f.*
88. & 93.—C. FASCICULARIS *Sow. Gen.—Wood Gen.
Conc. t. 2. f. 6.*—C. DISCREPANS *Brown Ill. Conch.*
Oblong, strongly keeled by a dorsal, striated rib; valves
beaked, reniform, finely granulated at the sides, disunited
at the extremities; margin smooth, hairy, fasciculated;
inserted laminæ broad; colour various. ⅓...1. *Not
common.*

FISSURELLA NUBECULA: *Macg. Ab. p.* 345.—
PATELLA N. *Turt. D. p.* 142.—Ovate oblong, conical, little elevated, brownish red rayed with reddish
white, with about fifteen broad ribs alternating with
smaller, and somewhat reticulated with concentric inconspicuous lines; interior purplish white with a ring
of pale reddish purple around the thick whitish marginal
rim. 0,30...0,16. *Aberdeen.*

BULALÆ CATENULIFERA *Macg. Ab. p.* 187.
Oblong-cylindrical, very thin, transparent, brittle, pure
white, truncate at the right extremity, wider and rounded at the other; aperture extending the whole length,
narrow for a fourth only, then dilated into an oblong-
truncate form : outer lip very thin, pillar exposed and
gently waved: white with regular distinct divergent
longitudinal striæ which are moniliformly marked, or

present the appearance of two undulated lines intersecting each other. ⅓...⅓ *Aberdeen.*

BULLA CANDIDA. *Macg. Ab. p.* 189.—DIAPHANA C. *Brown Ill. Con. t.* 38. *f.* 13, 4.—Broadly ovate, thin, semitransparent, glossy white; apex rather prominent, obtuse, two very small volutions being apparent, but with a slight scrobiculus ; aperture wide, ovate-oblong, acute behind, the columellar margin a little thickened and reflexed, outer margin thin. *Aberdeen* ⅓...0,14.

B. PUNCTURA *Johnston in Edin. Phil. J.* 19. Oblong-oval, opaque, white, thickish, marked with numerous close, transverse, punctured striæ; apex with a very narrow perforation 0,33. *Berwick. Shape of B. Ampulla of Montague.*

B. MINUTA. *Macg. Aber. p.* 334.—DIAPHANA M. *Brown. Ill. Con. t.* 38. *f.* 7, 8.—Ovate cylindrical, of two very thin transparent hyaline white glossy turns, nearly smooth ; broadly truncate above, with a wide sutural groove, and a rounded mammillation which protudes a little; mouth oblong, anteriorly wide and rounded, moderately narrowed behind, extending the whole length of the shell : outer lip projecting conside-

rably behind in the form of a small lobe ; a false umbilicus. 0,09...0,06. *Aberdeen.*

B. Pellucida.—Bullina. P. *Macg. Ab. p.* 334.
—Volvaria P. *Brown. Ill. Con. t.* 38. *f.* 45, 6 Subcylindrical, hyaline white, glossy, faintly striolate the
whole length, a little wider anteriorly where it is rounded,
apex truncate; spire sunken, forming a wide and shallow
umbilicus; mouth very narrow but becoming oblong
anteriorly, and at its hind part projecting a little in the
form of a sinus beyond the extremity of the shell.
0,16....0,18. *Aberdeen.*

B. Producta. *Brown. Ill. Con. t.* 38. *f* 15, 6.—
Macg. Ab. p. 335.—Oblong cylindrical, thin, transparent, glossy, hyaline white with faint lines of growth,
the apex slightly umbilicated ; aperture extremely
narrow, the outer lip forming a narrow sinus projecting
considerably beyond the apex. 0,23...0,11. *Aberdeen.*

Natica Rutila *Mac. Ab. p.* 126—Subglobose,
rather broader than high, thick, glossy, dull greyish
red, with a white band margining the suture at which
the margin of the whorls is sharply inflexed, the base
paler ; spire very short and convex ; suture channelled
but narrow ; whorls four, very convex, longitudinally

striolate, the body ventricose ; aperture oblique, subovate, reddish white, inner lip nearly straight, thickened
slightly reflected at the strongly sulcated umbilicus but
not forming a prominence, operculum semicircular,
horny spiral. *Aberdeen. Between Rufa and Monilifera.*

TORNATELLA PELLUCIDA. *Macg. Aber. p.* 158.
Ovate-conical, subfusiform, very thin, transparent,
glossy ; the spire having a straight outline and tapering
to a small point ; whorls little convex, transversely
striated; the body nearly twice as broad as the length
of the spire, more deeply striated anteriorly and towards
the suture where there are two punctulate impressed
lines, the anterior striæ minutely crenulated : suture
distinct, edge of the whorls simply incurved : aperture
narrow oblong, much narrowed behind by the convexity
of the last turn; outer lip extremely thin, pillar with an
obscure obtuse plait, colour hyaline white, with two
very faint reddish bands on the first whorl. 0,20—0,12
Aberdeen.

SCALARIA TREVELIANA. Turreted imperforate,
thin, pellucid, glossy, of a uniform pale yellow ochre
colour, with very indistinct, lighter bands ; whorls eight
or nine, moderately rounded, about eighteen longitudinal

ribs which are narrow, equidistant, and as well as the interstices perfectly smooth. 0,65...0,33. *Rare.* *Scarborough.*

TROCHUS CONULUS *Lin. Gmel. p.* 3579.—*Chem-nitz. 5. f.* 1588.—*Lam.* 48.—*Dilw. p.* 798. Conical, smooth, polished, imperforated, variable in colouring being uniform gold or bronze or bluish white with chesnut longitudinal linear undulations; whorls six to nine, flat, with a smooth elevated belt at the lower extremity; base of the last whorl angulated and most delicately striated concentrically : apex acute ; aperture subquadrate, oblique, operculum corneous. *A single small but brilliant and live specimen was procured at Scarborough by W. Bean Esquire.*

TROCHUS MONTAGUI. *Wood. Sup. t.* 6. *f.* 43. Produced-conical, imperforated, rather dull, whitish tessellated with chesnut on the five or six rather distant little elevated spiral belts on each of the whorls ; whorls rather convex, suture indistinct; interstices of the belts minutely and obliquely striated ; base subangulated in colour and markings similar to the whorls; apex rather obtuse: aperture rather square. ↓ *Rare. Ireland.*

TURBO FULGIDUS *Adams in Lin. Tr.* 3. *p.* 354.—

Mont. p. 332.—*Turt. D. p.* 199. Somewhat conic, smooth, glossy, transparent; whorls three, the body very large, variegated with white and bronze generally in bands, terminating in a small obtuse point; aperture somewhat orbicular, margin acute. *Minute. Whitsand Bay, very rare.*

By the advice of several distinguished Conchologists, I have determined on the adoption of the genus

LACUNA.—TURTON.

Thin, conoid or somewhat globular clothed with an epidermis. Aperture entire, roundish or oval, with the lips disunited at the top. Pillar flattened, with a longitudinal groove which terminates at the upper end in an umbilicus . Operculum horny.

To this genus then will belong our Rufa (L. Puteolus) (fide Turton) Natica. Pallidula, Lacuna Turbo, Quadrifasciatus, Vinctus and Crassior.

LACUNA FASCIATA *Macg. Ab. p.* 145.—HELIX F *Mont. p.* 446.—(*Adams in Lin. T.* 5. *t.* 1. *f.* 20, 1.)— PHASIANELLA F *Brown Ill. Conc. t.* 46. *f.* 54.—Subglobose, broader than long, spire depressed, of three very thin transparent rapidly increasing volutions,

which are glossy and nearly smooth, the suture deep ;
body-whorl very large, with four white and three reddish brown bands, the central one being broader and
sometimes separated into two by a pale line ; mouth
roundish, peristome thin and whitish : a deep and wide
groove from the umbilicus, margined by the slightly reflected columellar margin. *Aberdeen*.

L. CANALIS *Turton Zool. Jour.* 3. *p.* 192.—TURBO
C *Mont. p.* 309. *t.* 12. *f.* 11.—L. VARIABILIS VAR.
Macg. Aber. p. 145.—Conoid, opaque, pale coloured
without markings ; outer lip hard and thickened.
0,37....0,25. *Southampton*.

LITTORINA—SOWERBY.

*Ovoidal, ovate-conical or subglobose ; the spire often
short, often acuminated ; the whorls convex, spirally striated, the last very ventricose ; aperture
elliptical, rather acute above ; pillar lip thickened
rather flat and generally covering the umbilicus ;
the outer lip thickened and bevelled to a thin edge ;
operculum horny, spiral, consisting of few volutions,
increasing rapidly in width.*

L. JUGOSA. *Macg. Ab. p.* 326.—TURBO C. *Mont. t.*
20. *f.* 2.—*Lin. Tr.* 8. *t.* 4. *f.* 7.—*Dor. Cat. t.* 19. *f.*

1.—*Turt. D. p.* 196. Somewhat oval, not much
pointed; whorls four, the first occupying three-fourths
of the shell, tumid in the middle, fulvous or dark purple with eleven spiral circular shape ridges (often
white or greenish black) which reflect a little upwards
(the middle are the stronger) ; aperture dark purple or
chocolate brown; lip thin, pillar broad, polished chocolate. 0,37....0,25. *Common.* At the advice of an
eminent Conchologist I have retained this shell as a
species, although considered by Fleming, &c. as the
young of Rudis, an opinion which 1 am inclined to
assent to.

L. ANATINA. *Gray Turt. p.* 87.—PALUDINA A.
Drap. Alder in Mag. Z. & Bot. 2. *p.* 116. Ovate,
perforated, thin, transparent; whorls ventricose, rounded
and the mouth ovate ; operculum horny and brown.
*Resembles Bithinia (Paludina) Ventricosa, but is
smaller and shorter and has a spiral and horny operculum ; the peristome is contiguous and the shell
generally covered with green Algæ.*

L.SAXATILIS *Johnston in Berw. Tr.* 3. *p.* 268.—
Macg. Aberd, p. 138. Subglobose-conical, as broad
as long, moderately thick, banded or tesselated with
dusky brown or green ; whorls three, transversely

striolate, suture deeply impressed, body somewhat flattened above and angulated towards its lower part ; spire
scarcely occupying one third of the shell, the apex
obtuse ; mouth very large, roundish, lip united at right
angles, throat chocolate brown. 0,33. *Aberdeen,
Wexford, &c. Very like the young of Rudis.*

L. PATULA *Jeffreys*.-Semi-globose, rather solid, grey-
chocolate colour with coarse and rather distant raised
spiral striæ ; whorls three ; the aperture occupying three
fourths the length of the shell, peritreme white, throat
glossy chocolate. 0,40. *Eddystone Rock.**

ODOSTOMIA SCALARIS *Macg. Ab. p.* 154.—Ovate-
conical, hyaline white, whorls five, transparent, glossy,
faintly striated, moderately convex ; the suture spi-

---

* Those who may adopt this genus (not considering
its type the common periwinkle to be a typical Turbo
and consequently that if that genus must be again de-
severed, the name at least should be retained for the
present group) must add to these species our Turbo
Littoreus (L. VULGARIS *Sow.*) Petræus. Rudis, Tenebrosus, Fabalis (*the note has erroneously been appended
at page* 167 *to that species*) and Neritoides.

rato-conaliculate towards which the upper margin is suddenly inflexed; mouth ovate, nearly half the whole length, peristome thin, columellar lip rather inflexed and terminating in a prominent plait on the columella; no umbilicus. 0,06...0,02. *Aberdeen.*

O. MARIONÆ. *Macg. Ab. p.* 156. Ovate conical, hyaline white, thin, transparent, rather glossy : whorls five, finely plicated lengthways and delicately striated spirally, the upper margin of each in the form of a plaited rib; mouth ovate, nearly half the whole length, peristome slightly thickened, not reflexed on the pillar but ending in a very slight plait behind the minute umbilicus. 0,04...0,02. *Aberdeen.*

O. ANNÆ. *Macg, Ab. p.* 157. Oblong-turreted, rather thick, opaque, glossy, destitute of markings, pure white; suture slight, whorls five, the body convex and proportionably large, the rest flattened; mouth ovate, nearly a third of the entire length, peristome thin, its columellar portion rather inflexed and terminating in a small plait on the pillar opposite the small umbilicus. 0,04...0,14. *Aberdeen.*

O. OBLONGA. *Macg. Ab. p.* 157.—Oblong, subcylindrical. very slightly tapering and ending in an obtuse point; of five flattened whorls of which the upper three are smooth, the rest longitudinally marked with numerous fine ribs ; suture deep, aperture a fourth of the whole length : ovate, the peritreme ending about the middle of the inner side in a prominent plait running into the interior 0,04...0,13. *Aberdeen.*

CINGULA PULCHRA *Johnston in Edin Phil. J.* 19. Conical, white, glossy, with two rows of oblong reddish brown spots on the whorls which are six in number, spirally striated, rounded and well defined : aperture roundish, narrowed above, with even margins and a slight perforation behind the pillar. ⅜. *Rare.*

C. (RISSOA) MURIATICA *Macg. Ab. p.* 148.— TURBO ULVÆ *Pen.*—CYCLOSTOMA ACUTUM *Drap. t.* 1. *f.* 23.—PALUDINA M. *Lam.*—P. ACUTA *Fl. p.* 315. Oblong-turreted, rather thin, transparent, somewhat corneous, pale yellowish or greenish grey : spire elongated, tapering to a small but bluntish point : whorls six, slightly convex, obscurely striated lengthways ; the body whorl rounded, without an angle ; aperture ovate, acute behind, peristome thin, considerably reflected on the columellar side, leaving a slight fissure but concealing the umbilicus: 0,20...0,09. *Aberdeen.*

C. (RISSOA) GRACILIS *Macg. Ab. p.* 152. Turreted, subcylindrical, of six thin pellucid glossy moderately convex whorls, the suture deep ; mouth about one fourth of the length, ovate, oblique, a little narrowed behind, the peristome complete, thickened externally on the outer lip, thinner and direct on the inner, leaving a very small cavity : hyaline white, brownish red around the mouth. *Aberdeen.* 0,102...0,025. *Very like Rubra but is less attenuated and the mouth rounder.*

A

SUPPLEMENT

OF

NEW SPECIES

CONTRIBUTED BY

W. BEAN, Esq.

CHITON HANLEYI—*Bean.*—Shell oblong oval, narrow, carinated, brownish white, granulated, with the granulations larger towards the margin which is covered with minute spines; inside pale green; length 3 lines, breadth 1½ lines.

Only two specimens of this beautiful shell have been met with at Scarborough attached to the under sides of rocks at the lowest spring tides. We have great pleasure in naming it after the author of " a Descriptive Catalogue of recent Shells."

CHITON PICTUS—*Bean.*—Shell oblong, smooth, depressed, subcarinated, colour dark red with a few spots of white, margin smooth and the fringe distinct, inside crimson. *Length ½ inch, breadth ¼ inch.·*

This shell is more depressed, not so broad, and the colour uniformly darker than C. Lœvigatus. It is rare, only three specimens have been detected in company with C. Lœvis.

PATELLA ATHLETICA *Bean.*—Shell oval with about twenty large tuberculated ribs which project beyond the margin and three or four smaller ones filling up the interstices between each, apex obtuse and never central. colour dull white but young shells are black between the ribs which gives them a beautiful appearance ; inside pearly. *Length 2 inches, breadth 1½ inch.*

The animals in this species are very hard and tough, our Fishermen call them Kennocks and never use them with the common P. Vulgata in baiting their hooks.

TROCHUS ELECTISSIMUS—*Bean.*—Shell conic, spires six, tapering to a fine point with numerous spiral striæ which are crossed by minute longitudinal lines of growth only visible with the aid of a good magnifier ; color brown, with darker longitudinal oblique bands; aperture subquadrangular, inside pearly. *Length* 4 *lines, breadth* 4 *lines.*

This rare shell differs from T Tumidus, in the striæ being stronger and less numerous ; the volutions are not so much rounded, nor are they flattened at the top as in that species.

SERPULA. SOLITARIA.—*Bean.*—Shell cylindrical, opaque, white, gradually tapering to a point and wrinkled transversely, fixed at the smaller end to Dentularia abietina or Plumularia falcata, round the stems of which it forms four or five volutions, and then projects forward in a straight, (or sometimes) undulating manner to the length of an inch. *Var.* With the volutions reversed. *Common on the coast of Scarborough.*

SERPULA. PLACENTULA.—*Bean.*— Shell strong, opaque, white, with three volutions, the outer one with a sharp keel-like ridge which is strongly wrinkled or serrated. *Diameter,* 4 *lines.* VAR With the volutions reversed. *Found on the same Zoophytes with S. Solitaria and equally common.*

NATICA LIVIDA —*Bean.*—Shell smooth, globular, of a livid greenish colour, volutions five, marked with very fine longitudinal striæ ; aperture roundish-oval, outer lip thin, pillar lip white, a little spread and forming a small perforation behind it. *Diameter* 6 *lines.*

M

Only five specimens have been met with on the Scarborough Coast, and four of them are very young shells.

LITTORINA. ZONARIA.—*Bean.*—Shell very strong, oval, not much pointed, body whorl very large occupying nearly three parts of the shell, volutions five, finely striated transversely and longitudinally giving the shell a beautiful decussated appearance; colour yellow with two broad dark purple bands ; outer lip thin, pillar lip spread, yellow and polished, inside purple. *Length 6 lines, Breadth 4 lines. Found in great abundance at Robin Hood Bay on the flat Lias scars at low water, in company with the common species.*

LITTORINA. NEGLECTA. — *Bean.* — Shell strong, smooth, glossy and nearly globular, volutions four, mostly ending in an obtuse point; body whorl large covered with numerous transverse dark interrupted bands ; aperture orbicular, inside pale purple. *Diameter, not 2 lines. This small species is found in company with L. Petræa and Fabalis on large blocks of oolite that have long braved the fury of the elements on the north shore of Scarborough.*

LITTORINA. RUDISSIMA.—*Bean.*—Shell strong, somewhat conic and pointed, with numerous raised spiral lines which never become totally obliterated in the oldest specimens; volutions five or six, rounded and well defined by the suture; color reddish brown and dark purple, rarely white; outer lip thin, pillar lip broad, white and polished, inside purple. *Length 5 lines, breadth nearly 4 lines.*

A very variable but distinct. species found in the greatest abundance on our piers and rocks at high water mark at Scarborough. It differs from L. Rudis in its raised spiral striæ and the body whorl being more patulous.

TEREBRA SPECIOSA.—*Bean.*—Shell slender, greenish white, tapering to a point; volutions seven, rounded, well defined by the separating line and marked with numerous very fine longitudinal beaded striæ, aperture roundish oval, with a very slight canal. *Length nearly 2 lines.*

Only one specimen has been met with in the shelly sand of Scarborough.

H. Fisher, Printer, Cross Street, Islington.

www.ingramcontent.com/pod-product-compliance
Lightning Source LLC
Chambersburg PA
CBHW031337070726
47496CB00017B/1181